John Salisbury is the pseudonym of an established author and playwright. His previous novel, *The Baby Sitters*, was an enormous best-seller.

John Salisbury

Moscow Gold

Futura Publications Limited

A Futura Book

First published in Great Britain by
Futura Publications Limited in 1980

ISBN 0 7088 1702 5

Printed in Great Britain by
Hazell Watson & Viney Ltd
Aylesbury, Bucks

Futura Publications Limited
110 Warner Road
Camberwell, London SE5

'The Olympic movement is a 20th century religion, a religion with universal appeal which incorporates all the basic values of other religions, a modern, exciting, virile, dynamic religion, attractive to Youth, and we of the International Olympic Committee are its disciples.'

Avery Brundage, President of the IOC,
Tokyo, 1962

PROLOGUE

Saturday, June 9, 1979

The news broke as the first editions of the Sunday newspapers were coming off the presses. It appeared on the Associated Press teleprinters at 18:22 GMT. Almost simultaneously, images of two young athletes, a man and a woman, took shape on the Mufax picture transmission machines.

Fleet Street editors hesitated: in all probability the story would merit a mere 150 words, tucked away at the bottom of a centre page. Yet years of experience also warned them that this particular story might suddenly get so big that no editor competing for the Sunday morning ratings could afford to leave it off his front page.

At 18:45 the teleprinters began to chatter again. The story was getting bigger, Soviet statements increasingly acrimonious. Gathering all available reporters in the news rooms, editors sent them out into a London summer evening in the vain hope of gathering that extra bit of information which would produce a scoop for the later editions.

At 19:01 an entirely new twist: Reuters and Agence France-Presse began to feed their client papers with reports of a feature story, 4,350 words long, which had just appeared in the first editions of *Paris-Etoile* and the Munich newspaper *Vaterland*. Hasty translations from the French and German confirmed that the events now taking place in London could have the most dramatic impact on world politics since the fall of the Shah of Iran.

Copy was passing from the sub-editors to the composing rooms. Columns of metal type were expelled from the front-page chases and replaced by new paragraphs quickly composed by the linotype operators. Picture plates of the two young athletes were rushed through the process departments. New flongs hurtled from the moulds to the foundries.

Ramsay Jordan, editor of Britain's leading quality newspaper, the *Sunday Monitor*, engaged in a sharp altercation with his most illustrious reporter, Bill Ellison.

'In my opinion we should run the story after all.'

'No way.'

'We have 4,350 words set up in type. We have exclusive British first serial rights. We have a scoop which could lift our final edition by 150,000 copies.'

'The story stinks, Ramsay.'

'But look what's been happening here in London today! We have the only eyewitness account, the only photographs of the vital moments.'

'I know. It's hard.' Ellison's tone was uncompromising. 'But the story still stinks.'

It was already 21:45 hours Moscow time when the first reports from the Soviet news agency Tass's London office hit the editorial desks of *Pravda* and *Izvestia*. The more serious news which came in twenty-three minutes later caused *Pravda*'s deputy editor, Constantin Zhikov, to put through a call to the weekend dacha of Alexander Martinov, president of the Press Control Commission of the Central Committee of the Communist Party of the Soviet Union, candidate member of the Politburo and favoured protégé of the First Secretary himself.

It wasn't only the news agency reports but also messages of increasing urgency from the Soviet Embassy in London which finally convinced Martinov, at 23:08, that the story was so big and ominous that it could neither be published nor be not published. This is the catch 44 of the Soviet bureaucratic censorship system; it involves, also, catch 55, which means instant dismissal for failing to consult the First Secretary and instant dismissal for disturbing his Saturday-night sleep, or party, or mistress.

Trembling, Martinov dialled the most closely guarded telephone number in the Union of Soviet Socialist Republics. Tremble he might: as one heart attack succeeded another and as rumours about Brezhnev's health abounded in the Western press, so the First Secretary's temper became increasingly unpredictable – and deadly. He had even deposed the President of the Republic and had taken his job, too, because Podgorny had had the temerity to express a view of his own about the Horn of Africa.

'Well?' The voice at the other end of the line sounded like a grizzly bear which had just discovered a bullet embedded in its rump.

In the Foreign Ministry and in Dzerzhinsky Square, headquarters of the Soviet secret police, the KGB, experts were being summoned from their weekend holidays to examine the mounting pile of de-coded messages from London.

Josef Arbuzov, head of the KGB's West European Counter-Insurgency Division, was in a foul mood when he reached Dzerzhinsky Square. His dual war against vodka and Armenian tobacco, which doctors had warned him could cost him his life within the year, set his deprived nervous system screaming and his big, sadist's mouth dribbling in uncontrollable rage.

'So, that Jewish pig has double-crossed us after all.'

The man he had in mind was a lawyer called Chaim Leonhard, normally resident in Vienna but temporarily staying in Paris. Leonhard's political brain matched his professional ability – two reasons why he had been invited to serve as counsel to the Israeli Olympic Committee. There was a third reason, utterly foreign to the sensibility of Josef Arbuzov: Leonhard had spent a brief but not easily forgotten period of his adolescence in Auschwitz.

Now Arbuzov understood why earlier that day Leonhard

had received a coded telephone message from Bill Ellison. The line had been tapped by a French telephone engineer whose loyalty was to the local Communist Party. The code hadn't been hard to crack; indeed, Arbuzov, once a student at the Sorbonne, regarded it as personal insult to his own intelligence, his own culture.

Ellison was due to meet Leonhard in Paris the day after tomorrow. The two agents whom Arbuzov now despatched to Paris via London would take care of both the Jew and the famous British journalist. Arbuzov had chosen them with care.

It was at 23:52 that Aeroflot's American-built Sperry Rand central computer in Lenin Prospekt received a KGB priority request for two seats on flight SU 581 departing from Sheremetyev International Airport for London at 10:55. All places on the Ilyushin were taken. Automatically the computer's multiple electronic censors interpreted the situation, scanned the passenger list data and dictated a telegram to the modest Moscow hotel where a retired couple from Novosibirsk were passing a sleepless night in excited anticipation of their first visit to the West. It was a reward, subsidized by the husband's trade union, for a lifetime's work in the bridge building industry. The Aeroflot cable informed them, without explanation, that their departure for London had been delayed twenty-four hours.

In Jerusalem, a hastily summoned meeting of the Committee for Security, having consulted with the director of Ha Mossad, Israel's crack intelligence service, decided to hold its hand until further clarification had been received from the Israeli Embassy in London.

And from Chaim Leonhard.

By midnight the normal Saturday-night calm of the Foreign Office in London was severely disrupted. At 23:15 the Foreign Secretary had used the telephone link to the Prime Minister's Somerset farm.

'What do MI5 say?'

'They've been caught with their pants down.'

'Perhaps you ought to phone Washington. On second thought ... it could all blow over. Storm in a teacup. One doesn't want to look foolish.'

'Quite. We could look pretty silly. On the other hand –'

'I'll leave it to you.'

The State Department remained, in fact, a very quiet place that night. The London Embassy had relayed a bland statement put out from the Kensington Hilton by the manager of the United States athletics team which had just concluded a two-day, triangular Britain-USA-USSR match. It was further south, in Langley, Virginia, that a small group of men stayed at their desks all night, linked to the Chief of Station, London. These men worked for the Directorate of Operations (Clandestine Services) of the Central Intelligence Agency.

As the night wore on, the London Station twice advised Langley that they might have a problem. The name of the problem was Bill Ellison, four times Journalist of the Year and universally acknowledged as the best investigative reporter in Fleet Street.

'Ellison's people have been much too active today,' the message read.

Leaving the *Monitor* building at three in the morning and heading home to Chester Place in his VW Passat, Ellison felt extremely tired. But his mind, as usual, would refuse to rest until his head hit the pillow. His thoughts, now, were squarely focussed on events which had taken place five years earlier, in October, 1974.

His first meeting with Chaim Leonhard.

CHAPTER 1

October 20, 1974. Vienna

Ellison landed at Schwechat Airport and took a taxi straight to Chaim Leonhard's apartment in Futterer, off the famous Jüden Platz. A widower, Leonhard now lived alone, surrounded by shelves of dust-covered books and periodicals. Ellison had heard of a daughter, Ruth, reputedly very beautiful and now studying at the University of Chicago.

The lawyer shook his hand warmly and led the way to a cosy study overlooking a tiny, dark courtyard.

'Where are you staying, Mr Ellison? Let me guess: the Ambassador?'

'The Sacher.'

Leonhard's eyes twinkled mischievously. 'But of course! They tell me that you now rank number one in your profession. Princes, presidents and oil companies quail at your approach! Where else should such a man stay but at the Sacher Hotel? So close to the Staatsoper, too. You will not miss our opera, I'm sure. I suppose you realize that at the turn of the century every important personality in the Austro-Hungarian empire stayed at the Sacher when he visited Vienna. You must ask to see the tablecloth that Madame Sacher made her famous guests sign: she had their signatures traced in coloured thread, an embroidered autograph collection. And then, of course, you won't miss the world-famous *Sachertorte* – a chocolate cake like no other chocolate cake. Alas, I can no longer indulge . . . but you are still young.'

'When did the Israeli Olympic Committee first ask you to serve as legal adviser in Europe?'

'You don't waste time on superfluous courtesies and cultural chit-chat. Straight to the point.' Chaim Leonhard sighed and sank his barrel-like form into a deep armchair. 'Two years ago, they first asked me, after the massacre.' His voice sank to a whisper. 'After the Munich massacre.'

'You were in Russia last year?'

Leonhard nodded. 'Yes, I have been dealing with the Russians. One has to. They have been arriving in Vienna all week for the crucial meeting of the International Olympic Committee. I assume that is what has brought you here – the contest between Moscow and Los Angeles for the dubious honour of staging the 1980 Olympics? Or course. You will find the new-style Russians quite unlike their dour predecessors of the Harry Lime, Four-Power-Occupation era after the war. They're very sleek now, very Madison Avenue. And they're not taking any chances after the fiasco of the vote four years ago, when Moscow lost to Montreal at the second ballot. And whom will you be seeing during your visit to Vienna? All the top brass, of course: Killanin, Exeter, Beaumont, Samaranch, Worrall, Berlioux, Pavlov. . . . How pleasant it must be to have every door swing open at your approach. My contacts, of course, are more humble. . . .'

Chaim Leonhard sat in his chair, small and round, observing his guest with keen intensity.

'I believe you know Armand Krohl,' Ellison said.

'Indeed yes! You'd like to meet him? By sheer coincidence he is to be one of my guests at dinner this evening. Perhaps you would honour us with your company? Yes? Delightful. We shall meet at the Altes Kerzenstuberl, Habsburgergasse 6, at half past eight.'

'How long have you known Krohl?'

Leonhard gestured vaguely. 'For some years. I knew him long before he was elected to the IOC's nine-man executive board. He's a great force for sanity and decency in a world conspicuous for its insanity and indecency.'

'I'm told he was a fine athlete in his youth?'

'I believe so. An accident of some sort prematurely ended his running career. After that, he devoted his energies to the administrative side of the sport. He was manager of the Benelux team at the London Olympics in 1948.'

'But he's not a full-time sports administrator?'

'No, no, no. He runs a chain of import-export businesses. The main office is in Amsterdam.'

'I assume you got to know him through his work for Amnesty International and Christian Care?'

Leonhard nodded. 'He has fought for the release of political prisoners in the Soviet Union and in southern Africa. And he's a good friend of the Jews.' Leonhard winked. 'We don't have so many, you know.'

Ellison rose abruptly. 'You're a busy man, I must go.'

Leonhard heaved himself out of his chair. 'Until this evening, then.' Almost as an afterthought, he added: 'My daughter Ruth will have the pleasure of meeting you. She is due to arrive from Chicago in half an hour's time.'

'From Chicago!'

Leonhard smiled cautiously. 'She is a student of journalism. Her course instructor told her she should not miss the opportunity of meeting you. It seems that your work is now legendary, Mr Ellison. I believe you have a daughter of your own: how old is she?'

'Faith is thirteen. She recently won a scholarship to St Paul's School. Pru and I are very pleased.'

'So you should be. Ruth is only a few years older.'

Was it a warning, or a plea?

Ellison took a taxi. From the moment he had left the airport he had been conscious of being under surveillance. Two men in a Peugeot 504 were waiting for him outside Chaim Leonhard's apartment in Futterer. They followed him to the Hotel Sacher.

Although he arrived early at the Altes Kerzenstuberl in Habsburgergasse, Leonhard and his daughter Ruth were already seated in the bar. He fell in love with her on sight. She was exquisitely beautiful, with dark, shoulder-length hair and eyes to match. Her smile, shy yet bold, seemed to establish instantly a kind of complicity between them, as if they had been destined to meet because they understood one another perfectly. Her slender hand rested in his.

'Ruth is infatuated by the world of journalism,' Leonhard said. 'I thank God that I gave her a sound education in philosophy at the Hebrew University in Jerusalem. Please don't misinterpret me, Mr Ellison, I – '

Ellison smiled. 'I understand. Journalism is to literature what plumbing is to physics.'

'Daddy is entirely old-fashioned,' Ruth said, with a feigned pout. 'My generation has had enough of poetry and fine phrases. What we want to know is how the world really works.'

Leonhard had turned to greet two of his guests. The choice of these two gentlemen, who arrived in harness, took Ellison by surprise. Sheikh Abdul Al-Rahmani, a wealthy IOC member from one of the Gulf States, was known to be lobbying hard on behalf of Saudi Arabia for the 1988 Olympics. With him came the vast, treble-chinned trombone figure of Sol Enders, America's most famous sports impresario, promoter in his time of six world-title bouts.

'You are wondering what we all have in common,' Leonhard said to Ellison, introducing them. 'Well, the Sheikh is an Arab and Sol is a Jew.'

'It figures,' Ellison said.

'Delighted to meet you, Mr Ellison,' boomed Enders. 'I hear you're one of the few reporters left whom money can't buy.'

'You could always try.'

'Sheikh, what will you drink?' Leonhard asked. 'Jaffa orange juice perhaps?'

'Double scotch on the rocks,' grunted the Sheikh.

'Those emirs and sultans out in the Gulf are crazy to have

the Olympics,' Enders explained to Ellison. 'And I say, why the hell not. Those Ay-rabs have the money, after all.'

'And the sand.' Leonhard gave Ellison a broad wink.

Ruth Leonhard remained at Ellison's side. He felt her finger tips touch his wrist. Or was it his imagination?

Leonhard's guest of honour arrived a few minutes later, limping on a stick. At first sight Armand Krohl reminded Ellison of a professor of jurisprudence; at second sight, of an international entrepreneur; at third sight, of one of those idealists whom totalitarian regimes make it their first task to destroy. Thick, steel-grey hair was combed back from his forehead with impressive rigour; his eyes were frank and searching. He greeted each of Leonhard's guests politely but without ceremony.

Ellison had one reason for wanting to meet him. Krohl's influence within the International Olympic Committee was reliably reported to be second only to that of the IOC's Irish president, Lord Killanin.

Leonhard led the way from the bar to the dining-room, whose walls were adorned by portraits of solemn, slack-jawed Hapsburg monarchs. Ruth had taken Ellison's arm, lightly but firmly; she made sure that she sat beside him at table.

'When I was a boy,' Ellison told her, 'my favourite painting was Titian's "Emperor Charles V". There you have a grave man, trapped between his spiritual and secular burdens, half monarch, half monk, a recluse in armour astride a horse, gazing at some distant dilemma which he alone has sight of. Tomorrow you and I will find time to inspect the original in the Kunsthistorisches Museum.'

'It hangs in Room XVI of the Prado, in Madrid. We could always take a plane, if you're anxious to see it.'

Her smile was worthy of the Louvre.

'Ladies and gentlemen, your orders, please,' said Chaim Leonhard.

Ruth chose sweetwater crayfish and wild suckling pig. Like a young boy half out of his mind with love, Ellison automatically ordered the same.

'Later,' she whispered, 'you will put your figure at risk with *Pfannkuchen Marie Louise*, a dessert covered with chocolate sauce. I shall insist.'

'I was warned this would happen in Vienna.'

'Oh? That what would happen?' Her gaze, this time, was openly provocative. Again her hand brushed his, under the table.

As conversation warmed round the table, Ellison lit a cigarette and left his tortoiseshell cigarette case lying open on the table.

'What a pretty little case,' she murmured.

'A present from my wife.'

'Rather rude, though....'

'What – to smoke?'

'To tape-record the voices of Daddy's guests.'

This time the talon of a stiletto heel raked his shin.

Leonhard was asking Krohl his opinion of the imminent IOC vote on the Moscow-Los Angeles contest. 'They say the outcome is as certain as a papal election in the Sistine chapel with only one Italian candidate.'

Krohl nodded. 'There will be red smoke from the Rathaus chimney.'

'There are two issues here,' Enders intervened. 'Do the Russians deserve the Games? And do they get the Games? I have a contract with the City of Los Angeles which means I stand to gain five million bucks if the Russians lose out.'

'My sympathies,' Krohl said acidly. 'It must be very frustrating to be constantly thwarted in your efforts to destroy the last citadel of true amateurism in world sport.'

'Now wait a minute,' erupted the vast promoter. 'You, Mr Krohl, are well known as a lobbyist for Amnesty International. How can you support giving the Olympics to a nation that regularly jails its dissidents?'

'That's a fair question,' Ellison said.

Krohl gave him a level, appraising scrutiny.

'Since 1952,' he said, 'when the Soviet Union first took part in the Games, her athletes have won 211 gold, 183 silver and 169 bronze medals at the summer Olympics. Two years ago, at Munich, the USSR won fifty golds; the United States won only thirty-three. As for the athletics matches between the two countries, beginning with the one held in July, 1958, we find that Russia has won nine and America two, with one drawn.'

'But Mr Enders asked about Russia's inhumane treatment of political prisoners,' Ellison pressed Krohl.

'Politics and sport don't mix,' Krohl snapped.

'You've touched him on a raw nerve,' Ruth whispered in Ellison's ear. But her father had hastened to intervene.

'You see, Bill – if I may call you by your first name – for Los Angeles this bid is simply a commercial calculation.'

'Besides,' Krohl cut in, 'LA has already staged the Games, in 1932. Moscow, never. Indeed, no Communist country has ever staged the Games.'

'The Russians,' Leonhard went on, 'were deeply hurt by what happened when the IOC met at Amsterdam in 1970. There were three candidates for the 1976 Olympics: Moscow, Los Angeles and Montreal. After the first ballot Moscow led Montreal by 28 votes to 25, with 17 for LA. Inexperienced in voting behaviour, the Russians took victory for granted and actually announced it, prematurely, through Tass. When 16 of the 17 LA votes switched to Montreal at the second ballot, the Mayor of Moscow, Promyslov, stormed out in a rage.'

'For the Russians,' Krohl added, 'this week's vote here in Vienna is a vital matter of national pride. No city has ever prepared its case in advance with such thoroughness. Indeed, we fear the Russians might even pull out of the Games if the vote went against them a second time.'

'So it seems that political calculations do intrude after all,' Ellison said.

Krohl again appraised him and then nodded. 'You're quite right, of course. It has always been the case. In 1896 Irish athletes had to compete as part of the British team. Peter O'Connor, world record holder for the broad jump, climbed 200 feet to fasten the Irish Republican flag to the masthead. In 1908, at the opening ceremony in London, the American team refused to dip their flag to King Edward VII. The Finns registered their protest against Russian domination by refusing to carry any flag. In 1956, at Melbourne, the Hungarians appeared wearing black arm bands and carrying the Kossuth Cross to protest the Soviet invasion of their country. And so it will always be.'

'You left out one little incident, my friend,' Chaim Leonhard said. 'The massacre of twelve Israeli athletes by Arab terrorists two years ago.'

'My apologies. I didn't feel it was comparable....'

'I'd like to ask the Sheikh here a question,' Ellison said. 'Does he feel that the present composition of the IOC is fair? There are 17 members representing the Americas, and 35 Europeans, but only 11 from Africa and 12 from Asia.'

'It is most undemocratic,' grunted the Sheikh darkly.

'You tell them, Sheikh,' Enders said.

Krohl shrugged urbanely. 'As you know, the IOC dates back to 1894. The Olympic ideal was revived by a European, Baron de Coubertin. He selected the first fifteen members of the IOC. Since that time we have worked on co-option. Democracy is not applicable. We depend on men who will jealously guard the independence of the movement.'

'And sham-amateurism,' growled Enders.

'I don't accept that characterization.'

Enders turned to Ellison. 'If you're British, you play

cricket, right? Did you ever hear of an Australian TV impresario called Kerry Packer? You didn't? Well, you will. I know the man. He's planning to turn cricket professional. And he'll succeed.'

'Cricket has been professional for years,' Ellison said.

'Oh sure. And what do top cricketers earn? Peanuts. Maybe £5000 a year. Kerry Packer plans to set up a travelling circus, with all the world's top players on contract, prime-time TV coverage, luminous ball, luminous clothes, floodlights, first-class promotion.'

'The national cricket boards of control will never allow it.'

'Just as the International Amateur Athletics Federation have a ban on Sol Enders. I'm enemy number one. But in the end, money talks. The cricketers that Kerry signs up and the athletes I sign up will be banned by the authorities, fine, they can cry all the way to the bank.'

'There may be more to life than money,' Krohl said.

Sol Enders's heavy face clouded: clearly he didn't appreciate the remark. His voice now rose several decibels.

'Did you ever hear of Big Jim Thorpe? He was an American Fox Indian whose real name was Bright Path. He won both the pentathlon and the decathlon hands down at the 1912 Olympics in Stockholm. All the lords and ladies lauded the guy: King Gustav personally received him. A year later it came out that poor Jim Thorpe had once been paid to play baseball in a minor American league. He was immediately stripped of his Olympic medals. Now that's the so-called amateur spirit for you – arrogant and cruel. I'm gonna sign up all the Olympic finalists on contract and take them round the world: those stars are gonna run and jump for real money. I have a real big deal with the Sheikh here, don't I, Sheikh?'

Everyone turned with some astonishment to the Arab, since he was a member of the IOC. The Sheikh remained inscrutable. Enders chuckled malevolently.

Later, as Leonhard's guests rose to disperse, Ruth squeezed Ellison's hand. 'Daddy and I will see you again tomorrow. Don't forget your pretty cigarette case – I hope you will play the tape back to me, one day.'

He watched her as she mounted the stairs on her father's arm. It was his first view of her whole body. Lust and guilt engulfed him in a sudden fireball of middle-aged misery.

'I hear you're staying at the Sacher, too, Mr Ellison.'

It was Krohl.

'Of course. Shall we share a taxi?'

Krohl limped at his side out into the street: clearly the left leg was shorter than the right.

'I have particularly admired your reports in the *Monitor* on Rhodesia,' Krohl said once they were seated in a taxi. 'It's a subject of acute interest to me. In Christian Care we look after the families of some two thousand Rhodesian Africans detained without trial. Do you intend to pursue your investigations of Rhodesian evasions of UN economic sanctions?'

'Possibly. My colleague Magnus Massey was in Bulawayo recently. He was able to take photographs of an oil tank farm owned by a sanctions-busting outfit called Transport Services.'

'The name rings a bell. Who runs it?'

'A South African called Coenraad Ventner.'

'Of course. They say he is a powerful man, a fanatical proponent of white supremacy.'

They had reached the lobby of the Sacher Hotel now. Krohl tucked his silver-tipped stick under his arm with a brisk movement, shook Ellison's hand warmly and limped away. Ellison noticed that Krohl's left shoe was supported on a platform sole two inches thick. The Olympic official's abrupt 'good night' disappointed him; this was a man he had come to Vienna to talk to.

If only to keep his thoughts from Ruth Leonhard.

CHAPTER 2

October 21, 1974. Vienna

When they met the following afternoon Chaim Leonhard was alone. Such was his disappointment, so ardently had he longed to set eyes on Ruth again, to feel the glow of her reserved smile, that Ellison felt more like eighteen than thirty-eight.

Leonhard, perhaps deliberately, made no mention of his daughter. And Ellison was too proud to be the first to mention her name.

'Tell me, honestly,' Chaim Leonhard said, regarding him out of the corner of his eye, 'Vienna – she appeals to you? Some cities ... it's a matter of chemistry, almost, as with women.' Was the cruelty deliberate?

It had been a long walk, starting in the Volksgarten, beside the Burgtheater, where beds of red tulips flower in the spring. Leonhard had led him past the massive Staatsoper, with its flanking winged horses, then past St Stephen's Cathedral, along Rotenturm Strasse, towards the Danube.

'I prefer Prague, since you ask,' Ellison finally said.

'Prague!' Leonhard was clearly hurt, even offended. 'But Wien was the capital of a great empire ... Schubert ... Mozart – where in Prague will you see a collection like that of the Kunsthistorisches Museum?'

They reached the Morin Platz, overlooking the river. Leonhard jabbed out an arm, pointing to a building below them, on the river front. 'That was Gestapo headquarters, Wien.'

'Yes.' Ellison felt embarrassed; he wanted to embrace the man beside him. Leonhard, he knew, had survived Auschwitz, but four of his brothers and sisters had not. Nor had his parents.

'Now I will show you the synagogue,' Leonhard said. 'Not as good as the Old Synagogue in Prague, of course,' he added sardonically.

Passing the Rupprechtskirche, more than a thousand years old, Leonhard led the way down Seitenstettengasse past the Kornhauselturm.

'Built by a famous 19th-century Viennese architect, proverbially to appease his jealous wife,' Leonhard commented.

'How did it appease her?'

'They say he never left it!'

'Is it my imagination or are we being followed?'

'For the past half-hour, yes.'

Abruptly Leonhard opened an inconspicuous door in the wall.

'The old synagogue,' he whispered. 'Razed by the Nazis in 1938, rebuilt after the war.' He lit a candle, slipped some coins into a box, ignored two old men who nodded to him out of their prayers and closed his eyes for about ten seconds. Though his mouth did not open, it was clear to Ellison that Leonhard was saying something, talking to someone – perhaps to God, perhaps to himself.

'The two men following us. . . .'

'They will not dare enter here. We will leave by another entrance to which I have a key. It was put in after the war . . . just in case. We all have a key: but there are not many of us now.'

Leaving the synagogue by a door in its rear wall, then snaking through narrow alleyways until they found themselves in the Fleischmarkt, the two men finally caught a red bus with a cream roof at a *Haltstelle.*

'Now you will be my guest at Demel's,' Leonhard said.

'It's your turn to be my guest.'

'Good! Demel's is very expensive. You will have to take

back delicacies for your family: the girls will wrap them beautifully in cardboard boxes.'

'So who was following us?'

'The Russians, of course, who else? Do you remember Harry Lime, that extraordinary moment in the Carol Reed film when Orson Welles came out of the sewers?'

'Why are the KGB following you, Chaim?'

'They don't trust me. Why should they? They are afraid that I am filling your head with anti-Soviet poisons. They even believe that I have campaigned against granting the 1980 Olympiad to Moscow.'

'Have you?'

Leonhard sniffed. They descended from the bus on Kohlmarkt and entered Demel's. Ellison's saliva glands were immediately activated by the spectacular display of pastries, chocolates, cream cakes, game salads, stuffed mushrooms, vegetable-and-cheese salads. The décor was a delight, like the smile of the girl who stood at their table waiting for their order. Ellison thought of Ruth.

'Every visit to Demel's costs one a year of one's life,' Leonhard said.

When they had ordered, Ellison pressed home his question: 'Have you campaigned against the Moscow Olympics? Or are you neutral on the whole question?'

'No Jew is ever neutral.'

'Particularly one who works on contract for Ha Mossad.'

'I shall ignore that remark. Listen: last year I went to Moscow for the World Student Games. I was officially accredited to the Israeli team. The PLO wanted us excluded, naturally, but the Russians didn't care – they wanted the 1980 Olympics too badly. At first the Russians treated us very correctly – not friendly, but perfectly polite. But dissident Soviet Jews who want to leave Russia naturally made contact with us, and we could hardly turn them away. The Russians were furious. Israel was scheduled to play a basketball match against Cuba: hundreds of Soviet Jews turned up to watch.

The KGB panicked, fearing that the Jews would applaud the Israeli team. Squad cars full of plainclothes agents rushed to the scene, the Jews were locked out of the hall, busloads of soldiers were brought in to fill their seats. Every time the Israeli players had the ball, the soldiers whistled and booed derisively. Before the match was half over I had launched an official protest. At first the Soviet officials responded in a truculent manner: if the "Soviet people" wished to express their anger at the crimes of "Zionist racism" etcetera, etcetera. I lost my temper, told them I had been in Auschwitz, likened them to Nazis. That didn't please them. They threatened to expel me for gross interference in Soviet internal affairs, etcetera. But the next morning they came to eat out of my hand; they grovelled; they crawled.'

'Why?'

'You should remember. A British journalist got hold of the story, it was published widely in the West, Western athletics officials in Moscow began to protest. Even worse, Lord Killanin himself was in Moscow at the time to observe the student games. Such importance was attached to his good opinion that he was received in person by Premier Alexei Kosygin. I had of course cabled Killanin: how could Israeli athletes expect to receive fair treatment at the Olympics if they were staged in Moscow?'

'So the Russians apologized to you?'

'Did they apologize! Listen if I had asked them to send the prima ballerina of the Bolshoi ballet to my room, I would have had her within ten minutes.'

Ellison laughed, his mouth full of chocolate cake.

'Then they offered me a two-week tour of Soviet sports facilities, all expenses paid.'

'Did you accept?'

'Accept! I don't know the difference between a diving board and a trampoline. Don't ask *me* which has the higher net, volley ball or tennis. No, my friend: I expressed a strong desire to spend two weeks in the USSR – at their expense, of course – talking to members of the Jewish community. In private. Without police surveillance.'

'They swallowed that?'

'They had to, didn't they? After all, I am not entirely unknown among the six million American Jews who make or break Presidents.'

'Long ago, Chaim, I asked you whether you had recently been campaigning against Moscow.'

'If I had, then every IOC delegate in Vienna, not to mention every visiting journalist, would have received a copy of this.'

From his pocket Leonhard took a pamphlet which he handed to Ellison. It was published in Paris, in four languages, by the League Against Anti-Semitism. On its cover was a cartoon displayed in May, 1972, by the Soviet magazine *Krokodil*, showing a six-legged octopus at the centre of which was a Star of David. Each tentacle of the octopus carried a word: these had been changed in the Paris edition from the cyrillic alphabet into French.

'You see the six aspects of Zionism,' Leonhard said. 'Aggression, provocations, adventures, anti-Sovietism, anti-Communism, terror.'

At the heart of the Star-Octopus was a bloated capitalist wearing a high black hat crowned with yet another Star of David.

Inside the pamphlet was reprinted a feature article issued by the Novosti Press Agency and the Soviet information bureaux in Paris and Rome. According to this article, 'Israelites' were given the following rules for life:

—Akums (non-Jews) should not be regarded as people;

—An Israelite must always rejoice at the death of an Akum and never try to prevent it;

—It is better to throw a piece of meat to a dog than to give it to a goy.

'Good God,' Ellison muttered.

'So, you see, my friend, had I wished to campaign against Moscow having the Olympics, I would have made free use of this pamphlet.'

'And why didn't you?'

Leonhard shrugged. 'We made a calculation. If we took the Games away from Moscow now, we would deprive ourselves of a valuable weapon.'

'To get the Soviet Jews out of Russia?'

'Just so. Until 1977 or even 1978 it would be technically feasible to remove the Games from Moscow to Montreal or Munich. Between now and then we expect the Soviets to grant some 90,000 exit visas. If they don't....'

Ellison had barely climbed out of his bath when there was a knock on his door. Two men without faces were standing in the discreetly lit corridor. He recoiled. Then one of them laughed softly. How well he knew that laugh!

'Good God, it's Joe! And Patrick! I didn't know they let blacks into a posh place like the Sacher!'

Grinning broadly, Joseph Mutobo and Patrick Okie stepped past him into the room.

'Nice pad you've got here. Where's the five-star brandy?'

In appearance, the two Africans formed a vivid contrast. Mutobo, a Manica from the eastern region of Rhodesia and a former guerrilla fighter for Zanu, liked to adorn his tall, muscular frame in hippie shirts and colourfully patched jeans. Okie, a slender, small-boned Nigerian lawyer, preferred dark Savile Row suits and matching silk ties.

Ellison took a bottle of cognac from the cupboard and poured out three generous helpings. 'Freedom!' he said.

'Freedom! Glad to see you've learned your lines, man.'

'How do you like Vienna?'

'I've yet to see a native under the age of ninety,' Mutobo chuckled.

Ellison regarded him with deep affection. It was Joe's contacts in Lourenço Marques and Salisbury which had enabled Ellison and his young colleague Magnus Massey to publish a devastating exposé of the techniques used by multinationals to evade economic sanctions against the rebel Smith regime in Rhodesia.

'So what brings you to Vienna, Joe?'

'Your brandy. Nothing else.'

'Joe has been seconded from Zanu to the Special Investigation Department of the Organization for African Unity,' Okie explained, sipping decorously at his brandy.

'Which in effect means that I have to spend my time with a bunch of corrupt characters called the Supreme Council for Sport in Africa,' said Mutobo.

The reference was to Okie, who had worked as legal counsel for the SCSA since 1972. Within relatively few years, the Supreme Council, led by President Abraham Ordia and Secretary-General Jean-Claude Ganga, had become a force to be reckoned with in the politics of world sport, notably athletics.

'I sense that you have come to lobby me,' Ellison said. 'Which is the choice of Africa – Los Angeles or Moscow?'

'LA,' Mutobo replied immediately.

'We're faced with a serious situation,' Okie said, bringing the finger tips of his two hands together in delicate balance. 'You no doubt recall, Bill, the manoeuvres of the Detweiler-Pomonti-Wagner clique two years ago, at Munich?'

'Certainly. They almost got Rhodesia admitted to the Olympics.'

'Those bastards knew it was no-go with South Africa,' fumed Mutobo, 'so they tried it on with little Rhodesia – the Trojan Horse. And it damn nearly worked!'

Okie nodded. 'Detweiler flew to Salisbury and convinced Smith and van der Byl that they could send a team to Munich if they would only agree to parade under the British flag at the opening ceremony.'

'For one day Smith would forget about his Unilateral Declaration of Independence. The Tory Government in London was delighted – it would teach the bloody blacks of Rhodesia a lesson for insolently rejecting the wonderful Smith-Home proposals for a settlement, One Thousand Years of Servitude.'

'Calm down, Joseph,' Okie said. 'As for the Germans – the Foreign Ministry in Bonn and the Olympic Committee – they didn't mind if the British didn't. The Detweiler-Pomonti-Wagner group got their friend Kurt Klostermann, owner of the second largest newspaper chain in the Federal Republic, to launch a "Fair Deal for Little Rhodesia" campaign instead of his usual full-frontal nudes.'

'But you boys scotched it,' Ellison intervened consolingly.

'Only just!' shouted Mutobo. 'Old Avery Brundage, president of the IOC, he was against us. "Keep politics out of sport" and all that shit! In the final vote, on August 22, the majority for excluding Rhodesia was only 36 to 31.'

'Are they trying again, here in Vienna?' Ellison asked.

'No,' Okie said. 'Those men never try the same tactics twice.'

'So?'

'It was your own Searchlight team, Bill, which turned up the dirt on Detweiler, Pomonti and Wagner. When you published that, we were sure they'd be expelled from the IOC.'

'I wasn't so confident. Their activities and business connections are by no means illegal. We found out that they, like Klostermann, were all connected with chemical and electronics firms involved in the nuclear development project at Stuttgart.'

'The so-called Centre for Nuclear Research,' Okie added.

'Right. With the help of you boys and a series of spectacular raids on South African embassies, we were able to show that the Stuttgart Centre had brought South Africa's uranium enrichment technology to the level required to produce a nuclear fission weapon.'

'Hence the real purpose of the Kalahari desert test site,' Okie said.

'For Detweiler, Pomonti, Wagner and Klostermann, the South African defence programme is worth millions of dollars,' said Joseph Mutobo.

'White South Africa is driven crazy by its exclusion from international sport,' Okie said.

'So how do they get back into the Olympics?' Ellison asked. 'The Canadians won't have them at any price, so you needn't worry about Montreal in '76. Which brings us to 1980.'

'It certainly does,' Mutobo growled. 'Can you imagine all those militant blacks who live in the Los Angeles area allowing South Africa to compete? Hell, the black American athletes who raised their clenched fists in the black power salutes at Mexico and Munich had their power base in California.'

Okie nodded vigorously. 'That's true. When Tommy Smith and John Carlos, gold and silver medal winners in Mexico City, were expelled from the US team for their black-gloved salutes on the victory rostrum, they were received as heroes in black California.'

Ellison smiled. 'You've convinced me. And what about the Russians? I thought South Africa regarded Communism as the ultimate enemy.'

'Oh shit,' growled Mutobo, 'the Russians make all these fucking declarations of principle, but all they care about is prestige and gold medals.'

'Maybe.'

'Maybe nothing. The Russians have just concluded a secret deal with the Detweiler South Africa lobby.'

'What's the deal?'

'Deweiler's boys vote for Moscow on Wednesday. Two years later, after a discreet interval, the whole Communist bloc within the IOC votes for the re-admission of South Africa.'

'We know the size of the Communist voting bloc,' Ellison

objected, 'but how many votes can Detweiler deliver?'

'I believe you met Sheikh Abdul Al-Rahmani, Bill,' Okie said. 'You no doubt heard of his discontent about the present power structure within the IOC.'

'He was hardly eloquent on the subject. But I got the gist.'

'Well, there are about thirty delegates who hold the same opinion. The new Third World nations strongly resent the dominance of America and Europe. The Detweiler group has pulled off a great coup and we're in real trouble.'

'May I guess? Detweiler persuaded the Russians to commit themselves to reform of the IOC; in the long run, of course. In return, Moscow gets the votes of the Third World group on Wednesday. Later, the Russians pay off their debt to Detweiler by admitting South Africa.'

'Correct,' snapped Mutobo.

A long silence settled over the room. Ellison refilled Mutobo's brandy glass for a third time – Okie's remained half-full.

Eventually Ellison forced himself to the point: 'May one ask how you know all this?'

'We have an impeccable inside source,' Okie said.

Ellison shrugged and glanced at his watch. 'Fine. Good luck.'

'Now, Bill,' began Mutobo, rising excitedly from his chair, 'you can't hang us up on this one. I mean, the only way we can beat this thing is by massive exposure right now!'

Okie nodded vigorously. 'Joe's right. This story has to make the headlines of the major Western newspapers before Wednesday's IOC vote.'

Again Ellison shrugged. 'Then put out a statement.'

Mutobo hurled down his glass in fury, but so thick was the pile of the carpet that it refused to break and merely rolled under the bed, leaving a brown brandy stain on the floor. 'You know damn well those motherfuckers won't take any notice of us! They'll dismiss it as black propaganda!'

'Sit down, Joe,' Ellison said quietly.

'Yes, Joe, cool it,' Okie murmured. 'I warned you that Bill would want a source for this story.'

'Some evidence,' Ellison said.

The two Africans stared at one another bleakly. 'We were told this in strict confidence by . . . a great friend,' Okie said quietly.

'Sorry, Patrick. I really have to check out a story like this one.'

After a long silence Okie said: 'Our source was Armand Krohl.'

Ellison picked up the telephone. 'Give me Mr Krohl, please. No, I don't know his room number.'

The two Africans stared at him, horrified. The tension in the room was now electric.

'Krohl,' Krohl said.

'Bill Ellison speaking, Mr Krohl. I have Joe and Patrick here. They bring me a big story, citing you as their source. If you'll confirm it to me, I'll print it without attribution, that goes without saying.'

'No.'

'No, what?'

'The risk, for me, is too great. I'm more use inside the IOC Executive Board than ignominiously expelled from it. That would please our common enemies a great deal.'

'I did promise to – '

'No. Very sorry.' And Armand Krohl replaced the receiver.

Ellison turned to the two Africans and raised his hands in a gesture of helplessness. 'I'm sorry, too, boys. It seems that we all have our reputations to guard.'

Mutobo took several steps in his direction. His eyes, red from too much brandy, blazed with anger. 'You coward, Ellison. You coward – after all I've done for you!'

It seemed for a moment as if he would strike the object of

his fury, but Okie wrapped his slender arms round Mutobo's rippling muscles and eventually succeeded in coaxing him back into his chair.

'Why don't we all go and have a consolation dinner,' Ellison suggested. 'It's on me, by the way.'

'Good evening, Herr Ellison.'

'Good evening.'

Some twenty minutes after returning from a rather unhappy dinner with Mutobo and Okie, and having dutifully begun to study a fat folder of expensively illustrated promotional material issued by the Moscow delegation, Ellison had been distracted by a tap on his door.

The young lady who stood stiffly in the corridor had long blonde hair and wore dark glasses. An ankle-length leather coat, trimmed with fur, protected her against the chill of an autumn night. She carried a leather briefcase, and her rigid expression reminded Ellison of the one adopted by Greta Garbo in his favourite film, *Ninotchka.*

'My name, Herr Ellison, is Anne-Marie Schubert. I am a graduate of the F. Engels Institute of Sports Science, Leipzig.'

'My name's Wolfgang Amadeus Mozart. You'd better come in.'

'Thank you.' She marched stiffly past him, surveyed the capitalist decadence of the room with obvious scorn, then tossed her long leather coat on the bed. Beneath it she was wearing a skin-tight, wet-look black jumpsuit and knee-high boots poised on stiletto heels. 'I represent the Soviet National Olympic Committee,' she added.

'I could have guessed – even before you took your coat off.'

'It is my task to answer any questions you may have concerning the 22nd Olympiad and to repair any gaps in your knowledge of that event. Now kindly turn your attention to the graphs, maps, tables of statistics and illustrations that I am displaying on the bed. Remember that Moscow, unlike Munich and Montreal, already possesses sport facilities sufficient to stage the Olympics tomorrow. We have 5,475 sports arenas, including 61 stadiums, 1,815 sports halls and 37 swimming pools.'

'Ah, but how many of them are heated?'

'That is of no account, since we do not plan to use any of them. Main athletic events will commence on July 19, 1980, in the Lenin Stadium – commonly called the Luzhniki by Muscovites – capacity 103,000. Not only will a new Olympic pool be built but also an Olympic village capable of housing 12,000 competitors, 3,500 referees and 800 officials.'

'Should I be taking notes?'

'These facts are all included in your information kit.'

'It's hot in here, don't you find?'

'Moscow already possesses 42,000 hotel beds. By 1980 this figure will have been increased to 78,000 bed units plus 30,000 hostel beds. Architectural competitions have been launched; tenders for a brand new international airport will be put out to foreign firms.'

'No brandy?'

'The Soviet National Olympic Committee plans to welcome no less than 7,000 journalists from all parts of the world.'

'And all social systems, you forgot that bit.'

'Yes, I – '

'Bend over, Anne-Marie.'

'No less than 1,200 seats will be reserved in the Lenin Stadium for television and radio commentators. The two electronic screens serving the stadium are each capable of carrying 512 symbols.'

'You must be exaggerating.'

The young woman was seated on the edge of the bed now;

one slender leg was delicately cocked over the other. Her expression remained impassive, her eyes inscrutable behind the dark glasses.

'Automatic Data Control systems will be employed to gather, process and distribute information. Negotiations are in progress for the purchase of a one-million-dollar Sperry Rand computer by the Soviet news agency, Tass. A new press centre at Luzhniki will be equipped with five hundred telex machines. Communications facilities include, of course, our magnificent Ostankino TV tower, at 592.9 metres the highest building in Europe.'

'Yes, I've always been puzzled by that "point 9" at the end. Was there some slight error, do you think?'

Anne-Marie Schubert had risen from the bed now and was pacing the floor with the grace and contained energy of a caged cheetah. 'You have heard, of course, of our orbiting space station "Mars" which guarantees high-quality colour TV transmission via Soviet satellites across the world.'

'Satellites? You mean Hungary, Czechoslovakia, your own German Democratic Republic, etcetera?'

She stamped her high-heeled boot with indignation. 'You are not trying to understand! Herr Ellison, I bring a message from Sergei Pavlov, Minister of Sport; Vladimir Promyslov, Mayor of Moscow; and Ignati Novikov, Chairman of the Organizing Committee of the Moscow Games.'

'Don't exaggerate, Anne-Marie.'

'During the next six years you, Ellison, British journalist, will be required to write at least one feature article per month lauding the achievements of the Soviet Union in preparing for the 1980 Olympiad.'

'And if I refuse?' he said softly.

'Then you will be . . . eliminated.'

'Whom do you really work for?'

'Please do not ask me that!'

With a quick, deft movement he lifted the blonde wig from

her head, then the dark glasses. He kissed her. Slowly Ruth Leonhard's arms encircled his neck.

'I'm old enough to be your father.'

'You don't feel like my father.'

'Chaim wouldn't like it.'

'Chaim isn't doing it.'

She drew him down to the bed; her tongue flicked tenderly into his mouth. Her slender, supple body filled him with an almost uncontrollable desire, the middle-aged man's yearning for the clear, soft, unbruised flesh of the fountain woman, for the bright light in her eyes, the innocent ambition, the scent of her smooth skin, the overspilling erotic energy. The pain he had felt, the disappointment, when she had not showed up as promised with Chaim had appalled him. You will not see that girl again, he had told himself; learn to live with it, and learn fast.

Her body now lay on top of his; her soft black hair tumbled round his face, her kisses grew longer, the motions of her small hand more feverish.

'Who are you really?' she murmured in his ear as she began to probe his sex. 'A ruthless, callous, unprincipled man. A dangerous man. A man who will stop at nothing to get his big story. A frightening man.'

'You don't feel frightened,' he whispered.

'But I am. Very.'

And then she showed him the effect that fright had upon her. The hour that followed ranked among the most beautiful, the most fulfilling, of his life. In the flesh she was everything, and more, that her enigmatic smile had promised; the spirit that commanded her exquisite body was more than a match for his own. If fame were the aphrodisiac, if his reputation and achievements inspired her love-making, he was happy. He had never set much store by his face; and a man, after all, is what he does.

He slept so deeply that he was unaware that Ruth had left

until the first light of day awoke him. Had it all been a dream? He ordered breakfast from room service, shaved and showered, then began to assemble his kit for the day. Transferring his tortoiseshell cigarette case from one suit pocket to another, he glanced inside it. The tape had gone. In its place was a tiny purple card: 'I couldn't resist, kisses, R.'

He smiled. Ambition. She would graduate *summa cum laude* from the University of Chicago.

Although he didn't realize it until some years later, Bill Ellison had made his second serious mistake within twenty-four hours.

CHAPTER 3

October 23, 1974. Vienna

An imposing array of chauffeur-driven limousines was drawn up in front of Vienna's magnificent Rathaus, the Town Hall. Designed by the Wurttemberg architect Friedrich von Schmidt one hundred years ago, the building presents a vast neo-Gothic façade, softened by Renaissance elements and decorated by statues of artists and public figures. At its 300-foot pinnacle the Rathaus is crowned by the famous 'Iron Man', the statue, ten feet high, of a knight in armour holding a spear 18 feet long.

There are 108 steps from the flowerbedded Rathausplatz to the council chamber in which the IOC session was due to meet. As the cameras clicked and turned the dignitaries arrived: elderly, dignified, exclusively male, not a few of them princes, peers, counts, sultans, sheikhs, rajahs. But the IOC's only reigning monarch, Constantine of Greece, had finally resigned when it became overwhelmingly clear to him that he was no longer reigning.

The journalists crowded forward. The influential Marquess of Exeter, chairman of the International Amateur Athletic Federation, had just arrived. As Lord Burghley, fresh out of Eton and Cambridge, he had won an Olympic gold medal for the 400 metres hurdles in the Games of 1928. The Marquess declined to answer journalists' questions or to state his preference between Moscow and Los Angeles.

Two minutes later a new wave of recognition greeted Comte Jean de Beaumont, senior vice-president of the IOC, whose preference for Moscow was already on record. Then came the influential Finn, Baron Erik von Frenckell, followed by Armand Krohl, a member of the Executive Board, equally well known to reporters and cameramen. And now, the key figure himself, Lord Killanin.

Elected in 1972 to succeed the famous guardian of amateurism, the American millionaire and art collector Avery Brundage, the portly, jovial Irish peer carried the burdens of the presidency comparatively lightly. He was both a Catholic and a liberal; the iron hand in the velvet glove. 'We all have our own beliefs,' he had said; 'we all have our friends and enemies; but the aim of the Olympic movement is to subjugate these in the fellowship which is enshrined in the intertwining Olympic rings representing the five continents of the world, wedded together in sport, peace and friendship.'

The Killanin family motto was 'Deus nobiscum quis contra nos' – If God is with us, who is against us?

Following an address of welcome by the President of the Austrian Republic, Herr Rudolph Kirchschläger, the playing of the Olympic anthem and music by Mozart and Schubert, the elderly members of the IOC Assembly filed into a lecture hall fitted up with a 16mm projector, a screen, various exhibit tables covered with scale models and a team of ten gleaming Soviet salesmen dressed in French suits of blue cloth designed by Pierre Cardin, Italian silk shirts and ties, and sun tans acquired in ultra-violet health clinics. With dazzling deftness and almost permanent smiles acquired from an intensive study of Madison Avenue marketing techniques, the Russians treated their hypnotized audience to a quick-fire show of slides, films, charts and lectures. They worked with the sleek precision of Ferrari mechanics in a Grand Prix pit stop.

Headphones for simultaneous translation into five languages had been provided.

Sergei Pavlov, chairman of the Soviet Olympic Committee, spoke briefly: 'Lord Killanin, honoured members of the IOC. Your Executive Board has already received the formal pledge of the Soviet Government guaranteeing that Olympic Games held in Moscow will conform to the rules and regulations of the IOC. May I make my own personal pledge that the Soviet Union will issue visas to *all* competitors recognized by the IOC, regardless of political or social system.'

Questions were fired at him from the floor.

'What about the People's Republic of China?'

'Yes,' said Pavlov calmly. 'If elected before 1980.'

'And Chile?'

'Of course.'

'Israel?'

'Yes, Israel, too.'

'What about Rhodesia and South Africa?' Sheikh Abdul Al-Rahmani asked.

'Gentlemen, they are not recognized by the IOC.'

'But suppose the IOC shall change its mind between now and 1980?'

Pavlov's English was quite good but not good enough to cope with the Sheikh's. There was considerable tension in the room while Pavlov waited for the translation.

'Yes,' he nodded vigorously. 'We will not stand in the way of any country recognized by the IOC.'

'How will the seats for spectators be allocated?' asked a member from Western Europe.

'Half the seats will be allocated to Muscovites and officials, one quarter to visitors from other parts of the USSR, and one quarter to foreign visitors. I should add that 7 million tickets will be on sale compared with 4 million in Munich.'

'How will you allocate the tickets reserved for foreign visitors?'

'There will be discussions in October-November, 1978, here in Moscow.'

This remark was greeted by laughter which Pavlov himself did not understand until a junior colleague in a beautiful blue suit stepped forward and whispered in his ear. It was a mark of Pavlov's confidence that he now felt himself to be at home in Moscow; it was also a mark of how many of the men sitting before him had recently visited Russia as official guests of the Soviet Olympic Committee.

'Will all visitors require visas?'

'Certainly, yes. But Soviet consulates will be instructed to issue visas almost automatically to all ticket holders.'

'You say "*almost* automatically to all ticket holders",' the questioner persisted. 'A Soviet visa is sometimes slower than a Soviet sprinter like Borzov.' (Laughter.)

'We don't anticipate any visa problems – not with bona fide sporting visitors. Of course, if certain criminal elements were to purchase tickets as a pretext....' Pavlov let the sentence evaporate; no one was prepared to pursue it.

A moment later, Pavlov was holding out economic bait. In September, 1976, immediately following the Montreal Olympics, a technical exhibition would be staged in Moscow; more than 300 firms from 25 countries were expected to take part. 'Remember, gentlemen, that we will be catering for between 100,000 and 120,000 visitors at any one time between July 19 and August 3, 1980. We will need refrigeration facilities, new running tracks, furnishings, buildings, food and drink in massive quantities to please foreign tastes, sporting equipment – we expect foreign firms to play a major role in providing these vital items, not to mention communications equipment and computers of the most advanced kind.'

Later the members listened to Mayor Bradley and the delegation from Los Angeles. But there was an air of unreality, almost of amateurishness, about the American city's sales pitch. Yes, yes, it was true that LA already boasted splendid tracks, stadiums, pools and student dormitories; so what? The political muscle was all on the Russians' side.

Later Lord Killanin, wearing a dark blue lightweight suit, a white shirt and a polka-dot handkerchief in his breast pocket, appeared before the assembled international press in an adjoining room of the Rathaus. Ellison noticed with a smile that the president was wearing his Garrick Club tie. Killanin's tone was crisp, confident, friendly; Eton, the Sorbonne and Magdalene College, Cambridge had left their stamp on the man. His job was unpaid but expenses were covered. Killanin himself estimated that he spent about a quarter of his time on IOC business, travelling some 100,000 miles each year. The telex was his favourite means of communication.

Despite the flashing cameras, the banks of microphones confronting him and the intense heat generated by the lights, Killanin remained unruffled. The limelight meant nothing to him, one way or the other.

'Good morning, gentlemen. The city selected to hold the Games of the 22nd Olympiad is Moscow.'

As the clamour of voices rose, demanding to know the vote, the president of the IOC smiled briefly, then turned on his heel and walked out.

Later, as the delegates dispersed for lunch, Ellison waylaid Armand Krohl on the steps of the Rathaus.

'What was the vote?'

Limping, Krohl led him away from the throng, out of earshot. 'There is a rumour going about that the vote was 39 for Moscow, 22 for Los Angeles.' A mischievous light glinted briefly in his eyes.

'And how, according to rumour, did the Third World delegates vote?'

'For Moscow – according to rumour.'

'And what, according to rumour, are the chances of South Africa gaining re-admission between now and 1980?'

Krohl's face clouded: the human rights activist abruptly took on the contours of the professor of jurisprudence.

'It depends if we are vigilant, Mr Ellison.'

CHAPTER 4

July, 1976. Switzerland

Magnus Massey checked into the Hotel des Papes a week before the opening ceremony of the 21st modern Olympiad. Delicate research lay behind his choice of a hotel. Apart from a suitcase, he also carried a large, leather hold-all containing expensive electrical equipment.

But no sooner had he taken possession of Room 204 than the entire electrical circuit in his room failed: lights, razor socket, ice-box, air conditioning, television. He complained vigorously to Room Service: this wasn't what he was paying 60 Swiss francs a night for.

The electrician arrived quickly. He examined the wiring and scratched his head: if the thought hadn't been absolutely absurd, you could have imagined that some bastard had quite deliberately and very deftly sabotaged the works!

He worked hard but it wasn't easy with this tall, blond Englishman pacing back and forth in a towering rage, complaining he would miss all his appointments. If only one could have moved the bastard to another room: but every hotel bedroom in the town had been booked months in advance!

But these Englishmen have strange temperaments. Quite suddenly the fellow eased up, offered a cigarette, chatted pleasantly. Quite a change! Easier to work under those conditions. And *mon dieu*, these wires were *foutu* in a most diabolical way.

The guest asked the electrician about his boss, the hotel's chief electrical engineer. Ah! Now that was quite a story, *monsieur*! Oh, yes! That Jean-Etienne Marchard was quite a fellow, mad on sport, the last of the big spenders, but supporting a wife, four children, an expensive mistress and an unbridled passion for golf, skiiing, yachting, surfing, skin-diving, tennis, fast cars... you name it!

Jean-Etienne Marchard was in debt, all right. And the bank was threatening to foreclose on his collateral. Marchard had even thought of suicide one weekend, but the weather was so beautiful that he took his mistress skin-diving instead. One was only human! And that girl, she wouldn't look twice at a fellow who drove anything less than a Jaguar. Besides, his wife demanded a little runabout car for the shopping and having her hair done – he could hardly refuse her.

'*Monsieur*, that Jean-Etienne Marchard is a man who cannot say no!'

When the electrician had mended the circuit and departed, Magnus put through a call and asked to speak to Monsieur Marchard. Within ten minutes the chief electrical engineer was knocking on his door.

'I'm sorry you had trouble, *monsieur*,' he said with dignity. 'I trust all is now well.'

Magnus closed the door, motioned Marchard to a chair and brought out a bottle of malt whisky. Marchard protested that he was on duty but it was only a token protest: as the electrician had said, here was a man incapable of saying no. To anything nice.

What Magnus Massey slowly removed from his wallet and let drop on the table was very nice indeed. One thousand dollars. Almost a month's pay. And tax free.

'Have another,' Magnus murmured, refilling his guest's glass.

'What... what are you asking of me, *monsieur*?'

Magnus told him. 'Room 310.'

Marchard shrugged. 'That is a big job, *monsieur*! If it came to light I would be out of my job with the worst references in Switzerland! Besides, there is the problem of the equipment.'

Magnus hoisted the large leather hold-all from the wardrobe on to the bed and invited the chief electrical engineer to examine the contents. Marchard whistled in admiration. 'Very pretty!'

'You'll find all the required fittings in the bag. I have some experience of this kind of job.' He handed Marchard a printed chart of circuit diagrams.

Marchard was whistling between his teeth. He felt nervous, so nervous in fact that he even asked: 'Perhaps you could tell me, *monsieur*, why you want to do this. I mean, are you a cop?'

'I'm a journalist. The gentleman who occupies Room 310 will be out of the hotel tomorrow morning from breakfast to lunch. The coast will be clear.'

The chambermaids proved to be the main problem, fussing about the rooms and corridors of the third floor, coming and going with clean towels and vacuum cleaners. As for the housekeeper, she was everywhere, vigilant, suspicious, poking her nose. And then you never knew when some sharp little messenger boy would walk in with a telegram, spot your game and promptly demand $500 for his silence.

The job took Marchard a couple of hours. He had to admit that they were lovely to handle, these miniaturized microphone-transmitters, manufactured by Schellen-Hahn GmbH, a German subsidiary of Tishika Industries of Osaka. They occupied no more space than a large walnut. One in the telephone, one behind the central light fitting, one behind the skirting under the bed, and every word that passed would be recorded forty feet away, behind the locked doors of the control cubicle which housed the fuse boxes, meter boxes and master switches controlling all the third-floor circuits.

Marchard agreed to remove the tapes twice a day from the control cubicle, bring them to Magnus's room and replace them with new ones.

They shook hands at Marchard's behest. 'I hope you get the big story, *monsieur*.'

'And I wish you a month's happiness.'

At this, the chief electrical engineer looked slightly nonplussed.

True to his word (and his $1,000), Marchard brought the tapes from Room 310 to Magnus twice a day. There was one tape which Massey played back until he knew it by heart.

First Man: 'We're still short of the forty votes we need to gain re-admission to the Olympic movement.'

Second Man: 'At my estimate, we have thirty-three votes in the bag.'

Third Man: 'When I pressed Novikov and Pavlov about our agreement, they hedged. They're playing wait-and-see.'

Fourth Man: 'Which is why we've got to make our big push in the West. Connie Mulder has called for maximum effort between now and the summer of '78. No expense is to be spared – I have that from Kruger at information. I believe Ellison might help us.'

Second Man: 'Ellison! He's enemy number one.'

Third Man: 'I've always told Hendrik he should be eliminated like a kaffir's mongrel dog. But Hendrik won't give the order. He's afraid of international complications.'

Fourth Man: 'I think we might pluck him now.'

First Man: 'Don't forget how close he got to your half-brother with his last Rhodesia story.'

Fourth Man: 'Not just close. Spot on. Ellison doesn't publish everything he knows. He plays a waiting game. Sometimes he's prepared to wait for years. Robert, you shall approach him.'

Second Man: 'When and where?'

Fourth Man: 'The Russians are due to hold a party on board the *Pushkin* during the Montreal Games. Choose your moment.'

Third Man: 'What about the Jews – Leonhard and Enders?'

Fourth Man: 'They're desperate. We have them in the bag.'

It was the Fourth Man who occupied Room 310.

July, 1976. Montreal

Ellison flew in to Montreal three days before the opening ceremony and checked in to the Hudson Bay Hotel. He and Massey dined that evening with Chaim Leonhard in a French-Canadian restaurant called the Coq d'Or.

'I'm on what's called a seafood diet,' Leonhard chuckled. 'If I see food, I eat it.'

It was their first meeting since Vienna, their first meeting since Ellison had made love to Leonhard's daughter. He wondered what this shrewd father knew, or had divined. The Jewish lawyer, however, could speak of one thing only, a subject which plunged him into an intense, all-consuming despondency.

'You have followed this Taiwan affair? It's a disaster for Israel.'

'I don't see the connection,' Massey said.

Leonhard glanced sardonically at Ellison. 'If he works for you, he should be bright.' He turned back to the younger journalist. 'Canada, as host nation, is brazenly flouting Rule 4 of the IOC Charter by refusing to admit the Taiwan team under the name recognized by the IOC, "Republic of China".'

'Presumably Ottawa is in no hurry to jeopardize its huge wheat-exporting deal with Peking,' Ellison commented.

'Don't give me excuses,' Leonhard said, tucking unhappily into a dozen snails-in-garlic. 'Just note the facts. The Canadians have come under sustained pressure from the most powerful of nations, the United States, to let in the Taiwanese. President Ford himself has lodged a protest: USOC

President Krumm has been conferring with the White House three times a day and has even threatened to pull his team of 425 athletes right out of the Games. Despite all this, Killanin has publicly admitted defeat. So what does this prove, Mr Massey?'

'That Russia can get away with barring Israel in 1980?'

'I knew you must be bright.'

Ellison asked Leonhard whether he now regretted not having lobbied on behalf of Los Angeles at the crucial Vienna meeting of the IOC two years earlier.

'Well, my friend, the Jews have been coming out of Russia. So far our policy has worked – give the Russians something they desperately want, the Games, on condition they behave themselves.'

'So you're not planning to change tactics?'

'Not for the time being. But I'm worried. This Taiwan affair stinks. I have spoken to Krohl. He has been trying to convince the IOC Executive Board that unless they take a firm stand with the Canadians now, the Russians will get away with murder in 1980.'

'What does a firm stand mean?' Massey asked.

Leonhard shrugged. 'Ultimately, in the last resort, it means withdrawing recognition. The Games then cease to be the Olympic Games.'

'But the IOC just can't do that at this late stage,' Ellison protested. 'The whole financial structure of the Olympic movement would collapse. Millions of dollars have been paid for franchises. Besides, the IOC's Contract is not with the Canadian Government but with the City of Montreal, which has plunged itself millions of dollars into debt.'

Leonhard nodded sadly. 'For Israel, it's not a question of franchises, it's a question of survival.'

'At a pinch,' Ellison said caustically, 'Israel could survive outside the Olympic movement.'

Chaim Leonhard laid down his knife and fork, wiped his

mouth with his napkin, rose, collected his homburg hat and walked out of the Coq d'Or.

An outraged Israeli or an outraged father? Ellison wasn't sure.

'Nice of you to come at short notice,' Armand Krohl said, ushering Ellison into his room in the Hotel de France. 'You know Joe and Patrick, of course,' he continued, as Mutobo and Okie greeted Ellison with the cool reserve that had characterized their attitude ever since he had declined to print their story of a Russian-South African secret trade-off.

Ellison noticed that Okie had now discarded his Savile Row suits for an American-style Afro haircut and a simple white tunic in the style of President Julius Nyerere.

'I asked you all to come and see me in a last-ditch effort to avoid the threatened African boycott of the Games,' Krohl explained. 'I personally sympathize with the sentiment inspiring the boycott; on the other hand, I am a guardian of the Olympic movement and I must deplore any attempt to sabotage it.'

'Blame New Zealand for that, not us,' Mutobo said.

'Either the IOC bans New Zealand or 21 African and Arab states boycott the Games,' Okie declared adamantly. 'The position of the OAU and of the Supreme Council for Sport in Africa is completely unequivocal.'

And then Emile Angel spoke. A huge, genial, bearded man who had once put the shot for South Africa until his conscience drove him to protest against apartheid in sport, Angel had lived in London for some years working for SANROC, the South African Non-Racial Olympic Committee. SANROC's offices in Charlotte Street, like those of the Anti-Apartheid movement, had become a primary target for agents of the South African Bureau of State Security, BOSS.

'I would have expected, Armand, that we could count on

your support. Is there some factor in this situation that we're missing?'

'It's very difficult for the IOC to conduct two battles simultaneously,' Krohl said. 'To be frank with you, the Taiwan affair is quite enough: the Canadian Government has presented the IOC with a fundamental challenge to its authority. What we in the Executive Board need is the full support of every member nation in resisting that challenge. Otherwise there is little doubt that the Russians will take the hint and throw up all kinds of barriers in 1980.'

'Against whom?' Okie asked.

'Well, Israel, for example.' Krohl looked to Ellison. 'Since you enjoy some credit with our friends here, I hoped against hope that you might persuade them that the pretext for the current African boycott is so trivial that it seriously risks discrediting our entire struggle against racism in Africa.'

Ellison lit a small cigar. He noticed that Joe Mutobo was glowering at him with undisguised hostility.

'It's certainly a hell of a pity not to be able to see athletes of the calibre of Kip Keino, Mike Boit and John Akii-Bua, or the great Ethiopian marathon runners.'

'They understand the sacrifice they must make,' Okie said. 'I have spoken with them: they realize that they must subordinate their personal ambitions to the general will of the African people.'

'That's just shit,' Ellison said.

Abruptly, high tension pervaded the room. Joe Mutobo's fists were clenched now. Okie adopted an expression of cold intellectual disdain.

'The only thing you fellows care about is politics, politics, politics,' Ellison went on. 'And what's it all about? A team of New Zealand rugby players – a non-Olympic sport – accepted an invitation to play in South Africa. Therefore you insist that all New Zealand athletes, who had nothing to do with the rugby players' decision, must be excluded from these

Olympics. It's a load of rubbish. You fellows come from countries where the government turns a switch and everyone has to fall into line. In New Zealand players can travel where they like, and play where they like, whether their government likes it or not. But you won't be happy until the whole world is at the mercy of your overbearing and autocratic *diktat*. You don't give a damn for all those African athletes who trained for years in anticipation of this supreme test and who are now sitting about the Olympic Village with their dreams shattered and tears pouring down their faces. And who will lose? They will. Black Africa will. As for the South Africans, I imagine they are laughing their heads off.' Ellison stood up and smiled bleakly at Krohl. 'Well, you asked for my opinion. Now you have it. *Adios*.'

Cruising effortlessly round the track, his nine-foot strides reducing his rivals to the stature of pygmies, the Cuban giant Alberto Juantorena swept up the final straight to take his second gold medal within a week: first the 400 metres and now the 800 metres. Spontaneously, the vast summer crowd gathered in the Montreal Olympic Stadium rose to its feet: what they had just seen was more than a great athlete; they had witnessed a phenomenon.

'Even so,' Ellison remarked to Magnus Massey as they left the Stadium, 'if I had to chose one idol from Juantorena and Lasse Viren, I'd go for the Finn. To take the gold in both the 5,000 and 10,000 metres in two successive Olympics is just phenomenal. And Juantorena must enjoy training – who wouldn't in a climate steady at 80° Fahrenheit all the year round? Imagine the young Viren slogging through the winter gloom of the Nordic forests at 20° below zero, day after day, mesmerized against fatigue, pain and frostbite by the fragile prospect of two days of glory in four years' time.'

'There's talk of blood-doping by the Finns, of course.'

'Jealousy.'

'Maybe. It's not illegal to remove a pint of an athlete's blood three weeks before a competition, allow him to make up the deficit during high altitude training and then reinject the pint to provide him with an enhanced oxygen supply.'

'It should be illegal.'

On July 24, the Soviet Olympic Committee threw a sumptuous party on board the motorship *Pushkin*, moored in the St Lawrence River. Top brass from the City of Montreal, the IOC and the media were greeted at the head of the gangway by Ignati Novikov, chairman of the Organizing Committee of the Moscow Games; Sergei Pavlov, Minister of Sport; and Vladimir Promyslov, Mayor of Moscow.

The Russians were doing it in style – unlimited caviar, vodka and champagne. Franchise-seekers, souvenir salesmen, politicians, courtesans and journalists mingled in a raucous atmosphere of artificial cordiality and cynical calculation. The presidents of the three major American television networks were on board, all bidding for the exclusive TV rights to the Moscow Olympics. In 1968 ABC had paid a mere $7 million for exclusive coverage; in 1972, $11 million; here in Montreal the price had upped to $25 million.

'And now,' Sol Enders was telling Ellison, 'the goddamn Russians are demanding $100 million. And it's cheap at the price! I have it from ABC that their Montreal investment will bring them a gross operating profit of $63 million within two weeks.'

Wearing a loud primrose summer suit, the great promoter had staggered aboard, surviving the crunching bear-hugs of his Russian hosts, followed by a retinue of lieutenants who looked as if they were stopping off on their way from Sicily to Nicaragua.

'How's your deal with the Sheikh?' Ellison asked, gesturing towards Sheikh Abdul Al-Rahmani, who was accompanied by two bodyguards wearing desert *kiffiyeh* and *dishdashas.*

'Big, real big. We have it all tied up for 1988.' Enders didn't elaborate but led Ellison away from the throng, out of earshot, lowering his voice. Abruptly the promoter shed his brashness.

'Chaim told me you were rough with him about Israel.'

'I know. It was just a silly remark.'

'Bill, I'm worried about Israel. You maybe assume that all Sol Enders cares about is making money. I'd like you to know that I have given in my time $3 million to the Jewish National Fund. Two years ago I tried to warn Chaim that he was making the biggest mistake of his life in not taking on the Russians. Now look at this Taiwan business. It stinks. Bill, I'm not a student of the British press but the people whose opinion I respect assure me that when you hit a target you knock it down. Chaim is still vacillating. Soon it will be too late. Bill, we've got to get the 1980 Olympics away from Moscow. This African-Arab boycott is just a rehearsal for cutting Israel out in 1980. The Russians won't resist.'

Ellison nodded and gave Enders his card. 'Call me in London any time I can be of help.'

'Bill, I appreciate that. It's good to know we Jews still have some friends left.' There was genuine emotion in his handshake.

They drifted apart. A moment later Ellison felt a light tap on his shoulder. He turned. A man wearing an expensive suit and a large white carnation in his buttonhole was extending his hand with a warm smile.

'Monsieur Ellison, I believe.' He spoke in French.

'Yes.'

'My name is Robert Pomonti, member of the IOC. Although we have not met, I believe we are known to one another. You were once kind enough to publish a 5,000-word description of my business contacts with South Africa, together with those of my colleagues Detweiler and Wagner.'

'I hope you found it accurate.'

'Have you ever given thought, I wonder, to the black South African athletes who remain frozen out of international competition?'

'Certainly.'

'Would it interest you to meet some of them?'

'So long as Pretoria continues to refuse me permission to enter South Africa –'

'Yes, yes,' Pomonti cut in, dabbing his forehead with a paisley silk handkerchief. 'If a working visit could be arranged by the Department of Information, would you accept the invitation?'

'I might.'

'All expenses would be paid, of course.'

'I always pay my own way.'

'As you prefer.' Pomonti again offered his hand. 'No one wishes to compromise your integrity.' He turned away with a smile which failed to touch his glassy eyes.

For a moment Ellison was alone, adrift with his own thoughts in a sea of intrigue, chicanery and insincerity. Looking down at the cool waters of the St Lawrence he recaptured the image of Lasse Viren's expression as he summoned from the depths of his being the supreme, lynching effort of mind and body to forge ahead of his rivals to the tape. The face of an honest man.

'So, you are dreaming.'

She was standing beside him, leaning on the rail, smiling.

'Ruth!'

'Yes.'

'Ruth.' He touched her dark hair. 'You're real.'

'I stole your tape, are you angry?'

'You're still lovely. More lovely.'

'Thank you.'

'Where have you been, all these months?'

'I was twice in London, wanted to call you, thought you'd prefer me not to. Was I right?'

'No. Yes.'

'And how are you, great and dangerous man?'

'Mucking along. Are you still a student?'

'I graduated *summa cum laude.* They gave me a job on the *Chicago Tribune.* So, you see, you must now treat me as an equal.'

'Does that mean not making love to you?'

She averted her gaze. 'Where will you be next weekend?'

'In London.'

'I thought of driving up to Quebec. Never been there. Have you?'

'Yes, once.'

'Is once enough?'

He leaned over the rail, smiling down at the water. 'I ought, of course, to study the Francophone separatist movement.'

'Mmn.' Her finger tips touched his. 'So where will you be next weekend?'

'In Quebec.'

'Does the sight of me please you?'

'Yes.'

'Do you love me?'

'Yes.'

'Do you want to sleep with me?'

'Only if you promise to be there in the morning.'

'Do you want to kiss me now?'

'Yes.'

'You can't. I can see my father talking to Sol Enders.'

'Your father . . . does he . . . I mean – '

She laughed. 'Of course not! He's a very simple man, really, not nearly so clever as you imagine.'

CHAPTER 5

October, 1976. London–South Africa

Two months after the Montreal Olympics, Ellison received an invitation from a body called the Fair Play Campaign, accompanied by a letter from the South African Government, extending the most cordial welcome to 'our beautiful but much abused country'.

The North London garden in which Ellison now sat on a mellow October afternoon belonged to Mr Emile Angel and his wife, Penelope, née Chosutu. They formed a striking physical contrast, and not only in colour: he, 6′ 3″ tall and weighing 257 pounds; she, a minute 5′ 2″, slender as a reed. Between them they had produced four laughing, cheeky children every shade of chocolate.

No flower or vegetable dared poke up its head in Emile's barren, crater-pitted garden: even the last tufts of grass had withered under the salt of his drenching sweat. For here he worked out with his $2,500 Schnell Trainer, engaging in two-arm barbell presses at 30 kilograms and full squats at 45 kilograms. Here, too, dreaming of the feats he might have achieved before vast summer crowds had not his conscience torn him from his native land, he heaved the shot 60 feet or more.

'So you have decided to accept the South African invitation,' Patrick Okie remarked coolly to Ellison.

'Yes. Any background information you fellows can give me would be helpful.'

'I thought you distrusted our information,' Joe Mutobo said belligerently. 'And our motives.'

'Obviously they believe they can buy you,' Okie said.

'They may be right,' Mutobo added.

'Hey, boys,' Emile Angel begged, handing round glasses of barley water, 'cool it.'

But the two Africans were relentless. 'I suppose you realize what a big propaganda scoop your visit will be for them.'

'Depends what I write afterwards,' Ellison said.

'No,' said Okie. 'You'll be on television stepping off the plane.'

'You're stabbing us in the back,' Mutobo said, 'just as you did in Vienna. And Montreal.'

'No, no, no,' Emile Angel intervened gently. 'With respect, Joe, Patrick, a reporter should go everywhere, see everything. Otherwise his opponents can always capitalize on his lack of first-hand knowledge. They can claim he's simply a dupe, a mouthpiece of propagandists like ourselves.'

'Thanks, Emile,' Ellison said, 'you're a real white man.'

A stunned silence – then Angel grinned. 'I'll tell you a joke about the proverbial Afrikaaner farmer van der Merwe, you can repeat it to your hosts in Jo'burg. Van der Merwe is taking his cows to market but one of them worries him: she's cross-eyed, he fears she won't fetch a good price. So he goes to the vet for advice. The vet says: "It's easy. Just stick a hollow bamboo up her arse at the right moment, blow with all your strength and her eyes will straighten out." When Van der Merwe gets to market he tells his black boy to stick the bamboo up the cow and start blowing. The boy blows like mad but it doesn't make too much difference to the cow's cross-eyes. "Give it here, boy," Van der Merwe snorts impatiently. He pulls the bamboo out of the cow, turns it round, sticks the other end up her arse and blows like mad. It works; he gets a good price for the beast. Later another farmer asks him why he pulled the bamboo out and turned it round before he started blowing. "Good God, man," he says, "you don't think I'm going to put my mouth where a bloody kaffir had his."'

Mutobo and Okie collapsed in laughter. The atmosphere

thawed; in a shrewd stroke, Angel had succeeded in turning the tension.

'I hear that SANROC had another break-in on Tuesday,' Ellison said.

Angel nodded. 'It's the third this year. Nothing was taken except our files and address books. The CID came, and then the Special Branch. They think we're all Commies.'

'The British Special Branch works hand-in-glove with BOSS,' Mutobo said, directing his remark towards Ellison.

Ellison nodded. 'No informed person could deny it.'

'I'll never forget the 1960 season,' Angel said. 'It opened my eyes. On four successive occasions Amos Bethonga bettered my distance in the shot: he even set a national record. But who won the National Championships? I did. Why? Because Amos was a Bantu, and Bantus weren't allowed to compete against whites.'

Okie jumped up from his chair. 'Do you know what South Africa told the IOC in 1966? "There are no blacks fit to take part in our Olympic team. They're all running around wild."'

To the delight of Angel's children, Joe Mutobo began prancing around the garden, with bent back and dropping arms, screeching like a demented baboon.

'South Africa was actually disbarred by the IOC in 1964?'

'Yes,' said Okie. 'But two years later she staged a counter-coup and gained re-admission. The Supreme Council had to act fast: by the Mexico Olympics in '68 we had lined up forty nations threatening a boycott. The IOC had to back down and later expelled South Africa, though Brundage didn't like it.'

'Dennis Brutus led the anti-apartheid opposition inside South Africa,' Angel went on. 'He was a real thorn in their flesh, an inspiration to all of us. On one occasion the police shot him in the stomach as he attempted to board a bus, then left him lying in a pool of blood for an hour. A passer-by, noticing Dennis's fair skin, called a "white" ambulance, but when it arrived and discovered that he was coloured, it drove away again. In strict accordance with the law.

'They deprived me of my passport and "banned" me under the so-called Suppression of Communism Act. That meant I couldn't write, meet friends, attend meetings or travel outside a restricted area. They sent Dennis to the notorious prison on Robben Island. When I met Penelope I knew I'd have to leave – sexual relations between black and white, including marriage, are *verboten.*'

The phone rang in the house. Angel went inside to take it. 'It's for you, Joe,' he called. When he came out again the huge athlete was carrying a large illustrated volume, which he placed in Ellison's lap. 'I was looking through Dr Robert Dietz's famous *History of the Olympics* the other day – borrowed it from the library. There you see two striking still photographs taken from Leni Riefenstahl's famous film of the 1936 Berlin Olympics. In the first shot you see one of the contestants in the first-round heats of the hurdles hitting a barrier and falling. Apparently he broke his leg in three places. The second shot shows him being carried from the field on a stretcher.'

'He's actually raising himself up on one elbow in order to deliver the Hitler salute to the *Führer.*'

'Amazing, isn't it, how radically the German athletes were indoctrinated. Look at his face: contorted in agony yet possessed by fanatical elation.'

'His name?'

'The odd thing is, Dietz searched through the German newspapers of the time but found no report of the incident.'

To Ellison, the conclusion was obvious. But he kept it to himself.

Mutobo returned to the garden wearing a haggard expression. 'Two of Christian Care's top staff in Rhodesia have been arrested: the Rev. Oliver Bikiti and a lawyer, Jackson

Ndiweni. The London office just had a cable from Armand Krohl. He's in Salisbury supervising the distribution of $100,000 of relief money to the families of 2,000 detainees.'

'If Krohl can't get Bikiti and Ndiweni released, no one can,' Okie said. 'The Smith regime hate his guts but they fear his influence.'

'Armand has arranged an interview with the Commissioner of Police.'

When Ellison returned to the *Sunday Monitor* he went straight to the press library and took down the volume of *The Times* beginning August 1, 1936, the day that Adolf Hitler opened the Berlin Olympics. The first-round heats of the hurdles were reported on the 5th. There was no mention of an athlete breaking his leg in three places or giving the Hitler salute. But if you broke your leg you had to come last: Ellison noted down the name of the last athlete in each heat, and then of the athlete listed second from last, just in case two had failed to finish in a particular heat.

One name interested him in particular.

His last instruction to Magnus, before leaving for Johannesburg, was to have the two photographs on page 213 of Dr Robert Dietz's *History of the Olympics* put on the photographic enlarger.

Ellison flew through a nasty tropical storm over Kenya, spent several nervous hours at Entebbe Airport in Uganda, where the plane had been diverted from storm-bound Nairobi, and then headed south to Jan Smuts Airport, Johannesburg. A four-man reception committee (three whites and a black) welcomed him warmly. Also on hand were reporters and photographers from the *Star*, the *Sunday Mail*, *Vaterland* and *The Flag*.

'Mr Ellison, does this trip signal a new policy on your paper? Is South Africa going to get a break at last?'

'I'm glad to be allowed to take a first-hand look at your country.'

'Mr Ellison, how would you assess South Africa's chances of sending a Springbok athletics squad to the Moscow Olympics?'

'That's what I've come to find out.'

He grimaced at the sight of a 'Slegs Blaankes' (Whites Only) notice over a toilet. Hendrik van der Groot, a wealthy businessman and Nationalist Party financial angel, who chaired the Fair Play Campaign, caught Ellison's thoughts.

'As a matter of fact, Mr Ellison, Jan Smuts Airport is now de-segregated as far as passengers are concerned. That toilet is strictly for staff.'

'Splendid.'

They housed him in luxury in the Carlton Hotel beneath the 50-storey-high Carlton Tower. He smiled wryly at the neat ivory push-button telephone and at the elegant Regency wallpaper surrounding him. Not every bug has twelve legs. Bottles of whisky and brandy, cartons of cigars, perfume for his wife (maybe) and a vaseful of dried flowers were waiting for him along with a fat brochure put out by the Fair Play Campaign. It reminded him of the Soviet push at Vienna. Would Anne-Marie Schubert appear?

The thought of her sent him to the shower. During an idyllic weekend in Quebec, they had shared a warm shower, trying to kiss away the water.

An hour later he arrived at the Fair Play Campaign's sleekly furnished offices in Commissioner Street. The walls were lined with offprints and posters of ads inserted in foreign newspapers. 'This is how we discriminate in South Africa,' announced one caption on a poster showing a collage of multi-racial sporting contests. In the largest photo a black boxer was knocking down a white one.

A pretty secretary brought coffee and cigars.

'This poster shows your British Lions rugby team playing

our black Leopards,' Hendrik van der Groot explained.

'Very impressive.'

'Yet you British extend hospitality to all the crackpot elements who leave South Africa to join SANROC and the so-called Anti-Apartheid movement. Throwing bags of flour on to tennis courts, that sort of thing.'

'Well. . . .'

Paul Shrivers, owner and publisher of a chain of newspapers and magazines, arrived at that point and asked Ellison what sort of entertainment he would like laid on for the evening. A sleek, handsome man wearing sparkling cufflinks and a silk bow tie, Shrivers had been the first to shake Ellison's hand at the airport.

'We don't know much about you, Mr Ellison, except what you write. We could take in a theatre; or I believe there's a ballet in town; or perhaps you'd like to skip the culture and inspect our night life in Hillbrow.'

Paul Shrivers winked.

'How about a visit to Soweto?' Ellison said, referring to the riot-torn township where one million blacks were confined, south-west of the white city.

Shrivers, van der Groot and Talbot Tashweni, the black secretary-general of the Fair Play Campaign, exchanged glances.

'That has to be arranged through the Bantu Administration Board,' Shrivers said quickly.

'I gather that black sportsmen are still barred from white clubs even though matches between white and black clubs are allowed,' Ellison said.

Talbot Tashweni smiled helpfully. 'The main reason that white and black players have played for separate teams in separate leagues is the *level* of their performance.'

'These things take time, believe me,' Shrivers added. 'You simply wouldn't believe how rapid the progress has been in South Africa during the last ten years.'

'Because of the international boycotts?'

A certain silence descended on the room.

'We believe,' van der Groot said eventually, 'that nothing is gained by keeping sportsmen apart. We all have much to learn and much to teach other nations....'

'Keeping sportsmen apart is precisely what the world accuses you of,' Ellison said.

The following morning Ellison rose early and took a taxi to the *Rand Daily News*, where he called on an old friend, assistant editor Graham Pollock. After a chat, Ellison asked if he could look through back numbers of the paper. Pollock led him downstairs, where he handed him over to the librarian.

'Hennie, I leave this famous man in your charge.'

Despite the librarian's desire to help, Ellison refused to commit himself to which year, month and week he was looking for. 'I'll just browse, if I may.'

As soon as the librarian had left him he plucked down the leather-bound volume containing the issue of August 5, 1936. On the sports page were three separate excisions: the results of the first-round hurdles heats had been clipped neatly out, a lead story was missing from the top left-hand corner and what must have been a photograph was now but a hole in the page. A further excision had been made on the front page.

Although already running behind the schedule set for him by van der Groot and Shrivers, he took a taxi to the offices of two other newspapers, one English language, the other Afrikaaner. In both he was courteously admitted to the press library; and in both he found that the editions of August 5, 1936, had been neatly operated upon.

They drove out of Johannesburg through the northern suburbs, cresting a series of ridges within the shelter of which the prosperous white enclaves nestled, protected from the wind-blown dust of the old mine dumps. It was a world of cricket pitches, tennis courts and bowling greens, of middle-class whites clad in spotless white sporting gear. Then, sweeping along broad highways in a Ford Fairlane, they headed for the gold mines to the west and north-west – Randfontein, Rustenberg, Transvaal Consolidated.

'Now,' said Shrivers, 'you'll notice that our friend Talbot Tashweni is travelling with us. I daresay your Anti-Apartheid friends in London told you a black can't travel in the same car as a white.'

'No,' Ellison said. 'But I daresay Mr Tashweni would have trouble boarding a white bus in Jo'burg, or a white railway compartment.'

'These things take time,' van der Groot grumbled.

'Do they take time, Mr Tashweni?' Ellison asked.

The African pondered; the pink palms of his hands were cupped in an expressive gesture; his smile was saintlike, forbearing.

When they reached the Borenstein Sports Club – a modern structure on which no expense had been spared – a reception committee was waiting for them: the manager of the Borenstein Gold Mine (Pty) Ltd, his recreation director, his public relations officer, a senior official of the South African Amateur Athletic Union, three journalists and a television crew.

After the handshakes, Ellison again found himself being interviewed.

'You know,' he said, 'I'm what one of our satirical magazines calls a hack. I'm not a VIP or a celebrity. I'm used to asking questions, not answering them.'

'Mr Ellison,' pressed one of the journalists, undeterred, 'is it true that you enjoy close relations with several influential members of the International Olympic Committee?'

'Like who?'

Shrivers laughed loudly. 'Now that's a smart answer, boys. I daresay Mr Ellison knows all the smart answers in the book. We here in South Africa are in a delicate position, and we certainly won't help our cause by naming particular IOC officials. Isn't that right, Mr Ellison?'

'What is your opinion of the Supreme Council for Sport in Africa?' asked a reporter with a thick Afrikaaner accent.

'I believe they're very sincere people.'

'But do you sympathize with their policy of boycotting sportsmen from this country?'

'That's what I've come to find out.'

A journalist from the liberal *Rand Daily Mail* pursued another tack.

'Mr Ellison, three or four of your books are banned in this country.'

'That's right. I've only written three or four.'

'Why do you think they are banned?'

'I've no idea.'

'How many times have you been refused permission to enter South Africa?'

'Twice.'

'Why do you think you were granted permission this time?'

'You must ask my hosts that question.'

The athletics track was built out of dust from the gold-mine dump. Lavishly equipped, with a first-class gymnasium and swimming pool, it nurtured some of South Africa's elite black athletes, of whom the most famous was the 1,500-metre ace, Cornelius Wakatama.

Ellison watched for half-an-hour while Wakatama was put through his paces by a white track coach wearing the green-and-yellow Springbok track suit. The SAAAU official had now been moved up, discreetly, to Ellison's shoulder.

'Cornelius is a remarkable athlete,' he said quietly. 'He comes from Swaziland, one of a family of ten, and used to work down this mine at 9,000 feet. I wouldn't want to call into question Cornelius's amateur status, but I'm authorized to tell you he doesn't go down the mine all that often nowadays.'

Only 5 feet 9 inches tall, Wakatama possessed a 7-foot stride. While Ellison watched, he was doing leg speed work and repetitions over 150 and 200 metres. At one stage he went through an impressive series of 120-metre sprints, rolling off the bend through the next 180 metres, then jogging back down the straight for recovery, before starting the cycle again. After half-an-hour of this his coach wrapped him in towels and brought him over to meet Ellison.

'What's your best time this year, Mr Wakatama?'

'Three minutes 39.4 seconds.'

'Did you run ten miles to school every day, like the Kenyan runners from the Kalenjin and Gusii tribes?'

'Don't talk to me about Kenyan runners! Earlier this year I was in a New Year's festival race in Brazil. The Kenyans withdrew in protest – because I, Cornelius Wakatama, was competing.'

'There you are,' Shrivers said. 'His fellow black men stop him competing because he happens to have been born in Swaziland.'

'Do you feel bitter about the international boycott?' Ellison asked him. 'What's your opinion of the Supreme Council for Sport in Africa?'

'I feel bitter – here.' The athlete jabbed his lean, flat stomach furiously. 'It hurts me. It punishes me, this ban. I'm not young for ever. Is it fair, sir? Some of these guys from the Supreme Council pretend they love black Africa ... you ask me, they love themselves and those fat-cat jobs they've got up there in Addis Ababa.'

An intense throng of some thirty men was now gathered round Wakatama and Ellison, almost as if South Africa's sporting future was to be decided there and then. Cameras turned, microphones were held close to their chins; each question posed by the British reporter was faithfully recorded.

'Do you think you'll be allowed to compete in the Moscow Olympics, Mr Wakatama?'

'I think so. It has to come. The world won't stand this injustice. Look how they treat their own athletes – you have to torture your body, day after day, to reach the top in athletics.' Wakatama gestured savagely. 'Take that African fake boycott at Montreal. For what? Because a few New Zealand rugby players came here!'

'Are you satisfied with progress towards multi-racial sport in this country?'

'Mister, look at my green track suit. You see that Springbok embroidered on the vest? A few years ago no black man was allowed to wear that.'

The crowd round them murmured warmly, appreciatively – things were going really well, Ellison was clearly impressed.

'But what about the grass roots level?' Ellison persisted. 'Swimming pools are still segregated. Most black kids don't enjoy anything like the facilities that white kids do.'

Wakatama looked at Ellison: eggs would have fried in their shells if those eyes had settled on them.

The mine manager led them to the clubhouse for lunch. A long table groaning with cold meats and salads had been laid for twenty guests. But not one of the black athletes, not even Cornelius Wakatama, had been invited to sit among them.

'If South Africa sent a mixed-race team to the Olympics, would the white and black athletes share the same rooms, toilet facilities and eating arrangements?'

'Absolutely,' boomed van der Groot.

'Then why not here?'

'Here, in the Republic, we face the pressure of public opinion.'

'You know,' the SAAAU official was telling Ellison, 'it was about ten years ago that the IOC sent out a three-man team to investigate us. At that time Prime Minister Vorster assured Lord Killanin that South African athletes of all races would form a single national Olympic team, travel together and share accommodation. That was ten years ago! Isn't that fair? What more can you ask?'

'Yet the pressure of Communist-backed movements like

SANROC, Anti-Apartheid and the SCSA was enough to thwart common sense,' complained Shrivers.

Shrivers interested Ellison. His tabloid daily, *The Flag*, stridently attacked all critics of the regime as agents or dupes of the Red Hand. Allegations that police tortured black prisoners or that the 'suicides' of these same prisoners were anything but genuine were dismissed as concocted in Moscow. Vorster, Botha, Mulder and other leaders of the Nationalist Party appeared frequently on the front page: whatever they 'explained', 'stressed', 'insisted' or 'revealed' was the plain truth.

So what was odd?

What was odd to Ellison's mind was the language in which *The Flag* was published: English. Fare like this was standard stuff in *Der Burger* or *Vaterland*, but the English-speaking readership was notoriously immune to Nationalist Party laager heroics.

Ellison had also checked through the advertising agencies on *The Flag*'s real circulation, which turned out to be much lower than the figure Shrivers had given him. In fact, the paper's ad pages were few and thin. So how did *The Flag* stay in business?

After lunch Ellison was taken on a conducted tour of the mine and then back to the track and gymnasium to watch a further work-out by black athletes of the Springbok squad. One of these, the sprinter Herbert Munganshuba, having driven himself through a series of dynamic 25-metre bursts out of the blocks, jogged over to Ellison and handed him a sealed envelope.

'That's my training schedule for the past year,' he said, 'and my best performances. I hope you'll write about me, sir – I want to be famous and win races against Don Quarrie and Haseley Crawford and that Russian guy Borzov.'

He grinned and skipped away. The white officials smiled patronizingly. Ellison pocketed the envelope. On the road back to Johannesburg, he questioned his hosts.

'There was some talk at Vienna, in '74, of a secret pact between the Detweiler group and the Russians.'

'That's news to us,' Shrivers said. 'The Russians are our deadly enemies, Mr Ellison; ever since Lenin they have sworn to destroy Christianity and Western civilization.'

Ellison had noticed a story in the Johannesburg *Star*. A group of twenty blacks had turned up in a Dutch Reformed Church to attend the funeral of their late employer, a white farmer. When the white pastor entered the church and saw the group of blacks huddled humbly in the rear pews, he refused to continue until they had been expelled. In Shrivers's tabloid, *The Flag*, the same incident had been depicted as a callous plot by the banned African National Congress to disrupt the funeral service.

'Who was your source for that story of a deal between us and the Russians, if I may ask?' van der Groot said.

'A member of the IOC Executive Board called Armand Krohl.'

There was a long silence in the car. Shrivers and van der Groot stared straight ahead, at the long ribbon of road passing under the car, at the vast blue dome of the African sky. 'You really ought not to take your information from Communists, Mr Ellison,' Shrivers said eventually.

'Krohl is a Communist? Surely not.'

'I'm not saying he's a Party member. But take his work for Christian Care, giving aid and comfort to black Marxist terrorists who are financed by the Soviet Union and Cuba.'

'Just relief to their families,' Ellison said quietly. 'I always thought of Krohl as a Christian. A crusader.'

'With respect, you made a big mistake. For me his recent return to the IOC Executive Board was little short of a disaster.'

Reaching his bedroom in the Carlton Hotel, Ellison opened the envelope given him by the African sprinter Herbert Munganshuba. The message inside was written on a torn-off sheet of lined paper:

'Dear Sir, I have done 10.13 and 20.54 which is WORLD CLASS. I need world competition [misspelt]. Tell your English people how it really is here for black people. It's hellish bad. They beat us, kill us. Don't take notice of that white nigger Cornelius Wakatama. He is too much ambitious, that one. Don't get me into trouble, Sir. Your friend, Herbert Munganshuba.'

Ellison committed the message to memory, then shredded the paper and flushed it down the toilet.

He reached the Tropicana nightclub in Hillbrow at 8:45, wearing a black tie, after declining his taxi driver's offer of 'the best coloured lays in town'. Shrivers and van der Groot rose to greet him. Sitting at their table were two men he had not seen before.

'Mr Ellison, I'd like you to meet Hans Kruger, the rising star of the Department of Information, and Pieter Jacobsdal, a . . . business colleague.'

If Paul Shrivers was a smooth customer, Hans Kruger positively gleamed like a new Jaguar in a Mayfair showroom. Fair-haired, square-jawed and blue-eyed, he spoke with the blend of solemn dedication and latent menace reserved to those who expect to inherit the earth. He never smiled, even when he poured laughter from his throat like a measure of gin from a bottle.

'So how did things go today, Mr Ellison?'

'Most impressive.'

'Great! Super, as they say in Rhodesia. If you're impressed, the world will be impressed.' He leaned across the table and fixed Ellison with an intense gaze. 'May I call you "Bill"?'

'Of course.'

'Jolly good, Bill. What will you drink for a cocktail? Scotch? Great. Now, you're a man of the world, I mean you've kicked around a bit. And you have principles, we know that. But you're not one of these homosexual idealists. I mean you get your hair cut when it needs cutting. And when you get into bed with someone, you make damned sure it belongs to the opposite sex. Am I right?'

'An in-depth portrait.'

Vast, sizzling steaks arrived from the barbecue, served on oval platters with chips, mushrooms and salads. Kruger continued to do all the talking.

'Now, my province is the press. To be perfectly frank with you, I'm responsible to the Minister himself, Dr Connie Mulder. He's boss of the Party in the Transvaal. When the Old Man moves on, heaven forbid, Connie will be in the big seat.'

'With you at his right hand?' Ellison inquired mildly.

Five seconds of laughter came from Hans Kruger's throat, but there was no smile. Ellison found the effect unnerving. He glanced at Pieter Jacobsdal, a young man possessing a massive neck and shoulders, topped by a small, delicate head, porcelain-white skin and a pencil moustache – not unlike King Gillette. Ellison guessed that Jacobsdal played rugby and was dreaming of the last time he raked his studs across the face of an opponent trapped at the bottom of a loose maul. This fellow smelt of a four-letter word: BOSS.

Kruger was leaning intently across the table, speaking in that soft, clipped accent used by all the nastiest whites south of the Zambesi.

'To be frank with you, Bill, we in the Department of Information have funds to float certain overseas operations. I'm not talking about peanuts either: I mean real money. But if you scrutinize the official budget or the list of parliamentary expropriations, you won't find that money. Are you with me?'

'I'm with you.'

Van der Groot coughed loudly and turned red. Possibly a morsel of prime veld beef was caught in his throat, but Ellison suspected that the old businessman felt that the brash young Kruger was spilling the beans unnecessarily.

'So,' continued Kruger, undeterred, 'we're talking about overseas propaganda operations on an unprecedented scale. We in Information have nothing against our Foreign Ministry diplomats, of course, apart from the fact that they're a bunch of slow-moving, pompous, bureaucratic bullshitters. We in Information are interested in results, not protocol – and we get results, Bill, even when we employ unorthodox methods. Are you with me?'

'I'm still with you.'

Shrivers snapped his fingers at the waiter. 'Two more bottles,' he called.

'Recently we purchased a controlling interest in two prestigious publishing companies, one in New York, one in London,' Kruger said.

'We?' Ellison asked quickly.

'Good question. We work through front men, of course; it must look like a legitimate business deal. But now we intend to go further. To be frank with you, what we need is a major British quality newspaper – your own.'

'I don't happen to own it.'

'But your proprietor, Lord Gowers, does. He has major business interests out here. We talked to him. Last time he was in Pretoria he was granted an interview by the Old Man himself. Gowers is on our side.'

Ellison shrugged. 'What more do you want?'

'You. Gowers is not master in his own house, all Fleet Street knows that. You and your editor, Ramsay Jordan, block him at every turn. Gowers is afraid of losing you to the rival *Sunday Dispatch* – and losing 300,000 readers into the bargain.'

'What's your proposition?'

'Jordan gets dropped, and you take over as editor. Now, we're not quite so primitive down here as some of you sophisticated Europeans imagine. We don't ask you to change the *Monitor*'s policy on South Africa overnight. If you did, people would smell a rat. Besides, Bill, your value to us is not only your personal prestige, but the fact that you're a card-carrying liberal with a small "l".'

Ellison nodded. 'I understand perfectly the kind of transformation you require: almost imperceptible but relentless. More and more "objective" reporting, offset by occasional protestations: "No one deplores apartheid more than we do. But, it has to be admitted that a real change is taking place in South African thinking...." Is that it?'

All four South Africans were watching him with undisguised pleasure.

'Name your price,' Kruger said. 'We can arrange for monthly payments into any bank account you care to name. And by the way – you might as well drop those investigations into Rhodesian sanctions busting; they don't go down well with Mulder, van den Bergh and the Old Man.'

'What's your price, Bill?' Shrivers pressed eagerly.

'Money's a wonderful thing, Bill,' Kruger continued. 'Before I joined Information I was working for the Bantu Admin on Rand 450 a month and I'd never been outside of South Africa. But since working for Connie I've taken eighteen trips abroad, six of them with my wife; I've been skiing in Switzerland, salmon fishing in Scotland, and I attended the Montreal Olympics. All expenses paid. We know you command the biggest salary in Fleet Street and when we ask you to name your price, we mean it.'

'Don't be shy, Bill,' said van der Groot. 'Hans is talking about real money.'

At this juncture the plates were cleared from the table, coffee, brandy and cigars were brought, and a writhing belly dancer launched the floor show. Five coloured harlots appeared at their table, wearing fixed smiles and thick white face powder to lighten their skins.

Shrivers leaned across to Ellison with a big wink. 'Take your pick,' he said. 'It's all on the house.'

The following morning Shrivers telephoned him at 6:15, sounding very excited.

'Bill, a car will pick you up from the Carlton at 7:30. We're driving to Pretoria. You are scheduled to meet General Hendrik van den Bergh, head of the Bureau of State Security. We are also notified that you may be received by a Very Important Person. This is an honour dispensed to only one foreign journalist a year.'

'I'm honoured.'

'Get some breakfast, then.'

The journey to Pretoria took less than an hour by road. Shrivers and van der Groot remained quiet throughout, both suffering, Ellison surmised, from a surfeit of drink, illegal sex and an uncomfortably early start. As they approached the outskirts of the capital, Shrivers asked nervously: 'Have you given more thought to our proposition, Bill?'

'I slept on it.'

In Pretorius Street scores of men in stiffly starched blue shirts, shorts, long socks and peaked caps were emerging from a building resembling at first sight a block of flats. They were all rigidly saluting each other. Here, then, was the headquarters of BOSS.

Kruger and Jacobsdal were waiting for them at reception. Kruger threw an inquiring glance at Shrivers; the latter's jaded shrug no doubt indicated that Ellison was playing it tight. A black servant brought coffee. For a while they sat in silence. Then Jacobsdal turned his opaque eyes towards Ellison.

'I was in Angola last year,' he said quietly. 'We could have had that place if the Cubans hadn't come in. I was taken prisoner at Nova Lisboa, tried by a people's court and sentenced to life imprisonment. I thought I'd had it. For a time I shared a cell with an American. Nice fellow; I believe he's operating up in your neck of the woods now.'

'What's his name?'

Jacobsdal stared at Ellison. 'You wouldn't expect me to answer that, Mr Ellison.' Again there was silence. But Jacobsdal needed to unburden himself further. 'I was in London four mouths ago, as a matter of fact. I did a job on your friends in SANROC. You should advise them on elementary security.'

'I take it the Special Branch were helpful.'

'Our Embassy people send them Christmas presents,' Kruger said.

Abruptly there was a flurry of activity. The signal had come: everyone was on their feet. Jacobsdal led the way to the lift. But Kruger, Shrivers and van der Groot did not follow.

'We'll wait here for you,' Kruger said. 'The General wants to see you alone.'

On the third floor a private secretary was waiting for them as they emerged from the lift. He led the way along a carpeted corridor: this time it was Jacobsdal who dropped out. Ellison noticed the intense silence: the outer world was blotted out, moral values suddenly dropped into limbo.

His first physical impression of van den Bergh was disconcerting – an intellectual was blinking at him from behind horn-rimmed spectacles. Clearly the General liked to talk; indeed, he spoke in a relaxed, informal vein for ten minutes, describing the deliberate campaign of calumny directed against the Bureau of State Security in the Western press.

'You can read all manner of stories about black prisoners hurling themselves from the windows of our police stations after being tortured. Am I about to deny that this has ever happened? I am not. And I'll tell you why I'm not. It's because I have ordered personal investigations of every such alleged case, and I have found that in two per cent the allegation was true. Two per cent!'

'You were, of course, imprisoned during the war as a pro-Nazi, like Mr Vorster himself.'

Van den Bergh laughed. 'It had nothing to do with Hitler or Germany, I assure you. We were fighting the old war between the Boers and the British, a war that we have only recently won.'

'But you know what it is to be imprisoned.'

'I do. And I believe that every police chief in the world should have personally experienced imprisonment. Without it, there can be no humanity of feeling.'

It was one of the few occasions in a long career when Ellison found himself bereft of words. He could find nothing to say or ask. It didn't matter. The head of BOSS had something to ask him.

'Suppose you were appointed Director of Overseas Propaganda by the South African Government. What first steps would you take?'

'I'd abolish apartheid and transfer power to the African majority.'

Van den Bergh declined to rise to the provocation. 'No, no. You are appointed Director of Propaganda, not Prime Minister.'

'I'd instruct my staff that not every foreign journalist will fall for a Swiss bank account and a coloured call-girl.'

Van den Bergh nodded. 'Your point is taken. Thank you.'

The interview was over.

At 2:30 the summons came from the Union Building, which rises tier upon tier, white, curved, imperial, above Pretoria. Jet fighters were swooping across the sky in a series of power-exultant runs as Hans Kruger halted before a heavily sealed iron gate, bent his knees to bring his face level with a mirror and simultaneously inserted a coded personal card in the electronic lock. There was a five-second pause while the computer assessed the convergence between Kruger's face and the data recorded on the card. Then a sharp buzz and click.

'Please follow,' he said.

His complexion was pale now, his voice coarse with anxiety. Gone was the smooth, arrogant, jet-setting whizz-kid of Information; exposed was the poor, skeleton-clerk of Bantu Admin. Ellison knew that van den Bergh had roasted Kruger for his blundering indiscretion; he also knew that proximity to Prime Minister John Vorster reduced even Cabinet Ministers to jelly. For here, and in the white-painted private residence called Libertas up the hill, resided the ultimate, absolute power in southern Africa. White Power.

An under secretary received them. 'Mr Ellison, the Prime Minister will receive you for twenty minutes. The interview will be off the record. Nothing the Prime Minister says may be quoted or paraphrased. Will you be so good as to sign this paper in acknowledgement of these ground rules?'

Ellison signed.

The under secretary led the way down a wood-panelled corridor, stopped before a small, unmarked door and opened it without knocking.

The Old Man behind the desk rose with difficulty; his breathing was laboured. His was a potato face, untouched by sun or laughter, pink-nosed, rheumy-eyed. Vaguely he gestured his guest to an empty chair.

'One day,' he said, 'the world will push us too far.'

CHAPTER 6

June 8, 1979. London

The Britain-USA-USSR triangular athletics match opened in warm summer sunshine with a spectacular winning high jump of 2.31 metres by America's Charlie Watts. The capacity crowd of 17,000 basking on the terraces of the Crystal Palace Stadium burst into delighted applause. The Soviet high-jump coaches prepared themselves for a period of agonizing reappraisal.

Already the women's pentathlon was under way.

On the fifth floor of Gowers House, headquarters of the *Sunday Monitor*, Ellison squinted at his television set while shovelling down one of his wife's salami-and-coleslaw-on-rye-bread sandwiches. The focus of his attention was a well-proportioned young woman, clad in the red vest and white pants of the Soviet Union, as she glided gracefully across the approach fan, turned sideways to the bar, propelled herself up with breathtaking power, arched her supple back, then flipped herself backwards over the bar. The bar held steady. As the crowd erupted the pretty young Russian picked her neat, creaseless buttocks out of the foam-rubber cushioning, smiled shyly, allowed herself a little skip of pleasure and trotted back to her track suit with her blonde pony tail wagging.

'That's Tatiana Larin,' Ellison remarked over his shoulder to his secretary, Cherry.

'Well, she's one woman you're not going to catch easily.'

The electronic scoreboard now registered 1.82 metres (1,049 points). Tatiana's team mates hugged her.

'She has something of the ingénue freshness and vivacity of that little gymnast girl, Olga Korbut,' Ellison continued to muse, half to himself, half to Cherry. 'Mind you, a pentathlete has to carry a lot of muscle – I bet Tatiana weighs all of 145 pounds.'

'It's Tatiana now, is it?'

'Definitely. If she wins this, she becomes Russia's white hope for Moscow. She's a born star. And, my God, the Russians need one after the recent traumas they have suffered in this event.'

The intercom flashed red on his desk, the editor's signal.

'Yes, Ramsay?'

'The chairman arrived in the building fifteen minutes ago,' Jordan said. 'He's in a foul temper. His plane from Munich was delayed by the Dutch air traffic control assistants' work-to-rule. He was stacked above a tulip field for over an hour. He's brought back a 4,000-word article he wants me to run this Sunday.'

'Who sold it to him?'

'Kurt Klostermann.'

'I might have known it. We should take the chairman's passport away.'

'I'm sending a copy down to you now. It's sensational stuff; in fact, the most sensational story I've seen in a year. You'd better read it fast: Gowers wants to see us in his office at 3:40.'

As Ellison turned back to his television screen, Magnus Massey, seated in the Press Box at the Crystal Palace, raised his binoculars and focussed them on America's leading pentathlete, Barbara Floris. It was this tall, blonde mesomorph from California who had taken the lead after the 100-metre hurdles, with a time of 13.25 (966 points), ahead of Britain's

Sue Kitson (953 points) and Tatiana Larin. The Russian girl had lost her stride rhythm after hitting the third hurdle but recovered in style to finish in 13.53 (927 points).

Before Larin's spectacular performance in the high jump, a battle of brute power was joined as the contestants took it in turn to hurl the 8lb 13 2/5 ounce shot put as far as muscle, balance, will power and months of intensive coaching would allow. Examining Barbara Floris through his binoculars, Massey concluded that she wasn't one of nature's good losers: the expression of furious determination on her face and the high, piercing shriek she emitted as the heavy iron shot left her hand indicated a fierce resolve to win.

The electronic scoreboard lit up and swivelled: 15.44 metres for Floris. Warm applause from the spectators.

Sue Kitson's turn came next. The British crowd willed her to excel herself and she did, but she was outclassed and failed to reach the 15-metre mark.

There was something about this Russian girl, Tatiana Larin, virtually unknown though she still was in the West, that immediately magnetized a crowd's attention. Star quality; poise; a certain beauty. Her drama was their drama. Her first attempt produced a groan as she stepped over the curved board before her throw landed and was promptly red-flagged. Floris, back in her white USA track suit, did a little jog round the Russian, just catching her shoulder as she went past, a neat stroke of gamesmanship to unnerve a newcomer to international competition.

It was an error of tactics. Angry now, Tatiana Larin unleashed two devastating puts of 16.04 and 16.20, the Russian team went wild, the American Team Manager registered a protest of some sort, no one in the Press Box knew what, and suddenly the Cold War was very cold indeed down there in the sunny London stadium.

'I suppose they'll insist on a dope test if Larin wins,' Magnus said.

'Whoever wins. It's standard procedure,' replied Charles Graves-Brown, athletics correspondent of the *Monitor*.

'Jesus Christ,' muttered Ellison, tossing the typescript onto his desk and flicking his intercom to contact Jordan. 'Ramsay, we can't run this.'

'But what if it's true? We'd scoop the pool. Klostermann gave the chairman exclusive UK rights.'

'But it can't be genuine. Just take a look at that Russian girl on your screen. What we have here, my dear Ramsay, is Klostermann's attempt at the most audacious fake since the Protocols of the Elders of Zion.'

'You could be right,' Jordan said with his usual equanimity. 'On the other hand, you could be wrong.'

Ellison put a call through to Massey at the Crystal Palace.

Two competitions were now in process simultaneously, the women's pentathlon and its equivalent male event, the decathlon. In the latter a tall, handsome American called Karl Petersen had just earned the accolade of the crowd by throwing the discus beyond the 60-metre mark. As the judges raised their white flags, Charles Graves-Brown happened to notice that a slim figure wearing a red track suit with the letters CCCP emblazoned on it had leapt to her feet and was applauding with obvious emotion.

'I say, Magnus, did you see that?' said Graves-Brown, who was a very nice fellow indeed and not so long ago had been Britain's second string in the 400 metres (or what Ellison annoyingly persisted in calling the 'quarter mile').

For reply he got only the rapid clicking of Massey's F2AS Photomic Nikon, equipped with two silicone photo diodes, A-1 Automatic indexing, and a DS-12EE aperture control unit, racing through a score of Kodak Tri-X black-and-white frames at 1/500th of a second, through a 135mm lens.

'Yes, I did,' Magnus murmured. 'How good is this Petersen?'

'His best score to date is 8,114 at the American AAU championships last year.'

'You'll have to translate. What's the present world record?'

'Bill Jenner's 8,617 at the Montreal Olympics in '76.'

'So Petersen is hardly a medal prospect for Moscow?'

'He's improving. But he's reputedly lazy and vain.'

The women were now warming up for the fourth event of the pentathlon, the long jump – called the broad jump in America. Tatiana Larin now held a useful overall points lead, with 2,936, trailed by Barbara Floris (2,713) and Sue Kitson (2,588).

'I rather suspect the crowd is behind the Russian,' Magnus said. 'Jolly naughty of them, of course....'

'I suppose you realize what the pentathlon means to the Russians,' Graves-Brown said earnestly. 'Not only is it the modern prestige event, the ultimate test of all-round athletic ability, but it has recently been the scene of considerable Soviet traumas.'

'Was that the Tkacenko affair?'

'Exactly. In 1977 Nadia Tkacenko took the pentathlon title at the World Cup final in Dusseldorf with a new world record of 4,839. Last year she confirmed her supremacy with a winning score of 4,774 at the European Championships in Prague.'

'Charles, you're a walking *Guinness Book of Records.*'

'But then,' continued Graves-Brown, undeterred, 'came the trauma. Tkacenko, Russia's hope for an Olympic gold medal and a member of the Communist Party besides, was disqualified, stripped of her title and banned from competition by the European Athletic Association. The evidence was plain: I saw it myself in Room 202 of the Grand Astir Palace Hotel, Rhodes, where the French Secretary of the

EAA showed me documents proving that five athletes had failed their anabolic steroid tests at Prague. In fact, four of the five were Russians, including another Soviet pentathlon star, Jekaterina Gordijenko.'

'But the Russians didn't take it lying down?'

'Two tests were used in Prague: gas chromatography and mass spectronamy. Both tests proved positive for anabolic steroids. But the Czechs, acting on their own initiative, no doubt to prove their loyalty to their Soviet masters, came up with a third, unauthorized test, radio-immunassy, which proved negative. The East Europeans marched with regimental unity into the Rhodes meeting of the EEA's Council and read out written speeches in a demonstration of political support for Leonid Khomenkov, the Russian delegate. The Russians also argued that the matter should be referred to the IAAF, the International Amateur Athletics Federation. Finally the vote went against the Russians, 8 to 6.'

'So Russia's two leading pentathletes are banned for life?'

'Maybe. They'll get back, but probably not in time for the Moscow Olympics.'

'Which brings us to Tatiana Larin?'

'She's their white hope now.'

For the moment the vendors of hot dogs, Coca-Cola and peanuts were ignored: all eyes in the crowd were focussed on the twin dramas being enacted at the long jump and pole vault pits.

In the men's decathlon, the handsome American Karl Petersen had elected, with a confidence bordering on arrogance, to make no intervention until the bar stood at 4 metres, or 13ft 1½ inches. Considering – as Graves-Brown quickly pointed out to Massey – that Petersen's personal best was only 14ft 10 inches, he was engaging in a psychological gambit against his rivals which could easily backfire and leave him without a score, thus putting him out of the running.

'The man seems more interested in the photographers than

the competition,' Graves-Brown remarked with distaste.

In the women's pentathlon, the long jump began shortly before Petersen consented to make his first attempt in the pole vault. Magnus noticed that as she paced out her 112-feet, 18-stride, run-up to the board, Tatiana Larin kept throwing anxious glances to the far end of the stadium. She even interrupted a strict warm-up routine of calisthenics to watch Petersen's first vault. He flopped badly, knocking the bar off from underneath, and almost simultaneously her shoulders seemed to droop. Her own sprint to the board, when it came, was lack-lustre and tense; she stuttered her stride five paces out, lost it, crossed the board without jumping and automatically incurred a red flag. No jump.

'Good grief!' muttered Charles Graves-Brown. 'That was almost incredible. I suppose you realize she practises that run-up six hours a week under the eye of the finest coaches in the Soviet Union?'

'Maybe she was naughty and took her birthday off,' Massey said. 'Anyway, she's got five more attempts.'

'Two more. In the pentathlon they have only three attempts.'

Chernov, the short, square, grizzle-grey-haired veteran chief coach of the Soviet squad, was now shouting agitated instructions towards Tatiana, a practice forbidden by international regulations.

Tatiana was clearly distracted. When Sergei Panov gracefully negotiated the pole vault at 4.00 metres in the decathlon, her team-mates applauded vigorously but Tatiana scarcely reacted. As Karl Petersen again positioned his fibreglass pole for the long run-up she turned her back; the pole dug cleanly into the 16cm-deep plant box but the upward thrust was ragged. A low sigh came from the crowd; Petersen disconsolately recovered his pole; for an instant Tatiana's hand went to her forehead.

Her second jump was red-flagged. No score. One to go.

A discernible exultancy was now evident in the warm-up routine of the powerful blonde from California, Barbara Floris. Charles Graves-Brown, who had spoken to her several times after training sessions, knew her quite well. Parents trapped in poverty, who had devoted every spare penny and every available ounce of enthusiasm to developing her talents, had implanted in her a burning ambition. Day and night, she dreamed of an Olympic gold medal, a ticket not only to fame but, nowadays, also to fortune. Two of the women who had stood between her and her dream had now been eliminated by positive anabolic steroid tests. Two others remained: Renata Flack, of East Germany, and nineteen-year-old Tatiana Larin. Larin had talent all right, but so far she had failed to record a single win in a major event. Now Barbara Floris began to understand why; the Soviet girl lacked the ice-cool nerves, the capacity for total concentration, for shutting out any and every extraneous influence, that a true champion requires.

Barbara Floris was skipping back and forth now, her long golden hair bouncing exultantly on her strong shoulders.

'I'd like to meet this Barbara Floris,' Magnus said to Graves-Brown. 'Where are the Americans staying?'

'At the Kensington Hilton.'

'I'm counting on you to introduce me.'

'You'd better be warned: Floris has quite a reputation.'

'For what?'

Graves-Brown blushed. A light flickered in Magnus Massey's sky-blue eyes.

At 3:40 Ellison and Jordan stepped out of the executive lift on to the thick pile carpet of the tenth floor and were confronted by the chairman's personal secretary, an aloof woman whose rhinestone-studded oval spectacles invariably provoked in Ellison a smile that she misunderstood.

'Won't you please take a seat, gentlemen?'

The two men sank into leather chairs which sighed on impact.

'He'll keep us waiting the statutory five minutes,' Ellison murmured.

But the electronically operated teak and bronze doors of Lord Gowers's office slid open almost immediately, revealing twenty feet of Penthouse-Supreme deep-pile carpet at the end of which, behind an enormous desk, was to be seen the fleshy, irascible, blood-red visage of the chairman.

He was watching television.

'Have a pew, boys.' Distractedly he waved them to be seated.

The cameras were focussed on the tense figure of Karl Petersen, now pawing the ground like a nervous horse in anticipation of his third and last attempt to clear 4.00m in the pole vault.

'If he makes it we'll be offered brandies,' whispered Ellison. 'If not, tea.'

Petersen made it. A moment later Tatiana Larin, launching herself into her final attempt, released a beautiful jump, soaring gracefully from the board, a late bicycle-kick of her long, powerful legs sustaining her forward momentum on the downward arc. A moment's hesitation from the judges; Tatiana froze, horrified; Barbara Floris had leapt to her feet.

White flag. Valid leap. The digits filled the electronic scoreboard: 6.83 (1,082 points).

'That's 22ft 5 inches,' Ellison said.

'What do you know about athletics?' Gowers said.

'I take a run in Regent's Park every morning, Chairman. I even possess an Achilles Club track suit.'

'You forget that Bill knows about everything,' Jordan said.

'He ought to, the salary I pay him.'

'Don't be vulgar, Chairman,' Ellison said.

'She'll win now, that Larin girl,' Gowers said contentedly, offering them his cigar box. 'What will it be, lads, cognac?'

Ellison and Jordan exchanged glances as Gowers pressed a button beneath his vast desk, a gift from the grateful people of a Third World state whose Esteemed Leader had recently awarded the Gowers Construction Company a £48 million contract. A signed photograph of the Esteemed Leader stood on the desk in a gilt frame. Now a cocktail cabinet emerged silently from the bowels of the desk.

'Of course,' said Ellison, lighting the Montecristo he had taken from the box, 'there's still one event to come in the pentathlon.'

'The 200 metres,' Jordan said. 'Even I know that.'

'You used to know it, Ramsay. Since 1972 it's the 800 metres.'

'Well, let's to business,' said Gowers. 'You've both read the article I brought back from Munich? You agree it's a world scoop and worth every penny –'

'How much did you pay Klostermann, Chairman?' Ellison asked.

Gowers jabbed a wet cigar end into his mouth; his signet ring flashed evasively. 'That's my business, Ellison.'

The man whose cold, steel-grey eyes met the chairman's was powerfully built, an inch short of six feet, with light brown hair cut short across a broad head, a flattish nose and a mouth which habitually twisted at the corners in mild mockery. Of whom – himself perhaps? – it was not always clear. Ellison looked his age: forty-three.

'Did you pay too much or too little?'

Gowers would never come to terms with Ellison's brazen insolence. No one, no employee in the entire empire of companies over which he presided, ever talked to Lord Gowers as Ellison did. Born into the humblest stratum of the Northern working class, Gowers demanded of his workforce a deference bordering on servility. And he got it, mostly. But when he plunged in to the world of newspaper proprietorship, he had no idea what he was letting himself in for. He had bought the *Sunday Monitor* out of hunger for prestige and influence.

Had commercial profit been his main motive, he would have invested in a television channel or a monopoly chain of provincial dailies. No, he wanted the world, the upper crust, the quality market, as his investment advisers called it, to believe in the things he believed in.

In practice, it wasn't so easy. He knew very well that the quality of a paper isn't the quality of its newsprint or even its lay-out; it's the quality of the men who edit it and write for it. He had vaguely imagined that his editor would be answerable to himself on a day-by-day basis, only to discover the sacred doctrine of editorial independence.

Well, he might fire Ramsay Jordan, but if he did Ellison would resign, cutting the *Monitor*'s circulation from 1.5 to 1.2 million and thus involving a loss of advertising revenue of £3 million a year. Yet what Gowers feared was not the loss of money but the loss of prestige; he sensed, with furious resentment, that Ellison could make him the laughing stock of the international press.

'I paid Klostermann £6,000 for British first-serial rights,' he said.

'That's ridiculously cheap,' Ellison said. 'There's something very fishy about this one.'

Gowers leapt to his feet, moisture collecting in rivulets and dams in the deep, red folds of flesh beneath his puffy eyes. 'Oh there is, is there? Of course I'm only a poor ignorant working man who happens to have made a fortune by means of drive, common sense and native wit: I didn't attend Winchester and New College, Cambridge like some people....'

'Oxford,' Ellison said.

'Chairman,' Jordan said, 'we'd like to suggest that publication this Sunday – the day after tomorrow – would be premature. In a week's time we'll know where we are.'

'Klostermann made one thing very clear to me. Our exclusive first-serial rights are conditional on us publishing this Sunday.'

Ellison glanced at Jordan. 'Which proves that what interests Herr Klostermann on this occasion is not so much reporting an event as creating an event.'

'Klostermann's chain of papers and mags in West Germany is second in size only to Axel Springer's,' Gowers said. 'And don't you forget it.'

Jordan intervened diplomatically: 'Chairman, I suggest we review the situation at noon tomorrow. In the meantime I'll have the story set up in type and the plates cast this evening; we'll use only employees of proven discretion.'

'At noon tomorrow I shall be trout fishing with Sheikh Al-Sabah on his estate at Barford.'

'I assume all your rods and reels carry radio telephones, Chairman,' Ellison said.

'Get out of here!'

Ellison reached his office just in time to see Tatiana Larin sweeping down the final straight in the 800 metres, her pony tail flying, 15 metres up on Barbara Floris and 30 metres ahead of Sue Kitson.

'Cherry.'

'Yes, baas?'

'Am I ever wrong?'

The nineteen-year-old Russian girl was now jogging round the Crystal Palace on a lap of honour, lifting her arms in acknowledgement of the applause which had greeted the announcement on the loudspeaker system: 'First, Tatiana Larin, of the USSR, with a New World Record score of 4,842 points!'

Growing bolder now, budding like a flower in spring, caressed by the warmth of the crowd, she trotted closer to the railings, occasionally reaching out to touch the forest of congratulatory hands extended to her.

Magnus came back from Ellison's second telephone call.

'Charles, I carry the normal press card but you carry special accreditation, right? I want you to get me into the television interview room.'

'Well. . . .'

'And fast. Bill needs this badly. Very badly.'

The thought of Ellison filled Graves-Brown with awe and emulatory energy. 'Right! Follow!'

This exchange was clearly overheard by Stanley Pirie, athletics correspondent of the *Sunday Dispatch*. Magnus was grinning as he followed Graves-Brown out of the Press Box.

'Stanley will be on the phone to our rival, Tim Powerstock. Tim will conclude that we're on to another anabolic steroids scandal. He'll get his knickers into a Saturday-night twist over it. And what the *Dispatch* will dish up on tomorrow's sports page will be their normal substitutes for investigative journalism: "Are Anabolic Steroid Tests Reliable? Two Views." '

Graves-Brown glanced shyly at his equally tall colleague. 'On a point of interest, what *is* going on?'

For an answer he got only a hearty slap on the shoulder. As they fought their way along the narrow, packed corridors towards the television interview room, arguing their way past a series of security-conscious attendants, the atmosphere became increasingly tense. On occasion journalists sense instinctively that a big story is about to break, even if they are not sure what it is. Inside the interview room itself producers, lighting men, sound recordists, editors and interviewers were milling about under bright lights, arguing, hustling, dominated by imminent transmission deadlines.

'Where's the make-up room?' Magnus asked Graves-Brown.

'Turn left, second door on your right.'

An iron-faced attendant at the door, sporting two rows of World War II ribbons across the tunic of his blue uniform, was quite adamant: 'No journalists!'

'But we're actually friends of Miss Floris,' Magnus assured him. 'If you'll be kind enough to take in my friend's press card here and show it to her....'

The leather-faced veteran was mightily reluctant. Security, he knew, is based on obeying rules, not exceptions. Even so, he hated to be hated; he took the card and opened the door. Magnus pushed in after him, gently but firmly, followed by Graves-Brown.

There were four women in the make-up room: the athletes Barbara Floris and Sue Kitson, seated in front of wall mirrors, a make-up girl in a pink apron who was attending to their hair, paint and powder, and a young woman of striking beauty, dark and seductive, who was carrying a small camera bag over the shoulder of an expensive leather jacket. They all turned, simultaneously, to scrutinize Massey and Graves-Brown, but it was Magnus who instantly magnetized their attention. (Ellison referred to his colleague's notorious sex-appeal as 'magnusetic'.)

What the four women saw was the face of a romantic poet drifting to perdition on the wings of a rampant sensuality he was powerless to quell. There had been a time, six or seven years ago, when his name had been linked to a succession of beautiful models, notably Claire Boothroyd and Kicky Rapp, whose gorgeous gowns and haughty, impassive stares he had photographed against chic Cockney backdrops: Covent Garden, Tower Hill, the Docks. He had even starred in a film called *Close-Up*. It had flopped; as co-producer Magnus had lost £50,000. Sulking, he had withdrawn to meditate in a fisherman's cottage on Skye. Emissaries from *Harper's & Queen*, *Vogue*, *19*, *Mademoiselle* and *Elle*, tipped off by Magnus's PR firm, had travelled north to discover that the hermit was disgusted by jet-set affluence and shallow materialism. So avidly did the readers of these magazines lap it up that Magnus's temperamental disappearances became an annual event, and every year millions of young women stampeded to discover whether this time he was utterly alone with

Claire Boothroyd or utterly alone with Kicky Rapp. Photographs containing the answer were invariably shot against a romantic background of sand, sea, rock and wind-swept sky: most of them were taken by Magnus himself, with the help of a tripod and a delayed-action shutter.

Then, one summer, he really did disappear. For several months there was no trace of him until a female graduate student spotted him – incredibly – in the Reading Room of the British Museum. All attempts by his agent and PR consultants to lure him out failed. When they heard that he had begun to write about political and historical topics they laughed sourly.

One day he walked into Bill Ellison's office clutching a pile of essays and asked for a job.

'Apply to the fashion editor,' Ellison suggested.

For half an hour the tall young photographer explained to the famous journalist the significance of the English Revolution of 1640, the Great Reform Act, Marx and Che Guevara.

'Try the colour magazine, Massey. If you've got a nice snapshot of Oliver Cromwell they might use it.'

Magnus nodded gravely, a little sadly. 'Nice of you to listen, all the same. I like your work.'

It was a year later that Ellison again came across Massey. General Arik Sharon had just forced a bridgehead across the Suez Canal and was thrusting his armour towards Cairo. Ellison and three fellow-correspondents accredited to Zahal were flat on their faces behind an Israeli Centurion tank at the height of an Egyptian artillery bombardment when bumping across the Sinai desert came an old jeep carrying a tall, blond photographer aiming a 500mm lens at the Egyptian gun and tank emplacements. Ignoring the warning shouts of the Israeli officers, Massey drove recklessly on and would no doubt have over-run the enemy positions if an Israeli sergeant hadn't put a bullet through the jeep's offside front tyre.

For twenty-four hours the Israelis held Magnus in detention; it took all of Ellison's influence to persuade them that he wasn't a spy. Only after Zahal's Military Intelligence had developed the photographs in his camera were the negatives reluctantly returned to him. After one glance at them Ellison offered to buy the lot. Magnus smiled gently.

'They're for my own story.' His tone of voice was almost apologetic.

'*Harper's* or *Mademoiselle*?'

'No idea. Haven't sold it yet.'

'By the time you do, the Yom Kippur war will be forgotten.'

Ellison was wrong. Magnus's story and photographs were published the following Sunday by the *Monitor*'s great rival, the *Sunday Dispatch*. The story was as good as the pictures. Ellison's own report was put in the shade. Ellison wasn't accustomed to being put in the shade, and he didn't like it. He offered Magnus a job.

It was Graves-Brown who, blushing profusely, broke the silence. 'Barbara, do you remember me, Charles – '

'Sure I do. What's this phenomenon you've brought with you?'

'Er, my colleague, Magnus Massey.'

'Does it talk or is one just supposed to stare at it?'

The old security attendant cleared his throat and was about to explain his orders, his duties and his dilemmas, when Floris cut him short: 'We're all friends. Let the guys stay.'

Magnus shook hands with the two athletes. 'Congratulations,' he said. 'Wonderful competition.'

'I daresay you're looking for the new world record holder,' Floris said caustically. 'Well, right now she's trying to pee into a bottle – it's one of the mandatory fruits of victory.'

Magnus had turned to the young woman carrying the camera bag. 'Magnus Massey,' he said softly, extending his hand.

She nodded with a slight smile. 'I know,' she said. 'You

met my father in Montreal. Ruth Leonhard.'

'Ah, yes, of course.'

Her dark eyes were examining his intently. 'Why "of course"? Does Bill speak of me to you?'

'Our relationship isn't a confessional one.'

A small cloud of anger passed swiftly across her face and was gone – his remark left her guessing about what he knew.

'What are you doing for dinner tonight?' he asked Barbara Floris and Sue Kitson simultaneously. 'Charles and I would be honoured if you would dine with us.'

'You don't waste any time,' Barbara Floris said.

'I'd absolutely love to,' Sue Kitson said, 'but I have to get up early tomorrow to put my wretched girls through their paces. We've got a grudge match against St Margaret's next week.'

Magnus was watching Kitson in the mirror as the make-up girl applied the final touches to her hair. Here was a jolly sporting, decent English gel, Sports Mistress at Dame Alice Proudfoot's School for Gels. Twenty-eight years old, rather plain, unmarried – just the wife to make Charles happy. And how proud her gels must be of her! Magnus went on looking at her in the mirror. Why was this naturally phlegmatic English woman *so tense*? Pre-television nerves? Hardly. Magnus had seen her on the box a dozen times; she always took it in her stride, jolly good. And why was this Ruth Leonhard standing behind Kitson almost as if she owned her; why had she looked so displeased when Magnus invited the two athletes out to dinner?

Why had Bill never mentioned that Chaim Leonhard had a daughter?

'Acton, isn't it?' he asked casually.

'Sorry,' Kitson said.

'Your school playing field.'

'No, Hillingdon, worst luck – Acton's the school itself.'

'I'm feeling neglected,' Barbara Floris purred. 'And I

didn't say I was busy, either. I don't even have to get up early.'

'Wonderful. I'm delighted. I'll pick you up at your hotel at 8:30.'

'Hey, you goddamn British eat so goddamn late! I'll be dead of starvation by 8:30. Are you planning on taking a female corpse out to dinner?'

'Eight o'clock, then.'

At that moment there was a commotion in the corridor outside, the sound of attendants arguing with reporters, and into the make-up room came Tatiana Larin, shadowed by a large Soviet matron who reminded Magnus of a full-back in a soccer team noted more for its physical approach than its skill. Tatiana and Sue Kitson embraced affectionately. The girl in the pink apron then hustled Tatiana into a chair, combed out her hair, re-tied the pony tail in a satin bow, then reached for the eye-shadow and make-up.

'No, no,' Tatiana said shyly. 'I never do.'

Magnus studied her features closely: at close quarters they were the coarse, robust features of the flat-nosed Slav peasant girl. The glamour, the charisma, resided in the grace of body and movement she displayed out on the track.

'Welcome, champ,' Barbara Floris said. 'Did they have to turn on the cold tap to help you pee?'

Magnus and Charles Graves-Brown slipped away as the three girls were led from the make-up room on to the floor of the television interview room, where a battery of cameras and lights were focussed on four chairs. Occupying the centre chair was the BBC's Norman Flower, whose hyperbolical phrases, torn from his throat at the climax of races, were the delight of every British schoolboy with a talent for mimicry.

The young woman called Ruth Leonhard cast Magnus a wistful glance. He fluttered his hand in polite *au revoir*; suddenly she gave him a smile.

He telephoned Ellison but didn't mention Ruth Leonhard.

He had a horror of intruding on Ellison's private life, or even knowing about it.

Ellison joined Ramsay Jordan in the editor's office to watch Flower interviewing Tatiana Larin.

'Tatiana's very self-possessed, isn't she. If she's really about to take a momentous decision, you'd never guess.'

'Just look at the fixed smile that American girl is wearing. You could wipe it away with a slightly damp cloth, like chalk on a blackboard.'

'Shut up, Ramsay, I'm trying to listen.'

Flower: 'First of all, Tatiana Larin, warmest congratulations on your victory in today's pentathlon and on your remarkable world record of 4,842 points.'

Larin: 'Thank you.'

Flower: 'Tatiana, how does it feel to hold a world record at the age of nineteen?'

Larin: 'I . . . I (smiles). I can't really believe it yet.' (Nervously flicks her pony tail, tosses her head.)

Flower: 'Now, Barbara Floris, you took second place today with a fine score but I know you're never satisfied – '

Floris (interrupting): 'Norman, you got there. I have to be number one.'

Flower: 'But there must be some consolation – '

Floris (interrupting): 'None at all, Norman, and that's the truth. I can do better and I'm gonna do better. (Smiles flatly at Larin.) I guess you and I will settle final accounts next year in Moscow.' (Larin averts her gaze from Floris.)

Flower: 'Now, Sue Kitson, you brought Britain into third place today and you achieved a personal best total in the process. You must be very pleased.'

Kitson: 'I'm delighted. I've been training hard and it's always awfully nice when hard work pays off.'

Flower: 'What did you think of Tatiana's performance?'

Kitson: 'Fabulous.' (Smiles at Tatiana, who responds with an affectionate grin.)

Flower: 'Now, Tatiana, if I may come back to you, the Soviet Union must now regard you as its great hope for a gold medal in the Olympic pentathlon?'

Larin: 'Well, you know, in my country there are many very talented girls – '

Flower: 'Yes, but the previous Soviet pentathlon champion, and world record holder, Nadia Tkacenko, has been stripped of her European Championships gold medal and banned from competition for life because she was found to have taken anabolic steroids. What can you tell us about the Soviet reaction to that?'

Larin (very unhappy): 'No, no, I don't want such questions, I mean – '

Kitson (indignantly, to Flower): 'I think it's jolly nice of Tatiana to come on British television and answer questions in English.'

Flower: 'Well, of course, we're delighted – '

Floris: 'Oh come on, man, let's cut this British bit, eh, all frightfully decent what. Everyone knows that drugs are a problem particularly in events which involve high muscular development. You didn't mention that not only Tkacenko was banned for life but also the Russian girl who came fifth in Prague, Gordijenko. Now what bothers me is this. It seems the use of these drugs is pretty widespread in Soviet Russia and Eastern Europe and I'm just wondering how strict those dope tests are going to be at the Moscow Olympics.'

Kitson: 'May I come in on this? The tests will be administered under the supervision of the Internal Olympic Committee.'

Floris: 'Oh sure. By doctors from Bangladesh. But if I was a doctor from Bangladesh and I found myself in Moscow I'd sure turn a blind eye to a positive urine sample if it came from a Russian girl.'

Flower: 'Tatiana, we all noticed today how you almost came unstuck at the long jump.'

Larin (tense): 'Yes. I was very worried. . . .'

Flower: 'How do you explain it?'

Larin: 'I don't know. An error of technique, perhaps. . . .'

Flower: 'I must say we in the commentary box had the distinct impression that your two no-jumps were closely connected with what was happening in the men's decathlon. Karl Petersen's failures in the pole vault seemed to break your concentration. . . .'

Larin (blushing): 'Oh no, no, well, perhaps a little. . . .'

Floris: 'Come clean, darling, you're in love.' (Laughs harshly, lights a cigarette.)

Kitson (clearly angry): 'I would have thought Tatiana's private life was her own affair.'

Flower (hastily): 'Tatiana Larin, Barbara Floris, Sue Kitson, thank you and many congratulations.'

The cameras reverted to the stadium for the start of the men's 800 metres.

In a London embassy a man with the title of First Secretary lifted his ivory-coloured telephone.

'Yes, Ruth?'

'Ellison is taking a keen interest.'

'That was to be expected.'

'Massey is having dinner with Floris tonight. I suspect he'll get at Kitson tomorrow morning – he winkled the address of her school sports ground out of her.'

'Not so good. You must warn her. Have the Russians got wind of anything yet?'

'Not yet. Pass on what I've told you to The Man. Is he still in Amsterdam?'

'He's right here, Ruth, sitting beside me.'

CHAPTER 7

June 9, 1979. London

At 6:35 in the morning Ellison removed the yale key from the breast pocket of his worn Achilles Club track suit and let himself into his house in Chester Place, Regent's Park. It was a handsome, cream-washed Regency house on five floors, built in 1826 according to a design by John Nash and adorned by plain Tuscan pilasters. Six years ago, when his income had suddenly spiralled, he had paid £53,000 for a sixty-year lease: the Crown Commissioners granted no freeholds in this exclusive enclave of central London.

Invigorated by his routine spin across the dew-moist grass and around the Inner Circle, passing the lake and the open-air theatre, Ellison showered and shaved and thought about Tatiana Larin. He slotted his Ronson back into its holder, jabbed an electric toothbrush into his mouth, then walked into the main bedroom and pinched his wife's ear. This was routine, so much so that Prue Ellison often complained that her right ear was now larger than her left.

Breakfast was in the ground floor kitchen. Ellison's never varied: two cups of medium-blend Kenya coffee (an extravagance they could afford on his income of over £30,000 a year), a bowl of Swiss muesli, two boiled eggs and a slice of rye toast without butter. He also consumed half a dozen newspapers, his eyes skimming the columns in rapid, raking sweeps. On weekday mornings his son Christopher would pad sleepily into the kitchen at 7:30 hunting for Rice Krispies and complaining that his school socks were nowhere to be found. But on Saturdays he stayed in bed.

'Shall I tell him you'll take him somewhere tomorrow?' Pru asked.

'Well . . . we have a possible crisis.'

Pru made a face. 'You're a walking crisis.'

He left the house promptly at 7:30, walked ten paces along Chester Place, placed the key in the lock of his VW Passat estate car – and then stiffened. He was abruptly aware of being under observation. Twenty yards away a man with a small dog on a lead was standing patiently while his pet cocked its leg in the gutter. The man had short, brushed-down hair, broad shoulders and enormous hands – the contrast between the hands and the effeminate, gold-chain dog's lead they held was particularly striking. Nor did the jackets of local residents normally swell so noticeably under the left armpit. The shirt was white: drip-dry nylon. The face, seasoned in linseed oil, weather-hardened in Kuprinol, was partly averted towards the cock-legged Peke.

'Amazing how they can keep their little leg up hour after hour,' Ellison said.

The man with the dog paid no attention.

Ellison wandered up to him. 'Haven't we met before?' he said.

The man was forced, now, to meet Ellison's gaze. The eyes were small, red, short of sleep but not of alcohol. He mumbled vaguely, negatively, anxious to conceal his voice, his accent, then turned, tugged most untenderly at the Peke and walked away smartly towards the Outer Circle.

As Ellison's car swept down to the Marylebone Road and turned east towards King's Cross, Magnus Massey rolled lazily in bed, averting his face from the bright summer sunlight infiltrating the curtains of a bedroom in the Kensington Hilton.

Delicate fingers ran lightly down his stomach; the tip of a

warm tongue touched his mouth; a faintly familiar perfume tapped a message on his dormant consciousness. Neither the fingers, the tongue nor the perfume, it became increasingly clear to him, were his own.

'You could have been an athlete,' Barbara Floris said.

'I don't want to be an athlete,' he murmured, hesitantly opening one eye.

Without further ceremony the American girl effortlessly flipped him on to his back as if he were a pancake, straddled his loins, and then fashioned for herself an instrument of pleasure with deft, confident motions of her hand. As she bent to thrust her darting tongue into his mouth her large breasts brushed against his chest; her long golden hair, ripened like corn in the California sunshine, cascaded over his shoulders. He scarcely moved: the need, the urgency, were all hers. He would not have expected, perched like a judge in the Crystal Palace Press Box, that so powerful a body could, once abandoned to intimacy, be so utterly feminine, so acutely sensitive to his touch.

He waited until she came.

Her head fell back on to the pillow. 'You're quite something,' she sighed, reaching out for the pink bedside phone. 'What do you eat for breakfast?' she said.

'Won't they think it's a bit odd – a member of the US team in bed with someone?'

'Oh crap that. You British are such hypocrites. Like that Sue Kitson: she bugs me down to here. Such a lady – yeah, but who's she taking this money from?'

'What money?' Magnus said, as casually as possible.

Floris dug him in the ribs so powerfully that he groaned.

'What money?' she said, imitating his English accent and intonation. 'Just watch yourself, Massey: my fast-twitch muscles are as good as my slow-twitch muscles.'

'Translate.'

'The fast-twitch give you speed; the slow-twitch, stamina.

You'd really like to know who's paying money to whom, eh? You're not the first reporter I've met who'd do anything for a good story. Don't bullshit me: I know why you're here.' She smiled. 'I said, what do you have for breakfast?'

'Just coffee.'

'How very sensitive and intellectual.' She grabbed the phone. 'Room service? Send up a half-pint of fresh orange juice – and I do mean fresh – two bacon pancakes with syrup and three boiled eggs. Oh yes, and a pot of coffee ... two cups.'

She disappeared into the shower. 'I do know that Kitson has been fingered, got at, you know,' she shouted above the running water through the open glass door. 'Floris sees everything. But just who these guys are, I do not know. That dark-haired girl, Ruth Leonhard, she's involved somehow.' She padded out of the shower, drying her hair, letting warm water run down her brown body on to the carpet. 'Your nice to look at, Magnus. Karl Petersen is nice to look at, too.' Her tone, suddenly, was bitter.

When the waiter tapped on the door Barbara Floris was halfway through a gruelling floor routine of finger-tip press-ups and knee jerks, and Magnus was in the shower asking himself yet again why, at 7:15 the previous evening, had he been obliged to divert his Aston Martin DB6 into an illegal 145 mph burn-up on the M4 motorway in order to shake off an Alfa Romeo GTV 2000 which had shadowed him for ten miles, through dense traffic, after he left the Crystal Palace. He had made a note of the Alfa's registration number: WMX 534T.

'So tell me about Karl Petersen,' he said, pouring himself a cup of black coffee as Floris wolfed down her bacon pancakes-in-syrup.

'I hate his guts,' she said. 'Next question.'

'Why do you hate his guts?' Magnus said evenly.

'Why? Why!' she screamed. 'Hey, you don't *look* dumb.'

'You and he are both sophomore students on generous

sports scholarships at Glenmore College, California, right? That's how you met? And you found you had a lot in common – the decathlon and pentathlon, after all, are the male and female versions of all-round versatility.'

'You're full of shit, Massey,' Barbara Floris said, but without hostility. 'What we had in common, schmuck, was his prick and my cunt.'

Magnus winced. The models who graced his tormented youth had never talked like that. He supposed that Floris could have broken any of them in half with a single motion of her arm.

'About three months ago,' he perservered, 'a squad of top Soviet athletes turned up at Glenmore for an intensive training spell. An exchange deal?'

'Yeah.' Her mouth was full of boiled egg.

'Did Tatiana and Petersen . . . I mean. . . .'

'He laid her quicker than the hen laid this egg. And that was some achievement. OK, I'm jealous. Do you feel better, now that I've confessed? Would you like to call your boss with the news? Say, would you like to round off your visit here by calling on a real shitty motherfucker? You would? Then take the elevator to the fourth floor and knock on door 403. On second thoughts don't knock, just step inside: you'll find Karl Petersen gazing at Mr Universe in the mirror. He may have a room-mate, I don't know. One thing's sure, it won't be one of our black sprinters.'

'He's not so keen on blacks?'

'It's pathological. Sometimes I figure Karl has been in the wrong places.'

'Where, for example?'

Floris threw him a sudden, disturbed look. 'Forget it,' she said. 'Did you know that he and Larin eloped, disappeared, for four days in the States? The Russians were frantic. They would have sent the bitch to Siberia if she weren't their only surviving world-class pentathlete.'

'Does she love him?'

'I'm not a psychiatrist. She's a stupid cow. That's what Communism does to you. I'd tell her what Karl's game is but she wouldn't believe me.' Floris surprised Magnus by reaching into her purse and pulling out a cigarette. 'Am I boring you, sir?'

'No.'

'Karl can't keep his mouth shut. If you could see into his bank account you wouldn't believe it belonged to a student on a sports scholarship. There you are: I'm jealous again, or maybe I should say envious. There were nine kids in my family. We never had any money. We weren't just poor, we were hitching lifts with our furniture on our backs; I mean, did you ever read *The Grapes of Wrath*? My father used to go into scrap yards at night to steal pieces of metal which could be melted down to make weights for me to lift. Once he came back with half his arm ripped away by an unchained guard dog. Now do you understand why I can't smile charmingly when I come second?'

'Yes.'

'I guess you never had to struggle, eh? Born into the purple, I daresay; posh school, Oxford, well?'

'That sort of thing.'

'Listen, if you're a crack investigative reporter, that door over there is my grandmother.'

'You were telling me about Karl Petersen's bank account.'

Floris stubbed her cigarette butt into a saucer with two savage stabs. Then she bounced to her feet, sank to her haunches and launched herself into a series of leg-springs.

'Listen, did you ever hear of Mark Spitz? He won seven gold medals for swimming at the Munich Olympics. Naturally the sponsors went crazy, he was never off television, he made a fortune. Just like Peggy Fleming, the queen of the ice. But Karl Petersen! That jerk couldn't do better than a bronze medal at Moscow even if no one else was competing! So why, why, you tell me?'

'Why what?'

'Why has he been promised television commercials, sponsorship appearances, breakfast cereals, toys, cars, underpants, you name it; not to mention a job with Sol Enders International Promotions, Inc. Why?'

'Did he tell you all this?'

A mocking, friendly smile spread across her tanned, freckled face; it was the face of a very young woman who had matured before her time. 'Come and screw me,' she said quietly.

Ten minutes later she gave a long cry and fell back on the pillow. Her whole body relaxed as if she had finally worked out of her system all the frustrations and tensions of yesterday's competition – her anger at losing to Tatiana Larin, who had also walked off with her man. Then she fell asleep. She was out. He dressed quietly and left the hotel by way of the fire escape at the back.

Crossing the dense traffic in Holland Park Avenue, he found a phone box and put a call through to Ellison. But even now he could not bring himself to mention Ruth Leonhard.

Joe O'Neill, junior member of the Searchlight team, was beginning to feel like a twig fallen from a fatally diseased Dutch elm into long, frost-soaked winter grass. Ellison clearly derived some perverse pleasure from assigning him to nightwatchman's duties, particularly when they involved sitting in his cramped Austin Allegro all night outside some mansion pulsating with wine, gluttony and bionic sex. Now he found himself fighting fatigue outside a drab South London hotel as the hands of his luminous watch crept past midnight towords the deadly small hours of the morning.

Twenty-six years old, thick-set, bearded, Joe O'Neill was the son of a Belfast shipyard worker and made no secret of his proletarian origins. He had qualified as a chartered accountant before some restless dimension of his character carried him, against his parents' advice, into the bleak pastures of provincial journalism. Two brilliant stories in the *Belfast Echo* had caught the attention of Britain's most famous reporter; within twenty-four hours of receiving Ellison's call O'Neill had caught the night ferry from Larne to Stranraer.

For what? To act as dogsbody for two upper-class sadists. That Ellison was driven by dark public-school authoritarian compulsions had been abundantly clear to O'Neill ever since his new boss, instructing him to keep a Dartmoor cottage under 24-hour surveillance in mid-winter, had remarked: 'I'm a sadist driven by dark public-school authoritarian compulsions.'

O'Neill stared glumly at the main entrance of the hotel, fifty yards away, nibbled at a packet of potato crisps, lit another cigarette. What would a squad of top Soviet athletes, many of them due to compete the next day, do but go to bed early and stay there? Did Ellison imagine that one of them would silently slide down a rope of knotted sheets and into the arms of her American Romeo? It was plain rubbish.

But Joe O'Neill kept his eyes open and alert. Ambition surged in him like the motions of the tides; he dreaded Ellison's withering displeasure as acutely as he longed for the smallest crumb of commendation that might fall from the great man's plate.

A blue-and-white Ford Granada police patrol car had pulled up roadside of him, its blue beacon flashing silently. The peak-capped officer who brought his head down level with Joe's window carried an expression of polite neutrality.

'May I ask what you're doing here?'

O'Neill was aware that a man who sat in a parked car all night outside a hotel in his native Belfast might find an army rifle jabbed into his ribs before the questions started.

'Joe O'Neill, *Sunday Monitor*,' he said, handing over his press card. 'I'm watching the Bywater Hotel.'

'For what purpose, sir?'

'The movements of certain Soviet athletes staying in the hotel are of interest to my newspaper.'

'At 2:30 in the morning?'

Joe shrugged. 'Am I breaking the law?'

'Your continued presence here has given rise to a complaint.'

'From the Russians? Well, they never did understand freedom of the press, did they?'

'My advice to you – and it's only advice – is to move on. It's my opinion – and it's no more than an opinion, you understand – that if you stay here certain persons may take the law into their own hands.'

O'Neill grinned. 'I'll need police protection then.'

The squad car glided away.

Joe weighed up the pros and cons of staying. In the end one factor outweighed all others – Ellison had told him to stick there.

The KGB, surely, would never have the audacity to eliminate him outside the hotel in which the Soviet team were staying. Unless. ... The thought, when it surfaced, startled him; he lit a cigarette.

An hour later he caught himself nodding off. He took a swig of cocoa from his thermos, switched his car radio to a station relaying punk rock, began to fumble for his cigarettes – and fell asleep over the wheel.

Ten minutes later the Alfa Romeo GTV 2000 glided up behind him. Its registration number was WMX 534T.

Ellison's VW Passat reached Ludgate Circus at 7:40. At this hour of the morning Fleet Street was at its quietest. The presses were silent. In twenty minutes' time the day-shift operatives would emerge from buses and tube trains to begin the work of breaking up last night's chases and melting down the stereo-plates; by 9:00 the first editions of the 'evening' papers would be hurtling off the chutes into the vans – but no longer on Saturdays.

Ellison turned down Carmelite Street towards the Thames Embankment, slowed, slotted a coded card into an electronically controlled barrier, then descended into the underground executive car-park of Gowers House, the £10 million headquarters of the *Sunday Monitor*. Reaching the fifth floor in the small executive lift, he walked through the deserted Features Department to the glass-walled cubicle which bore his name.

On his desk, as always, lay a cluster of wire tapes put out overnight by Reuters, UP, AP, Agence France-Presse and the Press Association. He went through them like a Virginian farmer sorting tobacco leaves, yet very little of the information he tossed into the waste bin failed to leave an impression; it was from this memory bank, probably unequalled in Fleet Street, that he dug out the leads and connections that periodically drove Lord Jacobs, proprietor of the *Sunday Dispatch*, to entertain Ellison and his wife at the Connaught – dinners that culminated in kirsch for Pru, armagnac for Ellison and the most favourable contractual terms ever offered to a British journalist.

—The death toll in Rhodesia had risen to 400 a week.

—Militants of the Jewish Defense League had been arrested after a bomb explosion had caused extensive damage at the Soviet Intourist offices in New York.

—Senator Dick Aronson, a declared candidate for the Democratic nomination in 1980, had renewed his attacks on the President's policy of détente with the Soviet Union. Aronson had again called on the International Olympic Committee to transfer the 1980 Olympics from Moscow to Montreal or Munich.

—Governor Walter Prendergast, considered to be the leading Republican contender for the Presidency, had urged the American Olympic Committee to declare outright that it would not compete in Moscow.

—A statement from Chairman Pavlov of the Soviet Olympic Committee reaffirmed that the USSR would grant visas to all athletes, including those from China and Israel, who were recognized by the IOC.

Shortly after 8 o'clock, Ellison picked up yesterday's *New York Times* and lit his first small cigar of the day. Within half an hour he had skimmed and gutted *Le Monde*, *Die Welt*, *The Economist* and *New Africa*, as well as a translation of lead items in *Ha'aretz*, sent to him every day by special messenger from the Israeli Embassy. He then placed a call through switchboard to the embassy and requested that First Secretary Solomon Rupin should return his call as soon as he was at his desk.

'Mr Rupin will not be in today, sir. It is the sabbath.'

'Of course. My apologies.'

'You're welcome.'

A few moments later Ellison got through to an unlisted number in Alvanley Gardens, NW6.

'Solomon, I wouldn't disturb you today but it's important.'

'God will understand. In my country Jews and Christians phone their Arab friends on Friday: "Salaam," they say, "I wouldn't disturb you today but it's important." On Saturday, Arabs and Christians phone their Jewish friends: "Shalom," they say, "I wouldn't disturb you today, but it's urgent." The following day, Sunday, is the turn of Arabs and Jews to disturb the Christians. Do you know what they say?'

'What?'

'They say: "When do you people ever get any work done?"'

'We have reason to believe that a leading Soviet woman athlete is about to make the front page. You probably know more about it than I do. Correct?'

'Is she Jewish?'

'Who ever heard of a Jewish Soviet woman athlete? Who ever heard of a Jewish athlete?'

'You interrupt my sabbath prayers just to insult me?'

'Where, according to your information, is Chaim Leonhard at this moment?'

'As a matter of a fact, a Jewish woman was included as a token propaganda gesture in the German team for the 1936 Olympics. Since you ask.'

'I didn't ask.'

'It would therefore come as no surprise to us if the Soviets were to adopt the same tactic for the Moscow Olympics. Their purpose, after all, is identical to Hitler's: to deceive the world.'

'Where is Chaim Leonhard? I can't get any answer from his flat in Vienna.'

'Chaim! He's in Paris. 38 Boulevard St. Michel. Odeon 82-75. Ellen wants to know why you and Pru have not been here to dinner for so long.'

'We dined at your place last Tuesday.'

'You did? So that's who you are. Are you sure this Soviet athlete isn't a Jewish girl?'

'Quite sure.'

'Then what interest can this have for Chaim Leonhard?'

The question surprised Ellison because it sounded sincere; if this was an Israeli operation was it possible that Rupin hadn't been informed? Ellison visualized the solemn and somewhat aggressive expression on his friend's face. Short, stocky, balding, Solomon Rupin was described in the diplomatic list as First Secretary but was known to Ellison as principal agent in Britain of the most ruthless of Israel's five intelligence agencies, Ha Mossad – officially, the Institute for Information. Together with Agaf Modi'in (known as Aman), the intelligence bureau of the armed forces (Zahal), Ha Mossad shared responsibility for Israel's intelligence and espionage operations abroad. It was Ha Mossad's specialist squads which had abducted Adolf Eichmann from Argentina in 1960.

And then came Munich – the decisive trauma in Chaim Leonhard's decision to represent the Israeli Olympic Committee as counsel and consultant.

At 4:30 a.m. on September 5, 1972, five men wearing track suits had climbed over the wire fence surrounding the Munich Olympic Village. The guards, assuming that they were athletes returning from a night in town, did not challenge them, even though they were carrying bags. The five Palestinians made their way to Block 31, where they were joined by three others who had found jobs on the Village kitchen staff. The eight then burst into Flat One and instantly shot dead Moshe Weinberg, an Israeli wrestling coach who had tried to raise the alarm. The Palestinians, all members of Black September, an extremist terror outfit created in response to King Hussein's September 1970 suppression of the guerrillas in Jordan, ordered the other Israelis living in Flat One to lead them to the rest of the team. The captive Israelis shrewdly bypassed their track athletes and led the terrorists to Flat Three, which accommodated wrestlers and weight lifters. The second Israeli death occurred as soon as Joseph Romano, a weightlifter, tried to resist. Meanwhile, the athletes in Flat Two managed to escape through windows and side entrances. They sounded the alarm.

German armed police sealed off the Village. The Palestinians now held nine hostages. All the day's Olympic events were postponed. Negotiations began. The Black September guerrillas demanded the release of two hundred Palestinian militants imprisoned in Israel. They set noon as their deadline, threatening to kill one hostage per hour thereafter.

The Israeli Cabinet convened from 9 a.m. to 11:45 a.m. As far as Ellison was later able to discover, its decision was unanimous: not a single Arab prisoner would be released.

General Moshe Dayan flew to Germany to make sure that the German authorities did not strike a deal with the terrorists allowing them to take their hostages out of the country – most probably to Libya or Iraq.

Police Chief Dr Schreiber and Federal Interior Minister Hans Genscher had taken charge of negotiations in Munich. Playing for time, relying on attrition to soften the terrorists' resolve, they offered them a safe air passage out of Germany – with their hostages. When they finally recognized that the Israelis were adamant in their refusal to compromise, the Black September terrorists accepted these terms.

But they suspected a trap and they were right. Police marksmen had been assembled to ambush the guerrillas as they left the Olympic Village. The guerrillas foiled this plan by refusing to leave by bus until after dark, thus denying to the police marksmen any possibility of picking off the Palestinians without risk of hitting their hostages.

When the terrorists and their hostages finally arrived by helicopter at Fuerstenfeldbruck military air base, where a Lufthansa Boeing 727 was waiting, the police had run out of time and exhausted all hope of securing the liberation of the hostages by subterfuge. The kidnappers had anticipated every trap, when, finally, the order was given for police marksmen encircling the Boeing to open fire. The fusilade failed to eliminate the guerrillas swiftly, a marksman in the airport control tower was killed by an answering burst and a long gun battle ensued. The police captain in charge decided that there was no alternative but to storm the terrorist position. As men fell in a hail of bullets a doomed guerrilla pulled the pin from a grenade and hurled it into the helicopter in which the nine Israelis were trussed.

The police found all nine dead. Five terrorists died; three others were taken alive.

All Olympic events were suspended for twenty-four hours from the afternoon of September 5.

Nothing like it had ever before desecrated a great international sporting occasion; after Munich things could never be the same again. Security became an obsession; and sport – magnified by its exposure to television audiences running into millions – assumed a new dimension, that of amphitheatre for raw power politics.

'Solomon, you're not coming clean with me about this Russian athlete.'

'Listen: the Committee of Security in Jerusalem has laid it down as policy: if you would tell your own mother, tell that goy, Ellison. If you wouldn't tell your own mother, don't tell Ellison.'

'That's the trouble. You people never tell your mothers anything. That's why your mothers are like that.'

'Like what?'

'Like they are.'

'Another insult!'

'Shalom!'

He dialled the Paris code, 010331, on a direct line which bypassed the *Monitor*'s switchboard, and then Odeon 82–75. There was no reply.

Already the nine floors of Gowers House had begun to rumble like a ship putting to sea. It was Saturday, the crucial day in the life of a Sunday newspaper. Ellison wandered to the window and looked down at the street below where the hoists were lifting reels of newsprint off the long Leyland 442 trucks into the first-floor storerooms of Gowers House. Each reel was 64 inches wide, 33,000 feet long, and weighed three-quarters of a ton. A normal run of the 72-page *Monitor* would consume 28 million feet of newsprint, enough to extend from Fleet Street to San Francisco. But what preoccupied Ellison was whether those reels of newsprint on the hoists below him would by that evening be carrying the story that Gowers had brought back from Munich.

From Kurt Klostermann, whose business connections and

political allegiances were well known to Bill Ellison.

His buzzer sounded. It was Magnus on the line.

'Picked up anything?' Ellison asked.

'I hope not, I spent the night with Barbara Floris.' Ellison laughed. 'She was having an affair with Karl Petersen before Tatiana came on the scene, and is bitter about being jilted. She claims that Petersen has been offered lucrative commercial pickings after the Olympics and already has a job with Sol Enders International Promotions.'

'Sol! Now that's a line I hadn't thought of. So the whole thing could be commercial rather than political.'

'Don't forget Enders has given $3 million to the Jewish National Fund.'

'True.'

'I'll go and look for Sue Kitson now. Floris thinks she's been got at.'

'Do you know her home address, it would be useful to have? She's not in the phone directory, and when I tried the Women's Amateur Athletic Association, I got an extremely stiff answer.'

'It's good to know that some standards still prevail in our public life.'

'But not in the Kensington Hilton, I gather.'

'For that I deserve a bonus. No, I don't have Kitson's home address. It seemed a bit heavy-handed to ask her in the make-up room with Barbara Floris and the other girl listening.'

'The other girl?' A long pause followed. 'Are you still there, Magnus?'

'I lost you for a bit, bad line. Have you heard anything from Joe O'Neill?'

'Not a thing.'

'Odd?'

'I suspect that this could turn out to be a nasty business.'

CHAPTER 8

June 9, 1979. London

Finding the playing field wasn't easy. Magnus detested suburbia, with its monotonous rows of mock-Tudor, semi-detached houses. He circled the Hillingdon-Brunel area for twenty minutes before he spotted the neatly painted signboard: 'Dame Alice Proudfoot's School for Girls. Playing Fields. He parked his Aston Martin DB6 next to a little Renault 4 (presumably Sue Kitson's) behind a rather tatty pavilion. In the distance a group of adolescent girls in white singlets were being put through their exercises by a woman in a red track suit.

Slowly he scanned the playing field and its environs with his binoculars. It was a quiet, reassuringly normal English scene – a Saturday morning like any other.

He kept out of Kitson's way until she dismissed her squad and sent them in a chattering stampede to the pavilion, his presence arousing them to squeals of excitement. As he approached Kitson, the girls had already begun to gossip.

'That was quite a work-out,' he said.

'Good morning,' she said, with a notable lack of enthusiasm. 'We have this grudge match against St Margaret's next week. Last year they pipped us at the post after our best runner was tripped in the 200 metres.'

'Deliberately?'

'Of course one would never say so.'

'Gosh, no.'

She picked up the irony in his tone. 'A pity that you journalists didn't notice how Barbara Floris was barging into

Tatiana every time she walked past her during yesterday's long jump.'

'You're surely not suggesting that's why Tatiana started with two no-jumps?'

The colour came quickly to Sue Kitson's cheeks. 'Well, I hope you didn't swallow all that nonsense of Norman Flower's about Tatiana being infatuated with Karl Petersen.'

He stared at her. Her gaze was averted. 'Miss Kitson, who exactly told you to say that to me? Who are these people?'

She lifted her chin defiantly. 'I have nothing more to say, Mr Massey. Good morning.' She began to march towards the pavilion.

'You could be in trouble,' he said. 'The kind of deal they offered you could wreck your amateur status.'

She stopped. 'I have no idea what you're talking about.'

'You're not a good liar.'

'How dare you!'

'Teaching physical education and games in a school is in some ways the perfect job for an amateur athlete. But where's the snag? The snag is our wretched British climate. For the athlete training for five events, like you, a winter of wind, rain, snow, ice, slush, not to mention constant coughs, colds and bronchitis, is less than ideal. One can't help envying rivals who can train on tartan tracks and in temperate conditions all the year round.' He paused. 'Like Barbara Floris, for example.'

Kitson shrugged, her breasts moving inside her red track suit. 'I've managed perfectly well up till now. I don't take my athletics all that seriously anyway. So what are you driving at?'

'Next year is different: Olympic year. You're twenty-eight, right? Last chance? So what did they offer you? A year in the sun? A sports scholarship in California?'

A denial was forming on her lips when she checked herself. 'I was told not to talk to you,' she said.

'Who by?'

'I have no more to say.' She was clenching and unclenching her large hands. Spotting a 9-pound shot lying on the grass, she stooped to pick it up, caressing its smooth contours nervously.

'Is that dark-haired woman, Ruth Leonhard, involved?'

'Journalists like you sicken me. You don't give a damn about people, decent, sincere people, so long as you can muckrake a sensational story.'

'And you really imagine that your new friends care? They're simply manipulating you and – '

'They've been extremely generous!' Sue Kitson burst out, then flushed. 'OK, so Tatiana and I became friends at the European Championships in Prague last year. What's wrong with that? What's wrong with helping a friend?'

'If the Russians found out, I wouldn't rate highly your chances of getting a visa to the Moscow Olympics.'

For a moment he thought she was going to hurl the iron shot at his head. Her eyes blazed. 'They won't find out, will they? Will they?'

They had now reached the pavilion. She unlocked a storeroom and tossed the shot inside; he had a glimpse of javelins, stacks of hurdles, rollers, buckets of whitewash.

'Look,' he said, 'I wonder whether we really need to quarrel.'

'If you know what's good for you,' she said, looking towards the road, 'you'll make yourself scarce. I do mean that. These foreign freedom fighters don't have our. . . .'

'Scruples?'

'I was going to say "sense of civic restraint".'

He followed the line of her gaze. Two men in grey suits and white shirts had disembarked from the car that had pursued him the previous evening, the Alfa Romeo GTV 2000, registration number WMX 534T. Immediately he focussed his Leica M3 on them and ran it through a dozen frames.

'You bloody fool,' whispered Sue Kitson.

Ellison tried Chaim Leonhard's Paris number again, got no reply, wondered whether Solomon Rupin had deliberately misled him, then dialled 0101 202, followed by a number in Georgetown, Washington, DC. The voice that answered was distinctly sleepy.

'Norman Prosser.'

'Bill Ellison here, Norman. I notice that Senator Aronson and Governor Prendergast have both delivered speeches demanding an American boycott of the Moscow Olympics. What's the state of play?'

'I suppose you realize what time it is here?' grumbled the *Monitor*'s Washington correspondent.

'Nothing like an early start to the day, Norman. We have a big story about to break here.'

'Well, Dick Aronson is currently making all the running to challenge the President for next year's Democratic nomination. A recent Gallup Poll showed Aronson leading the President by six percentage points among registered Democrats and by three per cent among a national cross-section. As for Walter Prendergast, he looks like the best bet for the Republican nomination. Both men are reaping dividends by accusing the Administration of appeasing the Kremlin.'

'What's the balance of Congressional opinion?'

'Hard to be precise. I'd guess that about 35 of 100 Senators are seriously opposed to holding the Olympics in Moscow. By "seriously" I mean they're prepared to link the issue to the ratification of treaties, to trade deals and to the SALT arms limitation talks. The good Baron de Coubertin must have smiled when he decided to slot the Olympics into the same four-year cycle as the American presidential elections.'

'What about the American Jews?'

'There you've put your finger on it. Aronson's major speech on this issue was delivered to the American Jewish Congress. Prendergast was the guest last week of the Jewish Defense League. The fact that Israel was barred from the Asian Games held in Bangkok in December last year made an impression here. So did the fact that the Russians went along with the decision despite a warning from the International Amateur Athletics Federation. When the United States Olympic Committee marked its move from Manhattan to Colorado Springs, a strong contingent of Jewish demonstrators made the journey to protest against American participation in next year's Moscow Olympics. Robert Kane, president of the USOC, is reported to have been bombarded by Jewish protest mail. There has also been considerable pressure on NBC to abandon its exclusive TV coverage of the Olympics, for which it paid the Russians a reported $80 million.'

Ellison recalled what Sol Enders had told him about that subject in Montreal.

'We also have the Women's Campaign for Soviet Jewry in the fray,' said Prosser. 'What else can I tell you?'

'Any sign of the White House yielding to all this pressure?'

'Not publicly. I had a word with the President's press secretary last week and he intimated to me that if the artillery gets any heavier the line may prove untenable.'

'Thanks, Norman. You can go back to sleep now.'

The press cuttings on Ellison's desk showed that the mounting anti-Moscow agitation was by no means confined to America. Simon Wiesenthal, world-famous for his relentless pursuit of fugitive Nazi war criminals, had demanded that Sweden should boycott the Olympics unless the Soviet Union provided a satisfactory explanation of the disappearance in 1944 of the Swedish diplomat Raoul Wallenberg. A member of the Red Cross, Wallenberg had saved some 25,000

Hungarian Jews from the gas chambers by issuing them with Swedish passports.

Ellison knew of Chaim Leonhard's profound respect for Wiesenthal's judgement.

The more he contemplated the evidence in front of him, the firmer became Ellison's conviction that Leonhard had changed tack during the course of 1978. The trials and imprisonments of such Soviet dissidents as Shcharansky, Slepak, Nudel, Orlov, Ginzburg and Piatkus had convinced many people that Russia's signature to the Helsinki Agreement was nothing more than a mockery. Foreign visitors to the Moscow Olympics, it was widely argued, would appear to condone the incarceration in labour camps and psychiatric hospitals of thousands of dissidents. The Kremlin wanted to stage the Games for the same reason that Hitler had wanted to stage them in 1936 – to bolster the image, the prestige, of a totalitarian regime.

Ellison lit a small cigar. It had to be the Jews. In Jerusalem, Prime Minister Begin himself had publicly called for a worldwide boycott of the Olympics so long as the Soviet Union refused all Jews the right to leave Russia. Was this statement not a tacit admission that Leonhard's tactics had failed?

Again he dialled Paris. Again he got no answer.

The two men in grey suits and white nylon shirts were within fifteen yards of them when Sue Kitson made a gesture – involuntary, Magnus sensed – which halted them.

'He's going now,' she said. 'He has promised to leave me alone.'

The younger of the two took a step towards Massey and held out a powerful arm. 'Your camera,' he said. 'The film.'

Massey noted with interest the man's accent.

'Of course,' Magnus said slowly, 'a highly publicized scandal involving an assault on a reporter would hardly help Miss Kitson's athletics career.'

The older man was obviously thinking this through: tick-tock. But the younger one plainly didn't appreciate Massey's style at all.

'He's got us on film,' the younger man grunted. His arm was still extended. He took two more paces forward.

'For God's sake, give them your film,' Sue Kitson begged.

'No. I never do that, on principle.'

It wasn't true: he had found himself in several tight corners round the world where the exposure of his film was a small price to pay for staying alive. He and Ellison shared the self-disparaging joke: 'Even if you offered me £1,000 a week, I wouldn't agree to be dead.

The younger of the two men was now only five paces away from him.

'I'm not asking you again,' he said. It was then that he pulled the Webley.

Shortly after noon Ellison made telephone contact with his wife. She was a busy woman – mother of two, headmistress of Crewe Hill Comprehensive School, wife of a man who put his work before his family seven days out of seven – despite the super-tax bracket in which he was trapped.

'Who's head of Dame Alice Proudfoot's School for Girls?'

'May Catchpole.'

'Do you know her well?'

'Quite well. We sit together on various committees.'

'Do you happen to possess her private telephone number?'

'If I did, I couldn't possibly impart it to a journalist.'

'What are those?'

'Derives from the word *jour*, meaning a day. A journal is something one writes on a daily basis: hence "journalist".'

'From a strict epistemological point of view, the description hardly fits he who writes once a week.'

'What do you want from old Catchpole? I warn you, she's quite a stick.'

He told her.

'Heavens! She'll never give you the phone number of one of her unmarried female teachers. You'd better leave it to me, I'll get it out of her.'

'What are your terms?'

'We'll negotiate later. Your son is clamouring for his lunch.'

'Give him my love.'

'That's one thing he certainly needs.'

Bill Ellison winced.

Magnus Massey walked into a tenth-floor luxury flat overlooking Primrose Hill and the London skyline spreading down to the Thames. He was paying £105 a week for the flat but money didn't bother him.

'And where were you last night?' the girl on the Habitat sofa asked.

'With an American athlete.'

'Male or female?'

'I'm still trying to decide.'

Julie Beavan followed him into the darkroom, where he removed a roll of Kodak TriX from the hidden compartment of his Leica and immersed it in developing fluid.

'I lost my dummy roll today.'

'Trouble? Violence?' Her arm went round his waist when he nodded.

'What's that smell you're using?' he said.

'Alliage. Like it? What do you think of this eyeshadow – it's Clinique's Ivory Bisque. And just a touch, very discreet, of Lancôme Maquicils mascara. Well, of course, a girl becomes a walking paintbox if you neglect her, doesn't she?'

Her smile, like her lilting voice, floated on the breeze straight out of the Welsh valleys. Abstractedly he let his free hand slide beneath her silk dressing gown and over her naked breasts.

'Oh don't, sweet,' she whispered, closing her eyes.

'Chap pulled a gun.'

'Ugh! Nasty.' He felt the jolt in her small body. Her love for him, he sensed, was the real thing. No mistress had ever pleased him more, which was why he had kept her for eight months, a record of sorts. And she could use a camera, too.

'Ellison rang twice,' she said. 'They put Joe O'Neill in hospital with concussion. Poor Joe, we people from the fringes have an affinity, you know! He needed twelve stitches.'

'How long will he be out of action?'

'Oh, sentimental you are!' She poured him a mug of coffee from the simmering pot on the stove and took a jug of cream from the refrigerator. 'Ellison also passed on Sue Kitson's address. Is that the one you spent the night with? Look, I've written it down.'

'If I'd spent the night with her, I'd surely know her address.'

'Not if you both went back to your place.'

'But this is my place.'

'So you tell me, boyo, so you tell me.'

He studied the address, consulted his A-Z street directory and told Julie to hurry herself into some clothes.

'Dress not to be noticed.'

She put her arms round his neck and let her thigh slyly nudge his groin. The tip of her tongue caressed his mouth.

'No time for loving, Mag, eh?'

At 2:10 Ramsay Jordan received a call from Lord Gowers demanding an assurance that the 'big story' would appear in the first edition due to run at 5:15 pm from the *Monitor*'s twelve giant Nohab-Ampress machines at the rate of 150,000 copies an hour. Jordan equivocated: he could put off a final decision for at least an hour. Gowers now threatened him with summary dismissal, the first time he had ever gone so far. Jordan buzzed Ellison.

'You're absolutely sure this story is a fake?'

'I'm absolutely sure. Bernie Holzheimer just called me from the *New York Times*, by the way. Sol Enders, the top American sports impresario, yesterday gave a press conference in Detroit, promising to pump $16 million into a global athletics circus starring the finalists of every event at the Moscow Olympics. More to the point, he promised to sign up a sensational husband-and-wife, double-gold-medal partnership. Of course he refused to name them, to protect their amateur status.'

'So you think – '

'Yes. Graves-Brown reports from the Crystal Palace that Tatiana has just left the stadium, wearing a white dress and looking relaxed and happy. The cause of her happiness, he surmises, has been the greatly improved performance today of Karl Petersen in the two-day decathlon. According to that incomparable statistician, Graves-Brown, Petersen is heading for his highest ever points total, an overall performance which would make him a hot candidate for a medal in Moscow: 10.81 in the 100 metres, 48.5 in the 400 metres, 15.01 in the 110 metres hurdles, 47 metres in the discus, 4.71 metres in the pole vault, and so on.'

'When will he leave the Crystal Palace, at a guess?'

'The javelin and 1,500 metres are yet to come. Assuming he wins, he should be through the victory ceremony by 5:15.'

Jordan groaned. 'We just have confirmation that *Paris-Etoile*, *Vaterland*, and the *New York Sentinel* are planning to run Klostermann's story in tomorrow's editions whatever transpires here in London between now and tomorrow.'

'Well, Klostermann owns all three papers. But he doesn't own us.'

When Magnus and Julie Bcavan reached Ockenden Road in Julie's battered Mini the familiar Alfa Romeo GTV 2000 was already parked outside Sue Kitson's front door beside her Renault. He told Julie to park in Wentworth Street, which gave them a fair view of the Alfa through binoculars but was far enough away to avoid attracting attention.

'I think I'm frighthened a bit, Mag. Men with guns is outside my province.'

He offered her a fruit gum and took a look at her. She was as pretty as a peach. From her earliest years the little Welsh girl from Brecon had loved pretty things, made pretty things, passed enchanted, mesmerized summer hours sitting by the roadside hedgerows weaving bouquets of wild flowers. She arrived at the Chelsea College of Art with an exorbitant thatch of strawberry hair and an accent bewitching to every musical ear. Almost her first question to him after she became his photographic model, assistant and pupil was: 'Am I number ten or number twenty?'

Forty minutes later, a smartly dressed Sue Kitson, shadowed by two grey-suited gentlemen in white nylon, drip-dry shirts, entered a fashionable Regent's Street shop called 'Town Girl'. Once inside the shop, the agents separated themselves from Miss Kitson and headed upstairs where, observed by Julie Beavan's Leica M3, they entered the office of the store detective.

'For God's sake, keep a low profile,' Magnus had begged her. Yet he knew her to be bold, impulsive and frightened. The responsibility of bringing her weighed on him but he had no alternative: Kitson and the two agents from the Alfa Romeo knew his own face too well.

He stationed himself outside 'Town Girl', close to the

entrance. And waited, buffeted by the buffalo crowds.

Then it happened – within five seconds his heart-beat had leapt from 55 to over 100. Descending from a taxi were two women and a man: Tatiana Larin, dressed in dazzling white, Irina Bulganova, Soviet discus thrower, and an unknown official of (presumably) the Soviet Athletic Federation. They entered the shop.

Positioned behind a rack of long dacron-and-polythene dresses, Julie's camera hurried through a couple of frames as Sue Kitson and Tatiana Larin warmly embraced. But their mood was clearly tense: in their vivacity was a false note somewhere, and their interest in clothes lacked conviction. Bulganova, on the other hand, seemed genuinely delighted with the array of brightly coloured finery surrounding her. It was the male official, perhaps, who cast a blight on their happiness to be three girls going shopping.

'It's a shame,' Julie Beavan said to herself. For a moment or two she forgot to be frightened. She pretended to be examining the gowns. The premonition that she was herself under scrutiny caught her like a vice; her courage revived out of no small ambition, a determination to prove herself in a game she had hitherto watched with humble admiration – Magnus's game. But where was he, her Mag?

She heard Kitson laugh. The English girl had purchased three large, psychedelic-bright plastic carrier bags, one for each of the women. Now Kitson and Tatiana were drifting away from the absorbed Bulganova. A middle-aged woman assistant approached Bulganova.

'Can I help you, madam?'

Trapped between two racks of flimsy summer dresses, the Soviet discus thrower blushed, stuttered a few words of English. But the assistant was persistent. Selecting a vivid turquoise frock, she held it admiringly up under Bulganova's chin, urged her to try it on in one of the changing cubicles, and obligingly divested the Russian of her carrier bag, on which was imprinted the Tower of London. Looking sheepish, Bulganova trundled away.

With a deft movement the assistant pulled two frocks off the rack, folded them and let them drop into Bulganova's carrier bag. Julie's camera clicked. The woman assistant swivelled in her direction, alerted; heart pounding, Julie turned away as casually as she could, drifting towards the blue jeans.

'Yes, madam, can I help you?' It was a man's voice, a soft voice with short, clipped vowels, not a foreign accent but not a British accent either. She wheeled round, feeling the blood rush to her face, heart hammering against her ribs. He was a tall fellow, smartly dressed, with hair polished down like glass.

'I thought I'd try one of these.' She took two pairs of jeans under her arm and walked away from him, towards the changing cubicles. She daren't look round as she went. When she came out of the cubicle carrying the jeans, both of them the wrong size, he was standing in exactly the same spot, watching her intently. Such was her terror of him that she went straight to the cash desk and bought them. Kitson and Larin had vanished now; all Julie could feel was helplessness and shame, to have botched the whole thing.

'Don't cry, you're doing nicely.'

Magnus was standing close to her elbow in the line at the cash desk.

'You bastard,' she whispered, 'where have you been?'

'I went down to Brighton for a swim.'

'Did you see that store detective?'

'I did. He was in half a mind to reach for your camera. Kitson and Larin are in lingerie now. You'd better wait outside, hail a taxi, give the driver a fiver, ask him to wait on the kerb.'

Although he didn't smoke, Magnus put a cigarette in his mouth, drifting cautiously towards lingerie. Kitson, Larin and

Bulganova were approaching the cash desk in lingerie, followed by the dogged, morose Soviet official. At that moment the two agents in grey suits from the Alfa surfaced close to the women. Magnus was only just in time to swivel away, averting his face. He could see them, now, in a large wall mirror; he took his Minox miniaturized 16mm camera from his pocket, directing its lens into the mirror. It looked like a cigarette lighter.

The store detective was very polite but also firmly insistent about the two unpaid-for dresses discovered in Bulganova's plastic carrier bag. The discus thrower had turned scarlet. The Soviet official had begun to splutter official protests. 'I'm sure it's a misunderstanding,' Sue Kitson said, but mechanically, without conviction. Magnus studied Tatiana's expression; it betrayed neither shock nor distress, only waves of calculation radiating out from narrowed Slavic eyes.

Magnus made several attempts to light his cigarette. Click.

It was agreed that Bulganova must accompany the store detective to his office, where the Soviet official could make all the telephone calls he desired. The Soviet official turned to Tatiana and spoke rapidly to her in Russian, as if insisting that she too must accompany him. She shrugged contemptuously: she would stay with her English friend. Reluctantly, torn between conflicting duties and fears, the official allowed himself to be taken from her side and disappeared upstairs with the weeping Bulganova.

Tatiana Larin's arm hooked into Sue Kitson's. The older of the two agents in grey nodded. The two women walked smartly out of the shop.

The Soviet star had defected to the West.

CHAPTER 9

June 9, 1979. London

The row that now broke out between Ellison and Jordan was their fiercest for years.

'If my understanding of the situation is correct,' fumed the editor, 'we now have direct confirmation from Massey (a) that Tatiana has given the Russians the slip, and (b) that she is now holed up in Sue Kitson's flat in Ockenden Road.'

'I don't dispute it.'

'We therefore possess *prima facie* evidence that Tatiana has in fact defected and that the story which Klostermann sold to the chairman is, after all, genuine – can you bear to have been wrong?'

'I'm not wrong.'

'Stubborn as a mule. If your pride is hurt, Bill, I'm sorry, but I'm the one who has to face the chairman in ten minutes' time. You realize that he's about to fire me on the spot?'

'He's about to try. I had a meeting with our printer, Stan Gilbert, and a number of key men in the production field. They're solid behind you.'

'Who did you talk to?'

Ellison had in fact conferred with the Father of the National Union of Journalists Chapel (an unpaid office which he himself had once occupied), the Imperial Father of the National Graphical Association Chapels, representing workers in the composing room, the foundry, the machine room and the publishing room, and the SLADE Father of Chapel, who spoke for the men in the Process (picture plates) Department.

'If a proprietor is generally out of sympathy with his editor's work, then he can fire him,' Ellison reasoned to them. 'But if the dismissal arises because the editor decides to print or not to print a particular item, then it becomes a threat to editorial independence – and therefore a trade union matter.' But he didn't need to explain or argue. The confidence these men had in him was total.

'Agreed,' said Bob Sutcliffe, Father of the NUJ Chapel and therefore the key official involved, from whom the others would take their cue. They nodded their unanimous consent.

'We can close the paper down at ten minutes' notice,' Stan Gilbert, the printer, said. 'That would mean loss of the Midlands and Home Counties editions: 900,000 copies, £1.25 million in advertising revenue down the drain.'

'Thanks, Stan. I only wish you didn't say it with such relish.'

Now Ramsay Jordan was growling down the intercom into Ellison's ear. 'Let's forget about my personal predicament, grateful as I am for your support, Bill. We know where Larin is at this moment, so now, surely, for God's sake, is our chance to take the Klostermann story to her. "Did you write this, Miss Larin? Is it authentic? Do we have your permission to publish it?" Christ, we even have Kitson's phone number. We could do it by phone.'

'Tatiana would confirm the story.'

There followed a long silence.

'Am I to understand,' Jordan said with slow deliberation, 'that if Larin says she wrote this story, and Ellison says she didn't, that Ellison must be right?'

'Yes.'

'Those less devoted to you than I, Bill, might detect here the first symptoms of oncoming megalomania.'

'Certain people wanted us to publish the story but have displayed considerable determination to prevent us following it up – '

'Simply fear that any outside snooping might alert the Russians and prevent – '

'Ramsay. These people put Joe O'Neill in hospital. They pulled a gun on Magnus. Now one doesn't just *do* that to British reporters on British Saturday mornings. I don't like it. And I mean to swing these characters by their balls.'

'I don't like it either, but an attitude of personal revenge –'

'Ramsay. Why, why, why, are they going to such lengths to make sure this little Russian girl defects? She's in love, that's all: she needs their help; she becomes a tool in their hands; they write anti-Soviet diatribes under her name and she, playing ball, says yes, yes, she wrote the Klostermann story. Who are they, what are they up to? I want – to – find – out.'

'Am I stopping you?'

'If you publish the Larin story as genuine, yes you are. And you can't publish it with a disclaimer, denying proof of its authenticity, because, as we know, the contract Klostermann signed with Gowers strictly precluded that. Klostermann is no fool. He wants us to stake our professional reputations on this story *precisely to paralyse our investigative capability.*'

'Holy fuck.'

'This is a family newspaper, please.'

'What will you do if I do run the story?'

'I'd pursue my investigations freelance and publish my findings through a worldwide syndication deal. Probably make more money that way.'

'Would you mention our, er ... disagreement this evening?'

'Good Lord no, I wouldn't want to make you look a fool.'

Ten minutes later Magnus came through. 'Karl Petersen has just arrived at Kitson's flat.'

'Nice one, Massive.'

'Do you realize I haven't had a bite to eat all day? And

when I think of those bacon pancakes I turned down in the Kensington Hilton. . . .' He rang off.

Jordan was on the line again. 'Look, Bill, we could approach Tatiana, just to find out what she has to say; I mean, it wouldn't oblige us to publish. . . .'

'It would simply reveal that we had succeeded in recording the day's events and would expose our reporters to the risk of even more violent attacks.'

Agency tapes from the News Room indicated that the Russians were now entering a slow but steady burn. An initial Embassy protest complaining about the 'frame-up' of Irina Bulganova in the shop 'Town Girl' was followed by a second statement claiming that her subsequent release, without charges, proved that the incident had been a 'deliberate provocation'. But the Russians, as yet, remained silent about Tatiana Larin.

Once again he dialled Chaim Leonhard's number in Paris. This time the call was immediately answered.

'*Allo?*'

'*Bon soir, monsieur, voulez-vous bien me dire si un Monsieur Degas reste chez-vous?*'

The man at the other end chuckled. '*Qui parle? Monet?*'

'*Renoir.*'

'Such elaborate precautions. Did I get my bit right? I thought you had a private line.'

'I do. But how did Fred Astaire dance?'

'Tap tap.'

'Yes.'

'Who gave you my number?'

'He who judges.'

'I think you enjoy this schoolboy rigmarole. In fact, it may explain a great deal of British history.'

'I must see you, urgently, in Paris. Monday, 2:30. I suggest a game of tennis, at Paul's place, but do come alone, I can't abide doubles. Or spectators. If your back aches, I'll understand. Return home and rest. Understood?'

'Perfectly. My daughter will be delighted to see you. She is due here on Monday.'

'Where is she now?'

'I have no idea. She is a free woman. She does not often confide in me, why should she? *Adieu.*'

As he put down the phone, Cherry laid a fresh agency tape on his desk. At 18:19 the Soviet Embassy had issued a statement complaining that Tatiana Larin had been 'abducted' with the connivance of 'certain British circles'. Two minutes later Ellison received a call from Anthony Rhoderick, number two on the USSR desk in the Foreign and Commonwealth Office.

'I have First Secretary Tretiakov with me here,' Rhoderick said. 'He claims that Miss Larin vanished from "Town Girl" in Regent's Street at about 4 o'clock this afternoon, in the company of a British athlete, Susan Kitson. Tretiakov says he has reason to believe that you may know something about it.'

'What reason has he to believe it?'

'I'm afraid he's reluctant to disclose that.'

'Tell him, he no talk, I no talk.'

Rhoderick cleared his throat. 'I quite understand your point of view, Bill, and I wouldn't for a moment want you to misinterpret what I have to say as any kind of interference with the freedom of the press, but – '

'You'd be awfully obliged if I'd help avert a nasty diplomatic incident.'

'Well, yes.'

'This I do know for certain: that whatever Miss Larin has done so far she has done freely, of her own choice. She may not fully understand the implications of her actions, but the decision has been hers.'

'Hmn. Where is she now?'

'I don't know.'

'My colleague Tretiakov here rather thought you might help us trace Miss Kitson.'

'Roddy, if – and I only say if – Larin has jumped, you

wouldn't want squads of KGB goons racing up to North London and snatching her back by force?'

'Good heavens, no! Obviously we would get to her first....'

'What about that £2.5 billion Anglo-Russian trade deal now awaiting ratification?'

'Er ... well ... that's a different issue altogether.'

'Is it?'

'What flabbergasts me,' raged the purple-faced chairman from behind his huge teak desk, 'is why two experienced journalists like yourselves should turn your backs on an exclusive scoop of monumental proportions! Damn it, the girl has jumped, hasn't she? What more do you want? I mean, you're not Communists, are you? You, Ellison, have written many fine exposés of repression in Russia and Eastern Europe. It's not like you to cover up for the Kremlin!'

Jordan, silent throughout the altercation, gazed bleakly down at the Penthouse-Supreme carpet. Outside the huge teak-and-bronze, electronically operated doors waited the Fathers of the Chapel, playing cards. Gowers got the message.

'Get out of here,' he growled.

She trotted into the empty house, light, fluffy and smiling, her high heels echoing on the floor boards. The young painter, clad in white overalls engagingly stained, looked up from his work, surprised by her beauty.

'Where's Magnus, then?' she asked brightly.

'Upstairs, first floor front. He's using the bay window.'

Magnus had spotted the young painter at work, putting the final touches to the decoration of a converted house some ninety yards down Ockenden Road from Sue Kitson's flat. It turned out that both he and Magnus were Chelsea supporters with unrivalled collections of Rolling Stones albums; that the young painter was fascinated by cameras and needed someone to talk to anyhow.

The bay window on the first floor gave Magnus an excellent view of Kitson's front door.

'Well,' Julie announced, 'I've brought you two ham sandwiches, coffee in a thermos, and one Aston Martin. As commanded. Sir.'

'Did you put mustard in the sandwiches?'

'I did, I did.'

'French or English?'

'Which should I have put?'

'Which did you put?'

'Bite it and see. It might be Welsh mustard.'

'Did you take the film into Ellison?'

'I did. I'm awfully obedient, you know. I don't think he fully trusts me. Now why should that be?'

'Where did you park the Aston?'

'Round the corner in Wentworth Street. As commanded.'

In the room below, the painter's transistor, turned up full blast on Radio 1, brought them a news bulletin, echoing up the uncarpeted stairway: the Russians had now gone so far as to accuse the British Government of unwillingness to search for the missing Tatiana Larin.

'World War Three,' giggled Julie Beavan.

'You can laugh, Welsh rarebit, but I guarantee there'll be a 50-megaton nuclear attack on this city before the night's out.'

'My God, Mag, is that very big?'

'Julie, I've made an awful mistake and I don't know how to rectify it.'

'Me, you mean? Don't worry, darling, I'll go quietly. Just tell me how much you're worth and I'll settle for fifty per cent.'

'When I visited the athletes in the make-up room yesterday evening, there was this dark-haired girl standing there, with a camera over her shoulder. She told me her name is Ruth Leonhard, daughter of Bill's Jewish friend, the Viennese lawyer Chaim Leonhard. But Bill has never mentioned her existence to me. Point one. And the way she looked at me when she asked whether Bill had ever mentioned her suggested, really strongly, that. . . .'

'They're lovers?'

'Just so. Somehow I couldn't bring myself to mention her to Bill this morning.'

Julie shrugged cheerfully, then hugged herself against the creeping evening chill as the sun slid down the pink summer sky. 'Does it matter so much?'

'I hoped it didn't. Until half an hour ago.'

'What happened half an hour ago?'

'Karl Petersen arrived at Kitson's flat in a taxi. Accompanied by Ruth Leonhard.'

'Holy cow! You'll have to tell Bill.'

'Yes. But I didn't. When I phoned him to report Petersen's arrival, I meant to, but I didn't. Each time I don't, it gets harder.'

Julie's eyes had opened saucer-wide. She was standing very close to him now, the top of her head barely level with his shoulders. 'You're a naughty boy, boyo,' she whispered. 'We may have to take away your NUJ card.'

'It gets harder and harder!'

He swung round to the bay window, raised his Nikon F2A Photomic, fitted with a 500mm lens, took a rapid light reading off the two silicone photo diodes, adjusted to f.4 at 1/500th and then recorded on Ilford HP4 the arrival of a large American car, probably a Buick, out of which stepped a chauffeur, carrying a silver-tipped walking stick. The chauffeur walked smartly round to the rear, nearside door and opened it, extending a hand as if to help out the passenger, but the passenger did not emerge. Instead the door of Sue Kitson's flat opened, the two agents in grey suits stepped out, scanned the street, then hustled four people out of the house into the big Buick.

Massey's Nikon was racing now. 'Kitson, Larin, Petersen, Leonhard. Wow!' He grabbed the Aston Martin keys from her and ran.

Standing in the bay window, Julie watched him sprint out of the house, discarding all caution, and across the road towards Wentworth Street. Involuntarily her little hands had clenched tight out of fear for him; yet, at the same time, she was cheering him on as if he were a Grand Prix driver racing for the grid. 'Go, boyo, go!'

The Aston Martin gunned out of Wentworth Street with a deafening roar, like some male battle cry, bombed into Ockenden Road with burning tyres and belted for Islington in pursuit of the Buick.

The Alfa Romeo GTV 2000, fitted with a 4-1962 engine at 122 bhp, snarled off the kerb in pursuit. They had been expecting Massey and now they had him where they wanted him, tied to the tail of the Buick. This time there would be no burn-ups on the motorway, where the Aston Martin's top speed of 145 mph gave it a 25 mph advantage over the Alfa.

It was opposite Euston Station, in the Euston Road, that the Alfa drew level with Magnus, just as the Buick ahead jumped a set of red lights and sped away towards Marylebone. The silencer on the Webley reduced the report to a dull 'phutt' – a neat hole appeared in his laminated windscreen only inches from his head. He ducked instinctively, at the same time swinging the wheel left-hand-down so that the front fender of his precious Aston ripped into the offside wing of the Alfa. The second bullet ricocheted off his steering wheel into his upper arm. The third knocked out his rear tyre.

With a fierce snarl, the Alfa disentangled itself and roared away, its horn blaring.

He felt as if his arm had been struck by a hammer; it was

the whole arm, rather than the point of impact, which hurt. There was blood, now, on his right hand.

A concerned, friendly face was staring at him through his window. 'Are you all right?'

He nodded. 'Damn,' he said.

'Inspector Coughlan of the CID,' Cherry said, showing the plain-clothes detective into Ellison's office. During the inspector's journey from reception to the fifth floor, all negatives and prints from the day's photography had been tidied away into a locked filing cabinet.

'Well, how are you, Inspector?'

'You look remarkably cheerful for a man who's had one reporter concussed and another shot in the arm!'

'For us hacks, Inspector, bad news is good news. Up to a point, of course. Now will you have some coffee? Or maybe some Irish coffee? Yes? Cherry, be a darling. Now try one of these little Dutch cigars. Good. I was up the Shannon at O'Brien's Bridge only last summer, excellent coarse fishing, my young son caught a 4-pound bream using a ton of ground-bait from the local creamery. I got in a couple of rounds at Limerick but I was slicing my woods.'

'Would you be giving me the blarney, Mr Ellison?'

'I might be, Inspector.'

'Would you kindly stop imitating my accent.'

'I can hardly help myself, Inspector, I'm that pleased to see you.'

'Would any of this have to do with the disappearance of Miss Tatiana Larin?'

'Now, Inspector, you don't want to be putting your big clumsy boots into journalistic privilege, otherwise I might have to display your large intestine all over the front page of the *Monitor.*'

'Mr Ellison, this is a serious business. Firearms. Attempted murder in central London. You've no right to be obstructing justice.'

'I suppose you've been talking to Anthony Rhoderick at the Foreign Office?'

Coughlan disregarded this remark. 'When Massey was shot, was he attempting to follow anyone?'

'I don't know. Ask him. He's conscious and *compos mentis* in University College Hospital.'

'I did ask him. I've just come from his bedside.'

'What did he tell you?'

'I'm asking the questions, Mr Ellison.'

'What did Rhoderick say to you?'

'You're trying to blur the issue, sir, by politicizing it. You're trying to compromise me. I am pursuing a strictly police inquiry. A serious crime has been committed.'

'Listen, Inspector. The *Sunday Dispatch* would pay you £20,000 for the information you have just asked me to divulge.' He picked up a copy of the *Dispatch*'s first edition which a spy regularly smuggled out of the *Dispatch*'s machine room shortly after 5 o'clock. 'Look at that headline: SOVIET STAR VANISHES – 96-point Century bold across two columns. However, if you look below the headline you'll find nothing of consequence, just a re-hash of the Soviet complaints and the Foreign Office reply.'

'Are you suggesting that I could be bribed to divulge confidential information?' protested Coughlan.

'Inspector, that filing cabinet contains a dossier this thick of cases of *proven* corruption in the Metropolitan Police Force during the past five years. Now leave me alone, Inspector, and don't apply for a search warrant from a magistrate because we'll counter-move for an injunction if you do.' He stood up. 'Besides, Coughlan, I have dirt on you I wouldn't hesitate to use.'

Cherry came in with the second edition of the *Monitor*. MYSTERY OF TATIANA.... He noticed that Jordan had inserted long extracts from 'Goodbye, Russia', the Larin story printed only an hour earlier in *Vaterland* and *Paris-Etoile.* Ellison smiled. Ramsay had got his little scoop after all, since the other British papers hadn't yet had time to pick up and translate the big story published by Klostermann's papers. But it didn't matter. The *Monitor* hadn't committed itself, that was the main thing.

Julie Beavan came in.

Ellison poured her a drink. 'How is he, then, that big Mag, eh?'

'Don't worry, dear,' Cherry said to Julie, 'he was doing an equally abominable Irish accent only ten minutes ago.'

'He's fine,' Julie said. 'He'd like to see you, of course, but the Sister said "No way". They're putting him to sleep.' Suddenly she burst into tears. 'I'm glad they didn't kill him.' Gratefully she accepted Cherry's comforting embrace. There was one thing she had meant to do, because Magnus had asked her to do it: to tell Ellison about Ruth Leonhard. But Julie Beavan was so upset now that she forgot.

By 2:30 in the morning Ramsay Jordan's office was cloudy with cigar smoke. Ellison was on his fourth scotch, and his editor was matching him in cognacs. There was, of course, no reason at all for Ellison to hang around, but they made a habit of it on Saturday nights, like midwives superintending the long, twelve-hour birth of a child. Far below them, in the bowels of the vast building, the twelve Nohab-Ampress machines, with sixteen stereo-plates locked into position on the cylinder of each unit, were roaring like the turbines of an ocean-going liner. As the huge sheets of newsprint sped out of the presses, slitters descended faster than the speed of an eye to cut the web; kites automatically folded the sheets. Complete, folded copies of the 72-page newspaper moved up the igranic wires to the publishing room above, where automated counter-stackers twirled quires of twenty-five copies into stacks of four, then despatched each stack along a conveyor belt to be wrapped in brown paper, labelled by destination and bound in yellow twine. At the end of their journey the bundles shot out of the chutes into the long line of vans waiting to rush them to King's Cross, Euston, Victoria, Waterloo, Paddington and Liverpool Street.

'Well, Bill. . . .'

'Well, Ramsay. . . .'

'Sorry if I was a bit sharp with you earlier on. . . .'

'On the contrary, I gave you a rough passage. . . .'

'I'm sure you were right. . . .'

'Yes, I expect so.'

It was already 21:45 hours Moscow time when the first reports from the Soviet news agency Tass's London office hit the editorial desks of *Pravda* and *Izvestia*. It wasn't only the news agency reports but also messages of increasing urgency from the Soviet Embassy in London which finally convinced Alexander Martinov, president of the Press Control Commission of the Central Committee of the Communist Party of the Soviet Union, that the story was so big and dangerous that it could neither be published nor be not published. Trembling, Martinov dialled the most closely guarded telephone number in the Union of Soviet Socialist Republics.

'Well?' The voice at the other end of the line sounded like a grizzly bear which had just discovered a bullet embedded in its rump. Brezhnev.

In the Foreign Ministry and in Dzerzhinsky Square, headquarters of the KGB, experts were being summoned from their weekend dachas to examine the mounting pile of decoded messages from London.

By 23:55 Josef Arbuzov, head of the KGB's West European Counter-Insurgency Division, had arranged places for two of his agents on Aeroflot's flight SU 581, leaving Sheremetyev International Airport for London at 10:55 the following day. Arbuzov's dual war against vodka and Armenian tobacco, which doctors had warned him could cost him his life within a year, set his deprived nervous system screaming and his big, sadist's mouth dribbling in uncontrollable rage.

That Chaim Leonhard was a Jew was sin enough in Arbuzov's eyes. He hadn't forgotten how Leonhard had threatened to make an international scandal over the affair of the basketball match between Israel and Cuba, held in Moscow in 1973, when Soviet troops had been imported to barrack the Israeli players. Now Leonhard had double-crossed him by masterminding the disappearance of Tatiana Larin in London – the day after she broke the world pentathlon record, too. Master-stroke! And why? To blackmail the Soviet Union into releasing more Jews.

Arbuzov stared hard at the two agents assigned to the mission. 'We have a tap on Leonhard's phone thanks to the help of a friendly telephone engineer in the French Communist Party. Leonhard is expecting a visit on Monday from Bill Ellison, the British journalist. Ellison is number one in his profession and considered even by Soviet reporters to be the best investigative journalist in the world. He achieves his results by team-work; only loyalty to his chief prevents Massey, his right-hand man, from accepting the lucrative offers made to him from all quarters.

'We must assume deep collusion between Leonhard and Ellison. Not only is the British journalist a frequent visitor at the Israeli Embassy, but his family dine periodically at the home of Rupin, principal Ha Mossad agent in Western Europe. This collusion is documented for us by a vital inside informant whose identity will be revealed to you when you contact a number I shall give you in Paris.

'And here, on this paper, is the loosely coded message exchanged today between Ellison and Rupin. By the time you board tomorrow's Ilyushin at Sheremetyev, I expect you to have de-coded it.'

Arbuzov's smile was not a pleasant one.

CHAPTER 10

June 10, 1979. London

Tempted though he was to disconnect the telephone when he finally crawled into bed beside Pru at 4:30 in the morning, it went against the Ellison grain. The telephone was the oxygen supply of his trade – the faint, interrupted voice of a distant, beleaguered correspondent surrounded by a menacing mob, the frightened whispers of an anonymous caller blurting out a truth. He had been asleep barely three hours when the phone rang.

'Bill, I'm sorry, there's no way I can go to bed until I've spoken to you.' It was Ellison's old friend, Bernie Holzheimer of the *New York Times*, calling from 229 West 43rd Street. 'I've only just seen news of Magnus's hospitalization on the UPI tape. How is he?'

'Asleep, I expect.'

'OK, point taken. I've also been reading "Goodbye, Russia" in the *New York Sentinel*. There's a rumour flying about here that you actually suppressed the *Monitor*'s exclusive British rights in that story. Can you confirm?'

'Yes.'

'Look, Bill, I'm sorry, I know you're tired. Is it true that your chairman, Gowers, brought the story back from Munich on Friday?'

'Yes.'

'So how come you didn't print it?'

'We're not convinced that the story is authentic.'

'Is Gowers convinced? Was there a row? Is it true he

threatened to fire Ramsay Jordan? Is it true you threatened to shut down the entire newspaper if he did?'

'Bernie, did I ever try and interview you about the Sulzbergers?'

'Is there a connection between the attacks on Massey and O'Neill and the Larin story?'

'Certainly.'

'What connection?'

'Why should I give you my story, Bernie?'

'Do you have any idea how the Larin girl gave the Russians the slip?'

'Same answer.'

'Or where she is now?'

'Same answer.'

'Bill, how big a story do you think this might turn out to be?'

'Very big.'

'Hold the line a minute, Bill.'

Ellison let his head fall back on the pillow and closed his eyes. Pru was fast asleep, immunized to interruption by twenty years of marriage to Ellison.

'Bill?' Holzheimer was back. 'I'm authorized to offer you $125,000 for the exclusive United States first-serial rights to the final Searchlight story, as published in the *Monitor*.'

'Talk to Bruce Stroud, our business manager. Try calling him now. He loves talking money at 7:30 on a Sunday morning.'

'I'm also authorized to offer you any help we can give you this end. I have a feeling the action might transfer to this side of the Atlantic, yes?'

Ellison sat up sharp on his elbow. 'The first thing you can do, Bernie, is to have Karl Petersen's CV checked out in depth.'

'Yes, sir!'

'I hope you're standing at attention.' Ellison disconnected the phone and crawled back under the sheet as the summer sunshine infiltrated the heavy damask curtains that Pru had once found time to make, eighteen years earlier, after the birth of their daughter, Faith. He fell asleep.

When he descended to the kitchen at 10:45 he found his family immersed in newspapers and lively speculation. Christopher was particularly excited by the shooting of his hero, Magnus, who occasionally took him to cricket matches. 'Was it a real gun?'

'We'll call on him in hospital this morning and ask him.'

Ellison glanced out of the window: there was no sign of anyone prowling Chester Place with a Peke dog or a bulge under his left armpit. He debated whether to discuss security with his family but concluded that he would merely create more alarm than actual security.

'What puzzles me,' Faith said, 'is why Larin should want to defect. After all, she enjoys all the privileges of the Soviet elite, and if she really wants to marry this American, Petersen, she could surely do so without denouncing the entire Soviet system.'

Ellison found difficulty in concealing the pride and love she aroused in him. She had just won a scholarship to his old Oxford college, New, which had recently gone co-educational.

'So what's it all about, Bill?' Pru asked, presenting him with a plate of bacon and scrambled eggs.

'It's my hunch that someone is trying to sabotage next year's Olympic Games.'

'Who?' yelled Christopher.

'And how?' asked Faith, puzzled.

Their father looked from one to another slyly. The few hours he could snatch with his family were the most precious of his week. 'How do I know you're not a secret stringer for Tim Powerstock?' he asked the boy.

Christopher leapt around the kitchen. 'You're holding back! He's holding back, Mum! It's the famous Ellison technique. Look – he's smiling, he admits it!'

Ellison, scanning the Powerstock centre page in the *Dis-*

patch, laughed. 'As usual, his third paragraph begins: "Now that the dust is beginning to settle, certain questions still need to be answered." '

Pru said: 'Tim – '

'Oh, it's Tim now, is it?'

'Shut up. Tim has less than half your salary and not a tenth of your reputation. Every six months Lord Jacobs invites us to dinner at the Connaught and offers you Tim's job. You should be ashamed to make fun of him.'

'I'm ashamed.'

'You're not, Daddy,' Faith said. 'You're a brute.'

He reached out to touch her hair and his heart gave a small leap at the memory of Ruth Leonhard, scarcely older than Faith was now, when he had first met her in Vienna. And tomorrow, in Paris. . . .

They all drove to University College Hospital, to see Magnus. The Sister in charge of Magnus's ward was by now running short of patience. 'It's like being under siege,' she complained. They found Magnus sitting up and looking cheerful, his bed covered with newspapers and Julie Beavan. 'I've been fending them off with my shepherdess's staff,' she said.

Christopher stared at Magnus's bandaged arm. 'Did it hurt?'

Magnus gave him a big wink. 'A real, muscular man doesn't feel pain,' he said.

Christopher absorbed this information slowly.

After ten minutes Ellison showed his usual signs of restlessness. With a few well chosen words he cleared them all out of the ward, then dropped his voice to thwart the curiosity of Magnus's fellow-patients.

'What did you tell Inspector Coughlan?'

'Nothing that Powerstock could use.'

Magnus rehearsed the entire sequence of events from the arrival of the Buick outside Sue Kitson's flat in Ockenden

Road to the shooting opposite Euston Station. Then his eyes fell. 'There's something I ought to have told you earlier.'

'Oh?'

'There's a woman involved. She was with the athletes at the Crystal Palace on Friday evening, she turned up in the same taxi as Karl Petersen yesterday evening and she left in the Buick with Larin, Kitson and Petersen – and the unseen person with the silver-tipped stick.'

'Any idea who this woman is?'

Magnus nodded. 'Yes. She told me. Her name is Ruth Leonhard.'

Whatever Ellison's immediate reaction to the news, Magnus took care not to know about it – he was examining his bottom pyjama button with absorbed interest.

Eventually Ellison said, in an even voice: 'That seems to confirm that this is an Israeli operation after all.'

'Not all the evidence of the last forty-eight hours points in that direction.'

'Ruth, of course, is a *Chicago Tribune* reporter. She may simply have got herself an inside scoop – chequebook stuff.'

Finally, Magnus allowed his eyes to meet Ellison's. They betrayed no emotion at all.

After a curry lunch at home and a game of chess with Christopher, Ellison took his family up Haverstock Hill for a walk on Hampstead Heath. Approaching Heath Street, he decided that a black Rover 3500 had pursued him through too many twists and turns to accommodate the law of averages. Abruptly he pulled into the kerb. The Rover swept past: two men occupying the front seats seemed (perhaps) to avert their faces. It may have been his imagination.

'Why did we stop?' Christopher piped.

'Daddy thought we were being followed,' Faith said.

'Gosh. Did you, Dad?'

'If nobody follows me, I must be losing my touch,' Ellison said.

Pru looked worried.

They began to walk across the Heath. Faith linked her arm in her father's. 'Every minute in your company,' she said, 'feels as if it may be the last. I keep expecting you to remember a vital engagement and vanish in a puff of smoke. Is it just conceivable that you're going to spend the whole of Sunday with your family?'

'He's flying to Bonn tomorrow,' Pru said. 'The odd thing, though, is that there isn't a flight to Bonn at the time he gave me.' Her tone was cold, hurt. 'I suppose mendacity becomes finally an all-consuming principle ... even with one's wife.'

He put his arm round Pru's shoulder. How hurt she must be, to say that in front of Faith! She had always suspected that his trips abroad involved affairs, but hers was not a confrontational style and he, for his part, retreated into a form of limbo, neither confirming nor denying.

Tomorrow he would meet Ruth again, after almost three years. Perhaps. The prospect had released in him a waterfall of desire, of longing, until Magnus had abruptly dynamited his assumptions. Ruth had been in London, involved in the Tatiana affair; Chaim had denied knowing where she was; if Magnus had held back, it could only mean....

Two men walked out of the copse ahead of them. The Ellisons were now entering one of the more remote areas of the Heath, a spot known for its muggings, assaults and suicides. Pru slowed her pace and reached for Christopher's hand.

'It's OK, it's Jack Knight,' Ellison reassured her. 'I thought I recognized him in that Rover which was shadowing us.'

'Who's the big fellow?'

'Ray Lawson, First Secretary at the American Embassy.'

Lawson shook everyone by the hand; Knight, inhibited, no one. He looked embarrassed and began to apologize to Pru for interrupting a family Sunday outing.

'You can have him for twenty minutes,' she said. 'We'll shadow you, though.'

'Nice of you to let us borrow your husband, Mrs Ellison,' Lawson said, throwing an admiring glance towards Faith. He was an attractive man, tall, thickening a bit round the middle, with a mop of curly hair, a matching beard and a relaxing smile. Dressed in jeans, sneakers and a T-shirt, he didn't at all resemble the Ivy League, Brooks Brothers image of the Foreign Service. He looked like the kind of graduate student you might find lounging under a tree with a stack of Beatles cassettes and the poems of Wallace Stevens. The glance that he had thrown in Faith's direction, and the evident impact his presence had on her, reminded Ellison of Lawson's reputation with women. Rumour had it that his constant infidelities drove his wife to join the Jim Jones Temple of Peace sect in Guyana. She and their young son had been two of the hundreds who had swallowed poison from a bubbling vat in November of the previous year. Lawson had told friends that he knew he ought to fly to Guyana to identify the corpses of his wife and son but he just couldn't face it.

To this relaxed, Bohemian image, Jack Knight offered the most extreme contrast: thin almost to the point of emaciation, pale as parchment, dressed invariably in cut-price, off-the-peg brown suits, he wore a dark tie forced into a tight knot and carried a grey-brown raincoat over his arm at all times of the year except during rain, when he put it on with relief.

Jack Knight was the sort of man you pass without noticing in the street: hair, skin, shirt and suit receded into a pale lifelessless. He would have blended into any street-corner betting shop, fag-end in mouth, eyes half-closed against the smoke, bad cough. The Inland Revenue and Social Security files showed that he worked for Section F4 (public order, firearms) of the Home Office's Police Department. The files however, were slightly deceptive.

Ellison had known Knight for many years. An investigative journalist is as good as his contacts; Ellison commanded a range of sources within the upper and middle-upper reaches of government which no rival could match. But Knight was different, for Knight, like Ellison himself, was a hunter. He worked for MI5.

Ellison waited. Normally Knight would begin by feeding him titbits of information, just as he tossed pieces of stale bread to the ducks in St James's Park. But it was the American who opened with a direct question: 'Bill, do you believe the Larin girl has genuinely defected? Or is she just holed up in some London pad, screwing Petersen?'

'Who knows?'

Lawson threw him a quick, sidelong glance. 'The Soviets claim that the arrest of the Bulganova woman on a shoplifting charge was a pre-planned set-up designed to lift Tatiana Larin. Do you have any views on that?'

'None.'

'Bill, you're holding out on me.'

'Am I on your payroll?'

Lawson laughed. 'No, you're not. But in the weeks ahead we might be able to help you with your investigation.'

'What investigation?'

Knight intervened. 'It can't be coincidence that you have two reporters in hospital. One of them was slugged outside the Soviet team's hotel; the other had spent the night more comfortably, in the company of Miss Barbara Floris.'

Lawson chuckled. 'He must have stamina, Massey. Personally, I'd sleep my way through the day after two stands with Floris. That girl can do sixty press-ups on her finger tips.'

'I had a word with Sergei Tretiakov,' Knight said quietly, referring to the KGB operative ('First Secretary' at the London Embassy) responsible for the surveillance of anti-Soviet Russian émigrés in Britain. 'He's convinced –'

'You mean he wants to convince you,' Lawson cut in.

'He's convinced,' Knight repeated with more than a hint of irritation, 'that this is a Zionist operation. After all, there are still 150,000 Jews waiting to get out of Russia, 2,000 of whom have been turned down flat for unspecified reasons.'

'Tretiakov could be right,' Ellison said. 'Or it could be the Copenhagen-based International Sakharov Committee at work. After all, they've stage-managed defecting ballet dancers, novelists, scientists and musicians – how about a leading athlete for a change?'

Lawson nodded. 'Last year was certainly a disastrous one for détente. Orlov, seven years in prison, five in exile; Ida Nudel, four years in exile; Vladimir Slepak, five years in exile; Ginzburg, eight years in a labour camp; Piatkus, three years in prison, seven in a labour camp, five in exile; Anatol Shcharansky, thirteen years in prison and labour camps. ... It's hardly astonishing if exiled groups retaliate.'

'On the other hand,' Ellison said, 'the whole operation could be a KGB trap. The stories which appeared in Klostermann's papers could have been planted.'

'Standard disinformation procedure,' Lawson said. 'The KGB's penetration of Russian-language publishing houses and literary agencies in the West is highly developed.'

Knight shook his head. 'I don't believe it.'

'That's because you're buddies with Tretiakov,' Lawson said.

'Offer a plausible motive.'

'Easy. The anti-Soviet *émigré* groups will latch on to Tatiana, they'll make wildly exaggerated claims, and then Tatiana herself will resurface, blushing, with her handsome beau, baffled by all the fuss and furore. "We just want to get married," she'll say. "I love my country." She will of course completely deny having written the "Goodbye, Russia" story. And the result? The *émigré* movement will be entirely discredited!' Grinning broadly at his own acumen, Lawson looked to Ellison to gauge the famous journalist's reaction, before continuing: 'If you ask me, the operation bears the thumbprint of Josef Arbuzov, head of the KGB's West European Counter-Insurgency Division. His doctors warned him to give up vodka and Armenian tobacco; since then he's turned very mean indeed!'

Ellison laughed. The ghost of a smile was allowed, fleetingly, to invade Knight's thin, pallid features.

'When did Massey last see Susan Kitson?' he asked Ellison suddenly.

Ellison simply let the question evaporate in the dry summer breeze. Jack, of course, had been talking to Tretiakov, just as Anthony Rhoderick, of the Foreign Office, had got his information from the same source. But who was tipping off the Russians about the movements of the Searchlight team? That was a question that Ellison needed answered, and answered fast.

'It's time we re-joined the ladies,' he said.

CHAPTER 11

June 11, 1979. Paris

An hour after his British Airways Trident touched down at Charles de Gaulle, Ellison was picked up outside the Bibliothèque Nationale in the Rue de Richelieu by a yellow Renault 4 with a right-hand drive.

'Bill!'

'John!' They shook hands warmly. 'You certainly make yourself conspicuous with a right-hand drive,' Ellison added.

John Coppola smiled through steel-framed spectacles. 'When your Government threw me out as a dangerous alien, it was all I had to take with me.'

'You're sure you weren't followed?'

'I'm sure. My apartment has been under round-the-clock surveillance since I arrived and it's probably bugged from top to bottom. But I always give them the slip. I was a student at the Sorbonne, you know; I learned then how to drive up a *sens unique* the wrong way with an air of baffled innocence. Things are harder when the Surêté Nationale do the "Company's" dirty work for them – those *flics* are harder to lose.'

Coppola lived in permanent exile now. Having broken his contract of silence with the CIA and published his exposé of the 'Company', he had been harassed and hounded from one NATO country to the next. There was no way he could return to his family in the United States without incurring immediate arrest and prosecution.

Nor was his life safe: at least one attempt had been made on it after it became known that he had supplied a list of CIA operatives serving overseas to the radical San Francisco magazine, *Last Chance*. Two of the agents named had been murdered by left-wing groups in Teheran and Frankfurt: a body called the Association of Retired Intelligence Officers was looking for vengeance.

Never had the CIA been more sensitive to criticism and adverse publicity. Years of shit had suddenly tumbled out of the bucket. One Congressional committee after another was subpoenaing the 'Company's' records and former directors, while also exposing the Agency's complicity in Mafia plots to murder foreign heads of government. The 'Company' was now a haunted place; it was several years since a single green leaf had budded in Langley, Virginia. In 1973 incoming CIA Director James Schlesinger had purged more than one thousand 'spooks'.

'What do you know about Ray Lawson, John?'

'You want to stop for a coffee or just keep driving?'

'You know best.'

'We'll keep driving. Lawson's assigned to the London Embassy now as a First Secretary – I guess you know that. The big thing in his ambitious life was Angola.'

'He was in *that*?'

'Certainly. Kissinger was determined to give the Russians a bloody nose after the Vietnam fiasco – which meant committing a cool $31 million in the summer of '75 to stopping Neto's Marxist MPLA from taking over Angola as the Portuguese pulled out. The result you know: the instant appearance in Angola not only of 15,000 highly efficient Cubans but also of a number of men with a lot of snow on their balls. About $200 million of snow, according to Kissinger, who claims the Russians made the first move.'

'And Ray Lawson?'

'Clandestine Services: recruiting European and American mercenaries to fight for Savimbi's Unita and Holden Roberto's Zaire-backed rabble; payment of bounty for stolen aircraft used to fly in arms. Later Ray was involved in farming out fake stories from Kinshasha, the capital of Zaire ... the *Sunday Monitor* published a few of them, I recall.'

'That was before we took you on our payroll as consultant,' Ellison said sardonically. 'What about the Pretoria connection?'

'You always get there, Bill.'

'Do I?'

'The South Africans got into the Angolan thing up to their necks – with "Company" backing. According to Paul Larabee and Joe Connolly, Ray Lawson was a key link man. He was taken prisoner at Nova Lisboa and shared a cell with a South African from BOSS. Later they were traded.'

'Is he a racist?'

John Coppola lit a Gitane. 'I wouldn't say so,' he said reflectively. 'Just an operative in the Allen Dulles-William Colby mould: all's fair in the Christian war against atheistic Communism. I know Ray quite well; at one time we even shared a mistress. The CIA lobby to which he belongs in Clandestine Services is determined not to "lose" southern Africa to the Communists. The geo-politics of that region, with its strategic sea routes and mineral resources, are regarded as vital to American interests. Ray and his friends hate Jimmy Carter, that's for sure, and they hate his black Ambassador to the United Nations, Andrew Young.'

'Because Carter and Young insist on regarding the struggle in Rhodesia and South Africa as one between minority White Power and Majority Rule?'

'Correct. Even though the Russians and Cubans arm and equip the guerrillas of the Rhodesian Patriotic Front, Young stays on good terms with the PF leaders Nkomo and Mugabe. Lawson and his friends in the "Company" wanted Washington to recognize the Smith-Muzorewa Government in Salisbury, but Carter and Young weren't buying it. Then things got a whole lot worse last year when Carter delivered an unprecedented public reprimand to the CIA, which he accused of failing to forecast Smith's air strike against Nkomo's camps in Zambia, which took place at exactly the moment when Smith was in Washington talking to Secretary of State Cyrus Vance. Carter discovered that the CIA had had clear warning of the Rhodesian air strike but decided not to inform the White House in case Smith and his black colleagues didn't get their visas to enter the United States.'

'In fact the Lawson group were collaborating with the pro-Smith Congressional opposition?'

'Oh sure. Their big hope now is Governor Walter Prendergast. Failing him, they'll settle for Senator Dick Aronson. Anything to get rid of Carter.'

'Every time Carter quarrels with the Russians, he patches it up again?'

'That's right, Bill. During the Human Rights argument last year, doubts were raised about the export to Russia of submersible pumps destined for the Urals–Volga oil fields, and of an electron-beam welding machine manufactured by Dressler in Texas. Yet before the year was out US Secretary of Commerce Juanita Krebs had flown to Moscow on Carter's instructions to announce the authorization of twenty-two licenses for exports of high-technology oil equipment. And don't forget that Carter appeared on TV prime time to oppose any boycott of the Moscow Olympics.'

'Hungry, John?'

'Why not?'

'How about the Calvet?'

'Great. Now what's all this about, this Ray Lawson stuff? I've just spent the weekend with a gorgeous lady down in Nice and haven't had time to catch up with the news.'

Ellison's pulse quickened slightly. Throughout lunch he kept glancing at his watch: it became almost impossible to pay attention to what Coppola was saying. Once again he felt as excited as a fifteen-year-old boy.

* * *

'I suggest a game of tennis, at Paul's place, but do come alone, I can't abide doubles. Or spectators. If your back aches, I'll understand. Return home and rest. Understood?'

He paid off the taxi at the corner of the Rue de Rivoli and the Place de la Concorde, at the north-west corner of the Jardin des Tuileries, then stood for a few minutes, absorbing his surroundings, the pulsing air of Paris, waiting for a shadow. ... Five years had passed since Leonhard had led him past the Rupprechtskirche and down Seitenstetten, shadowed by three agents whom they had lost in the synagogue. Five years since she told him that Titian's 'Emperor Charles V' hangs in Room XVI of the Prado; five years since Anne-Marie Schubert had knocked at his door in the Hotel Sacher.

At 2:16 Ellison turned and walked into the Jeu de Paumes. A stout guide in a grey skirt was telling a party of absorbed German tourists: 'Here, in this famous annexe of the great Louvre, is housed an incomparable collection of 19th century Impressionist and post-Impressionist masterpieces. The name Jeu de Paumes, meaning tennis court, owes its origin to. ...'

Ellison drifted out of earshot. Gradually his rudder was swinging him towards the room housing the work of Paul Cézanne. It was exactly 2:30.

By 2:45 Leonhard had not showed up. A bad case of back-ache, then: and probably of a tapped line. Nor did Ellison feel himself to be alone: a young man with smoothly brushed fair hair and blue eyes had been miming a not very convincing interest in Cézanne's landscapes ever since Ellison's arrival. The suit, shoes and shirt were French, of course – nowadays the KGB budget covered that, Yuri Andropov had insisted on it – but not the nose. Ellison closed on the young man and asked him the time.

'*Skolka vryemeni?*'

Involuntarily the Russian's left arm bent at the elbow, uncovering his wrist watch. Then he scowled, realizing his mistake. Ellison winked and walked smartly out of the Jeu de

Paumes, heading for the Rue Royale, hoping that confusion would lose the KGB man a few vital seconds. At the moment he spotted a taxi, the young, blond Russian emerged from the museum, looked about him desperately, saw Ellison and broke into a run.

'Taxi!'

Ellison lifted his arm and made a dash for the kerb. The taxi roared past him, across the Place de la Concorde. The Russian was only twenty metres away now and closing fast. At that moment a black car swooped out of the traffic like a Patagonian Condor, swallowed Ellison and swept him away.

Her mouth closed over his. He shut his eyes and drew her to him, let the unique, seductive scent of her envelope him, as the car skidded and screamed up the Boulevard Haussman, then snaked and snarled its way through the narrow, intricate streets of Montmartre towards the Seine. He ran his hand through her soft black hair, caressed her slender neck, kissed her eyes, her ears, her mouth, the tip of her nose. He dared not say anything for fear of saying something foolish.

Off the Rue de Vaugirard the chauffeur turned down the straight, narrow Rue Madame, driving parallel to the western edge of the Jardins du Luxembourg. They stopped outside a small, slightly shabby hotel.

'Chaim is here?' he asked.

'He will be. Later. Your coded messages are no match for the KGB, Elephant.'

She dismissed the chauffeur with a sharp word in French and led the way into the hotel. 'My parents stayed at this hotel when they were penniless students,' she said. 'It has hardly changed.'

She collected the key at the front desk and led him up the stairs to the third floor. 'The lift is a poor security risk,' she smiled.

He didn't mind: following behind her gave him a view of thighs whose perfect contours he had never forgotten. And she took her time.

The room was clean, simple, empty. A double bed made up with fresh linen. A wash basin. A note lying on the bedside table, addressed to 'Monsieur Ellison'. He opened it: 'Things are not easy, my friend. Our telephone conversation was intercepted, the code of an amateur broken by professionals. Wait here until I contact you. Your good friend, Chaim Leonhard.'

He took her chin between his hands. 'So you have been in London this weekend?'

As her long eyelashes dropped, so her cheeks dimpled: 'Yes,' she whispered. He sensed now a particular stillness in her. But the questions he wanted to ask wouldn't come: he was paralysed by passion, by an all-consuming desire to possess her. Very slowly the flat of her small palms moved up his chest, across his face and round the back of his head. His head was drawn down to hers; her long, cool tongue slid deep into his mouth.

'Have I changed?' she whispered.

'No. Yes. No.'

'Look at me, Bill. What do you see?'

'Anne-Marie Schubert.'

She laughed sexily, thrusting out a leg. 'Herr Ellison vonts some fital statisteeks? Yes? How many dooble-bedrooms in Moskva have zer locks on zer doors?'

He swept her on to the bed. Her lithe body arched up against his in passionate response, her arms enfolding his neck and her chiffon skirt sliding up her beautiful thighs as they locked round his. Again her tongue darted into his mouth, cool and ardent, while her hand slid cunningly into his trousers, rousing him to throbbing heat with sly, delicate touches. He groaned. She laughed in his ear and called him Elephant, guiding his hand into the soft flesh of her thigh. Wriggling out from under him she threw off her clothes in a few, swift movements, then stripped him as he lay on the bed, playing him like a musical instrument, coaxing out of him chords of unrestrained longing and lust, a helpless desire.

Bending, she took him in her mouth. He groaned and came. Humiliated, he forced her on to her stomach, stifling her protests in the pillow, then penetrated her from behind, thrusting almost angrily into small, neat buttocks, laying siege to her clitoris with his finger, driving her on relentlessly until, her fists pounding the mattress, she was forced to yield, to surrender to her orgasm, to lie limp and wet in his arms. But she had only begun. Slyly now, she shifted the rules of the game, drawing him down into her and enveloping him in the tentacles of a slower, more subtle sensuality. His growing sense of helplessness stemmed less from what she did to his body than what she said; she said things to him so personal, affectionate and touching that he wanted there and then to renounce his wife, his family, his job, his career, his self-respect, and to run away with this girl, for ever, to a Pacific island. Over and over he told her he loved her. Now she withdrew into her shell, tantalizing him with almost oriental obliqueness, rousing the simple, maddened bull in him, laughing as he loomed up above her, thrusting savagely, his eyes wide, his head tilted back, roaring his need of her. Again he came, she with him, their loins locked in fire. She took his head in her hands and searched his eyes. 'Again,' she said. 'Again.' Mischief caressed the corners of her mouth, the dimples in her cheeks, the dark, Jewish light in her eyes. 'Again.' She smiled mockingly. 'Or is my famous Elephant too old, is he past it now?' Gently she rolled him onto his back, spreading her thighs luxuriantly across his loins, her high, arrogant breasts swaying above his face, her buttocks thrusting and plunging with cruel, exacting expertise. He felt, as never before, the sensation of total surrender, of abdication, of losing himself – his control, his will, his identity. He was turned to fire and water. It didn't matter because nothing mattered except the joy of possession, of love. If she had pulled a stiletto from under the pillow and held it to his throat, he wouldn't have stirred; his love for her, his total immersion in her before she was lost to him again, a mere dream, for years at a time, had rendered him totally passive. He no longer belonged to himself, only to his need of Ruth Leonhard. He came again. A deep exhaustion was spreading up from his loins, through his limbs, like a general anaesthetic; and the last thing he saw, before he fell asleep, was the gentle smile of an angel gazing down at him.

When he awoke an hour later she was gone. But he was not alone.

Two men were standing either side of the bed. One, young and fair-haired, he instantly recognized as the KGB agent from whom he had asked the time in the Cézanne room of the Jeu de Paumes. Ivan, as Ellison automatically christened him, was staring down at him through impassive blue eyes – a neutral, professional gaze such as surgeons adopt over operating tables. The older man, whose dark Armenian features reminded Ellison of Anastas Mikoyan, was intently examining Ellison's wallet, address book, notebook and passport.

'Did you knock?' Ellison said.

'Why?' Mikoyan replied in English. 'Is it your room?'

'It's certainly not your room. So get out!' He reached for the bedside telephone. To his surprise neither Russian made any attempt to stop him.

'Go ahead,' Mikoyan said. 'Call reception. Ask them if room number 32 is rented by Monsieur Leclerc.' Mikoyan held out what resembled a perfectly in-order French identity card bearing the name and photograph of Marcel Leclerc. 'You are occupying my bed in my room.'

Ellison looked around for his clothes. They were nowhere to be seen.

'Where is my . . . friend?'

Mikoyan shrugged. 'Which friend?'

Ellison abruptly experienced an unpleasantly total recall of an incident ten years ago, when he was a resident correspondent in Moscow. The surveillance under which he had been placed was nothing exceptional – just tedious and exasperating – until he was accepted into the dissident and *samizdat* network. The day he called on Solzhenitsyn at his Moscow flat was the turning point. From that cold, 20°-below-zero afternoon he was shadowed continuously by a black Volga sedan, registration number (he would never forget it) LEB-23-26. Even to the shops. The tyres of his own car were repeatedly slashed. On one occasion he made a rendezvous to meet a notable dissident at the Hotel Rossyia. When Ellison emerged from the hotel an hour later, the steering wheel of his car felt abnormally heavy. On inspection, he discovered that a front wheel had been changed and that the substitute wheel had been fastened by two lag nuts screwed on to a depth of no more than a quarter-inch. Yet two policemen were standing outside the hotel, a few paces from where his car had been parked, watching him impassively – just as Mikoyan and Ivan were watching him now. When he complained that an attempt had been made to kill him, he was interrogated for an hour, the two policemen swearing solemnly that at no time had they noticed anyone tampering with his car. When the interview drew to its fruitless and frustrating end, one of the interrogation team had abruptly offered to introduce him to a couple of girls.

For a moment he pictured the six-storey building in Dzerzhinski Square. And the face of Comrade Yuri Andropov, successor to Beria, Yezhov and Yagoda.

'We wish to discuss certain things with you,' Mikoyan said.

As Ellison tried to jump from the bed, the younger Russian pulled the bottom sheet out from under him with such speed that he had no time to fend off the pillow that Mikoyan clamped down over his face. But this was no pillow fight: as he began to struggle, his genitals were suddenly and decisively in Communist hands – a nasty feeling at the best of times, which these no longer were after one sharp, excruciating jerk on his penis had brought a scream vomiting up his throat into the stifling soundproofing pillow.

He lay still. The hyperdermic, when it came, was quite skilfully inserted. Almost immediately his head began to spin and anaesthetizing clouds swept over him. He had one thought before he became unconsious: it's just like a movie.

Gradually the unfamiliar Paris hotel bedroom came back to him, discovering its final form through a kaleidoscope of merging cubes and rectangles. The afternoon was dying, the light on the walls was soft and pink, the sounds floating through the open window from the Rue Madame were evening sounds. Mikoyan's finger rested on Ellison's pulse.

'You ought to take my blood pressure, you know.'

Mikoyan showed no reaction: he continued to stare at the watch in his left hand. Ellison noticed that his own voice sounded distant and disembodied.

'How do you feel?' Mikoyan asked.

'Call room service. I could do with caviar and a dry martini.'

Ivan leaned down over the bed. 'What is the Russian expression for "What is the time?"' he asked, then grinned most unpleasantly. Evidently that little incident in the Jeu de Paumes was not forgotten.

'What are the rules?' Ellison said in French. 'You be Spassky, I'll be Fischer.'

Again his voice didn't sound quite real, quite his own. But the stinging slap Mikoyan gave him was real enough, and the face that took it was clearly his own.

'A leading and honoured Soviet athlete, Tatiana Larin, has defected to the capitalist West,' Mikoyan said sombrely.

'Maybe.'

'Maybe!'

The second slap made the first seem like a caress. Young

Ivan seized the little finger of Ellison's right hand and began to force it back.

'Stop!' Cold one minute, he was now bathed in sweat.

'You, Ellison, are deeply involved in this plot to undermine peaceful co-existence. We know all about your intricate links with Chaim Leonhard and Solomon Rupin, notorious agents of Ha Mossad and of Zionist imperialist terrorism. Only two days ago you phoned Leonhard in code. It so happens that there are working class militants among the telephone engineers in Paris.'

'I see.'

'As for your code, it was an insult to our intelligence and our culture.'

'Sorry. I'll do better next time.'

'There may not be a next time.' Ivan was smiling.

'Ah.'

'Why did Leonhard not campaign in 1974 against Moscow staging the Olympics?' Mikoyan asked.

'He wanted to get the Jews out of Russia.'

'Good. Continue to tell the truth. Have many Jews been granted exit visas since 1974?'

'Yes. But Leonhard was not wholly satisfied. When Israel was banned from the Asian Games in '78, despite warnings from the IAAF, he saw the writing on the wall. The USSR would surely do as Canada had done to Taiwan, at Montreal. The Begin-Sadat meeting and the Camp David Agreement sharpened Soviet hostility towards Israel. In '78 Leonhard was twice refused a visa to enter Russia.'

'But Begin himself called for a boycott of the Moscow Olympics!'

'Do you want to understand Leonhard or have a discussion?'

Mikoyan corrected himself at once. 'Can you confirm that from the summer of '78 Leonhard reversed his policy and began to work secretly for a boycott of the Moscow Olympics?'

'It's possible. The pressure on him from the Jewish Defense League was very strong. There was an international outcry against the trials of dissidents – '

Mikoyan nodded calmly, to indicate that he knew all about that. He lit a Russian cigarette, then offered Ellison one as an afterthought.

'I'd prefer one of my own cigars.'

Mikoyan nodded to Ivan, who flung open the wardrobe. Ellison saw his clothes hanging neatly on two old-fashioned wooden hangers – no doubt the sort that Ruth's parents had used during their impoverished honeymoon thirty years ago. Ivan tenderly placed a baby cigar in Ellison's mouth and lit it.

'So,' said Mikoyan, 'Ha Mossad may have re-computed its resource options.' He perched on the edge of the bed like a solicitous physician and blew smoke through his nose. 'Two months ago,' he continued, staring at the ceiling, 'the Larin girl travelled with ten other Soviet athletes to Glenmore College in California for a six-week exchange-training programme. Right, Mr Ellison?'

'So I'm told.'

'So you're told.' A slightly menacing edge had re-invaded Mikoyan's voice. 'Five of the ten athletes were females – I'm afraid our Soviet athletic authorities show more good will than common sense. Our Soviet chief coach soon reported that Tatiana was "dating" (as they say) the decathlon star Karl Petersen. Was it a simple and touching case of young love, Mr Ellison?'

'I have no idea.'

'Mr Ellison has no idea. Perhaps you have no idea why Chaim Leonhard appeared on the Glenmore campus three days after Tatiana and the other Soviet athletes arrived?'

'None.'

Mikoyan leaned forward until his face was a few inches from Ellison's.

'Or why Leonhard met with the Zionist sympathizer Armand Krohl and the Jewish sporting impresario Sol Enders in the Pasadena restaurant, Los Angeles, two days after Tatiana first went to the movies with Karl Petersen?'

'It's news to me. Thanks for all the leads – I never expected such assistance from the KGB. But don't worry: I never reveal my sources.'

He shouldn't have said it; even as he said it he knew he shouldn't have said it. But somebody else, some ventriloquist's dummy perched on his shoulder, seemed to do the talking. Besides, he wasn't amused by his predicament. It was natural to hit out with the only weapon at his disposal. But foolish. And not very professional.

They lifted him bodily off the bed, Mikoyan taking his feet and the huge Ivan supporting his head and shoulders, dragged him to the wash basin (the bedroom had no bathroom), filled it with cold water and forced his head under. The first few seconds were rather refreshing.

Ten minutes later he lay on the floor gasping and coughing while Ivan knelt on his back and kneaded water up out of his lungs.

Mikoyan, meanwhile, was busy with an apparatus which turned out to fill the whole of his 'briefcase' – the lid and box of the case were shaped and moulded to fit exactly the plugs, adaptor, leads and electrodes. One lead ran from the 115-volt mains socket in the wall to the adaptor: the second joined twin electrodes to both the adaptor and magnometer. It remained only to fasten the electrodes to Ellison's penis and scrotum.

'Much activity down here today, eh?' Ivan grinned as the first, mild shock brought forth a cry from Ellison's throat. But the sound was entirely muffled by the pillow that Ivan clamped over his face.

Ellison had written much about torture. But it was a subject he had always been content to research at second-hand.

'Very well,' Mikoyan was saying, as they heaved his naked,

sweat-drenched, scorched body back on to the bed, 'let us dispense with the jokes from now on. Agreed?'

Ellison agreed.

'You won't deny that you dined in Vienna on October 21, 1974, in the company of Leonhard, Krohl and Enders? Yes? You even tape-recorded Krohl on a machine disguised as a cigarette case. Why? And here you are in Paris trying to make contact with Leonhard, following a coded phone call made on the very day that Tatiana Larin disappeared from London. Yet you ask us to believe that you have no knowledge of this conspiracy? Who took the decisions, and when? What is their contingency plan for the immediate future?'

Ellison now experienced difficulty in speaking at all. His throat was sore, his tongue like frizzled bacon. Solicitously Ivan offered him a glass of water and gently raised his aching head.

'I have not seen Leonhard since the Montreal Olympics, three years ago,' he managed to say. 'I came to Paris to find out if he was involved . . . in any way. That's all.'

Again the morose Mikoyan leaned down over him. 'But you are of course aware of the deal we did with Leonhard only three weeks ago, following the first short disappearance of Tatiana with Petersen?'

'I had no idea they had disappeared. What happened?'

'I am the interrogator here!' He seized Ellison by the shoulders and began to shake him in genuine exasperation. 'Why, why, why, why did Leonhard break his promise? Why has he double-crossed us? Who is behind this decision?'

'I don't know!'

'Yes you do! Only yesterday you met the American CIA agent Lawson in London. Only yesterday. Now why, why, why?'

Ivan glanced at Mikoyan. 'Again?' he asked in Russian.

Mikoyan stepped back from the bed, sighed, lit another cigarette, ran his hand through his short, dark, curly hair.

'I have told this swine more than he has told me. It is a serious situation. He is the best informed journalist in Britain. Yes, again: starting at 60 volts this time.'

On the second round even Ivan's pillow could not entirely muffle Ellison's screams. But it wasn't the sort of hotel where guests ask questions.

As for the management, they had strict instructions not to intervene. From Anne-Marie Schubert.

CHAPTER 12

June 13, 1979. New York City

The temperature in mid-town Manhattan was in the nineties as television crews and over one hundred reporters crowded into a small lecture theatre on the 18th floor of the Jason Stern Building on East 52nd Street. The shirt-sleeved crowds in Lexington Avenue were groggy from the sheets of heat beating off the high stone ramparts and sizzling off the side-walks. The streets were black with burnt rubber. In the suburbs kids were cooling themselves in the fire hydrants and the Fire Department was heading for a collective nervous breakdown. 'All we need is a power failure,' Bernie Holzheimer of the *New York Times* remarked to the *Monitor*'s Norman Prosser in the express elevator to the 18th floor offices of the National Committee for Soviet Liberty. 'Luckily I'm made of drip-dry nylon,' Prosser said, 'and can wring myself out.' The heat inside the lecture theatre, intensified by the Klieg lights, was unbearable. 'No point in fainting,' Holzheimer murmured, 'there's nowhere to fall.'

At 11:30 Eastern Standard Time officials of the National Committee for Soviet Liberty (an umbrella organization) and of the Jewish Defense League walked on to the platform accompanied by Tatiana Larin and Karl Petersen. The Russian girl's pony tail bobbed nervously as she stepped before the banked microphones and cameras, blinking under the lights.

'She's cute,' Holzheimer murmured. 'No wonder Magnus followed her all over London. How is he, by the way?'

'Mending disgustingly fast,' Prosser said. 'But Ellison disappeared in Paris two days ago and Jordan is seriously worried.'

Speaking in excellent English, Tatiana read out a short prepared statement. She and Petersen had formed a friendship, 'as happens between young people'. They had become secretly engaged and wanted to marry at the first opportunity. But the Soviet coaches and athletics officials had warned her that this was out of the question; she was expected to return to Russia, continue training and win a gold medal at the Olympics before a Soviet crowd.

'I am not a political person,' Tatiana told the press conference. 'I am an ordinary young woman with a love of literature, especially the great writers in the English language. But my recent experiences have taught me that my own lack of personal freedom to lead my own life in my own way reflects the general suppression of human rights in Soviet society. My eyes have been opened. I am therefore seeking political aslyum in the United States.'

Although expected, it was nevertheless sensational.

Karl Petersen made an even shorter statement, playing the male equivalent of the dumb blonde. He loved Tatiana and wished to marry her. He had been shocked by the pressure to which she had been subjected as soon as the Soviet authorities caught wind of their innocent romantic feelings. Now she had escaped: it was a blow for freedom. Petersen seemed to enjoy the limelight.

The assembled reporters now fired a barrage of questions at Tatiana while the first video-tapes were rushed out for the major network news bulletins.

'Miss Larin, how did you give the Soviets the slip in London?'

Tatiana shook her head, eyes downcast. 'Sorry,' she said softly. It was a word she was to use repeatedly during the next twenty minutes.

'How did you reach the United States?'

'Sorry.'

'Did the British or American Governments assist your passage in any way?'

'Sorry.'

'Miss Larin, did you write the story "Goodbye, Russia" published over your name last Sunday in the *New York Sentinel* and several European newspapers?'

For a moment she had seemed to look for guidance towards the officials of the National Committee for Soviet Liberty. 'Yes,' she said.

'You did write it?'

'Yes.'

'Did you write it in Russian or English?'

'In English.'

'Did anyone help you?'

'Yes, but I cannot say who.'

'Was it the CIA, Miss Larin?'

'Sorry.'

'Was it the Jewish Defense League or the Committee for Soviet Liberty?'

'Sorry.'

'Were you paid for the article, Miss Larin?'

'Yes. Some money.'

'Who paid you? Was it Kurt Klostermann? How did he obtain the story?'

'Sorry.'

'Why do you refuse to explain these things, Miss Larin?'

'I do not want to bring any trouble to anyone. Some people have been very kind to me. . . .'

'Did anyone put you up to this, Miss Larin?'

'I beg your pardon?' Tatiana blinked into the blinding lights, seeking out the voice that had asked the question.

'Who suggested to you that you might seek political asylum in the West?'

'No one. I knew that many famous Soviet artists and writers had done it.'

'But you are the first athlete?'

'I believe so.'

'Where will you live in the United States?'

'At Glenmore College. I have been offered a scholarship there by a very generous gentleman, Mr Sol Enders.'

There was uproar in the conference room. As the first batch of reporters returned from their telephone calls the next batch raced out. Within minutes the switchboards of the College and of Enders International Promotions, Inc. were jammed.

'When was that scholarship arranged, Miss Larin?'

At this point an official tried to intervene but the protests were so vigorous that he stepped back. Larin shook her head: she would say no more about Glenmore.

'Miss Larin, does this mean you won't compete in the Moscow Olympics?'

'I don't know. I hope to compete.'

The questions were being fired so fast and furiously now that she could scarcely sort them out.

'You hope to compete as a member of which national squad?'

'The American, of course.' She said it very calmly.

'But you would have to become a citizen, Tatiana.'

'Yes. Karl and I will be married as soon as possible.'

'But would you risk going back to Moscow for the Olympics?'

'As an American citizen – of course.'

'Do you think the Soviets would grant you a visa?'

'I think they must if I am chosen to represent America.'

At 14:20 Eastern Standard Time the following statement was released by State Department spokesman DeWitt Mason: 'The United States Government had no prior knowledge that Miss Tatiana Larin would seek political asylum in this country. At no stage has the Administration or any of its agencies encouraged, aided or abetted her to take such an action. Her application is now under study.'

Asked where, when and by what means she entered the United States, he declined to comment 'in the interests of national security'.

The American reporters, in particular, picked up their phones seething with anger. 'In one breath he tells us Uncle Sam had nothing to do with it; in the next, he puts it under top security wraps.'

Almost simultaneously, a Foreign and Commonwealth Office spokesman in London denied that the British Government had any knowledge of how, when or where Larin and Petersen had left British soil.

At 15:30 EST, 20:30 GMT, sharply worded protest notes were delivered by the Soviet Ambassadors in London and Washington. The latter demanded immediate access to Miss Larin and was told that this would be granted if the young woman consented. But only if. It soon turned out that she didn't consent.

A spokesman for Governor Walter Prendergast, leading Republican candidate for the 1980 Presidential nomination, at that moment visiting Taiwan, urged the Justice Department to grant Miss Larin asylum with all possible speed. Prendergast termed the girl's decision further proof that human decency and human love will survive even the most oppressive, godless totalitarianism. It was time to discard the present Administration's policy of abject retreat and appeasement.

Moving equally rapidly on-stage, Senator Dick Aronson, the front-running Democratic Presidential aspirant and an influential member of the Senate Foreign Affairs Committee, hoped that the Administration would not allow its laudable desire to reach agreement with the Soviet Union on trade and arms limitation to blind it to its simple duty in the 'utterly human case of this nice little girl from Russia'.

Next morning the American papers carried scores of statements from pressure groups, rights groups, ethnic groups and religious groups, all urging the United States Government to grant Tatiana a refuge. Photographs of Tatiana and the handsome Karl, hand-in-hand, were spread across the front pages under 96-point bold headlines:

TATIANA SENSATION!

RUSSIAN STAR QUITS!

I Want to Run for America – Tatiana.

But all attempts to persuade her to kiss in front of the cameras failed. 'We Russians are really very private people' was one quote that the *Christian Science Monitor* found more interesting than did the *New York Post*. In the *Post*'s working manual, private life was great – so long as it was made public, preferably on an exclusive basis.

The only quote available from Sol Enders was very short: 'I'm a Jew. I just wanted to help this girl for the sake of all those people, Jews and others, still trapped inside Russia.'

One or two newspapers showed signs of quick research into the all-American boy, Karl Petersen. Interviews with teachers and coaches at Glenmore College revealed that Karl wasn't maybe the brightest thing on two legs but he rated high for sincerity, beef and sex appeal, scoring slightly lower on reliability and hard work. 'Loves life, girls, America,' decided the sub-editors.

Feeling the heat and aware that here was a dilemma it was going to have to live with, the United States Olympic Committee issued a statement from its new headquarters in Colorado Springs at noon the following day. The USOC spokesman, Brodie Short, looked about as unhappy as newsmen had even seen him.

Yes, he confirmed, the USOC had received a message from the Soviet Olympic Organizing Committee expressing its 'extreme indignation' at recent events and demanding that Miss Larin, who had been 'led astray' by elements determined to sabotage peaceful co-existence should be 'allowed' to return to the Soviet Union. The Soviet Committee gave an assurance that no disciplinary measures would be taken against her and that her prospects as an athlete would not be adversely affected.

'Gentlemen,' Brodie Short pleaded to the faces he knew so well, and drank Bourbon-on-the-rocks with, 'this thing is out of our hands. If it's political we don't touch it.'

'What the hell do you mean "we don't touch it", Brodie? This girl says she plans to seek naturalization papers, to become a United States citizen. How can you turn her down?'

'Did I say anything like that?' Brodie Short groaned. 'How about you fellas quoting what I did say rather than what I didn't say? Any American citizen may compete in our national Olympic Try-outs next June. The first three in each event represent the United States in the Olympics. Period.'

'How do you imagine the American pentathlon girls are going to feel about this, Brodie? Barbara Floris, for example – Tatiana just mopped the floor with her in London and it's common knowledge that Barbara's sweet on Karl Petersen.'

'I'm not a psychiatrist or a marriage counsellor,' Short snapped.

'Brodie – a nasty question.'

'I'm used to it, Hal.'

'Do you think this business could wreck the 1980 Olympics?'

The following day's newspapers quoted Brodie Short as replying, firmly, 'Absolutely no way.' But what they omitted to mention, however, was that it took the USOC spokesman all of ten seconds to find an answer.

June 13, 1979. Vienna

Obtaining no reply from Chaim Leonhard's telephone numbers in Paris or Vienna, Ellison took a taxi to 38, Boulevard St Michel. The concierge told him that Monsieur Leonhard had departed for Vienna the previous day in a great hurry. At what time of day had he departed? In the evening. Had he been alone? Oh no, his daughter was with him. Smiling grimly, Ellison thanked the concierge and caught the first available flight out of Charles de Gaulle to Vienna. On arrival next morning he took a taxi to Leonhard's flat in Futterer. He pressed the bell for five minutes, without response, then rang for the concierge. An old woman with a bent back and frightened eyes eventually crept to the door and opened it a few inches, on a chain.

'Where is Herr Leonhard, please?'

'Who are you?' she whispered. 'You're not the police, you're foreign.'

'I'm English, yes, and a close friend of Herr Leonhard.'

She stared at him. 'The police were here ... last night.'

'The police? Why?'

'They came to arrest Herr Leonhard ... and to search his flat. You never saw such a mess.'

'Did they wear uniforms, these police?'

The corners of her thin, bitter mouth curled down in scorn. 'In the old days, a policeman wore a uniform. But not nowadays, oh no – '

'How do you know they were police?'

'I'm not a fool, sir! They showed me their identity cards. And when they went in there, into his apartment, Herr Leonhard he went right off his head. Such a quiet man, twenty years he has lived here, you never know the real truth about people, do you?'

'He went off his head, you say?'

'Shouting, biting, screaming. And do you know what he was screaming to me?'

'What?'

'"Frau Brunner, call the police! Call the police!" How do you like that? The police come for him – an extremely serious crime, one of the young detectives told me, though I don't know where he had been to school, his accent was that strange – and there was Herr Leonhard calling for the police!'

'And the men took him away?'

'In handcuffs. Gagged, too. It took three of them to drag him into their car. I'll never forget his eyes, Herr. . . .'

'Ellison.'

'Herr Elleesson. Terrible. Quite mad, I think.'

'And Mr Leonhard's daughter, have you seen her recently?'

'Fräulein Ruth? Poor girl! She arrived here just half-an-hour after the police took her father away. How she cried! She told me she had to go back to America . . . she has a job there, you know.'

'I see. Might I take a look at Herr Leonhard's flat, Frau Brunner?'

She stared at him with fear and hostility. 'No, no, I can't do that, not a stranger. Vienna used to be such a peaceful city.'

'Then you'd better call the police.'

'The police! Again!'

'The men who took Herr Leonhard away last night were not police, they were agents of the Soviet Union. He was not arrested, he was abducted. Which is why he begged you to call the police.'

Frau Brunner noticed that tears had suddenly sprung to the Englishman's eyes before he turned and walked away down Futterer. And the way he walked, clearly his health was poor. His suitcase seemed a burden to him.

June 15, 1979. London

The typed report that Joe O'Neill placed in front of Ellison was three pages long. 'Mind you,' Joe warned him nervously, 'I'm no international lawyer.'

'Now he tells me!' Ellison winked at Cherry. But he didn't

feel like winking at anyone. He felt sadder than at any time he could remember.

Section 312 of the relevant American Act required a candidate for naturalization (citizenship) to be able to read, write and speak words in ordinary usage in English. (Tatiana Larin would have no difficulty.) It also required a knowledge and understanding of the fundamentals of American history and of the American system of government. (Ditto.)

More serious: the candidate must reside continuously in the United States, after being lawfully permitted to reside permanently, *for at least five years* immediately preceding the date of filing the petition for naturalization. (This apparently closed the Larin file – the US Olympic Try-outs were only twelve months away.)

But: any alien married to an American citizen need have resided continuously in America *for only three years*, provided the marriage was in being throughout those three years. (Still too long for Tatiana's purposes.)

But: Section 319(b) provided that any alien whose spouse was an American citizen and in employment of the American Government, or of an American firm engaged in the development of foreign trade, and who in the course of such employment was regularly stationed abroad, might be naturalized *without any prior residential presence in the United States* – provided that the alien declared before the US District Court his or her intention to take up residence in America as soon as the American spouse's work permitted him (in this case) to return home.

Here, then, was the loophole through which Tatiana might pass into the US Olympic team. Yet Karl Petersen, to whom she was not yet married, was not visibly employed by the American Government or by an American firm engaged in foreign trade, or by anyone at all. Nor did he reside abroad. He was a student on an athletics scholarship at Glenmore College.

Which meant that even if they married tomorrow, Tatiana would have to wait three years: good enough for the Los Angeles Olympics but not the Moscow ones.

Ellison turned to his junior colleague. 'We haven't found the way through this legislation but you can be sure they have. By "they" I mean the gentlemen who gave you that bandaged head.'

'We don't know enough about Karl Petersen.'

'Quite so. I asked Bernie Holzheimer to check out his CV. Did Bernie call from New York?'

'Not so far.'

At the entrance to Kensington Palace Gardens, once called Millionaires' Row, Ellison's VW Passat was flagged down by a commissionaire. Only when a call had been made to the Israeli Embassy was the barrier raised. The embassy itself was fortified by an iron grille, six feet high and tipped with spikes. At the gate he spoke into the intercom, waited for the buzzer to signal the release of the electronic lock and then, monitored on closed-circuit television, walked towards a massive steel door. It swung open as he reached it.

Short, stocky, balding, Solomon Rupin received him in a spartan office lined with maps of Greater Israel. Ellison and Rupin didn't see eye-to-eye about Israel's present frontiers, but the journalist had not on this occasion come to discuss the Sinai or the West Bank of the Jordan.

'This time you'd better come clean,' he said.

'That sounds like pawn to king eight. Are you circumcised yet?'

'Some weeks ago Chaim was involved in a deal with the Russians involving Tatiana Larin. When I called you last Saturday to find out where Chaim was, you didn't say anything about that deal.'

'No. And you didn't say anything about Tatiana Larin –

just a Soviet athlete who wasn't Jewish. Of those there are many.' Rupin shrugged powerful shoulders. 'If Chaim chose to tell you about it, that was his decision, and it was a decision that he alone could make.'

'He didn't. The KGB told me about it. Want to see the finest pair of roast chestnuts in the Western world?'

It certainly wasn't in search of sympathy that he now invited Rupin to take a look; he was merely in a hurry to unlock the Israeli's tongue.

'That's nasty, Bill.' Rupin was clearly shaken. Rupin wasn't easily shaken. He had once finished a prayer in progress before returning the fire of Black September commandos and killing two of them in the courtyard of the Israeli Embassy in Stockholm. 'You say the Russians did that? In Paris?'

'Yes. And now I'm going to tell you something which it goes against the grain to tell you or anyone else. But I judge it to be necessary. Immediately preceding the laceration of this fine instrument you see before you, it had spent an hour in close congress with Ruth Leonhard.' Ellison pulled up his zip and fastened the buckle of his belt. 'Who is an agent not only of your Ha Mossad but also of the KGB.'

Rupin stared at him, dumbfounded. Then suddenly, moved by uncontrollable agitation, he gripped Ellison's arm like a vice.

'Where is Chaim? Where is Chaim?'

'Behind the Iron Curtain. He was abducted from his flat in Vienna on Tuesday evening. I'm afraid they've got him, Solomon. They think he double-crossed them and they don't care for that. I daresay Josef Arbuzov is interrogating Chaim at this minute – an Arbuzov deprived of the vodka and Armenian tobacco he craves.'

Rupin nodded slowly, staring at Ellison. Then he flicked a switch on his intercom and barked a series of curt directives in Hebrew.

'If Ruth is a KGB agent, it's a disaster, a calamity. But

why should you imagine she has worked for us? Because Chaim does? No, no, no.'

'How do you account for the fact that she was physically involved in the defection of Tatiana Larin last Saturday?'

'She was *what*! Ruth? Are you serious?' Ellison had known Rupin too long to doubt that this astonishment was genuine. 'How do you know that?'

'I'll tell you that when you come clean with me about the deal Chaim did with the Russians some weeks ago. I gathered from the KGB that Sol Enders was involved, and also Armand Krohl. True?'

Rupin nodded and began to speak in a rapid, businesslike way. 'Krohl contacted Chaim a few days after the Soviet squad arrived at Glenmore College. He asked Chaim to approach Sol Enders – Krohl has never been personally on good terms with Sol – '

'Yes, I remember an acrimonious exchange between them in a Viennese restaurant five years ago, over the vexed issue of amateurism.'

'Exactly. Anyway, Chaim arranged for the three of them to meet for dinner in Los Angeles, at Krohl's request. Krohl had a proposition. He had learned that Karl Petersen was dating the Larin girl and that she had taken a shine to him. He urged Enders to approach Petersen with an unwritten contract.'

'Commercial endorsements worth millions of dollars provided Petersen (a) won a medal at the Olympics and (b) did so as the husband of Tatiana Larin?'

'If you wanted to pass yourself off as a Jew, Bill, no one would know. But more than that: in the immediate future Sol offered Petersen a job in Enders International Promotions.'

'A job requiring service outside the United States, of course?'

Rupin gestured helplessly with hands that could render

Chopin with soufflé touch or strangle a man with fastidious economy. 'What can one tell you?'

'You can tell me what Krohl got out of all this.'

'That's not complicated. As you know, Krohl is a human rights activist. He and Chaim made the same calculation in 1974 when they supported Moscow's Olympic application. They both calculated that the Russians would be better behaved if they got the Games than if they didn't. But the repressive line adopted by the Kremlin during 1978 shocked Krohl. He was looking for a way of turning the screw on the Russians.'

'And found one in Tatiana's infatuation for Petersen?'

'Yes.'

'How did he find out about that?'

'I don't know, Chaim didn't tell me. Chaim, you see, was of the same opinion as Krohl, particularly after Israel was successfully excluded from the Asian Games in Bangkok at the end of last year. Nor is Jewish emigration from Russia proceeding rapidly enough.'

'And Chaim was able to appeal to Sol Enders's pocket and his sentiment simultaneously?'

'Sure. You know Sol, he dreams of professionalizing athletics. He can take an agency commission on the commercial endorsements he arranges for Petersen and Larin, but that's peanuts. Every time I meet Sol he tells me the same thing, it obsesses him. When a leading golfer or tennis player plays for big money or appears in commercials, their status as a tennis player or golfer rises! They head for the next tournament. But when Mark Spitz or Bill Jenner or any of the other photogenic Olympic gold medal winners start to endorse Wheaties or Y-front briefs, they may cream in millions of dollars but they simultaneously bring down the curtain on their careers as athletes. Spitz won seven gold medals at Munich and picked up over $5 million in endorsements. His poster sold more than any since Betty Grable's. But Mark

Spitz never again dived into a pool to compete against the world's leading swimmers. As a pro, he was ineligible. Compare his predicament to that of Jimmy Connors or Chris Evert-Lloyd or Jack Nicklaus.'

'You should really take a promotion commission from Sol Enders. Only your face is wrong.'

'Well, Sol, he wasn't slow to see that if Petersen married Tatiana it would be a romance on the cover of every magazine in the world. If the nineteen-year-old Russian girl was growled at by the grizzly Bear, every momma would adopt her; if she went on to win a gold in Moscow, every papa would, too. Sol would have the perfect couple to launch his pro circus.'

'Which would hardly please Armand Krohl, member of the IOC Executive Board and guardian of amateurism.'

Rupin nodded. 'That brings us to chapter two. Both Krohl and Chaim were manipulating Sol: he was dreaming of the long term, they were just twisting the Bear's paw. After a few weeks Sol suggested to Petersen that he take his Tatiana to Sol's mansion at Jones Beach, Long Island, for a four-day screw-in. Sure enough, the couple drove away from Glenmore, took a trans-continental flight to La Guardia and vanished.'

'The Russians began to worry?'

'So Chaim visited Ambassador Dobrynin in Washington. "Look," he said, "this girl likes Petersen; she likes beltways, blue jeans and ice-creams in twenty-five flavours. She wants to marry the schmuck. The only question is whether she marries him now and stays in America or whether she returns home to Moscow, trains hard, wins a gold medal for the Soviet Union and then marries him.'

'Ambassador Dobrynin thought that was a big difference?'

'He did. And Chaim put it to him that what would make the difference would be the release of an additional 50,000 Soviet Jews by the end of the year. Plus a new written assurance to the IOC that Israel would participate in the Olympics. Plus a pledge to amnesty a list of named Soviet dissidents incarcerated in labour camps and psychiatric wards.'

'The Russians gave all that?'

'They bargained. They haggled a bit. But they granted 15,000 additional exit visas to Soviet Jews.'

'Tatiana was returned to them? Why didn't the KGB bundle her aboard the first plane back to Moscow as soon as they laid hands on her?'

'Why do you think they didn't? Twenty years ago, that's what they would have done. They're more sophisticated now. Clearly Tatiana was deeply in love. She trained harder and performed better when she could be close to Karl Petersen. Didn't she break the world record a week ago, here in London?'

'So why did she decide to defect?'

Rupin shrugged. 'Don't ask me. I assume that she decided she couldn't live without the guy.'

Ellison had turned white with anger. 'I told you what has happened to Chaim, I alerted you to Ruth, and you're still holding out on me!'

'Holding out nothing!'

'This was a big operation! And you people pulled it!'

'I swear to you, Bill: I spoke to Chaim on the telephone on Sunday afternoon and he asked me what it was all about!'

'Then why did his daughter Ruth inform the KGB that Chaim was responsible? Why did they abduct him to Russia and fry my balls?'

Solomon Rupin extended his arms in a gesture of innocence. 'Bill, I don't know. This is what we have to find out.'

'Have you spoken to Sol Enders since Tatiana defected?'

'Sure. He was as amazed as you are. But delighted. Sol had felt very let down when Chaim had given her back to the Russians.'

'And Krohl?'

'Krohl phoned me on Monday complaining he couldn't reach Chaim. He wanted to know why Israel had embarked on such a dangerous operation without consulting him and why Chaim had betrayed their bond of mutual trust.'

Ellison left the Israeli Embassy with plenty to think about and one or two conclusions which he felt no inclination to share with Rupin. Waiting on his desk at the *Monitor* was a message asking him to call Bernie Holzheimer in New York.

'Have you checked out Karl Petersen's CV yet?'

'Sir, I've done my best, please don't fire me.'

'Sorry, Bernie. We're still in the feudal era over here.'

'Maybe feudalism works. We have, first of all, a rare interview that Petersen gave to the magazine *Track and Field* about a year ago. According to that one, his father, Conrad Petersen, a British subject, died when he was two. He was brought up by his American mother in Norwalk, Connecticut. She died when he was ten. He then attended Anderton Hall school in Vermont, staying with an uncle during vacations.'

'Where?'

'Abroad. Mainly Britain. Our next source is his birth certificate. If we search further, for a marriage certificate, we don't find one. In fact, Karl's mother, Alice Petersen, never did marry a Mr Conrad Petersen. Well, she's not here to answer questions.'

'Who *is* here to answer questions?'

'Alice Petersen had one sister, Mrs Jessie McGuire, who lived in Bloomington, Indiana. She, of course, decided to die six months ago, so – '

'How did she die?'

'In a car crash. She was coming out of her front drive when a car travelling fast slammed in to her, extricated itself and ran. It turned out to have been stolen and was later found abandoned. The driver was never discovered. Mrs McGuire and her elder daughter were both killed instantly.'

'There's a younger daughter?'

'Sure. Dorothy. She works as a Peace Corps idealist in Tanzania. Or did.'

'She had a little accident, too?'

'A week before she heard about the deaths of her mother and sister in Bloomington she was driving a Toyota Land-cruiser on a remote dirt track in the south-west of the country when it was ambushed. She put her foot hard down, screaming and yelling, as she describes it, and was lucky to get away without a scratch. The police counted twenty-five bullet holes in the Toyota. Apparently there are bandits in the area. Or blame it on Idi Amin next door, in Uganda. She flew home for her mother's funeral. After the service a man she couldn't describe placed an envelope in her hand and walked away. It was addressed to Ms Dorothy McGuire, With the Condolences of the Bloomington Peace Corps. By now her nerves were so on edge that she handed the package to the police: it was a letter bomb.

'The local District Attorney suspects that her mother and sister were hit deliberately, but he has no evidence and no motive, apart from a hunch that some local nut has harboured an irrational sexual grudge against the McGuire women.'

'Which the nut is prepared to pursue in remote south-west Tanzania?'

'There really are bandits down there. Dorothy is not the first Peace Corps person to have been shot at. Two have been killed.'

'Can Dorothy be found?'

'Mobilizing our unequalled worldwide network of sleuths, we finally tracked her down to her mother's house: her own home, in fact. She now lives under police protection, of a kind. When she opened the door to me, she said: "I suppose you want to know if I ever jilted any of the local boys or made a pass at an old man in a bar."'

'Which was what the local reporters had asked her several months ago?'

'Correct. I said, no, I wanted to ask her about something nice and cheerful, her famous cousin Karl Petersen. At this she perked up immediately. I gather she writes him "Remember little me?" letters to Glenmore College, but he never replies.'

'Not surprising. And if he does, she'd be wise not to open the package.'

'Wow! Is that how you interpret the deaths of her mother and sister?'

'How much does Dorothy McGuire remember from the time when she and Karl Petersen were kids?'

'Not much. They hardly ever met. It's at least twelve years since she last saw him. But she does recall what her mother told her. Apparently her aunt, Alice Grant, at that time a rather shy student at Bernard, was invited by a co-ed friend to spend the weekend with her at the Long Island home of the co-ed's fiancé, a wealthy Jew. There were several other house guests and a great deal of sailing, water skiing, swimming and other boisterous activities. One of the guests was a manly sporting type called Conrad, who instantly seduced Miss Grant. She spent one night alone with him; Dorothy suspects it was the only night in her entire life that Alice Petersen spent with a man. She never saw him again.'

'But she became pregnant?'

'She did. But who was the father of her child? She didn't even know his second name, let alone where he lived. Conrad had described himself as British, although his accent didn't resemble that of the British actors she heard on the movies.'

'She wasn't the abortion type, either.'

'I guess not. After some hesitation she went to the wealthy Jew and demanded to know who was the sporting Conrad who had seduced her and gotten her with child. The Jew refused to divulge Conrad's identity but informed her that he was a married man, with two children, a pillar of his community, and that she should put him from her mind for ever.

At this Miss Grant became incensed, sentimental and a bit calculating, although the amorous Conrad, of course, had never promised her anything. Despite the difficulties of bringing a paternity suit against an unknown man in an unknown country, her lawyer sufficiently intimidated the rich Jew with threats of subpoenaing him as a witness that he promised to contact Conrad. The upshot was a settlement of $200,000. Everyone, including her lawyer, advised Alice to give the child her own name, which she eventually did. Even so, she falsely entered the father's name as "Conrad Petersen" on Karl's birth certificate and always maintained to Karl the fiction that his father had died when he was two years old. But to her sister Jessie, in Bloomington, she confided the sad truth. The two sisters had always been very close.'

'You haven't told me the Jew's name.'

'Dorothy McGuire doesn't remember it; indeed, she's pretty certain she never knew it. There was a certain anti-Semitic ambiance in that family: he was always referred to as "the rich Jew".'

'OK.'

'When Karl was ten, his mother died. Jessie McGuire came from Bloomington to collect him, she was his only relative. Abut six months later, after Karl had settled into a local Bloomington school, the uncle arrived.'

'The uncle?'

'Dorothy isn't too clear, she was only nine at the time. All she recalls is that he wasn't American and that he limped on a stick, a silver-tipped cane. The uncle was very interested in young Karl's athletic ability. Anyway, he produced the money to put Karl in a boarding school with a first-class sporting tradition, Anderton Hall. After a while – Dorothy can't remember exactly when – Karl stopped coming home to Bloomington during the vacations.'

'Where did he go?'

'To stay with the uncle somewhere overseas – she thinks.

To her it's all rather vague and remote, not something she thought about until Karl sprang into national prominence a year ago.'

'Give me Dorothy McGuire's address and telephone number, Bernie.'

Holzheimer did so. 'You don't trust me, eh? Don't forget we have the American rights on your story ... if it turns out to be your story. We might get there first.'

'The day that happens I'll retire.'

June 18, 1979. Bloomington, Indiana

Ellison caught flight TW 771 out of Heathrow at 12:30, arriving in Chicago at 15:00. After a two-hour stopover he caught the Allegheny flight AL 582, which brought him into the tiny little airport outside Bloomington, Indiana, at 19:20. By this time it was after midnight on Ellison's inner clock and he fell into bed at a place called the Poplars Motel, where a congress of Jaycee rowdies kept him awake all night. When he telephoned Dorothy McGuire at 8 o'clock next morning there was no reply. He waited an hour, called again, got no reply. A taxi set him down outside the address that Holzheimer had provided: a modest, whitewashed, one-storey house. The shutters were drawn over all the windows. He banged on the front door in vain. A jolly young mother with freckles and a baby at her breast spoke to him from the neighbouring garden. Dorothy McGuire had been killed in a street accident two days earlier.

'*If* it was an accident,' said the young mother. 'Another hit-and-run job, exactly like when her mom and sister were killed just there, almost where you're standing. I was the first person to get to their car. Have you ever seen blood?'

Ellison walked away through the quiet, sedate streets of Republican Bloomington. In his briefcase were several portrait photographs and a tape containing the voices of four men. One of the portraits and one of the voices, he suspected, belonged to Karl Petersen's uncle.

Maybe Dorothy McGuire wouldn't have remembered, anyhow. He called in at the funeral parlour and left a bunch of flowers.

These girls don't enjoy it, they hate it. What they enjoy is conquering it. A masochist enjoys losing. Now, since I'm a sadist, I'll show you something.'

Forty-pound sacks of sand were strapped to the backs of each girl, using shoulder harnesses and a waist belt. They were then made to squat on their haunches and told to frog-hop for forty metres. After ten metres three of the girls had either keeled over or were resting on the flat of their hands. After twenty metres the field had been reduced to four; after twenty-five metres to two, Larin and Floris, who were level. Every new upward thrust of their thighs against the mounting oppression of the sandbags brought a fierce contraction of their lungs, a renewed effort of will, an expression of palpable pain. At thirty metres Floris faltered, fought to keep her balance, thrust herself up and forward in desperate contention with the force of gravity, snarled at Larin, keeled over. Tatiana herself fell forward on her hands only two hops later. Both girls lay anchored to the ground, groaning.

'But note the speed of recovery,' Mike Strong called to Magnus as if they were two seigneurs inspecting a stock farm. 'Both Tatiana and Barbara will come down from a pulse rate of 150 to their normal fifty within a minute, a symptom of high cardiac efficiency and aerobic capacity.'

'What's that?'

Barbara Floris hauled herself to her feet and threw him a sly look. 'Aerobic capacity is how long you can fuck with your mouth wide open,' she said. 'Anaerobic, how long you can fuck with your mouth closed.'

'Aerobic capacity,' Mike Strong explained, 'signifies the maximum amount of oxygen that can be absorbed, transported and used per minute of sustained work. If you follow a training routine you'll find girls like Barbara and Tatiana are put through at least two and sometimes three ten-kilometre runs per week to develop faster circulation from the heart through the arteries, arterioles, capillaries and veins to the lungs and muscles – and back to the heart.'

'That's the easy stuff,' Barbara said. 'But when you compete, man, it's anaerobic. You incur an immediate oxygen debt; and it hurts.'

'The muscular effort required for the 100-metre sprint theoretically requires seven litres of oxygen,' explained Strong. 'But the lungs can't supply more than half-a-litre during those ten seconds. Consequently the muscles incur an oxygen debt and gather lactic acid. The higher your aerobic oxygen uptake level, the bigger the oxygen debt you can carry. Clear?'

'Clear.'

'These things have to be demonstrated in bed,' Floris said.

The morning session lasted three hours. By the time they broke for a light lunch Magnus had come to the conclusion that what separated Larin from Floris was not speed, strength, willpower or even talent. It was technique. From the age of ten Tatiana Larin had benefitted from superb coaching facilities at the Central Institute of Physical Culture and Sports. At the age of sixteen she had been selected to spend three months at the famous Leipzig Institute of Sports Medicine in East Germany, where she had been pampered by coaches, physiologists, psychologists, even gynaecologists. But Barbara's father had stolen into big-city scrap metal yards at night, braving savage guard dogs and murderous vagrants, to steal heavy metal which could be melted down into weights for his gifted daughter. And he had died young, of tuberculosis.

At the end of the day, in July, 1980, she would stand on the rostrum, her big brave smile washed in tears, as the band played the American national anthem in honour of a Russian-born girl. And when the victor leaned down from the winner's raised platform to offer her hand, it would be a hand as soft, gentle and limp as the paw of a kitten asleep in front of a fire.

Later Barbara drove him back to her room. 'Does no one at Glenmore College object,' he asked, 'when Karl Petersen publicity during the first month of Olympic year. The bride, wearing a $2,000 gown whose train was supported by six bridesmaids, looked stunning in her Revlon Touch and Glow make-up, Helena Rubinstein mascara and Christian Dior Tartar Black pencilled eyes. Everyone knew that the big, proud man with a white carnation in his lapel on whose arm she leant as she walked up the aisle, had footed the bill; and the Hollywood producers crowding into the white-painted Episcopalian church of Glenmore also knew that it was Sol Enders they must first approach with their deals and projects. No fewer than twelve scripts were on offer from the major studios, each one describing how a Russian girl athlete fell in love with....

Glenmore, that day, was packed with celebrities and national figures. Experienced reporters noted, also, the high ratio of impassive, watchful eyes among the crowd and invited guests: the G-men were out. It was a cheerful scene, a ceremony of celebration, watched by millions of television viewers around the world: hardly a magazine on the news stands had neglected to portray the handsome, smiling couple on its front cover. MOSCOW, HERE WE COME! cried the local *Glenmore Herald*, innocently employing a verb that no big-city paper would dare to use for a wedding caption.

Discreetly tucked into the middle paragraphs of the women's magazines would be the really interesting information: like other athletes, Tatiana regularly took the pill anyway, to suppress debilitating periods.

And this was election year. Among those on hand to offer the bride the biggest of kisses and the groom the heartiest of handshakes were Senator Dick Aronson, now running the President neck-and-neck among registered Democrats, according to a recent poll, and Governor Walter Prendergast, currently trailing the President by only two percentage points among a national cross-section. 'This wedding, the consummation of their love and their faith in one another, represents a striking affirmation of American values,' Prendergast told two hundred reporters on the steps of the church.

But there was a sad side, of course: neither bride nor groom could produce a single relative. Everyone remarked on it and the women's magazines sighed about it. Tatiana's parents and sisters remained confined to the Soviet Union, where their application for a temporary exit visa had been turned down flat. The Kremlin was giving Tatiana the same treatment as it had handed out to the Soviet chess grand master, Victor Korchnoi; the same treatment that Martina Navratilova, the Wimbledon tennis champion, had received from the Czech Government after she had settled in Texas.

As for the groom, his total lack of relatives was more puzzling. Following the ceremony, Karl Petersen expressed his sadness to the media in a voice whose contained emotion would bring tears to feminine eyes from Seattle to Miami.

'I guess my family is just fated. First my papa, when I was two, then my beloved mama, when I was ten, and then this last year my Aunt Jessie McGuire and her two daughters, my only cousins.'

Bernie Holzheimer of the *New York Times* asked Petersen about the kind uncle to whom he had referred in his interview with *Track and Field.* Petersen nodded sadly.

'Now there was a remarkable man, Arthur Lionel Petersen, who did everything for me my father would have done, and more. But I told you, my family is fated, so much so that I seriously doubt whether I ought to have any children, though Tatiana tells me that's just superstition.' (A rash of flash bulbs exploded as the couple exchanged loving glances.) 'It was only three weeks ago that I heard that my poor uncle had been drowned during a deep-sea fishing expedition in the Pacific. As of now, they still haven't recovered his body. . . .'

Which, Holzheimer pointed out to Ellison when he telephoned him in London half-an-hour later, was nicely thought up. No body yet, no death certificate and therefore no documentary investigation of Arthur Lionel Petersen.

'What about the photographs of the guests?' Ellison asked.

'Your Honour, we did our best to follow your instructions. You ordered saturation coverage; our resources are not minimal ... when we try. We flew in not only four of our most experienced staff photographers, but we also commissioned a further half-dozen amateur enthusiasts from southern California. The film is at this moment being rushed to you by air freight. Sir, please may I keep my job for another week?'

Holzheimer now joined the cortège sweeping up the ocean highway to the District Court. There Karl Petersen swore and produced documentary evidence and witnesses attesting that he was an American citizen of necessity working overseas in the employ of an American company engaged in the promotion of foreign trade. He also swore that he intended to return to reside in the United States as soon as his work permitted.

When Tatiana Larin-Petersen, still wearing her bridal gown, stepped out of the District Court, she was a naturalized American citizen. The reporters crowded round the couple on the courthouse steps:

'Karl, when do you expect to be able to return home to resume serious training?'

'Well, as a matter of fact, Mr Enders has just suggested to me that now might be as good a time as any!'

The President of Enders International Promotions beamed proudly before the flashing cameras.

'Tatiana, how does it feel to be an American?'

'Great! Just marvellous! I can't believe it's really true.' The smile never left her face.

'So what are your immediate plans, Tatiana?'

'Karl and I have a pretty heavy schedule during the next five months leading up to the Olympic Try-outs.'

'So you definitely hope to represent America at the Moscow Olympics?'

'You bet! The Olympics is what it's all about.'

'Tatiana, if you win a medal in Moscow, would you see that as a blow for freedom?'

'Absolutely. No question about it. I fully expect the Soviets to try every dirty trick in the book to keep me off that victory rostrum. I know what I'm talking about. Don't forget I was brought up under the Soviet system. We were taught to win at all costs for the glory of the fatherland and the socialist set-up. For example, the taking of anabolic steroids is standard practice among Soviet athletes: the authorities don't only connive at it, they encourage it. They insist on it! It was one of the reasons I defected, as a matter of fact – I refused to take any more of the powder they gave me to swallow. They threatened to strip me of all my privileges. You can also expect a number of women athletes from the West to fail their gender tests at the Olympics – unless the IAAF refuses to let the Russians fix the laboratory results. In events like my own, non-Soviet competitors will be kept standing about in draughty corridors between events while the Russian girls keep supple in secret warm-up areas. Hell, this is going to be the dirty tricks Olympics.'

'Holy cow,' muttered Ellison as the transcript of this outburst came off the agency wire machines. 'They're certainly turning the key in the girl's back now.'

'The question is, can the Russians resist the provocation?' Ramsay Jordan said.

'There's no way the Russians could face having Tatiana win the pentathlon in front of a Moscow crowd,' Magnus said. 'Imagine the humiliation of watching their golden girl mounting the victory rostrum and saluting the Stars-and-Stripes.'

'What puzzles a simple mind,' Jordan said with laborious sarcasm, 'is why Tatiana should now be speaking in precisely the tone she adopted in her 4,350-word story, "Goodbye, Russia" which, a leading authority still assures us, was a fake.'

Ellison lit a cigar and regarded his editor with evident compassion. 'My dear Ramsay, if I may be bold enough so to address you: the English version of that story contained fourteen instances where a common noun had been typed with an initial capital letter. In German all nouns begin with a capital, but in Russian and English, only names and titles. If Tatiana had written that story herself, you may rest assured that she would have written it in Russian. Yet the version we received had clearly been carelessly translated from the German – hence the rash of illegitimate capitals. You may rest assured that "Goodbye, Russia" was in fact written by a Klostermann hack.'

Magnus nodded. 'A scholarly touch is always nice but why, as Ramsay asked, is she laying the anti-Soviet diatribes on so thick now? She must realize that they can only ruin whatever slim chances she still has of competing in Moscow.'

Ellison shook his head. 'No, she doesn't realize it. Clearly she has been advised, and believes fervently, that the Russians simply dare not refuse her a visa.'

'But why so vehement – remember that innocent little girl in a pony tail?'

'We have to face it, Tatiana is now a true convert.'

Jordan rose and walked out of Ellison's office in a huff. 'One day, perhaps, you'll admit that you were wrong from the beginning!'

The following day, the Searchlight team assembled in front of a screen to watch the projection of over 300 35mm colour transparencies taken on Ektachrome ASA 160 by Holzheimer's army of photographers at the Petersen-Larin wedding. Julie Beavan, projectionist for the occasion, had been instructed by Magnus to sift the transparencies in advance, eliminating all females, all children and all males indisputably under thirty years of age. 'If in doubt, show it.'

On either side of the projection screen Massey had fastened to cork pinboards blow-ups of two black-and-white photographs of a middle-aged man whose stern, pallid, unsmiling features indicated a lack of human warmth, a capacity for hard-bitten calculation and, perhaps, an ultimate allegiance to a cause, a faith, greater than himself.

The gaze of Ellison and Massey swivelled continually from the projection screen to the blow-ups. For they both believed that – only a chance in a hundred, perhaps – the man in the blow-ups might have travelled alone to Glenmore to observe the wedding from the anonymity of the crowd.

The hypothesis that Ellison and Massey had constructed during hours of analysis was the product of five years' investigation and the sifting of hundreds of small clues. Ellison's genius resided not only in his capacity to pick up vibrations which less sensitive divining rods passed over, but also in his ability to make connections where others saw only unrelated fragments.

A month earlier, in December, 1979, he had received a cable from Joe Mutobo and taken the first available flight to Nairobi, transferring there to a Lusaka-bound plane and then flying on from the Zambian capital to Maputo in Mozambique. The speed with which he reacted to Mutobo's cable could be understood only in the light of a similar journey he had made six years earlier, in late '73, a subsequent conversation in Vienna and a tape recording extracted from Room 310 of the Hotel de France, Montreal.

In 1973, of course, Maputo was called Lourenço Marques, and Mozambique belonged to the Portuguese, staunch allies of white Rhodesia and white South Africa.

CHAPTER 14

November, 1973. Mozambique–Rhodesia

On the quayside of Lourenço Marques, Ellison had tipped enough Customs officials and port supervisors to be allowed to photograph the tanker *Table Mountain* unloading crude oil from Iran into a tank farm owned by a company which coyly declined to state its name. One hundred metres away, parked on the quayside railway track, stood a number of coupled oil-carrying wagons. Although these, too, were unmarked, a close examination revealed a small documents box welded to the side of the wagon and carrying a bill of lading with the following specifications: 't/car No. 474302; cap. 41050 litres at 20°C; temperature 26; SG @ 20°C, 7350; product, Premium.' The fact that this card was written in English was in itself interesting, ruling out domestic Mozambique consumption. Ellison was just about to leave the quayside, alerted by the approach of a Portuguese police officer whom he hadn't yet had the opportunity to bribe, when his eye picked up two letters embossed on the wheel bogies of the wagons: RR.

Rhodesian Railways.

A coded cable to Massey in the Seychelles had sent the tall Scot into Bulawayo, principal city of Matabeleland in Western Rhodesia, via Jan Smuts Airport, Johannesburg. Once there, working on a contact whom Ellison got from Joe Mutobo, he had visited the headquarters of the all-black Union of Railway Operatives on Lobengula Street. John Ndhlovu, assistant general secretary, ushered him into a conference room lined with photographs of union officials, offered him a Kingsgate cigarette, folded his hands on the table and regarded Magnus with undisguised suspicion.

When Magnus mentioned Joe Mutobo's name, Ndhlovu's attitude softened a bit, but not much: there were plenty of Rhodesian Special Branch officers who knew Mutobo's name; not a few of them were capable of posing as a liberal white journalist from London.

When Ndhlovu finally decided to trust him he offered him coffee. For the next fifteen minutes the African was on the phone, speaking rapidly in Sindebele, interspersed with such English terms as 'railhead', 'wagon', 'loco' and (most often repeated) 'management'. Ndhlovu was chain-smoking in a high state of tension.

'This is classified information, you understand? We have very harsh punishments in Rhodesia for anyone divulging information pertaining to the evasion of sanctions regulations.'

Magnus walked down the shabby, peeling stairwell with its torn Pepsi poster showing a smiling coloured girl, guarding in his inner pocket a list of names whose strange clusters of vowels he could not hope to commit to memory. The street was full of men in khaki fatigues, mine-proofed vehicles with wide-wheel axles, and young white women modelled out of tinned peaches and vanilla ice cream. He drove his little Renault, hired from Echo Car Hire (Pvt) Ltd, due south to inspect the lonely grave of Cecil Rhodes in the boulder-strewn Matopos hills. The chances of getting knocked off by Joshua Nkomo's guerrillas were, in those days, not yet inhibiting. But Rhodesia was not a place where a man like Magnus Massey could afford to relax. He had left nothing but clothes and tourist brochures in his hotel room at Meikles Southern Sun; he didn't doubt that the Special Branch would greet his arrival in Rhodesia by toothcombing his possessions.

It was almost dusk when he passed the Antelope Mine and approached the suburb of Hillside along the Matopos Road. A green truck of the Rhodesian Railways' Maintenance and

Supply Department was standing in a quiet corner of the car park outside a large, mock-Tudor hotel called the Churchill Arms. He slowed to check its number plate.

The two Africans in the cabin of the truck wore Rhodesian Railways dungaree uniforms and caps. The driver nodded to him and gestured to the rear of the truck with a slight movement of his head. Magnus locked the Renault, climbed into the back of the truck, secured the double doors from inside and lay down on the floor under a pile of empty coal sacks from the Wankie collieries.

He timed the journey at eighteen minutes, correlating each turn of the truck with a section of the Surveyor General's 1 : 33333 street-map of Greater Bulawayo imprinted in his head. As expected, they were waved down outside the police station on Mafeking Road; to his relief, all the voices were African. The truck crunched into bottom gear and lurched away. In Birkenhead Road, outside the Cold Storage Commission railway depot, they were halted again; this time he heard the soft but authoritative accent of a white male Rhodesian.

'Open up, boy.'

The rear doors swung open: a strong torch beam raked the interior of the truck. Magnus lay still.

'It's an emergency repair, you say?' the white police officer was asking the truck driver suspiciously.

'Yessah. Rear axle, wagon TMA 30665, platform 7, Transport Services.'

'Where's your authorization, boy? For all I know you could be a terr planning mischief in there.'

'Here, boss: document signed by Mr Corbishley, Chief Engineer, South West, yessah.'

'I'll phone him, then. Wait here, boy.'

'Yes, boss.'

Five minutes later the white Rhodesian returned.

'Very well,' he said softly. 'Proceed.'

The black security guards at the entrance to Transport Services' sidings were easier to deal with: the Corbishley document was enough for them. Again the truck lurched forward, moving slowly now over pitted roads and sunken steel tracks. Finally the rear door opened.

'Be quick, my friend.'

The whole area was a mass of oil storage tanks: at a glance Magnus reckoned the Transport Services tank farm stretched for two hundred yards on either side of a double track. Using Ilford HP4 film with a flash at f4, he photographed a series of bills of lading taken from the small documents boxes welded to the side of the railway wagons. The number sequences and the specifications of load coincided closely with those noted down four days earlier by Bill Ellison at the quayside in Lourenço Marques.

The following day he met Bob Corbishley, District Chief Engineer, South West Railways, twice: a brief, cagey encounter in Corbishley's office in the morning and a more relaxed, friendly discussion at Corbishley's home in the evening. Corbishley insisted on picking him up in the bar of the Great Northern Hotel, near the main railway station.

'I wouldn't want your car to be seen parked outside my house, nor would I like to be seen with you in your hotel. Yes, things are that bad here, Mr Massey – this is a police state.' After a moment he added: 'I was against Smith's Unilateral Declaration of Independence, you see. I've always been loyal to the Crown, to Britain.'

Corbishley spent twenty minutes explaining the intricacies of sanctions-busting.

'It's really an elaborate paper-chase. Oil, solvents and other imports under UN sanctions are sold in South Africa to dummy companies operating under special accounts at post office box numbers in Durban and Jo'burg. These goods are then re-sold to front companies in Salisbury, so that at no stage do the names of the actual importers appear on the invoices. Here, for example, you have a railway advice note for 41,754 litres of Ormoil-2552 sold by Galaxy (South Africa) to Mitron No. 2 Account on August 4, 1973; the price is Rand 1,350 and the invoice number is 245748. In fact, what you have is a shipment from a major international oil company to Transport Services of Rhodesia. That's how we keep going out here.'

'Who runs Transport Services?'

'Transport Services is a wholly owned subsidiary of a South African company, Brandon Holdings. But of course it has to operate here under Rhodesian law – which is the law of the outcast.'

'Who is the controlling shareholder? Is there one man behind the whole operation?'

Corbishley glanced at his wife, rose and refilled Magnus's glass with sanctions-busting scotch. 'You do protect your sources, I suppose?' he asked with an apologetic smile.

'Always.'

'I did you a real favour, getting you into the Transport Services tank farm. If that ever got out I'd lose my job and spend five years in Khami.'

'That's a prison?'

'It certainly is. Now you're asking me to stick my neck out even further. I mean, you can take off for the UK tomorrow, but I have to live with the consequences.'

'After all,' said Mrs Corbishley, 'yours is a rich paper.'

'Ah – you want to be paid?' Magnus asked Corbishley.

'Well ... I didn't like to ask ... but educating two sons at English public schools is very expensive. Frankly, a sterling cheque on a UK bank would be very helpful.'

'Two hundred pounds, Mr Corbishley. Agreed? Good.'

'Have some more of our local Rhoplonk?'

'Thank you.'

'The man who owns and directs Transport Services is an Afrikaaner businessman who has become, in the space of ten years, Rhodesia's most successful sanctions-buster. He is also a power behind the political scenes, a financial angel of the Rhodesian Front, the key intermediary between Smith and Vorster. He lives in a large mansion in the Mount Pleasant district of Salisbury, protected by an electric fence, guard dogs and foreign mercenaries. Apart from a 25,000-acre ranch near Gwanda in Matabeleland, he also owns a lucrative coffee farm of some 1,900 acres at Chipinga, near the Mozambique border. Most of his domestic staff are not native Shona or Ndebele people, whom he regards as security risks, but immigrants from Malawi. The labour force in his various economic enterprises is honeycombed by black informers for the Special Branch. He is a very thorough man, who leaves nothing to chance. I know a good deal about him: a large proportion of his freight passes over my railway lines.'

'You're a friend of his?'

'I wouldn't say that. My political principles, after all, are diametrically opposed to his. We do share an interest in fishing, though – he has a boat down on Lake Kyle, near the Zimbabwe ruins. I've been invited down there once or twice.'

'You still haven't told me his name.'

'Ventner. Coenraad Ventner.' Corbishley spelt the Afrikaaner version of the Christian name for Magnus's benefit.

'Is he married? Children?'

'Yes, two sons, both attending Afrikaaner schools in South Africa. The family firm, of course, is based in Johannesburg.'

'Do you have a photograph of him? A press cutting, perhaps?'

'I told you, he avoids the limelight like the plague. I don't think I've ever seen a picture of him in a newspaper.' Corbishley took down a leather-bound album from his shelves and showed Magnus a couple of shots: one of Corbishley and Ventner fishing together on Lake Kyle, the other of Ventner fondling a black Labrador at a picnic.

Massey flew out of Bulawayo for Johannesburg the following morning, but not before taking the precaution of sending his notes and film by post from the central post office. And the two snapshots of Ventner, for which he had paid Corbishley an extra £50. It was just as well: on his way out Immigration officials confiscated the film in his camera, searched his bags and stripped him to his underpants.

A white Special Branch officer wearing a khaki shirt and shorts handed him an official letter. 'You're PI'd,' he said.

'PI'd? What does that mean?'

'It means, Mr Massey, that from now on you are a Prohibited Immigrant to Rhodesia.'

December, 1979. Mozambique

'This time,' Pru Ellison had declared, 'I put my foot down! I'm prepared to write you off at weekends, and I fully expect you to rate the current shock horror story as more important than our annual holiday. But there is one day of the year when you are always at home: Christmas. Think of Christopher! And you know perfectly well that my sister's family are coming to stay, with three small children.' Ellison's wife burst into tears at the sight of his dead-bat, obdurate unresponsiveness.

Christopher, a pale twig tucked into a corner of the room, had followed suit. Only once or twice in his life had he seen his mother cry.

Bill Ellison had flown out of Heathrow on Christmas Eve. At Johannesburg he changed to a South African Airways flight to Maputo, arriving in the capital of independent Mozambique on Christmas afternoon. He was met at the airport by Joe Mutobo, Patrick Okie and Henrique Chassinga, an official of the ruling party, Frelimo.

'On behalf of President Samora Machel, welcome to Mozambique, Mr Ellison. And happy Christmas.' With a shy smile Chassinga presented him with a small box of cigars; and it was only then that the guilt and distress he felt about deserting his family truly caught up with Ellison.

Chassinga drove them through the suburbs to a large house set in a secluded garden and guarded by two Frelimo sentries of lethargic demeanour. Clearly Mutobo and Okie were delighted to see him again; the hostility they had built up during the Vienna-Montreal period had been dramatically reversed by a series of punishing articles that Ellison had published after his return from South Africa. His early revelations about the Department of Information financial scandals in Pretoria during 1978 had delighted them even more. Ellison was once more *persona grata* in black liberation circles.

The two captured Belgian pilots, Jansen and Dubesque, were playing cards in a stiflingly hot room. A large electric fan suspended above their heads refused to turn. Seeing a white man, they immediately began to complain in French, pleading for an amelioration of the conditions under which they had been confined since being shot down, a week earlier, in Mozambique air space.

'*Monsieur, c'est affreux!* It's unendurable to be without mosquito nets during the wet season. Look, we're bitten from head to toe! And they keep forgetting to bring us malaria tablets!'

'What does the bastard say?' muttered Mutobo. This had been one of the problems during the past week: the Belgians spoke neither English nor Portuguese. For some ten minutes the pilots unburdened themselves. Clearly the interrogation techniques employed by Frelimo and Zanu had become increasingly direct and physical; Jansen and Dubesque were frightened men. But Jansen was the hard one.

'I assure you it was not our intention to violate Mozambique air space,' he argued. 'We had clearance from air traffic control, Lusaka, to proceed over Zambia, but committed a small error of navigation at night.'

'You were flying a DC-8 for La Compagnie Gabonaise d'Affretements Aeriens?'

'*Oui, monsieur.* Affretair, as we call it.'

'It's a pity, for you, that you were carrying Alouette helicopter parts to Salisbury from Gabon. My friends here are rather sensitive about Alouettes: the Rhodesian Special Air Service, Selous Scouts and Fire Force units use them to raid Zanu camps in Mozambique. Recently over two thousand people were massacred at Chimoio, mainly women and children.'

The Belgians stared at the floor, silent. 'We were only doing our job,' whispered Dubesque.

'Where did your journey really start?' Ellison asked.

'Gabon, *monsieur*.'

'Alouettes are not made in Gabon and I wasn't born yesterday. Nor were my friends here. Your alibi isn't helped by the fact that your DC-8 had been re-sprayed. In scraping away the new paint and AA-LVK Affretair registration number from the fuselage, my friends here have discovered the old registration number RTS – which means Rhodesian Transport Services.'

The Belgians shrugged. They knew nothing about that. Ellison believed them. The plane had probably been nominally transferred to the dummy company, Affretair, long ago, after the United Nations introduced sanctions against white Rhodesia in 1968.

'How big is Affretair's staff in Gabon?' Ellison asked.

Jansen and Dubesque exchanged glances. 'You represent the Surêté Nationale, *monsieur*?' Jansen asked cautiously.

'I'm a United Nations investigator.' Since the Katanga affair in 1961, he realized, Belgians, and particularly Belgian mercenaries, had hated the UN. But at this moment Ellison wanted to be feared, not loved. 'What is more, I am informed by my friends that you will be brought before a military tribunal and shot as spies tomorrow if you don't come clean.'

A tremor passed across Dubesque's face. Jansen remained outwardly calm. He was the hard nut: and his expression indicated ill-concealed hatred. Dubesque was in it, no doubt, for the money, the job, the adventure; but Jansen was defending the West, Christianity, the White Man.

'In Gabon Affretair has perhaps one hundred, perhaps 150 employees, *monsieur*,' Dubesque said.

'And what proportion of them are Rhodesians or South Africans?'

Dubesque shook his head. 'I don't speak English. An American, an Englishman, a Rhodesian, a South African, an Australian. . . .'

'Yes, yes,' Ellison interrupted, 'I take your point. *Je vous comprends.* How many trips have you made to Salisbury from Amsterdam?'

'Ten or twelve.'

Jansen emitted an oath under his breath. '*Crapaud.*' His co-pilot had blown it.

Ellison kept his gaze fixed on Dubesque. From the silence of Mutobo, Okie and Chassinga he inferred that he was getting further than they had during the week since the DC-8 was brought down over Tete province by a Soviet-built heat-seeking missile.

'You admit that Affretair of Gabon is just a cover for Rhodesian Transport Services?' he pressed. 'You pick up goods in Europe nominally consigned to Gabon, then you fly them on to Salisbury? Yes?'

Dubesque nodded. Perhaps he had a family; perhaps he felt he was too young to die.

'Correct. I am short of cigarettes, *monsieur.*'

Ellison tossed him a packet of cigars and two packets of Benson & Hedges. 'Where were you recruited?' he asked.

'By a man in an Amsterdam bar,' Jansen suddenly cut in. 'He spoke poor French, we don't know his name. The pay was good, we signed on.'

Dubesque reached for one of Ellison's cigars. Ellison walked over to him, took it from his hand and pocketed the packet, along with the cigarettes. 'If you're to be put on trial tomorrow it's silly to smoke today. You want to die healthy, don't you?'

Dubesque began to tremble. 'It's true we were approached by *un type* in a bar,' he said, exchanging livid glances with Jansen. 'After that we were summoned for an interview at the Affretair office at Schiphol Airport. They kept us hanging about while they scrutinized our licenses and documents. They seemed very worried about spies infiltrating their organization.'

'They? Who did you talk to? Who interrogated you?'

'Several people,' Jansen intervened. 'They weren't forthcoming about their names. I wasn't playing the detective. It seems a man can't take an honest job in this world without some gang of Marxist-inspired snoopers poking in their fucking noses and – '

Joe Mutobo didn't fully comprehend what Jansen was saying, but the tone adopted by the Belgian was enough for him. The two Frelimo guards were summoned, and Jansen was forcibly dragged outside. A few minutes later a shot rang out, followed by another. Presently Mutobo came back into the room carrying an AK 47 rifle. He sat down and pointed it at Dubesque's stomach.

'Talk,' he growled. '*Parlez!*'

Ellison opened his briefcase and spread a number of photographs out in front of the trembling Belgian, the front of whose pants, he noticed, had surrendered to a spreading wet stain since the shots were heard.

'We'll have an identity parade by proxy,' he said. 'Have you seen or spoken to any of these men since you began work for Affretair? Maybe in Amsterdam, maybe in Gabon, maybe in Salisbury.'

Dubesque gazed fixedly at the twenty-odd photographs,

his teeth quite literally chattering with fright. Ellison knew that Joe wouldn't have shot Jansen, but Dubesque didn't know it. He put a cigarette in the Belgian's mouth and lit it. 'If you tell the truth,' he said, 'I guarantee you'll leave Mozambique tomorrow on the same plane as I do.' He turned to Mutobo and repeated himself in English.

Dubesque threw a nervous look at Mutobo. The African nodded in confirmation.

'Two of these men I have met,' Dubesque whispered.

'Point, then.'

'This man here definitely. This man here, possibly, I'm not at all sure.'

'Their names?'

'Coenraad Ventner is the boss of Rhodesian Transport Services. During our first stop-over in Salisbury he asked us a lot of questions about our beliefs and opinions. That man, he is a fanatic, *monsieur*.'

'The other man?'

'I don't know his name. He never spoke to me. I happened to see him when I was leaving Affretair's office at Schiphol Airport, Amsterdam. He was getting into a chauffeur-driven Mercedes 450 SEL. I can't be sure, it was just a glimpse, I had my mind on other things.'

'Anything else you can remember about him?'

'*Oui, monsieur*. He had a limp and carried a silver-topped stick.'

January, 1980. London

'Next one,' Ellison said for the 200th time as another face from the Larin-Petersen wedding in California was projected on the screen.

Bernie Holzheimer had employed four professional and six amateur photographers with the result that many of the faces – invited guests, crowd, security men, press – repeated themselves. So far not one face had matched the two blow-ups suspended either side of the screen.

'I suppose it was too much to hope,' Ellison said to Massey when the exercise was over.

'He's a prudent, calculating man: why take the risk?'

'Yes, yes. But it must be hard for a proud father to keep away from his son's wedding.'

February, 1980. London

A thin, gaunt man in a 1940's brown trilby and a lifeless brown suit, carrying a drab raincoat over his arm, was tossing stale bread into the pond in St James's Park.

'Couple of fine crested mallards there,' Jack Knight commented.

'Every time you fall short, the tits and pigeons grab it. Filthy, bloated creatures.'

'I spoke to Sergei Tretiakov,' Knight said. 'He confirmed that Chaim Leonhard has been moved to Kolyma labour camp. I told him you have evidence that Leonhard is innocent and that Ha Mossad had nothing to do with the operation.'

'What did Tretiakov say?'

'That Leonhard has confessed.'

'Oh shit. Poor bastard.'

'I'm afraid the idea of anyone trying to sabotage their precious Moscow Olympics brings out the psychopathic side in them.' Knight finished the bread, screwed up the paper bag into a ball and dropped it, with civic scruple, into a waste bin. 'Tretiakov tells me they very nearly abducted you as well, it was a close-run decision. Arbuzov took it to Gromkyo, who said "No".'

'How's your friend Ray Lawson?'

'I don't have friends. He's back in the States now.'

'You knew he worked for the CIA?'

'Yes. On the other hand, that Sunday we followed you to Hampstead Heath, there was plenty that I didn't know – that HM Government didn't know – about Lawson.'

'Like what?'

'Larin and Petersen had been ferried out of the UK the previous night, from the US Air Force base at Brize Norton, in Oxfordshire, in a cargo plane owned by one of the Agency's dummy companies. They landed at a CIA base in Maine. Lawson supervised the whole operation.'

'How did you find out?'

'The Immigration Division of Justice screamed at State; the White House screamed at State. Finally the Secretary of State ordered one hell of an inquiry and the truth came out: it had been a minority job within the "Company".'

'And Lawson was sent home in disgrace?'

'Maybe. Have you seen those latest opinion polls?'

Ellison nodded. 'The President has his back to the wall now.'

'Of course the Russians insist that we had a part in it. For the past eight months they've frozen ratification of the £2.5 billion Anglo-Russian trade deal.'

'And you're not getting any help from Sergei Tretiakov – which means that the moles planted by his KGB rival Zarobin are running amok under your own turf. Our counter-espionage is at a standstill?'

Knight gazed at the ducks gloomily. 'I suppose you *do* know more about Operation Russian Girl than anyone else?'

'Apart from those who staged it.'

'It would be vulgar to ask you who they are, since you haven't yet gone to press.'

'Quite. But if I could convince the Russians, your life would be easier. Go back to Tretiakov. Tell him to have Chaim Leonhard brought to the East German border. I'll walk across to their side and tell them everything I know.'

'In return for Chaim Leonhard?'

'Yes.'

'I doubt you'll be able to convince the Russians.' Knight looked up from the ducks and gave Ellison a rare, point-blank appraisal. Everything about the relationship of these two men was oblique, indirect, awkward – not once in ten years had they ventured into a pub together, so insuperable was the difficulty of deciding who would buy the first two pints. 'After all, you're obviously not confident yet that you can convince your own readers.' Knight turned and took a few steps. 'Why do you care so much about that Jew lawyer, Leonhard, anyway? To maintain your Ha Mossad links? Or because of Leonhard's daughter?'

Ellison gritted his teeth, stifling the expletive pushing up his throat. He knew that Knight was utterly without malice and utterly without a trace of human curiosity extending beyond the strict perimeters of his work – the pursuit, exposure and arrest of foreign espionage agents operating in Britain. Not for the first time, he was testing the weight of Ellison's coin.

If Knight was to go back to Tretiakov, hat in hand, that coin had to be good.

'You'll listen?'

Knight nodded. 'Why not?'

'It all goes back to the early months of '78. South Africa's champion of non-violent black struggle, Steve Biko, had been callously beaten to death by the police while under interrogation. The United Nations slapped a trade embargo on South Africa. In February, 1978, the US Department of Commerce extended the list of embargoed goods, including computers, computer parts and computer data destined for use by the South African military or police. A month later Britain forbade the export of military and police riot control equipment.

'In '76 I had been granted an interview by Prime Minister Vorster in Pretoria. He has two chins, a red nose, a lugubrious doughnut of a face, and rheumy eyes – which makes it seem that he is permanently weeping with indignation at one's callous, British questions. He said to me: "The time will arrive when South Africa will say to the world, 'so far and no further – do your damnedest'." I often let that phrase jog round the big empty spaces of my mind.'

Jack Knight appeared to be absorbed in ornithology, but Ellison was in no doubt that the MI5 man was absorbing every word.

'In the spring of '78, you'll recall, a scandal began to break in South Africa. The devious yet clumsy attempts of the Republic's top men to cover it up eventually reached Watergate-like proportions. The epicentre of the storm was the Department of Information, which had been funnelling secret funds, running to millions of rand undisclosed to Parliament, into expensive covert propaganda activities both at home and abroad.

'Even more serious had been the attempt to buy up, quite literally, the English-language press, which alone maintained a critical stance towards the Nationalist Government of John Vorster. South Africa was perhaps three-quarters of the way to becoming a one-party police state; papers like the *Rand Daily Mail*, the *Cape Times*, the *Sunday Times* and the *Sunday Express* were determined to prevent it going four-quarters of the way. All are owned by an umbrella company called SAAN. The Government tried to buy SAAN – and failed.

'What the Department of Information did succeed in doing was financing, to the tune of Rand 12 million, a new pro-Government tabloid rag called *The Flag*, owned by a certain Paul Shrivers, a leading figure in the Fair Play Campaign, whom I met in South Africa. Its influence on English-language readers may well have accounted for the Nationalist Party's unprecedentedly sweeping election victory in 1977.

'This was taxpayer's money that was being covertly grafted into private hands. A lot of money. Every leading politician knew what was going on and approved of it: Prime Minister Vorster, Information Minister Connie Mulder, and General Hendrik van den Bergh, head of BOSS.

'Vorster appointed van den Bergh to conduct an inquiry. It was a simple cover-up assignment. It didn't work. Emerging from comparative obscurity was the spider at the centre of the web, Dr Eschel Rhoodie, Secretary of Information. Rhoodie did a flit to Europe. Mulder, who had boldly assured Parliament that no public money had ever reached *The Flag*, was forced to resign. Finally Vorster himself had to go.

'The whole leadership was implicated. Pieter Botha, who had succeeded Vorster as PM, made desperate efforts to contain the disaster, to suppress information, to mislead the world. Supreme Court Justice Anton Mostert was crudely relieved of his commission to investigate the Department of Information after he ignored the Prime Minister's instruction to conceal what he knew. Leading editors and journalists of the English-speaking press were subpoenaed and harassed under the Criminal Procedures Act.

'The crack-down began. The *Verkramptes* (hardliners) took over from the *Verligtes* (pragmatists) within the Party. The extremist elected to lead the Transvaal party, Dr Andries Treurnicht, made no bones about his opposition to mixed-race sport, religious worship and entertainment.

'That was the great turning point. That was when the elite who run South Africa, the secret Broederbond, embarked on their new course.

'Para-military police were poured into Rhodesia to bolster the white regime as it came under increasing pressure from the guerrillas. In Namibia, the South Africans defied the United Nations and the Western Powers by insisting on holding phoney elections under their own control.

'Back to the *laager*.'

Ellison had stopped now, but Knight behaved as if he expected the journalist to resume.

'Well, that's it,' Ellison said eventually.

'You expect me to take that to Tretiakov?'

'Well. . . .'

'Bit hypothetical, wouldn't you say? How does it all tie up with Lawson's role?'

'The Angola connection.'

They walked on in silence towards Piccadilly. 'Fact is,' Knight said, 'you're holding out on me – the key personalities, I mean. The villains of the piece.'

Ellison had known all along that Knight's sense of direction was sufficiently sound to force Ellison to choose between Chaim Leonhard's life and his own investigation.

'Forget it,' he said.

It was never their habit to shake hands or even to exchange farewell salutations. There just came a moment, somehow, when they found themselves walking in opposite directions.

February, 1980. Amsterdam

'Thank you for finding time,' Ellison said, as Armand Krohl courteously drew up a chair for him beside his desk. 'And what a splendid view of the Amster. I confess, this ranks among my favourite European cities. You were born here?'

'No, I was born in the Dutch East Indies – Sumatra. My father was in business there. Later he sent me to Holland to take over at this end.'

'It seems to me, now that Tatiana Larin-Petersen is a naturalized American with a declared wish to represent the United States at the Games, that the IOC must soon declare its position.'

Krohl ran a hand through his thick grey hair and adopted

his professor-of-jurisprudence demeanour, severe and exacting.

'Is that a statement or a question? If a question, then it is a hypothetical one.' Suddenly he smiled. 'After all – and heaven forbid – the lady may break her leg on the stairs.'

'Has the Executive Board of the IOC discussed hypothetical solutions to hypothetical problems – such as the declared refusal, at some future date, of the Soviet Union to grant a visa to a naturalized American athlete?'

Krohl pondered this, gazing out of the tall window at the canal below. 'Really,' he said, 'I am not at liberty to discuss that – even off the record.'

'Let's discuss something else then – your meeting with Chaim Leonhard and Sol Enders in a Los Angeles restaurant last summer.'

Abruptly Krohl appeared vulnerable, almost defenceless, the human rights activist that totalitarian regimes delight in depriving of liberty. 'Who told you?' he inquired mildly.

'Rupin. He maintains that the idea was yours – that it was you who had learned about Tatiana's attachment to Karl Petersen.'

Krohl nodded. 'Rupin, of course, would say that. I hear rumours that the Russians have abducted Chaim Leonhard. Can you confirm?'

'Yes. The Russians believe he double-crossed them. According to Rupin, you also feel that Leonhard betrayed your trust.'

'I can tell you the truth of the matter, provided we are off the record. Even though my involvement was not what Rupin claims it was, any public exposure of this business and I would of course have to resign.'

'Off the record, then.'

'The love affair between the Soviet and American athletes was something I discovered from Chaim. He in turn learned of it from his friend Sol Enders. I have good evidence but not incontrovertible proof that Enders secretly signed up Petersen on a pro contract some time ago – the boy looks like a TV ad. I only wish I could prove it, just as I wish I could prove that Petersen has been fiddling his athletic travelling expenses and taking prize money for his own use out of the World Superstars tournaments in the Bahamas.

'There is no doubt in my mind that Enders prompted the boy to have a go at this extremely talented and rather attractive little Russian girl. After all, it would raise Petersen's commercial value; and if she could be persuaded to defect, all the better, Enders could sign her up too!' Krohl smiled sadly. 'She wasn't a world record holder at that time, but she was the best in the USSR.'

'And your own involvement?'

'Chaim came to me. He was worried about current Soviet attitudes and saw an opportunity to put pressure on them. He asked my advice. He also wanted to use my name in negotiating with the Russians, to prove to them that the Jews were not on their own.'

'Did you permit him to do that?'

'No. I warned him that although he might get results, it was an extremely risky enterprise which could backfire, particularly if Enders was involved.' Krohl scratched his head and rang the bell for more coffee. 'I'm afraid Chaim always accused me of prejudice against Enders.'

'But why did you agree to meet both Chaim and Enders in Los Angeles?'

Krohl looked at Ellison very directly. 'To be frank, I wanted to put the frighteners on Enders.'

'By threatening to launch a full-scale inquisition into his financial dealings with Petersen?'

Krohl nodded. 'And all his other "clients".'

'I see.'

'Why did Rupin give you a different version? Because, whatever their protestations to the contrary, Ha Mossad did indeed engineer Tatiana Larin's defection. I feel desperately sorry for poor Chaim in his ghastly predicament, but the Russians are no fools, you know. I suggest you telephone Enders here and now. Report to him what I have said and challenge him to deny it.'

'May I?'

'By all means. Do you have the number?'

Krohl read out the number of Enders International Promotions as Ellison dialled. The journalist got through to the impresario without difficulty and put Krohl's statement to him bluntly. There was a pause.

'Mr Ellison, you're not going to quote me on this one?'

'Off the record.'

'What Krohl says is true.'

CHAPTER 15

May, 1980. London

When Ellison decided to send Magnus yet again to California early in May, the situation was becoming desperate. The Olympic Try-outs were only five weeks away, the Games themselves only nine weeks ahead. Since the end of '79 Ellison and Massey had been in no doubt who had engineered the defection of Tatiana, yet every effort to dig up evidence which would convince a sceptical world had failed.

Morale on the rival *Sunday Dispatch* was said to be at an all-time peak. From the George to the Old King Lud, the rumour up and down Fleet Street was that Ellison had at last bitten the dust. For the first time in five years, Lord Jacobs, proprietor of the *Dispatch*, had not invited the Ellisons to dine at the Connaught early in the New Year. In an exultant gesture of revenge for years of humiliation and anxiety, Tim Powerstock had invited Joe O'Neill out to lunch, got him to confess that the Searchlight team were stymied and then offered him a job on the *Dispatch* without a rise in salary.

News of this *démarche*, carefully fanned by Powerstock's men, was related at cocktail parties all over London. Jokes were made on television. It wasn't that people disliked Ellison, although dedication such as his inevitably touches a chord of suspicion among the British. But one witty columnist got pretty close to encapsulating Ellison's image when, in a reference to a famous Yorkshire and England cricketer noted for his dour dedication, he called Ellison 'the Geoff Boycott of Fleet Street'.

Much more serious to Ellison and Massey was the mounting evidence that the Tatiana operation remained crack on course for its target. Ellison termed it a heat-seeking rocket – and the heat was becoming more apparent by the day. Although the Russians had not yet explicitly announced that Tatiana would be refused a visa to participate in the Games, the increasingly hysterical Soviet diatribes ruled out any other possibility. At best, the Russians would wait until after the Olympic Try-outs in the vain hope that she would fail to qualify.

Politically, the situation was polarizing to an alarming degree; the Cold War showed signs of becoming colder than at any time since the Cuban missile crisis of 1962. Capitalizing on the refusal of the Russians to pledge that they *would* grant Tatiana a visa, Senator Dick Aronson and Governor Walter Prendergast were now campaigning for the Presidency on a 'boycott the Games' platform, supported by vociferous pressure groups.

The results were frightening, not only to Ellison but also to the White House. Whipped on by the Manchester *Union-Leader*, Aronson had captured the support of 62 per cent of 98,000 registered Democrats in the New Hampshire primary of March 7. In Massachusetts, on April 22, the President had held the line, narrowly, with 327,000 votes (53 per cent), but in Ohio, where for the first time Tatiana Larin-Petersen and her husband appeared in a pro-Aronson television plug, the Senator took 79 out of 153 delegates to the Democratic Convention, with a vote of 499,000.

Ellison telephoned both Norman Prosser and Bernie Holzheimer. Prosser told him the President's situation was 'serious'; the *New York Times* man used the term 'desperate'. Holzheimer wasn't given to hyperbole, either.

'When are we going to get the big story, Bill?'

Ellison ignored the question, although his pride was by now in a raw state. 'Aronson and the President are both aiming for the magic figure of 1,509 committed delegates at the

August convention. What's the state of play as of now?'

'So far 8.7 million Democrats have voted in the primaries. Of that vote, Aronson has 4 million, with 548 delegates; the President has 2.7 million, with 369 delegates. But the really big test comes on June 3 in California. Not only does that State return 217 delegates to the convention, but the winner on a plurality takes them all.

'In California defense industries are a big thing, although the generally liberal college vote is a factor, too. Aronson's local campaign vanguard are already equating the President's anxiety to secure Congressional ratification for the SALT 4 Treaty as bad news for employment in California. I have a reliable tip-off that Tatiana and her husband are not only scheduled to push Aronson on TV but also to make platform appearances in this, their home state.

'An equally reliable source in the White House informs me that the President is preparing to switch tack dramatically. He may even lay down an ultimatum to the Russians about Tatiana before voting day in California.'

'Christ.'

'Yes. It sure is bad, Bill.'

Later that afternoon Ellison talked to Massey. 'You'd better catch the first plane to California and stay there until Floris talks. Take Julie with you – she can be very useful.'

'In the circumstances, I'd rather have Joe.'

Ellison smiled sardonically. 'Handling two women isn't exactly a novel experience for you, Magnus.'

May, 1980. California

Magnus and Julie arrived at Los Angeles after a thirteen-hour flight over the Pole in the course of which Julie claimed to have photographed a polar bear from 36,000 feet.

'It'll turn out to be a white elephant,' he told her.

'Cruel man.'

In the airport bar, Charles Graves-Brown, who had just completed a pre-Olympic survey of West Coast track stars, handed over the keys of a hired car. Julie called him Gravity and made him blush to the roots of his hair: anyone or anything sexually desirable made the *Monitor*'s athletics correspondent blush.

'What's the latest on Tatiana and Karl Petersen?' Magnus asked him.

'Their performances have been good, although Tatiana is beginning to look tired – one coach at Glenmore used the dangerous word "stale". Indoor winter performances, of course, can be misleading: the maximum sprint distance is 60 metres, one circuit of the track is only 160 metres, and there's no way a decathlete can throw the discus or javelin in the confined space. So – '

Magnus touched Graves-Brown's arm affectionately. 'Just the gist, Charles.'

'In January, soon after their marriage, they both competed at the Sunkist International event on a track painted, believe it or not, orange and lemon yellow, before a crowd of 12,243. Tatiana won the 60 metres sprint, the broad jump, the high jump, the shot and the 800 metres.'

'Against hot competition?'

'Against the best. Including your friend Barbara Floris. I saw her two days ago, she was asking after you.'

Charles Graves-Brown winced and bravely stifled a groan as the toe of Magnus's shoe bit into his shin. The delicious Welsh girl wasn't looking at all pleased.

'Also in January, they both took part in the famous Philadelphia Track Classic. Tatiana's winning time in the 800 metres, 2.06, was exceptionally fast for an indoor track. But she was helped by a rabbit over the early laps.'

'A what, Charles?'

'A rabbit means a pace-maker over here. In March Karl won the pole vault at the NCAA indoor championships at the Cobo Arena.'

'That's the colleges?'

'In America all the top athletes belong to college teams, not clubs or areas as with us. The presence of Tatiana in the Glenmore women's team put it in really serious contention with the top squads like University of Texas-El Paso, which has won five times in six seasons, Washington State, the Cougars, who have those fantastic Kenyan long-distance runners, and Villanova, the Wild Cats. Tatiana notched up four tens and an eight: fantastic. The crowd went wild and the press went crazy.'

'And where did Ms Barbara Floris go?' Julie asked acidly.

Magnus turned gentle blue eyes on her. His voice was silk-soft. 'I don't suppose you have come all this way, at considerable expense to the *Monitor*, just to act out a parody of the jealous little wife.'

She fled in a flood of tears towards the door marked Exit. Magnus focused on Graves-Brown. 'Pray continue.'

'Don't you think – '

'She'll be back.'

Graves-Brown was a good-looking fellow, a fine athlete, a nice, decent chap. Why was it, when women walked away from him, which they often did, that they didn't come back?

'You said Tatiana notched up four tens and an eight. Translate.'

'At the NCAA championships the scoring goes 10-8-6-4-2-1. Her high jump of 6′ 2″ was her best ever; at the same time she's putting the shot right up into the sixties now. Fabulous. There's currently no one in the world to touch her – the only remote challenge comes from Renate Flack of East Germany and – well ...' He broke off and shrugged.

'Who?'

'I was going to say, "Barbara Floris". I'm convinced, you see, that she's not realizing her potential in competitions. She's holding back. One afternoon at Glenmore I wandered into the gymnasium. There was no one about except Floris: she was practising the high jump. As I walked in she went over the bar with a beautiful clean-lift Fosbury flop. I was standing in the doorway, she didn't see me for a while. She raised the bar and went over again, first attempt – at an incredible 6′ 1½″.'

'Is that incredible?'

'For a girl who had never bettered 5′ 10½″ in competition, yes. When she did finally see me she kind of scowled and stopped practising at once.'

'Good work, Watson.'

'What?'

'The Olympic Try-outs will be where?'

'At Mahlon Sweet Field, Eugene, Oregon – the University of Oregon track. On form Tatiana is sure to qualify. But Olympic trials are cruel. Take the famous case of Harrison Dillard, world record holder in his day for the 110 metres hurdles. Between May '47 and June '48 he won 82 consecutive hurdle races. But in the final Olympic Try-out he stumbled and failed to finish. As a result he was automatically excluded from the hurdles event at the London Olympics.'

'Point taken.'

The journey down to Glenmore wasn't much fun. Julie sat in the back of the Datsun and sulked all the way. Aware of what he had to do, Magnus feared that his precious relationship with Julie might go on the rocks down here, in southern California. Arriving at the Holiday Inn in Glenmore, he asked the reception desk for separate rooms. Inevitably, this provoked a new outburst.

'You're planning to bring that Barbara Floris woman here, is that it?'

'No.'

'Lying bastard! Is that the only way you can find things out – by screwing?'

He walked to his own room and phoned Floris.

'Hi!' she said cheerfully. 'It's my favourite Englishman. When do I see you? When do I feel you?'

He spent an hour with Julie, feeding white lies into her

sweet Welsh heart. Taking her small, perfect body in his arms, he showed her that in the New World everything is back to front: she loved it that way and milked him so hard that tides of moisture rippled down his body in harmony with the ebb and flow of her own pleasure. Then he ran her under the shower, dried her hair and handed her a letter from the editor of *Woman's Weekly* of London, commissioning Julie Beavan, freelance writer-photographer, to undertake a 3,000-word feature article on Tatiana Larin-Petersen.

'Her life, her love, her hopes, her fears, her man.'

'Doesn't sound like the Ellison-Massey style to me. What's the real angle, boyo?'

'You go take a close look at the Petersen domestic set-up. And if you can walk out of it with their cheque stubs and bank statements in your bra, I won't complain.'

'I don't wear a bra, sir.'

'And try her local supermarket. Americans love to talk – they believe in publicity.'

Later in the day he left a note for her: 'Sorry, my darling, urgent call from the big city, had to drive to LA, back tomorrow, Kisses.' He drove uptown to the smart middle-class suburb where Barbara Floris now lived. Six months ago she had changed apartments and cars: a four-roomed luxury duplex overlooking a park replaced her old downtown bed-sitter with a view of a service station, and a Mustang replaced her old VW beetle. He also cast an eye over her wardrobe while she was in the shower: there were definitely smart shops, even couturiers, in San Francisco, which had recently received visits from an international girl athlete with a problem – broad shoulders and narrow hips.

He didn't say anything about this new-found wealth, nor did she. But he noticed a twinkle in the slumgirl's fierce blue eyes.

Next day they drove in separate cars to the Glenmore College track, stopping on the way for her regular milkshakes and bacon pancakes. He bought a *Los Angeles Times* which carried the banner headline which he and Ellison had been dreading: MOSCOW BARS TATIANA. The Soviet Olympic Committee had finally sent a message to the USOC insisting that in no circumstances could a visa be granted to Mrs Tatiana Larin-Petersen were she to be selected to represent the United States at the 22nd Olympiad.

'Someone's just given me a gold medal,' Barbara Floris said without apparent emotion.

'What about the East German girls, and the other Russians?'

'They're just pussies stuffed with anabolic steroids.'

'And Sue Kitson?'

'*Who?*'

'Come on – the English girl who came third in the Britain-USA-USSR match last summer, remember?'

'Oh, *her*. She's got a good throwing arm but she couldn't jump over a bag of hay.'

'Have you seen her out here?' he asked casually.

'Should I have done?' Barbara Floris asked with sudden aggression. 'Do you have hot pants for her, too? How about trying Tatiana while you're about it? But watch out – there are some determined characters guarding *her* pussy.' She softened equally abruptly and kissed him. 'Don't look at me like that, smug bug. OK, Kitson *was* out here soon after Karl and that Russian bitch surfaced from England. She came down to the track to train for . . . hell, I can't remember how long . . . not long. I recall she gave some interview to the local paper and then vanished.'

'Which paper?'

'There's only one. The *Herald*.'

'Do you have the cutting?'

'I'm not a public library.'

'Who would the reporter be?'

'Ed Shields, he covers athletics.'

While Barbara drove on to the track, Magnus called in at the *Herald*. Shields was older than he had imagined, small, gnomelike, amiable.

'Coffee out of a paper cup, Magnus?'

'Thanks.'

He read through Shields's interview with Sue Kitson. Two points emerged: (a) she had been granted a year-long Sports scholarship at Glenmore; (b) she had been intimately involved in Tatiana's escape from the Russians in London. But she didn't specify how.

'Pity she didn't say more,' Magnus said.

Shields chuckled. 'She was prepared to – for five thousand bucks. A shrewd lady, that. We don't have that kind of money here, so we went to a famous East Coast paper offering to sell them the story. They wanted to see it first. I called Sue to make her the offer but she had vanished. Strange? Hasn't been seen for eight months. We all assumed she had returned to England. Homesick, maybe.'

'What about her apartment, her belongings?'

'Packed and gone, very tidy. I also checked with the utility companies: someone paid off her accounts.'

'Who?'

Shields smiled. 'They wouldn't say.'

'Can I make a collect call to England?'

'Go ahead.'

He got through to Joe O'Neill, who had already covered every angle on Kitson as a matter of routine: the Amateur Athletic Association, the secretary of the Belsize Ladies' Athletic Club, the flat in Ockenden Road, Dame Alice Proudfoot's School for Girls. All negative. She had vanished.

'Thanks, Joe. Keep checking, anyway.'

'The story of my life,' said the young man from Belfast in the voice whose only emotional variation was between gloom and despair.

Agency reports on the big Tatiana Larin-Petersen story

were chugging on to Ed Shields's desk. Questioned by reporters at Colorado Springs, a United States Olympic Committee spokesman admitted: 'This has to be the hottest potato ever to have landed in the USOC's lap.'

In Washington, a State Department spokesman strongly rejected the Soviet Olympic Committee's message and called on the Soviet Government to consider carefully the implications of barring an American athlete in contravention of the IOC's rules. But the spokesman declined to spell out those implications. 'We are, after all, a nation of immigrants,' he added.

In Lausanne, the International Olympic Committee Secretariat refused to comment.

In Moscow, the Soviet news agency Tass put out a statement by Foreign Minister Andrei Gromyko describing the whole Tatiana Larin affair as a 'gross provocation engineered by reactionary circles determined to wreck the Olympics and to sabotage peaceful co-existence'.

'Gromyko could be right, for once,' Magnus murmured.

Something of a silence followed. And then Ed Shields had a word to say.

'Magnus, I'll be frank with you – it's no use fishing with me. Sol Enders keeps Glenmore athletics afloat; Glenmore's track team is the pride of Glenmore College; Glenmore College is the glory of Glenmore. And the *Herald* would be out of business overnight if it ever forgot that.'

Magnus drove to the college track to watch Karl and Tatiana Petersen in training. He wasn't alone: at least two dozen other photographers and pressmen had showed up, hoping to learn the Russian star's reaction to the new Soviet move.

She didn't surface at first. Karl Petersen arrived alone in his new Thunderbird, brushing the reporters aside with a sour, almost limp gesture. It was the first time that Magnus had studied Petersen's face at close quarters: a weak, spoilt, petulant face, painted with vanity. The reporters were persistent.

'Where's your wife this morning, Karl?'

'How do you read the Soviet ban, Karl?'

'Do you feel the USOC statement is fully supportive?'

'Karl, can you clarify your exact relationship with Sol Enders?'

Petersen's face suddenly reddened. 'Why don't you motherfuckers go fuck yourselves,' he snarled, marching into the clubhouse.

'Can't print that,' grinned the reporter next to Magnus.

Petersen and his coach devoted the first half-hour of training to the pole vault run-up. With the modern, 5-metre glass-fibre pole, the higher the grip the vaulter can take on the pole, the better – so long as he can still control the thrust of the pole into the plant box. Using a grip of about 4.50 metres from the end of the pole, Petersen was now generating formidable kinetic energy at the moment of the plant and achieving vaults of 5.2 metres.

The reporters had to be impressed.

Even so, there was an idle, listless quality in Karl Petersen. He seemed too conscious of the photographers. Finely built an athlete though he was, there was something effeminate about his walk – and he ran his hand through his corn-coloured hair too often.

'You keep expecting the guy to whip out a pocket mirror halfway over the bar,' the American photographer crouching next to Magnus remarked.

Towards mid-morning Tatiana drove up in her Porsche 924. The assembled reporters, who instantly converged on her, whistled softly as she climbed out of the car: tinted hair, heavy make-up, skin-tight leopardskin pants, platform shoes, she was scarcely recognizable. The shadows under her eyes suggested a night spent weeping vodka. The face of this Russian girl, once so shy, modest, and innocent, was now possessed by worldly cynicism.

At the other side of the track, Karl Petersen glanced across, shrugged, continued with his training: it didn't take a genius to divine that the couple had been quarrelling. Tatiana took a packet of Kent cigarettes from her bag, lit one with a pearl lighter and pink finger nails, then turned to the reporters.

'You want my reaction to this visa business? Sure, I'm bitter,' she said. 'Either you fight for freedom or you don't deserve it. This morning's statement by the USOC from Colorado Springs made me throw up. It gets me here, right here, in the *gut* –' savagely she stabbed her muscular abdomen – 'to witness this rank, snivelling cowardice. I can tell you this: Brezhnev, Kosygin and Gromyko will be laughing like drains this morning. I know those men; I was brought up under the Soviet system; I was indoctrinated in the Communist ideology from an early age. They don't believe in God, or the soul, or the conscience: a materialist believes only in naked force and cunning. The only thing he respects in an opponent is ruthlessness.'

'To be fair, Tatiana, the State Department did say –'

'They said nothing. What do you expect: Washington is crawling with pink pansies and Ivy League perverts –'

Uproar. This was dynamite! The Russian girl was talking the language of the late Senator Joe McCarthy!

'Tatiana, do you feel you have been betrayed?'

'That's exactly what I feel.'

'Who betrayed you, Tatiana?'

'When Karl and I decided to get married, we were promised that if the Russians tried to bar me from the Olympics, the United States would boycott the Games and bring the Russians to their senses.'

Uproar again.

'Who promised you that, Tatiana?'

'Was there a deal?'

'Was it Sol Enders, Tatiana?'

'Was it the CIA?'

The world record holder seemed to recoil now, realizing

for the first time, perhaps, how far she had gone. She was looking for a route of escape from the microphones and cameras when two big cars swept into the car park with a screeching of tyres, the rear car disgorging a half-dozen plainclothes agents who kicked and elbowed their way into the throng of reporters, swinging punches, kicking shins and smashing cameras, then picked Tatiana up bodily and carried her towards their car, surrounded by enraged, clamouring newsmen.

Instinctively Magnus had made a dash for the front car, a Lincoln convertible, while everyone's attention was diverted by the angry mêlée round the star athlete. His hand rapped the offside front window of the car less than a second before his Nikon EL2 automatic, set at 1/500th, came up at hip level to flash repeatedly at the faces turned towards it inside the car. He didn't even have time to look inside with the naked eye before a powerful hand grabbed his collar. Magnus swung round.

He knew this man. Here was a face he would never forget – a massive neck and shoulders topped by a small, delicate head; porcelain-white skin, a pencil moustache. 'He always looks,' Ellison had commented as they studied the photographs of Pieter Jacobsdal that Magnus had taken at the Hillingdon playing field, 'as if he was dreaming of the last time he raked his studs across the face of an opponent trapped at the bottom of a loose maul.'

Pieter Jacobsdal, who had escorted Ellison into the presence of General Hendrik van den Bergh, head of BOSS; Pieter Jacobsdal, captured by the MPLA in Angola, who had shared a cell with Ray Lawson.

Pieter Jacobsdal, who had tried to kill Massey in the Euston Road.

Magnus's boot flew hard into the South African's groin, drawing an agonized gasp, an instant doubling up; lovingly he brought the weight of his camera down on Jacobsdal's carotid artery. The BOSS agent rolled over on the ground, clutching his stomach. Bending low, he whispered in the man's ear, 'You black Commie coon,' then pulled back as a second South African agent, enraged, drew a gun. The man was immediately overwhelmed by a phalanx of outraged reporters, not all of whom were as unfit as they looked.

'Get going, Magnus,' someone said.

He drove out of town fast, to Oceanside, where he anxiously supervised the processing of his film by an employee of Fotofast Services, Inc. Rarely had he shot a subject of which he had no view at all; rarely had he awaited the emergent positive images with such curiosity.

'Looks like they resented your presence,' the employee commented, scrutinizing the prints.

Magnus sent off two sets of prints by registered airmail – one to the *Monitor*, one to Chester Place – then put the third set on the wire-photo machine in the local UPI office.

He found Julie sulking in her room at the Holiday Inn, buried under West Coast women's mags full of male nudes, and assured her he had spent the night in LA with a *New York Times* stringer called Bob. 'You can phone him if you like.'

'As if I would. You men always cover for one another.' But the dimples had come back into her cheeks now; she even let him nibble her ear while they were waiting for their Spanish omelettes. But he said nothing about the morning's events, even though physical violence was profoundly repugnant to his nature and always left him shaken for hours afterwards.

'Any luck with Tatiana, by the way?'

'Luck, say you! She was delighted to see me, boyo, needed the company; I've never drunk so much vodka, I could hardly take a note by the time I was through. She spent half an hour on the phone berating Sol Enders for having miscalculated the State Department position. Then phone calls kept coming from right-wing pressure groups, Jewish groups, and the campaign managers for the various Presidential candidates. They all want her to make personal appearances on their behalf during the California primary. She said to me: "How the hell do they expect me to keep fit and behave like a film star?" She's very Americanized. She drinks too much, too. I said to her: "How did you like your wedding, Mrs Petersen; wasn't it lovely with all those flowers and photographers, but I bet you missed your parents, though, such a shame, what with Karl having no family." '

Magnus touched Julie's hand across the table. 'Good girl.'

'She began to cry, then. She showed me a photo of her parents and her sisters; her dad's an engineer, her mum's a teacher. She stared at me with red eyes, holding the bottle permanently in one hand, then she said, very slurred: "Karl's father is still alive. Karl sees him secretly. Karl thinks he's a great man. What kind of a man refuses to come to his son's wedding? And Karl's uncle, too, why didn't he come, eh?" She looked at me as if I were responsible. Then she said: "Karl hates America. He despises America. He believes in eugenics." Tatiana filled her glass. "So do I," she said.'

'You deserve a carrot,' Magnus said.

'She was very drunk, that Tatiana. Very unhappy. It's awful when you marry the wrong man, isn't it?' Julie gave Magnus a long, searching look. 'But it may be more awful when you don't marry him.'

Later, at 16:20 Pacific Time, 00:20 GMT, he put through a call to Ellison's unlisted number in Chester Place. At the first purr the receiver was lifted.

'You were awake then?' Magnus said.

'No, I'm still asleep as a matter of fact. It's a trick you'll learn. Joe brought me the Mufax print-offs of your day's work half-an-hour ago. I must say, our Tatiana looks unrecognizable. What are her recent performances in training like?'

'So far, good. But her coaches are worried – it's an open secret. What about my shots of the people in the Lincoln convertible: anyone you know?'

'Item: a certain Ray Lawson, CIA operative deeply involved with Pretoria during the Angola fiasco of '75, until recently accredited to the US Embassy in London. Item: a certain Hans Kruger, of the South African Department of Information. Item: a dark-haired lady known to me in more senses than one as Ruth Leonhard. You may wonder what Pru thinks of that – as soon as I saw your shots I decided to receive your call in the spare room.'

'Jacobsdal was on hand, too. I kicked him into touch.'

'Literally? Are you serious?'

'Yes. And I was inside my own twenty-five at the time, too.'

'You're in trouble. Any luck with Floris?'

'Give me time!'

'Time is what we haven't got.' The receiver went down in London.

Magnus knew that the man on the other end of the line would be asleep again before his head hit the pillow. What he didn't know was that before the night was out the ground-floor windows of the house in Chester Place would be raked by machine-gun fire.

The accompanying note which came through the door contained just two words: 'DROP IT.'

CHAPTER 16

May, 1980. London

The voice on the line sounded familiar, perhaps someone he had known or met a few years ago; it was a strained, frightened voice, unwilling to divulge its name on the telephone, begging for help, hinting darkly at disclosures involving dramatic repercussions. The voice of an English-speaking South African.

'If you won't come to the *Monitor*, meet me at my club at four o'clock this afternoon. It's the Oxford and Cambridge in Pall Mall. Take care not to get yourself followed.'

Ellison phoned Jack Knight. 'I think it's a man called Paul Shrivers, though I couldn't be sure on the phone. I'd like you to come, just to listen.' Then, betraying the underlying drift of his thoughts, he could not help adding: 'And Chaim Leonhard, is he still alive – according to Tretiakov?'

'Just.'

'Squash court bar, Jack, four o'clock.'

Ellison then rang Emile Angel at the offices of the South African Non-Racial Olympic Committee, which had recently enjoyed an unusually long spell free from burglaries and bomb incidents. 'We must be losing our touch,' Angel had laughed. Ellison interpreted the respite along different lines. If South Africa had secretly dropped her campaign to gain admission to the 1980 Olympics, why bother to attack those who worked to keep her out?

When Paul Shrivers was shown into the squash court bar by the desk porter, Ellison and Knight were already waiting for him.

'You remember me, Mr Ellison?' the South African asked obsequiously.

'Yes, Mr Shrivers. May I introduce a friend of mine, Mr Knight?'

'A friend?' Shrivers was rigid with suspicion.

'Yes. What will you drink?'

'A scotch, please. Make it a double.' Shrivers lit a cigarette with a shaking hand. 'I'll be perfectly honest with you, Mr Ellison.'

Ellison examined the man's features. The sporting suntan had faded, crow's feet had broken out, the flesh round the jaw was looser now; the sleek blond hair looked dry and scruffy, what was left of it. The eyes were bloodshot, the fingers stained with nicotine.

'We had a Prime Minister here. Every time he used the word "honest", one knew he was about to tell a lie.'

'But I'm on the level. I have to be.'

'As I recall, you were a leading light in the Fair Play Campaign, a successful businessman, and an energetic publisher of *The Flag*, and *National Life*. You were tied-in with Hendrik van der Groot and with Hans Kruger, of the Department of Information. And now?'

'All that's over now. I'm an exile, on the run. The South African Government want to have me extradited from this country. I have reason to believe that the British police are looking for me. I need your help.' Shrivers lit a new cigarette from the butt of the old one. 'I always knew it was a mistake to try and bribe you. I told van der Groot and Kruger, they wouldn't listen....' He paused, glanced round the empty bar and lowered his voice. 'There's a warrant out for my arrest in South Africa.'

At that moment Emile Angel walked in with his bushy beard and vast shoulders. There was no question of him shaking hands with Shrivers, though Shrivers would at that moment have made love to a rattlesnake if the other party had been willing.

'What will you drink?' Ellison asked Emile.

'Pint of bitter.'

Ellison stared at his guest's waist-line. 'How about half a glass of water with a slice of lemon?' He turned to the barman. 'Pint of bitter.'

'Look,' said Shrivers, 'I'm going to be perfectly honest about this.'

'So you said.'

'The Fair Play Campaign was always, from the very outset, a project of the Minister of Sport and the Department of Information. Kruger was the link man. Van der Groot put in some of his own money. He was our cover, if you like. I was the honorary treasurer. OK, I'll be honest with you: some of that money found its way into my private business enterprises.'

'How much?'

'Say Rand 3 million.'

'When did they find out?'

'One thing leads to another.'

'Philosophy I don't need.'

'They found out after the decision was taken to wind up the Fair Play Campaign. The Commission of Inquiry investigating the Information Department scandals took a look at the FPC's accounts. . . .'

'And they had some questions to ask you?'

'I didn't wait to see. I sent my family abroad on holiday, shipped out what assets I could strip off my businesses in a week, and hopped it.'

'How did you get out?'

'By private plane. From Maseru in Lesotho. I had taken that precaution.'

'Why was the decision taken to wind up the Fair Play Campaign?'

Shrivers glanced nervously from Ellison to Knight to Angel. His hands, once accustomed to gripping rugby balls, cricket bats and tennis rackets, now twisted and untwisted in a ceaseless dance of anxiety.

'I don't suppose I could have the other half? Would it be quite out of the question for me to pay?'

'Another double scotch,' Ellison told the barman.

'The FPC was always a Government smokescreen,' Shrivers said.

'We know that,' Angel said. 'Ellison asked you why the Government chose to wind it up.'

'When the Broederbond decided there was no way back into the Olympics. The Russians had double-crossed us.'

'So there really was a deal made at Vienna in '74?'

'Certainly.'

'I always told you,' Angel said to Ellison. 'Joe Mutobo and Patrick Okie also told you. You wouldn't listen.'

'You see, gentlemen,' Shrivers continued ingratiatingly, 'the Broederbond had decided by the end of '78 that South Africa's survival as a White State depended on sabotaging détente between Russia and America. The situation was intolerable! There was the Sovet Union arming the Patriotic Front terrorists in Rhodesia and the Swapo terrorists in Namibia, while Carter, Vance and the black Marxist Andrew Young were lending these same terrorists moral support and diplomatic assistance! Quite intolerable!'

There was a twinkle in Emile Angel's eye. 'Andrew Young is no Marxist. He believes in free enterprise and says so constantly.'

'That's what he says but –'

Angel held up a huge index finger as in warning. 'I think Mr Shrivers is forgetting that Mr Ellison only buys double scotches for certified liberals.'

'Well –'

'So the aim was to sabotage détente,' Ellison said. 'To drive the Americans back into a Cold War posture in southern Africa. To force the United States to shore up the white regimes in Rhodesia and the Republic. Of course, you had one powerful ally in the highest counsels of the American Government.'

Shrivers nodded. 'Brzezinski, Security Adviser to the President.'

'And you say the decision was taken by the Broederbond?' Angel said.

'Every important decision in South Africa is taken by the fifteen-man executive council of the Broederbond, the Band of Brothers. There you have the ruling elite: 11,980 members, including the President, the Prime Minister, every Cabinet minister except two, the vast majority of the 175-man Nationalist Party caucus, the leading Dominees of the Dutch Reformed Church, the heads of almost all the Afrikaans schools and universities, the head of the defence forces, of BOSS, of state radio and television, of the Iron and Steel Corporation ... need I go on? They are the self-appointed custodians of Afrikaaner power. They operate under conditions of complete secrecy.'

'Now, Mr Shrivers, you want my help,' Ellison said.

'Here's a paradox, Mr Ellison. I'm on the run, in hiding. Yet I need publicity. I want you to convince the British public that there's a political basis to my case. It isn't just that I misappropriated public funds....'

'You calculate that the British Government won't attempt to extradite you to South Africa if it can be shown that you're a genuine bedouin opponent of apartheid?'

'Apartheid is something I have always abhorred. Many of my best friends, I assure you, are black.'

Emile Angel almost collapsed laughing.

'The thing is,' Shrivers said, leaning towards Ellison with a desperate intensity, 'that I know too much.'

'You do? What do you know?'

At this indication of Ellison's interest Shrivers leaned back in his chair, lit another cigarette with a steady hand, smiled, gaining in confidence by the moment. He was ready to bargain now – even to enjoy bargaining.

'What I ask of you is a story in next Sunday's *Monitor* depicting Paul Shrivers as a political exile persecuted by one of the most ruthless regimes in the world. If you do me proud, Mr Ellison, I'll sing like a lark.' He winked. 'Exclusive.'

'But what will you sing about?'

'How the Russian girl operation was set up, who is involved, how the link with the CIA was forged, how Larin and Petersen were lifted out of Britain, how the Jews were manipulated. . . .' He smiled, basking in the glow of their close attention. 'Did you ever consider Karl Petersen's ancestry . . . on his father's side?'

'And would you be able to tell me how you recruited a young woman whose initials are RL?'

The knowing leer that Shrivers gave him made his stomach turn over. 'You have a deal,' Ellison snapped.

Later he walked with Jack Knight up Pall Mall. 'Well, are you convinced yet?'

'I'll have a word with Tretiakov.'

May, 1980. California

Magnus awoke from a painfully deep sleep. Although he never touched alcohol and didn't smoke, his head felt like a dustbin; it was several minutes before he identified the source of his migraine in Barbara Floris's all-American central heating.

She was exercising on the floor, punishing her body through a series of isometric muscle contractions at 40–50 per cent of her maximum strength. He lay there, watching her progress through four sets of finger-tip press-ups, each set containing fifteen repetitions, followed by a series of full squats with a 40-kilo barbell across her shoulders.

'It's a lovely pad, yours,' he said.

'I have a sugar daddy. Don't interrupt me. Women with small brains find it hard to concentrate, didn't you know that?'

He smiled. When he had first encountered Floris in the Kensington Hilton his dominant impression had been one of crass vulgarity; of a vagina like a sucker plant surrounded by a sierra of muscle. But the more he knew Barbara the more he admired and liked her; he could make love to her now with a dimension of genuine affection, even tenderness. She sensed it; she thrived on it.

She came out of the shower half-wet, pulled back the sheet covering his recumbent body and took him in her hand. 'Want to know who my sugar daddy is, English?' He came erect. 'So you do, eh?' Tumescent, he began to swell and throb under the sly art of her fingers. 'You really do want to know!' Her large breasts with their hard, swollen nipples swayed over his face as she straddled him.

'Say you love me.'

'I love you.'

'Say it better. Say it real, Magnus.'

A familiar voice, Ellison's, urged him on. Every day that passed now jeopardized the peace of the world.

'I adore you, Barbara.' He reached to touch her in a certain spot in a certain way; as usual she came on uncontrollably, crying out, then falling into the pillow as if felled by a rock.

Time is what we don't have, Ellison reminded him.

'I'd like to marry you, Barbara, if you'll have me.' He lay still, crippled by self-disgust.

Her head remained buried in the pillow. When she looked at him there was a vast noon of happiness in her eyes. 'What are your prospects, sir?'

'Poor.'

'Sol Enders is my sugar daddy,' she said. Gently her hand caressed his face. 'But you don't have to be jealous, I don't shack up with Sol. I simply handed over a dozen letters and a packet of photographs. Sol gave me one duplex, one Ford Mustang, plus $6,000 and a contract.'

'Terms?'

'To turn pro after Moscow. All I have to do is take the Olympic silver or bronze.'

'Not the gold?'

'That's reserved for the Russian bitch.'

'He made that clear?'

'Very clear indeed. After Moscow she and I both join the Enders Circus and travel the world in undying rivalry, me strutting about like a witch in platinum hair and scarlet tights while she bows her modest head and dresses in pure white.'

'Humiliating, Barbara.'

'Listen, English, I was born very low down at the bottom of the heap. I've know a week without food. I saw my father die of consumption. If I've got to wear scarlet pants to earn $40,000 a year, I'll wear scarlet pants.'

'Enders has offered you that much?'

'Yeah. But nobody knows except you. I'm an amateur, remember? I'm trusting you, Magnus, as I never trusted anyone.'

'Why did Sol Enders want your letters and photos so badly?'

'Because they were from Karl.'

'So?'

'Don't be dumb. Sol knew I was real upset when that jerk stood me up for a cheap tart from the Soviet Union. He came to see me about it . . . I guess he was shit scared I might go to the press and cash in. Mr and Mrs Karl Petersen are nothing but properties in the portfolio of Enders International Promotions, Inc . . . in case you want to know.' She sat up in bed, cross-legged, and studied Magnus with deep, ungovernable affection. 'Gosh, you're real nice,' she whispered. 'When do we get married? Today?'

'Why not?'

For a moment, a decisive moment, she read him – then jumped halfway across the room, removed a side panel from the refrigerator in the kitchen and returned to the bedroom carrying a package of papers and photographs wrapped in a plastic bin-bag. She tossed it into Magnus's lap.

'That's the Karl archive, sweetie.'

'But I thought you handed it all over to Enders?'

'Yeah. I did. But I took a set of photocopies first. Go on, go on, open it.'

Instinctively he reached first for the photographs.

One still, 6″ × 4″, dominated his attention. It showed a young athlete, carried on a stretcher, raising himself up on his left elbow, by a great effort of will, to give the Hitler salute. His fanatical eyes were fixed rigid on some distant point, probably on the *Führer* himself, high in the Olympic stadium. The young athlete's face was torn between the agony of the injury he had sustained and the ecstasy of hero-worship.

'Who's this?' Magnus asked.

'Karl wouldn't say. Karl's a real nasty Nazi, by the way.'

Magnus was now looking at another photograph, depicting Petersen in the company of two young men and a black Labrador. Extracting a magnifying lens from his camera bag, he focussed it on the floppy bush hat that Petersen was wearing.

'Did he ever discuss the emblem on the front of that hat?' Magnus asked.

'He used to drool over it, you know; something big in his manly life, I couldn't figure out what....'

The magnification showed an emblem-standard at the top of which was an osprey with outstretched wings. Below it were two bull horns bound in elephant hide, and a zebra skin. From the tips of the bull horns extended wildebeest tails on silver chains. There were two words: Pamwe Chete.

'Why did you call him a real Nazi?'

'He hates blacks. I told you that. Two seasons ago I got an

invitation to compete in Durban, South Africa, all expenses paid, first-class hotel, wow! The AAU here said I couldn't go because of apartheid. Karl blew his top: he called the AAU a bunch of nigger-loving Commies.'

'He used the word "nigger"?'

'Maybe. I don't know. He had a whole dictionary of words for blacks.'

'Like?'

She shrugged. 'I'm no scholar.'

'Was "kaffir" one of the words he used?'

'Yes.'

'And "coon"?'

'Spot on. Where did you get all this? Are you a Nazi, too?'

'How about "munt"?'

'You scored three out of three.'

Magnus turned his attention to a small pile of letters that Barbara had received from her lover during the Glenmore vacations. They were all postmarked 'London SW1'. It didn't take long to read through them: Whatever his gifts as a decathlete, Petersen was no Shakespeare.

'Not one of these letters carries the same date as the postmark on the envelope.'

'Well, it was always a miracle he wrote at all. I guess he often started a letter and didn't finish it till later . . . or maybe he just forgot to post it.'

'Barbara, in three instances the postmark date from London SW1 *anticipates* the date on the letter.'

'So what! Karl's dumb, he gets things wrong, just like I do.'

'Did you ever write to Karl during the college vacations?'

'Did I write! I wrote twice a day.'

'Starting when?'

'Starting the day he left for London.'

'Yet not one of the letters he wrote during the short Christmas vacations acknowledges receipt of a letter of yours.'

She shrugged. 'Karl's like that. What *is* all this, anyway, this interrogation? You sound like Scotland Yard.' Her antagonism, however illogical, was rising dangerously: she still loved Karl Petersen, albeit with a bitter, twisted hate mixed in to it.

'Listen, Barbara, you'd be wise to get rid of those photocopies.'

'Oh sure! Sure! And give them to your fucking quality nooosepepper!'

'Burn them. In making those photocopies you double-crossed Sol Enders. If they ever find out, they might kill you.'

'Balls. Sol wouldn't hurt a fly.'

'Sol might not. But the men behind him would. Look what happened to Sue Kitson.'

'Nothing *happened* to her. She's probably back in London trying to jump over a bag of hay.'

'No. She's nowhere. I've checked it out: she vanished because she knew too much.' He was dressed now and combing his hair in the bathroom. 'Ever noticed any odd characters hanging about since you moved in here?' He could see her in the mirror, standing behind him. Her rage had ebbed as rapidly as it had arrived.

She nodded. 'They look like . . . hell, G-men, I don't know. They never bother me. They're just there . . . sometimes.' She put her arms round his neck. 'Sorry I was sore with you.'

'Can I take the photos?'

She kissed him. 'Sure.'

It was a ten-foot jump from her rear balcony to the garden below. Scaling the wall, he edged to the corner of the building, took stock, then made a break for it, sprinting fast across the fifty yards that separated him from a sheltering copse. Cutting down back alleys towards the ocean, he managed to pick up a taxi on the Pacific highway. The Datsun that Graves-Brown had hired from Avis he intended to leave where it now stood, four blocks from Barbara's duplex.

'Stop at the first pay phone,' he told the driver. The taxi halted outside a drugstore.

He called Julie at the Holiday Inn.

'Where were you last night, boyo?' she said coolly. How's Ms Floris this morning? Well serviced, I trust.'

'Shut up. I'm short of dimes.'

'Dimes or dames?'

'Who have you talked to since I last saw you?'

'*You* ask *me* that, you bastard, why you –'

'Has anyone approached you with personal questions about me?'

'Only an extravagantly pretty lady journalist called Jane who claimed she had met you years ago in London and wanted to know what you were doing here. Another of your conquests, I assume.'

'Describe her.'

'Medium height, slender, dark curly hair, brown eyes, American to judge by her accent. Said she worked for CBS and asked whether you were the photographer involved in the fight at Glenmore track yesterday. Were you, boyo?'

'Did she make any arrangement to see you again?'

'Begged me to call her at the Sheraton as soon as you surfaced.'

Ruth Leonhard.

'OK. Pack you cameras, your film, your notebooks, your typewriter and your travellers' cheques. Leave your clothes. Instruct the reception desk to tell anyone who calls that we'll both be back this evening. Then take a cab to the UPI offices at Oceanside.'

He climbed back into the waiting taxi. 'Fotofast Services, Drayville Street, Oceanside,' he told the driver.

At Fotofast, Inc., the young employee greeted him with a broad grin. 'You must be famous.'

'Why?'

'Two people came in yesterday afternoon asking whether

you had been here to develop any photos. They said that your name was Mr Massey and they were friends of yours.'

'Describe them.'

'Pretty lady with dark hair, man with a funny accent ... could have taken him for a G-man.'

'What kind of an accent?'

'I don't know how to describe it. Not any kind of American accent I'd recognize; not the kind of English English accent you have; but not a foreign accent either, if you know what I mean.'

'Did he talk to you like I'm talking to you now, with short, clipped vowels and a soft tone, a mild, guttural "twang" in the voice, like this?'

'Hey! That's just it! Brilliant!'

'What did you tell them?'

'Said I'd never seen you in my life.'

'Why did you say that?'

'Because I remembered one of those shots of yours, you know, those angry folk glaring out of that car. And I kind of recalled that this pretty woman who came in here with him was in that photo.'

Magnus put ten dollars on the counter. 'Thanks.'

The employee pushed it back haughtily. 'My profession,' he said with injured dignity, 'has its ethical basis like any other.'

Magnus nodded. 'Sorry.'

'After all, sir, if I'd taken your money I'd have taken theirs.' He paused dramatically. 'They offered me more than ten dollars. A great deal more.'

Magnus walked to the nearest post office, cursing himself for having told Julie to meet him at UPI. It was too obvious, just the kind of place they would keep under surveillance. He put a call through to London, chafing at the delay. It was now 09:15 Pacific Time, 17:15 GMT.

Cherry answered. 'Bill's out, darling, and no way can I track him down. But I do take shorthand.'

'Yes, but do you have the required security clearance?'

She giggled. 'I'm waiting. Like all the other women. How's your Welsh rarebit, anyway?'

For five minutes he dictated notes on the progress made that morning with Barbara Floris; then, still fascinated by the unsolved enigma of the emblem on Karl Petersen's bush hat, he asked the West Coast operator to get him the London offices of the South African Non-Racial Olympic Committee. Abruptly a fifteen minute delay on calls to London surfaced. 'I'll wait,' he said, grimly standing his ground in the post office cubicle and drumming his fingers impatiently on the ledge. Julie would by now have arrived at the UPI office and would be sitting sweetly about like the proverbial duck. They were short, very short of time. He was on the verge of abandoning the call when the instrument made a beckoning noise.

'Your London number is ringing,' the operator said.

'SANROC,' said a voice.

'Is Emile Angel there?'

'Sure. Hold on.'

'Greetings, stranger,' boomed Angel.

Without mentioning Karl Petersen by name, Magnus described in detail the figures and symbols on the hat badge emblem worn in the photo by Petersen, and then felt something like a fool when Angel burst into deep, rumbling laughter.

'Man, what you have just described is the regimental emblem of the nastiest tracker unit in the world: Rhodesia's Selous Scouts. They specialize in knocking off missionaries and then blaming the guerrillas. As trainees they learn to live among wild animals and to drain the stomachs of antelopes for food. One of them, a South African called Captain Christoph Schulenberg, is the only holder of Rhodesia's Grand Cross of Valour. He is always photographed at ceremonies with his back to the camera. The Selous Scouts revel in secrecy. The motto "Pamwe Chete" is Shona for "Forward Together".' More laughter rolled in across the Atlantic.

'What amuses you, Emile?' Magnus said curtly.

'You sleuth, ha, ha! Didn't you know that ever since Haight Ashbury became the hippie Mecca in the sixties, the regimental emblems of Nazi and Fascist units have been worn as a chic cult?'

This friendly derision stung Magnus, robbing him of his judgement. 'Well, this one was worn by someone who isn't my idea of a hippie: Karl Petersen.'

'Holy cow!' roared Emile Angel. 'Hold on, Magnus, God will pay the phone bill. We have a joint SANROC-Christian Aid Committee in session here and this is something they have to hear.'

An alarm bell sounded in Magnus's head but it was too late to call Emile back to the phone. He could hear the huge man's baritone booming round the room. Presently Angel returned.

'One comrade here doubts very much whether it means anything. He suspects that young Petersen paid a visit to Haight Ashbury, period. Or one of his many girl friends did.'

'Who's the comrade?'

Emile Angel's voice fell to a confidential whisper. 'Armand Krohl,' he said.

Magnus walked back to the UPI office in Main Street, his heart hammering. A large car was parked outside – he recognized the Lincoln Continental, whose occupants he had photographed the day before at the Glenmore track car park. Two men were standing on either side of the car, studying his approach.

Hans Kruger.

Pieter Jacobsdal.

He was within twenty feet of the Lincoln when a voice spoke quietly but authoritatively from behind him.

'Mr Massey, I think it's time we had a serious talk,' Ray Lawson said.

Lawson opened the rear door of the car. Two women were sitting inside.

One reached out to Magnus with passionate relief.
Julie Beavan.
One regarded him with sardonic contempt.
Ruth Leonhard.

CHAPTER 17

May, 1980. London

Jordan and Ellison decided, after a conference of the inner editorial cabinet, to run the Shrivers story on page 4, down six column inches, without a byline: 'Preliminary investigations suggest that the self-exiled South African businessman Paul Shrivers, whose extradition from Britain is sought by Pretoria, nominally on a charge of embezzling public funds, is now a target of South Africa's political police. . . .'

He met Shrivers by arrangement on the deserted Sunday morning platform of Warren Street tube station. The South African looked grey, haunted; his eyes were never still and his breath was rank with overnight whisky.

They took an empty compartment on the southbound train.

'I thought you'd give me more space, more of a push,' Shrivers complained.

'Better to build you up week-by-week.' Ellison sat back and waited.

Shrivers lit a cigarette. 'You want the whole story, then – Operation Russian Girl?'

Ellison nodded.

'Fifty thousand,' Shrivers said. And sat quivering.

'I thought we'd get to that. If the material is good, ten would be the outside.'

'Forty, then.'

'Ten.'

'In cash.'

'We don't carry that kind of money round. You get a contract. You deliver. You get paid. But if you want ten, you'd better whet my appetite now.'

'A young South African athlete broke his leg in the hurdles at the Berlin Olympics. Do you know about that incident?'

'No,' Ellison said. Even now he could not discount the possibility that Kruger had Shrivers on a string.

'As he was carried off in agony, he raised himself up and delivered the Hitler salute to the *Führer*. After the Nationalist Party came to power in South Africa, the Broederbond had the episode scissored out of all the newspaper libraries.'

'Are you a member of the Broederbond, Mr Shrivers?'

Shrivers smiled thinly. 'I'm not an Afrikaaner, am I.'

'Why did they go to so much trouble?'

'Because the athlete concerned, having spent the war in South Africa as a clandestine Nazi agent, later settled in Europe under deep cover. Amsterdam family import-export business. His step-father and half-brother had been interned in South Africa, like Vorster and van den Bergh, as Nazi sympathizers.'

'How about some names now?'

'How about thirty thousand pounds?'

'Ten at the outside.'

'I could go to Powerstock on the *Dispatch*.'

'In that event the *Monitor* would be morally obliged to press for your immediate extradition to South Africa.'

He caught Shrivers's expression out of the corner of his eye; in the end a man will assume that the world is no better than he is.

Although Ellison cleared the £10,000 payment to Shrivers with Ramsay Jordan, he didn't hear from the South African the following day or the day after that. His anxiety mounted: for here, potentially, was the ultimate inside squealer, a real blow-torch.

On Wednesday the call came through shortly after eleven. 'You've prepared the contract?' Shrivers said.

'No problem.'

'I've hired a car: a yellow Ford Escort, registration number SWE 776T. We'll take a night drive. You'll find me parked on the Thames Embankment at Cheyne Walk, fifty yards west of Battersea Bridge.'

'Facing which way?'

'Facing west. Make it ten p.m.

At three minutes past ten Joe O'Neill's Allegro moved slowly along the Embankment – this wasn't a rendezvous that Ellison was anxious to make alone.

'There she is, then,' Joe murmured. 'SWE 776T.'

'Drive past her fairly fast, Joe.'

Ellison saw only one man in the Ford, Paul Shrivers himself, seated behind the steering wheel, staring fixedly down the road in front of him.

'Drive round the block, come at him from behind again and pull in level with him.'

'Didn't seem to be anyone else about.'

'Maybe.'

Joe turned and made his second run-in, slower this time. When the two cars were parallel, he stopped.

Slowly, Ellison wound down his side window. But Shrivers, only three feet away, showed no awareness of his proximity, continuing to stare fixedly along Cheyne Walk.

'It seems as if he's drugged,' O'Neill said. 'I'll take a look.'

Ellison caught his arm as he began to climb out. 'No you don't, Joseph, I'm not sending any late-night cables to your people in Belfast. Just drive me to Chelsea Police Station in Lucan Place.'

Two hours later the Bomb Squad opened up the booby-trapped car and extracted the corpse of Paul Shrivers. BOSS had moved again.

'At your age,' Jordan said, 'it's madness. Suicide.'

'What do you mean, my age? Don't forget I'm young enough to be your grandson.'

'What does Pru say?'

'Look, I have to get at Ventner himself. Only then can we make the whole thing stick together sufficiently to go to press. And the only way I can get into Rhodesia is overland, via Mozambique, with a Zanu patrol. If I took a flight to Salisbury, I'd be arrested on arrival. Joe Mutobo is prepared to help. So I'm going.'

'But Maputo is swarming with South African technicians and BOSS agents. That means the Selous Scouts will be waiting for you when you try and cross the Rhodesian frontier. Besides, no white journalist has ever made it across that frontier since it was closed five years ago.'

'I'll be the first.'

Bernie Holzheimer came on the line from New York. 'It looks as if Magnus and Julie are in hot water. They were picked up yesterday in Oceanville by a CIA agent Ray Lawson and several other characters whom we suspect may be connected with BOSS, though we're not sure.'

'Their names are Hans Kruger and Pieter Jacobsdal. Kruger works for the Department of Information in Pretoria; Jacobsdal it was who tried to kill Magnus in London on June 7 last year. That information may help you to get Magnus and Julie out.'

'OK. We've alerted the FBI but that's a delicate business in view of the "Company's" involvement in this affair. The Lawson crowd are going to plead "national security" and "national interest" and to hell with *habeas corpus*. Our own stringers on the West Coast are also monitoring their movements. Right now, Magnus and Julie are held in a big house belonging to the CIA in the Bay Area.'

'Well, get them out of there.'

'It may not be easy, Bill.'

'Now, if I toss this lighted cigar out of that window, Magnus, I could start a fire. Starting fires happens to be my mission, my contribution to the global imperative. The problem is, you and Ellison have misapprehended your own mission as reporters, which I respect. You have confused the investigative function with the prophylactic-action function. That's out of bounds, Magnus. Freedom of the press doesn't cover that.' Ray Lawson turned to Ruth Leonhard and squeezed her hand. 'Besides,' he murmured, 'fuck the First Amendment.'

Today Lawson was in one of his hippie-bohemian moods, blue jeans, a psychedelic shirt, existentialist paperbacks, lots of pot for everyone. Much of the day – the last before the California primary poll – was spent watching television. When Tatiana and Karl Petersen appeared for thirty seconds at prime time in the Dick Aronson slot, Lawson sighed with satisfaction. 'What a kid.'

'A verry noice gel,' Jacobsdal agreed.

But Lawson and his friends were not committed to Aronson or Governor Prendergast as individuals. What was music to their ears were the increasingly belligerent anti-Soviet speeches issuing from all candidates, including the President of the United States. And he had one advantage over all his rivals: he would be chief executive of the Republic before, during and after the Olympics, until January, 1981. The others could propose, he alone could promise.

And he did, at nine in the evening of June 2. 'If the Russians refuse a visa to any athlete nominated by the USOC in accordance with IOC rules, I shall advise the USOC to boycott the Games and urge the IOC to withdraw recognition. Visas will not be granted to any Soviet sportspeople, artists or performers during 1980. All trade agreements with the Soviet Union will be subject to unilateral revision by our side. Sales of wheat to the Soviet Union will not receive Government authorization this year.'

The President was asked whether he intended to continue giving moral support to black guerrilla groups in southern Africa who received their material from the Communist bloc.

'We are in the process,' the President replied, 'of rethinking our entire African strategy.'

Would he reappoint the black civil rights activist and former aide to Martin Luther King, as US Ambassador to the United Nations if he won a second term of office?

'Obviously,' replied the President, 'a change of policy, to be effective, necessitates a change of personnel.'

And so, asked the news commentators, who would pick up California's 217 delegates to the Democratic Convention? The key-precinct analyses of both CBS and NBC showed the President strong in northern California, running behind Dick Aronson in conservative San Diego County, and well behind him in the heavily populated working-class areas of Los Angeles, particularly the aerospace districts of Burbank and in blue-collar Huntington Park. Aronson was also ahead in the lower-middle-class Jewish precincts of the Fairfax district.

The verdict? 'It has to be Aronson,' concluded CBS's pundit Roger Preslee.

'Yes, Magnus,' Lawson said, 'it has to be Aronson. You are an educated man; we are in communion here with an historical imperative.'

'Why don't you tell me how the whole operation was planned from start to finish?'

'Well, we're not quite finished, are we? My vanity may be considerable, Magnus, but not that considerable. If and when I get authorization to terminate your life-span, I promise not to put you to sleep without a preliminary briefing before your descent into the Marxist hell.'

'He's just a pompous shit,' Julie said to Magnus.

Lawson wasn't too keen on her frank appraisals.

'Fifty grams of heroin, that's an awful lot, you know,' he said, referring to the narcotics he had planted in her purse when seizing her outside the UPI office in Oceanville.

'The CIA has no law enforcement powers,' Magnus reminded him. 'Your own failure to notify the FBI is itself a crime.'

Ruth Leonhard laughed. "The Company,"' she said softly, 'is above the law.' Clearly Lawson's attraction for her was overwhelming: one need look no further for the cause of her recruitment.

But how and why had the KGB recruited her? Magnus repeatedly pressed her on this, without effect.

'I'm not on the *Sunday Monitor* payroll,' she replied contemptuously.

At ten that evening a phone call aroused considerable agitation among the South Africans, notably Hans Kruger and Pieter Jacobsdal.

'Ellison is reported to have arrived in Maputo,' Kruger told Massey. 'Our intelligence suggests that he's crazy enough to try and get into Rhodesia overland, with a Zanu unit commanded by the kaffir terrorist Mutobo.'

'The Selousies will be waiting for him,' Jacobsdal said softly. 'And when they get him, oh boy, oh boy. . . .'

June 1980. Mozambique–Rhodesia

The Zanu patrol moved cautiously, Indian file, through the dense rain forest and shoulder-high elephant grass of western Mozambique. An hour earlier they had parted company with their two trucks and said goodbye to their Portuguese-speaking Frelimo drivers. Now, as they entered the Chimoio border area, Joseph Mutobo avoided open ground at any price. It was less than twenty minutes before they heard the first high drone of a Trojan tracker plane from No. 4 Squadron of the Rhodesian Air Force; shortly afterwards a deeper throbbing at a lower altitude heralded the approach of two Alouette scout helicopters. The patrol buried themselves in elephant grass.

Ellison had a fear of snakes.

His head had begun to ache as the morning sun rose higher in the sky. As the day wore on his feet increasingly resembled grilled steaks, and the murderous assaults he had suffered all night long from mosquitoes kept him scratching at his sweating skin. His face and arms were camouflage-blackened with burnt cork; the khaki combat fatigues and forage cap he wore were a gift from Frelimo. But Joe Mutobo could not persuade him to carry an AK 47 rifle.

'When the Rhodesians hit us, you'll be sorry,' the African said.

'I'm a reporter, Joe.'

After resting in a small village of mud huts, some of which had been burned out by a recent Rhodesian air raid, they moved on towards the Vumba mountains south of Umtali, Rhodesia's fourth city. Ellison increasingly found it hard to keep pace; he had been forced to decline the meal of *sadza* and boiled chicken the villagers had offered them, restricting himself to drinking water purified with iodine tablets. He knew that hunger could foster weakness but hoped to stave that off with the cubes of food concentrates he carried in his pack. He also knew that even a mild attack of dysentery could knock him out of the game.

They spent the night in a village where the pinkish hair of the pot-bellied children indicated kwashiorkor, a disease rooted in malnutrition. For the second night in succession the mosquitoes consumed his flesh, denying him a moment's sleep; and when they got going, shouldering their AK rifles, their Stalin Organ rocket launchers, fastening their grenades and tightening their ammunition bandoliers, he began to wonder whether irregular jogs round Regent's Park really prepared a middle-aged journalist for this kind of life. The tall grass hid deep holes and treacherous ruts; clusters of roots, creepers and vines snared his legs and head. As the temperature climbed to 33° centigrade, his throat turned to sandpaper and his tongue to parched leather.

Joseph Mutobo was keeping an eye on him. 'You don't look so good,' he said during a short break and insisted on taking Ellison's temperature. It registered 102° Fahrenheit. With some glee Mutobo jabbed a hypodermic into his bottom and filled him with penicillin.

'If the Rhodesian Air Force sees your white bum shining in the sun, we're dead men,' Mutobo chuckled. The whole patrol fell about laughing.

It was at that moment that the Alouette helicopter gunship roared in over the tree tops virtually without warning. The patrol hurled themselves into the grass, but one guerrilla, caught urinating in the open, was ripped apart by machine-gun fire from the sky. As they retreated deeper into the dark recesses of the rain forest, the Alouette circled overhead like an angry, thwarted hornet. Presently it was joined by a second, then a third.

'They're putting down troops,' Mutobo whispered, 'about a mile away. If they're Selous Scouts, they'll pick up our spoor in no time.'

The word made Ellison feel like a hunted animal. He had been warned on arrival in Mozambique that South African Intelligence would alert the Rhodesians to his impending attempt to cross the frontier south of Umtali. As the patrol beat a rapid retreat eastwards, away from the frontier, keeping close to tree cover, he visualized the Selous Scouts' emblem that Magnus had described to Cherry over the telephone from California. Maybe he would see it, in the flesh, soon enough.

Not until darkness fell did the helicopters and Rhodesian trackers call off their pursuit and permit the Zanu guerrillas to sink down into the earth, exhausted. Despite the mosquitoes, cumulative fatigue immediately carried him into a deep sleep. When he awoke nine hours later the Africans were cooking *sadza* and chattering softly. Mutobo thrust a thermometer under his dry tongue, but the fever had abated.

Towards three in the afternoon they finally crossed the frontier into the blue-green Vumba mountains, skirting the sandbagged Forbes border post on the Umtali-Beira road, over which flew the Zimbabwe–Rhodesia flag. Negotiating the two hundred-metre-deep minefield laid on the Vumba side of the border was a delicate, painstaking task entrusted to the guerrilla patrol's chief scout, Simba Selukwe.

Threading their way south, they passed through the wastelands of the Cashel Valley where more than a hundred white farms had been abandoned. Many of them were burnt out, their fields overgrown, their dip tanks destroyed, their livestock long since rustled or destroyed by the rampant tsetse-fly. Crossing the main Umtali-Birchenough road, they penetrated the Maranke Tribal Trust Land, a dead world in which all schools, clinics and grinding mills were closed, all stores burnt out and looted.

'That's martial law for you,' Mutobo murmured, falling back to Ellison's side. 'How are your feet, man?'

'You tell me where they are, I'll tell you how they are.'

They spent the night deep in Maranke in a village where they were greeted as liberators and hospitably fed on chicken, *sadza* and locally brewed beer. Despite the curfew and the shoot-on-sight powers which permitted the security forces to perpetrate one massacre after another, the mood was convivial, carefree, even joyous. Ellison, whose white face was now patchily streaked with burnt cork, was regarded as an object of profound curiosity. And when Mutobo introduced him, with a mischievous grin, as 'the best reporter in

Maranke', women lined up to tell him how they had been raped and pillaged by the soldiers.

He knew it already.

Lying under the stars, absorbing the alien, pungent smells of the African village, he wondered about Magnus.

When he awoke next morning, Ellison glanced at the date on his watch. The Olympic Games would begin in exactly thirty days' time.

CHAPTER 18

June, 1980. Oregon

Normally the United States Olympic Try-outs attracted only American sports reporters, but this year, 1980, the entire international press corps was represented, so keen was the political interest in the outcome of the women's pentathlon. Such was the fear of dirty tricks and desperate expedients that journalists from the Communist countries were constantly shadowed by the FBI. Tatiana herself was surrounded by armed guards not only outside the arena but also round the periphery of the track itself. Only the combined protests of the other girls in the pentathlon had persuaded the AAU officials to bar the security guards from the competition area.

Certainly the Russian girl had changed in appearance. Gone was the fresh, innocent, healthy bloom of the young maiden. The smile had coarsened now, and the mouth hardened into a thin, sardonic line.

The town abounded with rumours. Tatiana was said to be smoking too much, drinking too much, drugging herself, fighting with her husband, having a lesbian affair, planning to re-defect back to Russia, in the process of signing a $2 million promotion contract, a $5 million endorsements contract, a $10 million covert pro contract. . . . Two bets were drawing the heaviest money in the press box and the reporters' hotels: (a) the world record holder was in a class of her own and would qualify with both hands tied behind her back; (b) the most dramatic upset in modern athletics was about to take place. Remember what happened to Harrison Dillard.

They reached St Anselme's Mission, south of Umtali, the following afternoon. Father Gregory, who hadn't been back to Ireland in ten years, greeted them with the news that four of his African brothers had been taken away by the Special Branch the previous evening. 'They'll keep them for a week in tiny cages, beat them, spit on them and then send them back to me. What can I do for you, boys?'

For Ellison the long walk was over: he enjoyed his first bath and his first 'European' meal in a week. That night, despite the curfew and despite the high risk of ambush by comrade guerrillas on the main Umtali–Salisbury road, they set out in two of the mission's VW vans. Father Gregory drove the first van, Ellison the second, on the premise that any road block manned by white police wouldn't search a vehicle driven by a fellow-white.

By first light they had reached the mission's headquarters in a Salisbury suburb. Here black and white parted: Joe Mutobo and his men pressed on to the comparative security of Highfield, the largest African township in Rhodesia. He and Ellison fixed a rendezvous point and a fall-back, then shook hands warmly.

Having slept for a couple of hours, Ellison breakfasted with Father Gregory. 'What's the situation, Father?'

'Appalling. Scenes of chaos at the airports as whites literally fight for seats on aeroplanes out. Women and children trampled underfoot, survival of the fittest, very ugly.'

'What about the exit by road through Beit Bridge?'

'That's the direct route to South Africa. The guerrillas hit the armed convoys every day.'

'If I took a plane to Bulawayo, I'd presumably have to provide identification documents?'

'You would. And you'd be luckly to get a seat. Now that the roads are so dangerous, all internal flights are jam-packed.

Ten whites have been killed in a single week on the Salisbury–Bulawayo road.'

'Train?'

'Very slow. Twenty-four hour journey – and you'll still get hit. Who do you want to see in Bulawayo?'

'A man called Bob Corbishley, chief engineer, South-West Railways. Has God a spare vehicle, Father?'

'Question is, does God have any spare petrol coupons? You know that the allocation has been drastically cut since the fall of the Shah terminated Iran's oil supplies to South Africa?'

'I'm not even a Christian, Father.'

'Nor am I, my boy. I'll see what can be done.'

At 8:30 that night, Ellison pointed one of the mission's VW vans towards Norton and set out on a 500-kilometre drive across Rhodesia. He drove for two hours without seeing a single vehicle on the road, or a single human being beside it. As his headlights raked the shadows and black forest walls of the African night, phantom guerrillas constantly leapt at him out of the darkness, small points of light glinted on raised weapons, fireflies raced into his windscreen like tracer bullets.

All you need now, son, is a puncture.

He reached Corbishley's house in Abinger Road, Bulawayo, shortly after dawn. The railway engineer shook his hand warmly. 'What you need, Mr Ellison, is a plate of bacon and eggs,' Mrs Corbishley said.

Ellison immediately succumbed to the relaxing, friendly atmosphere. 'You did Massey a great service six years ago,' he said.

'I've always been a Crown loyalist, you see. I never agreed to UDI.'

'And now?'

'Now? We'll leave when we can. I'm spending $10,000 shipping our furniture and our car by road through Beit

Bridge. Can't get insurance on it, though – chances of it being hit in an ambush are too high.'

'Why not sell the furniture and the car, then buy new ones when you emigrate?'

'Because,' Mrs Corbishley intervened, 'Exchange Control regulations limit each couple to $1000 in cash. And they mean it, too: they're stripping people at the border.'

'There's the problem of this house, too,' Corbishley added. 'It should be worth R$40,000, but today I'd be lucky to get R$10,000 for it. And what could I do with the R$10,000: bury it in the garden?'

'Mr Ellison hasn't come all this way to hear our little troubles,' Mrs Corbishley said.

'I wanted to ask you about Coenraad Ventner,' Ellison said.

Corbishley nodded. 'I guessed as much. I know Ventner well because half of his freight traffic passes over my railway lines; because when guerrillas blow up the line, I repair it; and because what I don't know about Ventner's sanction-busting tricks, no one does. He used to sweeten me with all manners of gifts and winter holidays in Switzerland; he virtually paid for the public school education of my boys in England, if the truth be told. I don't think I mentioned that to your colleague, Massey.'

'And you . . . you found it, I mean. . . .'

'I know what you're thinking: how the hell could I bring myself to accept? Particularly when I opposed UDI and supported the spirit of sanctions. The flesh is weak, Mr Ellison. And yet I betrayed Ventner behind his back. I helped your Massey get into the tank farm of Transport Services here in Bulawayo.' Corbishley shrugged. 'When I get to the pearly gates, there'll be a long discussion.'

'Will Ventner stay – stick it out?'

'I don't know. Although he never joined the Rhodesian Front, he poured money into it and became the chief link between Ian Smith and Vorster. When Vorster put the screws on

Smith in '76, at the time of the Kissinger proposals, it was Ventner who brought the nasty news from Pretoria.'

'How does he get his profits out of Rhodesia?'

'Simple. His Rhodesian-registered companies export to his South-African-registered companies at a low, below-cost price. The result is nil profit in Rhodesia. His South African companies then re-sell on the open market and the profit is creamed off in the Republic.'

As Mrs Corbishley laid bacon, eggs, toast and coffee on the table, with a huge jug of orange juice, Corbishley casually picked up a machine-pistol leaning against a bookcase. 'This is the L75, manufactured by guess who: Coenraad Ventner. It operates on the blow-back system: the breech block and fixed pin are held in the rear position after cocking. I bought it for my wife, actually. At R$160 it's a fair rival to the Rhogun, the Rhuzi, the Mamba, the Barad, the Cobra and the LDP, all locally made of course.'

'What about Ventner's family?'

'They have a mansion in Jo'burg, a couple of big farms in the Transvaal, a large house in Mount Pleasant, Salisbury; I don't know, there must be others.'

'Have you met his half-brother?'

'Didn't know he had one.'

'What about his children?'

'Ventner has two sons. Maurice and Hendrick both work for the family firm and both are first-class rugby players. Maurice was fly-half for Northern Transvaal in the Curry Cup team; there was even hope of him becoming a Springbok but he didn't make it. I believe he's working in Amsterdam now.'

Ellison laid on the table one of the photographs that Magnus had sent from California. It showed Karl Petersen, wearing his Selous Scouts bush hat, with two young men a few years older than himself. A black Labrador lay at their feet, its tongue lolling in the heat.

'That's Maurice and Hendrik Ventner, with Ventner's

bitch, Polly,' Corbishley said without hesitation.

'Have you ever seen the young man in the bush hat?'

'I'd say . . . not. Odd though: there *is* something familiar about his face. Well-built lad, isn't he?'

Ellison drove back to Salisbury. Ten miles west of Gwelo he was waved down by a police roadblock – only twenty minutes earlier there had been an ambush at this point in the road. A camouflaged ambulance was still lifting the remains of a white family hit by a Katyusha rocket out of their wrecked car.

A white police reservist in a floppy blue hat took down the number of the VW van and asked him for his name and identity card. Ellison described himself as Clifford Moses and apologized for having left his ID card at home. The police reservist stared at him steadily.

'You realize it's an offence not to carry your card, sir?'

'OK, sorry.'

Reaching Salisbury several hours later, he parked the van and joined the tense pavement crowds. Long queues had formed outside South African Airways, the only commercial airline servicing Rhodesia; women wept openly. The jewellery and 'antique' shops were packed as people hysterically threw away their useless local currency for rings and broaches they might legally take out of the country. It reminded Ellison of an event two thousand years earlier, when Vesuvius had erupted suddenly and buried the town of Pompeii in lava. Or, more recently, of the final, panicked exodus from Vietnam. Fights broke out in the food shops and supermarkets as people attempted to buy up and hoard dwindling supplies of food. Half the country's cattle had now died of ticks and tsetse-fly: the price of beef had rocketed. The streets were crowded with soldiers and weird, mine-proofed, camouflage vehicles with corrugated steel flanks and wheels fixed to wide axles designed to blow off when they hit a mine. Yet even now, at the eleventh hour, white women in the smart means solely due to her rivalry with Mrs Larin-Petersen – a rivalry exacerbated, of course, by Miss Floris's previous friendship with Karl Petersen. As Floris explained to the *Sunday Monitor* last night in an exclusive interview, in recent weeks two other American pentathletes have dramatically improved their performances, putting themselves in serious contention for the highly coveted Olympic team places. They are Wendy Clarkson and Mary-Lou Okatovsky.

'When the hurdles heats finally got under way, they confirmed the lack-lustre shotput performance of the Russian-born favourite. Larin-Petersen struck the fourth hurdle, hesitated at the fifth, lost her stride rhythm and finished third in her heat in the poor time of 13.77 seconds (895 points). Floris again performed well, with smooth power, recording a time of 13.34 (953 points).

'After two events, then, the first four placings (only three go to Moscow) were as follows: 1. Floris: 1,913; 2. Clarkson: 1,820; 3. Larin-Petersen: 1,790; 4. Okatovsky: 1,780.

'Mrs Larin-Petersen could now be seen prowling around the arena, angrily remonstrating with herself, morose, sullen, unapproachable.

'The third event was the high jump. Here Barbara Floris almost encountered complete disaster. Having put in a "safety net" early jump of 5′2″ (775 points), she made no further attempt until the bar had been raised to 5′9″. Normally she clears this height without effort. Justifiably satisfied with her performances in the shot put and hurdles, she decided to conserve her energy. But when she attempted 5′9″, she hit the bar with her shoulder at the first attempt, flicked the bar with her heel at the second and then, after an agonizing bout of nerves preceding her third, fought for a moment of total concentration and maximum lift. When she fell on to the foam rubber padding, the bar was still trembling on its pegs; by the time she had risen to her feet, the bar had fallen.

'Wendy Clarkson and Mary-Lou Okatovsky made no attempt to conceal their jubilation. Against all the odds, they were now in with a chance. Barbara Floris burst into tears while the tall, lithe, gazelle-like Okatovsky gathered in a useful 1,049 points.

'Tatiana Larin-Petersen showed signs of her true form in this event, with 1,082 points, relying on the straddle jump style which she perfected under her Soviet coach, Antonin Rodzenko.

'And so, with three of the five events completed, the overall scores stand as follows: 1. Larin-Petersen: 2,872; 2. Okatovsky: 2,829; 3. Clarkson: 2,794; 4. Floris: 2,688.

'It looks, then, as if Tatiana Larin-Petersen has taken a commanding lead. It also looks as if Barbara Floris, until recently America's leading pentathlete, may not qualify for Moscow.'

June, 1980. Rhodesia

Ellison was driven after dark to a house in Highfield township. There Mutobo introduced him to the top Zanu command operating inside the capital of Rhodesia.

'We're hitting Ventner's oil tank farm in the south-west industrial area tonight,' he was told. 'You may accompany us if you wish – the first white journalist ever permitted to witness an operational mission.' The guerrilla commander, shaded by dark glasses and smoking a cigar, addressed him with a certain condescension. 'During the course of the week the entire Ventner empire will be wiped out. White morale will be further undermined. You will have a world-exclusive scoop.'

'I wish you luck. But I didn't come to Rhodesia to watch firework displays,' Ellison said.

He saw a note of warning, almost of entreaty, pass across Mutobo's face, but he believed he would get his way, in the such a pace might ultimately finish her. It didn't matter: the battle for a place at the Moscow Olympics was squarely joined between these two women.

'On the second bend Floris actually drew level. Suddenly the shoulder-charging and elbowing between them grew vicious and purposeful; the Russian girl was clearly kicking her feet high behind her in the hope of spiking the American.

'Now Larin-Petersen, the natural runner, flew down the home straight towards the bell. Clarkson passed a labouring Floris at the bell and set out in pursuit of Larin-Petersen, now some seven metres in the lead. At that stage Floris began to fall back, her morale apparently sapped; by the end of the bend she was twenty metres down on the Russian. I saw Floris turn to look back at Okatovsky, the lanky Iowan trailing about twenty-five metres behind her. At that moment, I'm sure, Floris, transferred all her calculations from the Russian to Okatovsky. If she could only finish seven seconds up on Okatovsky, she could still snatch from her that ticket to Moscow! Floris's brown arms thrashed with effort, her head tilted back, her teeth were gritted. She drove herself desperately down the back straight.

'The crowd now had fallen silent. It was almost as if the events we were witnessing were so portentious as to exclude the normal hubbub of a sports meeting.

'Two hundred metres to go. The early pace had been killing. Suddenly, almost simultaneously, the two famous girls began to wilt. Clarkson, against the form books, glided smoothly up to Tatiana's shoulder and past her; simultaneously Okatovsky began to close down the gap on Floris. So Floris, after all, was doomed.

'But was she? The amazing sight now confronting us was of the world record holder almost dead on her feet. Clarkson was streaking to victory; Okatovsky, in fourth place, was closing on Floris rapidly and so assuring her own passage to Moscow. But Floris, meanwhile, exhausted though she was, found herself inexorably gaining on a completely exhausted and demoralized Tatiana Larin-Petersen!

'Out of the final bend, Okatovsky passed Floris, raised a hand in jubilation, moved up level to the Russian girl, then spurted easily past her. Tatiana's stride shortened, her body rolled in desperation. Floris, now in agony herself, was still closing that gap: fifteen metres, twelve metres. . . .

'If Floris could hold her to five metres at the line, Floris would go to Moscow!

'And then the crowd began to shout. For Floris. It was an amazing moment and I can't account for it. It was as if, all of a sudden, we recognized the struggle of the individual against a giant publicity machine. And many of us, I suspect, could no longer repress within ourselves the hope that the eclipse of Tatiana would mean the survival of the Olympics.

'With forty metres to go, Floris had closed to within ten metres of her rival. At the thirty-metre mark, the lead was cut to eight metres; at twenty-five metres from the line, Floris found an untapped source of energy from the depth of her gut and actually spurted level with her deadly rival. The crowd had gone mad. Tatiana threw a desperate glance to her right, almost as if begging her rival to be merciful.

'At twenty metres out they were level.

'At fifteen metres from the line, Floris's legs buckled. One moment she was running and the next she was flat on her face on the track. By the time she had picked herself up Tatiana Larin-Petersen had crossed the line. The American girl managed to stagger home in fourth place.

'It made no difference. Tatiana Larin-Petersen had qualified for the American Olympic team. Barbara Floris had not.'

Charles Graves-Brown was not the only reporter to have noticed that Floris had picked up a white envelope dropped by an AAU official shortly before the start of the 800 metres.

But Floris was giving no interviews. She dared not. For the envelope had contained a cheque from Sol Enders for $10,000 and the message, 'Throw this race, Barbara.' Her first reaction had been: Fuck him, fuck them all! And that reaction had sustained her right up to the moment when, twenty metres from the line, she drew level with Tatiana.

Sol Enders had given her a fat pro contract for after the Moscow Games. But that contract was conditional on continued rivalry between herself and Tatiana – no use at all if Tatiana never got to Moscow, never won a gold. To eliminate her, then, was self-defeating – except for the sake of honour, pride, everything worthy in this life.

And then, fifteen metres out, the girl from the slums, the girl whose father had stolen scrap metal to make weights for her, had grabbed at that $10,000, telling her legs to collapse. They obeyed.

CHAPTER 19

June, 1980. Rhodesia

When Ellison drove up to the heavily guarded gate of Coenraad Ventner's residence in Mount Pleasant at first light the following morning, the whole city of Salisbury was covered by a thick pall of smoke from the two dozen oil tanks hit during the night by Zanu tracer bullets and Stalin Organ rockets. So great was the conflagration that the Fire Service ran out of foam and men: help had to be flown in from Johannesburg.

It was a vast mansion, set in five acres of garden, with stables, two swimming pools, tennis courts and lavish servants' quarters. The high electric fence surrounding the house was patrolled by guard dogs and white mercenaries. Ellison arrived in a Rix Renault taxi. The driver, trembling, refused to enter the front gate as it swung silently open like the jaws of a shark. Ellison got out and walked up the long winding driveway, lined with jacarandas, bougainvillaea and flame trees.

Silently the gates closed behind him. He paused to take photographs. Whether he would ever get the film out was another matter.

A black butler in a red fez and cummerbund received him at the door and led him along a corridor lined with tropical plants to Ventner's study. Two mercenaries frisked him, removing his camera and tape-recorder, before the door was opened and he was admitted to a room filled with light. It was painted white.

Ventner was standing rigidly at the far end of the room, tall and erect, with grey-white Calvinist features devoid of human warmth. Paintings depicting the Boer War and the British concentration camps in which Boer women and children had died hung from the walls. Ellison walked round the room, studying the family photographs in their silver frames. Nothing of interest: Ventner wasn't going to make it *that* easy for him.

'I believe you have come here with some kind of proposition,' Ventner said. 'Take a seat, Mr Ellison.'

'They say that an Afrikaaner farmer will never turn even his worst enemy away from his door.'

Ventner nodded. He spoke with the thick, guttural accent of the true Afrikaaner. 'We have our backs to the wall down here, just as my father's generation did when your troops burned their farms and massacred their families. It is a strange thing: we occupy such a small fraction of the globe, yet the world will not leave us alone. My family came to the Cape three hundred years ago. And yet, because my skin is white, I am denied the honour of being an African by Indians, Eskimos and Russians in the United Nations. How do you account for that, Mr Ellison? And then there is this other strange thing: we have built up a modern economy here in Rhodesia, and down in the Republic; no one compels the Bantu to come from their homelands to work in our mines and factories; they come because the wages are better than anywhere else in Africa. Yet the hypocritical world cannot tolerate such a state of affairs; it is dedicated to destroying our way of life. And for what end? Who will gain? Not the black people, that's for sure.'

'The Communists, you think?'

'I do.' Without moving his ground Ventner turned to the french window, indicating with a nod of his head the heavy pall of black smoke hanging over Salisbury. 'Your friends were busy last night. Tomorrow night they will be busy again, is that it? So you have come to blackmail me.' He coughed contemptuously. 'No doubt, from time to time, you talk of the high moral code of your profession.'

'If you speak freely and frankly to me about the Olympic Operation, there is a . . . chance that the attacks on your installations will not be pressed home for . . . the time being.'

'Ha! You hesitated twice. Do liberals, perhaps, have something in place of the consciences that God gave to His People?'

'His People?'

'The Elected.'

'Did your God command you to rake my home with machine-gun fire, try to murder my reporters, and kill witnesses who wanted to talk to me?'

Ventner's back stiffened. 'We can be pushed so far and no further, Ellison.'

'You put your illegitimate son Karl in the Selous Scouts to harden his fanaticism, his blood-lust, I assume?'

Ventner said nothing. His eyes never left Ellison's.

'I'm told Karl wasn't all that keen on life in the bush. He's vain, he's lazy. He'll never succeed you and your father into the Broederbond.'

The recoil in the tall, muscular Afrikaaner was brief but unmistakable: for a moment he quivered with uncontrollable anger and pain. 'What other filth will you hurl at me?'

'Your half-brother.'

'I do not have a half-brother.'

'Your mother married twice: one son from each marriage. You were the younger and it was under the roof of your father, Marius Ventner, that both boys grew up in a spirit of rigid fascist fanaticism. The spirit of the Broederbond. I have it all from Shrivers, you know.'

'That scum! He knew nothing, nothing!'

'Besides, Sol Enders is so incensed about being double-crossed that he has begun to sing like a bird.'

'What has he said to you?' The agitation was breaking through, the rigid self-control breaking down. 'I will not horse-trade with you, Ellison! Let the black terrorists indoctrinated by Moscow destroy everything I possess, everything I have built, here in Rhodesia! My own affairs are a trivial matter! God has no sight of them! But I warn you: if we must surrender the laager, the homeland, we, God's people, will scorch the earth and destroy the cattle! We will carry the evil world down with us! But that moment has not yet arrived! Our vitality remains, our will to survive is strong! For that reason we are determined, we of the Broederbond, that the Olympic Games shall not take place! For years we made the mistake of begging the world on our knees to allow us to compete on equal terms. The world rejected us with contempt. So be it! The battle, the final struggle between atheistic Communism and the People of God, is now joined! And you shall not thwart us!' He pointed to what appeared to be an old chimney breast in the wall, lined with book shelves and Sèvres porcelain. 'There is my six-lever lock safe, cast in a single bell. Within it is your story, Ellison. I need only activate two switches in sequence and it will self-destruct.'

'The story is already set up in type in London, Mr Ventner.'

Ventner grunted. 'But it must not be published – not until the Olympic movement itself is destroyed and the two Super Powers are finally locked in combat. Your presence here is, I think, the best guarantee of your newspaper's absolute silence.'

Ellison turned: the two mercenaries had entered the room silently and were standing close behind his chair.

'So that was why you agreed to see me?'

'Yes. As a matter of fact, your laborious passage into Rhodesia across the Mozambique frontier was quite unnecessary. From the moment that I was alerted to your plans, we – the Rhodesian Government and I – decided not only to admit you but to detain you. I confess that our security forces experienced some anxiety about your movements until you surfaced at the house of Bob Corbishley. You look shocked, Mr Ellison. Let me tell you this: no white person who remains in

Rhodesia today can afford the luxury of being true to his liberal principles. Corbishley hopes against hope that I will allow him to leave Rhodesia in one of my Transport Services aircraft, or my private Cessna jet, so that he can evade Exchange Control regulations. Not surprising, then, that he is anxious to do me every possible service.' Ventner smiled grimly. 'Fear is a great leveller.'

'Except among certain priests and missionaries.'

'Maybe. Maybe. We have arrested Father Maurice – it certainly wasn't sensible of him to lend you his van. I'm told he is too frail to endure torture for long.'

'Was it really necessary to murder all the McGuire women in Bloomington?'

Ventner succumbed to the sad, rheumy gaze perfected by his master, Vorster. They had, after all, shared imprisonment as Nazi sympathizers during the war. 'My wife is unaware to this day that Karl is my natural son; she believes he was adopted by my. . . .'

'Your half-brother?'

'God alone knows how you pieced all this together, Ellison. It's a pity that you turned down the offer we made you during your visit to South Africa: an intelligence such as yours should be harnessed to a worthy cause.'

'What will you do when all this comes out?'

'It won't come out. I have a telephone called booked to London, to your editor, Mr Jordan. He must be made to understand that your life is now in our hands.'

Ventner walked to the window and stared with fury at the oily black smoke still hanging over the city. His movement caused the black Labrador lying behind his desk to raise her head.

Ellison spent the night in a luxurious guest bedroom fronting on to a verandah and swimming pool. A white mercenary from Texas, who stood on permanent guard outside the french windows, told Ellison that reinforcements had been brought up from the Rhodesian Light Infantry barracks in anticipation of a guerrilla attack on the house.

In one corner of the room stood a magnificent mahogany wardrobe. It was double-locked. Timothy, the black servant from Malawi who brought him his food and laundered his clothes, appeared not to understand when Ellison asked whether he could lay hand on the keys to the wardrobe. But the following evening, when the security guard from Texas was relaxing over a beer, Timothy appeared in his room holding a bunch of keys. Silently the African gestured to Ellison to follow him into the bathroom, where he turned on the taps full blast and closed the door to intensify the echo.

'You be moved one hour. Ventner expect boys attack tonight. Last night boys completely destroy Ventner small-arms factory.'

'Do you know where I'll be taken?'

'Maybe ranch near Shabani. Maybe Special Branch interrogation centre Goromonzi, where they torture Father Gregory.' Timothy's hand rested fleetingly on Ellison's shoulder. 'Joe Mutobo send message; don't despair.'

'How long have you worked here, Timothy?'

'Only one month.'

'Have you ever seen Ventner's half-brother here?'

Timothy shook his head and handed Ellison the keys to the wardrobe. 'Be quick, please,' he urged. 'I take keys from master's desk.'

The wardrobe contained several suits of clothes, mostly of tropical material, three pairs of shoes and a framed photograph.

'Most times photograph hang on wall in this room,' Timothy whispered. 'I think master take it down when he know you coming.' The African reached into the back of the wardrobe, behind the hanging suits, and produced something Ellison hadn't noticed. 'Very nice, eh?'

It was a silver-topped walking stick.

'Very nice,' Ellison agreed.

The shoes, too, were very nice, with the left sole of each pair two inches thicker than the right. Hand-made, too, in Amsterdam.

June, 1980.

Like Plains, Georgia, Colorado Springs was one of those places where reporters from the metropolitan newspapers preferred not to be. Nevertheless, an alert put out by the USOC that it would be issuing a statement at 10:15 the following morning brought a scramble for seats on planes. This was too important to leave to the wire services.

The *Washington Post* and *New York Times* both carried stories that the American Ambassador in Moscow had been summoned to the Foreign Ministry and harangued threateningly by Andrei Gromyko. In Paris, *Le Monde*, quoting a well placed source in the Quai d'Orsay, reported that the Russians had urged France to intervene with her American ally before it was too late. *Le Monde* added that no such *démarche* was attempted in London, since Moscow still blamed the Foreign Office for complicity in the Tatiana affair.

The Jewish Defense League and the National Committee for Soviet Liberty inserted full-page ads in major East- and West-Coast papers, urging the USOC to stand firm. 'No Soviet Bullying! No Soviet Blackmail!'

A Pentagon spokesman confirmed at 19:17 Eastern Standard Time that the nuclear-powered aircraft carrier *Madison* had been diverted by the White House from the Indian Ocean towards the Cape. No explanation was given.

At 10:15 the following day reporters crowded into the United States Olympic Committee headquarters at Colorado Springs to hear a statement by USOC spokesman Brodie Short.

'Following the recent Olympic Try-outs in Oregon, the USOC intends to honour its promise to award places in the United States Olympic team to the first three competitors in each event. Mrs Tatiana Larin-Petersen qualified in the pentathlon. She will therefore represent the United States in the pentathlon.

'The decision was conveyed to the Soviet Olympic Committee in Moscow yesterday. We have this morning received a telegram from Sergei Pavlov, President of the Soviet Olympic Committee.'

Brodie Short adjusted his spectacles and mopped perspiration from his brow while the cameras turned. You could have heard a pin drop.

But what dropped was no pin.

'The Soviets reaffirm, to our great regret, that in no circumstances will a visa be granted to Mrs Larin-Petersen to take part in the Olympic Games. President Pavlov insists that Mrs Larin-Petersen is a Soviet renegade, that she has insulted the Russian people and that her selection is a provocation.

'We have repeatedly stressed to the Soviet Committee that: (1) this lady is now an American citizen enjoying the full rights of an American citizen; (2) the USOC is completely neutral and without preference as regards which athletes represent it in Moscow – everything depends on the performances of the athletes.'

'Come to the point, Brodie!' yelled an exasperated reporter, unable any longer to tolerate the tension. 'What's your decision?'

Brodie Short glared at him reprovingly. 'Regretfully, and with a heavy heart, having searched our consciences and deeply pondered our duty to the Olympic ideal, to amateur athletics, to our athletes, and to our country, the USOC has resolved that if a visa is not granted to Mrs Tatiana Larin-Petersen then the USOC will not send a team to the Moscow

Games. The USOC, moreover, will press the IOC to withdraw recognition from the Moscow Games on the grounds that the Soviet Committee is flouting Section 24 of the Olympic Charter and the pledges it expressly gave in 1974, at Vienna.'

Short let fall his prepared statement and took from the table a batch of cables.

'We have already received from the Olympic committees of the following nations messages of support, coupled with assurances that they too will withdraw from the Moscow Games if we do: Australia, the United Kingdom, the Federal Republic of Germany, Italy, Spain, Israel, Yugoslavia, Egypt, Saudi Arabia, Iran, Japan, the People's Republic of China. . . .'

The reporters stampeded for the telephones and telex machines.

On the following day an emergency session of the IOC Executive Board in Lausanne concluded with a statement 'regretting' the Soviet position. Pressed by reporters, Armand Krohl, on behalf of the IOC, refused to be drawn on whether the IOC would now withdraw recognition from the Moscow Games.

'Surely it's preferable to talk, to reason with people, rather than to issue threats,' Krohl said.

This remark incensed American reporters who suggested that the IOC was capitulating to Moscow.

'No, no,' Krohl said. 'If you want my personal opinion, I think the Americans have shown very little tact or understanding of Soviet feelings on this issue.'

This comment, however 'personal' to Krohl, precipitated a storm of angry editorials in the newspapers of the West.

Campaigning in New York for the Democratic nomination, Senator Dick Aronson came out in warm support of the USOC stand. 'This great nation of ours will not be pushed around. We desire peace and friendship with all, but we refuse to compromise our honor, our beliefs, our way of life.'

Passing through London the following day for talks at 10 Downing Street, the Secretary of State confirmed that the SALT 4 talks in Geneva, then reaching a vital stage on the neutron bomb issue, would be suspended indefinitely until the Soviet Union lived up to its obligations as host to the 1980 Olympics.

A reporter asked him whether he did not agree with the late Avery Brundage that politics should be kept out of sport.

'I agree absolutely with that sentiment. I suggest that you impress it on Mr Gromyko rather than on me.'

In Moscow the 750 deputies of the Supreme Soviet gathered in the heart of the Kremlin, surrounded by onion-domed churches, for the second session of 1980. When Gromyko rose to speak he was greeted by prolonged applause. Seated in the side galleries, the Western ambassadors listened impassively to a diatribe against enemies of peace, wreckers and Zionist plotters. Gromyko spoke of the dignity of the Soviet Union. Even so, the ambassadors prayed that the Soviet Foreign Minister would even now, at the eleventh hour, announce a generous concession.

'We will not allow this renegade to return to our soil under a foreign flag.'

Outside, the American Ambassador and his British colleague exchanged a few words. 'It looks as if it's all over.'

Later that day the President met with leading senators in the White House to discuss the easing of economic sanctions against South Africa and Rhodesia. Resistance to 'Soviet expansionism' in the area would be the new priority, the President told them.

A Presidential spokesman told reporters: 'We don't want to wait until we see daily on television white nuns being raped by black guerrillas with red stars in their berets.'

* * *

Ellison was taken from Salisbury after dark in a convoy consisting of a Mercedes saloon and two machine-gun support trucks, fore and aft. They circled the city along Rotten Row and then plunged south-west through the industrial area, following Beatrice Road towards Enkeldoorn. So it was to be the Ventner ranch at Shabani, not the Special Branch interrogation centre at Goromonzi.

If Ellison felt a faint relief, he was not inclined to communicate it to either of the two mercenaries who had him sandwiched in the back seat. One, an Australian, was by nature silent; the other, a Texan, claimed to have served with the Green Berets and kept talking about the 'crippled eagle' and 'why we lost Vietnam'. He talked ceaselessly.

Until the ambush occurred.

They were hit shortly after midnight, several hundred kilometres south of Salisbury, near the Gokomore Catholic Mission north of Fort Victoria. A blinding flash and a deafening explosion indicated that the front support truck, although travelling over a tarmacked surface, had been blasted by a claymore mine detonated from the side of the road. The Mercedes, travelling at 120 kph only seventy metres behind the front truck, braked sharply, swerved, tried to drive through the debris of the front truck and promptly had its front tyres shot out by murderously accurate AK 47 fire from a *kopje* overlooking the road.

Ellison found himself lying face-down on the floor of the Mercedes with the overweight Australian on top of him. The Texan had rolled out of the car and crawled behind the rear fender to return fire with his FN automatic. The rear support truck was also returning fire now, until a direct hit from a Katyusha rocket silenced it.

Suddenly all firing stopped.

It was only then that Ellison became aware of the dreadful screaming of the front truck's driver, who had been blown twenty metres out of his cab by the claymore blast, losing both his legs in the process. Closer to the Mercedes, the young Texan was rolling over and over in the road, sobbing and clutching his perforated stomach. It seemed as if he was going to lose Rhodesia as well as Vietnam.

All four army reservists of the rear support truck had been incinerated by the rocket strike, but two of them took a long time dying and were crawling about in the bush at the roadside, sobbing and begging for water.

Time passed. Ellison lay still, with the Australian on top of him.

Then came the soft footfall of men approaching from the *kopje.* Ellison felt the Australian's automatic suddenly jab into his gut.

'You'd do better to run for it, son,' Ellison said.

The remark produced the vital moment of hesitation in the mercenary; a moment later the door was flung open and black hands hauled the weight from Ellison's back. A torchbeam was shone in his face; he heard words muttered in a Shona dialect. A single shot rang out – the Australian had died as silently as he had lived.

'Ellerston?' the guerrilla commander said.

'Bill Ellison.' The guerrillas, wearing blue denims, were standing in a tight circle, watching him.

He walked up the road to where the legless driver of the front truck lay moaning, blood pouring from the stumps of his legs, his young face deadly white, his parched tongue begging for water. Ellison immediately succumbed to overwhelming nausea and vomited – it seemed to him, in that instant, that he was looking down into the crushed face of his own son.

'Put him out of his misery,' he told the guerrilla leader.

'Because he's white?'

'Because he's human.'

'Nothing white is wholly human, man.'

Ellison stared at them in astonishment: he had never seen such blind hatred in the faces of men. Picking up the FN rifle of the young American mercenary, whose breathing had now stopped, he walked back to where the legless Rhodesian soldier lay, crying like a baby. Ellison took aim, but his hand trembled with horror – the Military Cross he had won as a platoon commander in the Parachute Regiment during the Malayan insurrection was of no help to him now. He raised the gun again, focussing along its sights, then squeezed the trigger, bracing himself for the violent report, the splintering of the dying lad's skull. But nothing happened, the chamber was empty: the young American, though wounded, had fired until his magazine was empty.

He threw down the FN in disgust and walked away.

Within twenty minutes both front tyres of the Mercedes had been replaced. Four hours later the car crossed the border south of Plumtree into Botswana and headed for Francistown.

At one point on the journey he had expressed surprise that the security forces had not come in pursuit of them. The guerrilla leader had laughed contemptuously.

'At night, man, this country is called Zimbabwe.'

CHAPTER 20

Saturday, July 5, 1980. New York City

He had lived with her for a year and yet had never set eyes on her. He had watched her on television and studied her movements on film, but not until now had Ellison been in the same room as Tatiana Larin-Petersen.

She entered Sol Enders's eighteenth-floor office on Park Avenue like a queen, extending her hand with regal grace when the 260-pound impresario mumbled introductions to the three men who had been making his life a misery for the past twenty-four hours: Bill Ellison, Bernie Holzheimer and Solomon Rupin. Tatiana didn't quite catch their names, but her ear was quick to respond to the drum-beat of a powerful newspaper; her smile flashed through heavy make-up.

Karl Petersen wore a permanent arrogant sneer. His handshake was perfunctory, disdainful. The tone he immediately adopted towards Sol Enders confirmed Ellison's suspicions – for all his money, the impresario was cringing.

'So what's the big deal, Sol? We have exactly two weeks until the Olympic opening ceremony! We're supposed to be in strict training at Glenmore! I mean, why the hell didn't you come out to the Coast?'

Enders stared at him through beads of perspiration, although the air conditioning in the office was efficiently keeping at bay the fierce heat of mid-summer Manhattan. 'Karl, you *still* imagine that you're going to compete in Moscow?'

Petersen, dressed in a smart navy-blue yachting blazer and flared white trousers, was jingling coins in his pockets. 'I have word that the IOC has today sent Moscow a final ultimatum. The Russians will cave in by tomorrow.'

'You don't believe that,' Ellison said. 'You merely want your wife to believe it, to keep her wound-up until Operation Tatiana has achieved its purpose.'

'Who is this guy?' Petersen asked Enders.

'Bill Ellison, *Sunday Monitor*, London,' Ellison said quietly.

The young athlete's recoil was instantaneous. 'Hey, what's going on in here?' he snarled at Sol Enders.

Enders gestured wearily towards the pile of proofs and the supporting photographs that lay strewn across his desk. He had spent the entire night studying the 40,000 words of 'Operation Tatiana' and consulting with his lawyers, one of whom, Jackson, was now staring frostily down at the traffic in Park Avenue below.

Tatiana picked up one of the proofs with an expression of baffled puzzlement and read the byline aloud in a quiet voice from which the Russian accent had almost disappeared.

' "Operation Tatiana." By Bill Ellison, Magnus Massey, Joe O'Neill and Julie Beavan. A Searchlight Report. In collaboration with Bernie Holzheimer of the *New York Times*.'

'What you hold in your hand, Tatiana,' Sol Enders told her sadly, 'will start rolling from the presses of the *Sunday Monitor* in London in two hours' time and from the presses of the *New York Times* five hours later.'

'Then you've got to stop it!' yelled Karl Petersen, seizing a telephone and dialling 415 followed by a number in the Bay Area. His connection was rapidly made. 'Ray? Is that Ray Lawson? Hey, did you hear about this big story that – You did? Who? The FBI have your place surrounded? Well, what are we going to do? We can't just let this bunch of kaffir-fucking pansy liberals get away with – What?'

Karl Petersen slowly replaced the receiver, picked up a proof of 'Operation Tatiana' and slumped into a chair.

'Look, gentlemen,' Sol Enders began after a long silence, 'I figure there must be a deal here somewhere. O.K. my lawyers tell me you've got me skinned back and front, cooked in parsley butter and served up for dinner. My lawyers also tell me that if I threaten you with a libel suit or an immediate injunction I'll just end up tasting like curried chicken. OK, Mr Ellison, send a copy to the White House, a copy to the Kremlin, a copy to Jerusalem, a copy to 10 Downing Street, ten copies to the IOC in Lausanne, ten copies to the USOC in Colorado Springs ... but don't publish it! Give me a break! Solomon, this guy is a friend of yours....'

Solomon Rupin shifted in his chair uncomfortably.

'OK, OK,' pleaded Enders, 'newspapers are in business to publish. And you have this big deal sewn up with Orbit Books ... there'll be 2.5 million paperback copies out on the newsstands by Wednesday. So it's big money, this. Name your price, come on, boys....'

'Sol –' His lawyer Jackson had wheeled round from the window. 'Now listen, Sol, this conversation is not privileged.'

The several chins of Sol Enders wobbled like blancmange in an earthquake. 'Mr Ellison, I want you to believe me, I was taken in, I was duped by this guy Krohl. To think of the money I've invested in these two kids here, Tatiana and Karl, in the confident expectation that they would bring back Olympic medals! Sabotage the Games! Me! You have to be crazy! It's goodbye to all my agency commissions on the endorsements; it's goodbye to my pro circuit!'

'Maybe Krohl was too smart for you, Sol,' Rupin said angrily, 'but you duped Chaim Leonhard, your friend Chaim, your co-religionist Chaim, and look where he is now!'

Sol Enders almost choked with anguish and shame. He was not, Ellison was increasingly convinced, a malevolent man, merely one with an abnormally high capacity for self-deception.

'After all,' Rupin continued, jabbing the air like a prosecutor, 'you never told Chaim that this young man here was conceived in your own Long Island house, or that you knew the identity of his father, or that his uncle, Armand Krohl, had sworn you to secrecy many years ago. When you, Chaim and Krohl met in that Los Angeles restaurant last summer and Krohl announced that he had "been told" that a Soviet athlete called Tatiana Larin had taken a shine to someone called Petersen, you knew damned well that Krohl had engineered the whole operation – even though you were later coward enough to "confess" to Ellison quite falsely that you yourself had set it up. You said that because you were afraid of Krohl and his power to launch a punishing investigation of your secret contracts with amateur athletes. Yes? In reality, it was poor Chaim who was led by the nose.'

'But then Chaim double-crossed me!'

'How?'

'How? Chaim went off to see Ambassador Dobrynin and patched things up with the Russians. A Soviet girl defecting to the West and marrying an all-American hero is big money; the same Soviet girl remaining loyal to the USSR and maybe engaged to the same all-American hero is just *schmaltz*.'

Tatiana was staring at the fat impresario with horror. When she turned to Ellison she was showing her first signs of profound disturbance.

'Who is this Armand Krohl? I have never heard his name before.'

'He's your husband's uncle, a man whose cover has taken years to bring to its present perfection: a liberal, a friend of the black Africans, a friend of the Jews, a friend of political prisoners, a leading figure in the World Council of Churches, a dedicated opponent of apartheid – the second most powerful man in the international Olympic movement.

'The man who, using your love for Karl Petersen, conspired to sabotage the Moscow Olympics on behalf of his native South Africa.

'Krohl's father died when he was small. His mother remarried. Krohl lived thereafter under the influence of his step-father, Marius Ventner, an Afrikaaner businessman, a member of the secret Broederbond and an admirer of Hitler. A fine athlete and hurdler, Armand Krohl represented South Africa at the Berlin Olympics, broke his leg in three places in the heats and saluted the *Führer* while being carted away on a stretcher. Photographs of this incident were removed from all library copies of South African newspapers after the Broederbond came to power in the 1950's. Krohl's liberal disguise had to be protected.

'When the Nazis invaded Holland in 1940 Krohl was working in the Ventner family import-export firm in Amsterdam. In 1941 the Germans put him ashore from a U-boat in South Africa. He spent the rest of the war passing messages to the German navy about the projected passage of Allied shipping round the Cape. His step-father and half-brother Coenraad, meanwhile, had been imprisoned as Nazi sympathizers.

'Krohl's name helped him evade exposure when he returned to Holland after the war and set up a series of new companies to replace the one discredited by the name Ventner. There was no Allied dossier on Armand Krohl. He took a keen interest in amateur athletics, dug generously into his own pocket, was appointed manager of the Benelux team at the London Olympics of 1948, and by the mid-fifties had been elected president of the Benelux Olympic Committee and a member of the IOC. By the mid-1970's he was a force to be reckoned with in its powerful nine-man Executive Board.

'Meanwhile his half-brother prospered and rose to a position of political influence under the regimes of Malan, Strijdom, Verwoerd. As tension built up between Britain and the Rhodesian Front, led by Ian Smith, Coenraad Ventner moved into Rhodesian business and politics. He became sanctions-buster number one – assisted, at the European end, by Armand Krohl.

'Krohl has been South Africa's mole in the highest counsels of the Olympic movement, skilfully sheltering behind front men such as Detweiler, Pomonti and Wagner. It was Krohl, of course, who almost master-minded Rhodesia's admission to the Munich Olympics, though if one had tried to convince Mutobo or Okie of that, one would have been considered insane.

'His real genius, this man Krohl, is his ability to manipulate other people. Karl Petersen here could, of course, have been commanded to seduce a Russian girl athlete simply out of loyalty to his father, his uncle, the Broederbond and the Selous Scouts. But Krohl knew that a suspicious world would ferret about for a sinister intrigue. Thus the conspiracy had to be double-insulated against exposure.

'Hence his use of Enders. Karl Petersen on the payroll of Enders International Promotions was just the kind of cynical commercial deal to fool reporters who pride themselves on their worldly sophistication. Ditto Tatiana Larin on a sports scholarship at Glenmore College, whose beneficent angel, all sophisticated reporters know, is the same Sol Enders.

'Consequently, Krohl needed a second layer of insulation, to baffle the Russians. Here Krohl set up Israel, Ha-Mossad and Chaim Leonhard as the decoys. Arbuzov and Tretiakov fell for it – that was important. I very nearly fell for it myself.'

'I am still not clear why you came to suspect Krohl in the first place,' Rupin said.

July 5, 1980. California

Shortly before dawn agents of the FBI surrounded the secluded house in the Bay Area. A senior official of Clandestine Services, CIA, Stanley Lamont, attempted to drive up to the main entrance but was forced back by shots aimed at the tyres of his car. Lamont then engaged Ray Lawson on the telephone.

'I have an order from the Director, Ray. Come out of there and bring your hostages.'

'Well, you know who appointed the Director,' Lawson replied.

'Yes, I do. The President of the United States.'

'And you know who appointed the President of the United States.'

'He was elected, not appointed. By the people.'

'He was appointed by the Kremlin.'

'Ray, that kind of talk went out with Welch and the Birch Society fifteen years ago.'

'Who says they went out, Lamont?'

'Ray, it's an order!'

'I take my orders from some place else, Lamont.' Lawson slammed down the phone and dialled the unlisted number of Armand Krohl in Amsterdam.

July 5, 1980. New York

'I first met Krohl in Vienna in '74,' Ellison said in reply to Rupin's question. 'I noticed that he seemed interested in our investigations of Rhodesian sanctions-busting.'

'That was natural enough,' Rupin interjected, 'in view of his own work for Christian Care.'

'Oh yes,' Ellison smiled, 'Krohl had perfected his cover. In Vienna Joe Mutobo and Patrick Okie brought me the story of the Russian-South African secret deal. Deciding to build up his liberal image for my benefit, Krohl had planted the story on the two Africans, knowing that they would hurry to me with it and that I would insist on being told their source. But by refusing to comment Krohl could safely kill the story for the time being: he knew that I don't deal in unsupported speculation.'

'So he did in fact fool you?' Rupin said.

'He fooled me so much that we took great care to bug his hotel room in Switzerland, where he held a secret meeting with Pomonti, Wagner and Detweiler before the Montreal Olympics. Now listen to this bit of dialogue off the tape:

(Detweiler:) 'Don't forget how close he got to your half-brother with his last Rhodesia story.'

(Krohl:) 'Not just close. Spot on. Ellison doesn't publish everything he knows. . . .'

'You mentioned Ventner to Krohl in Vienna?' Rupin cut in.

'Yes. The inference that Krohl was Ventner's half-brother became very real once we heard that tape. He then instructed Pomonti to approach me with an offer to visit South Africa. Later Emile Angel produced the photograph of the young athlete delivering the Hitler salute from a stretcher at the Berlin Olympics.' Ellison walked across to Enders's desk, selected the picture from a pile and gave it to Tatiana. 'We had it blown up. One could detect some resemblance to Krohl, but forty years is a long time in the life of a face. Angel assumed that the athlete must be a German. But if a German, why had the good Dr Deitz found no reference to the incident in the German press of the day? I took a look at the hurdles heats as reported in *The Times* and found that in heat 4 the last man in was A. Krohl, South Africa.

'So you began to think again about Krohl's limp, stick and platform sole?' Rupin suggested.

'Yes. The incident had been excised from the South African newspapers, leading me to believe that the athlete concerned was indeed South African and was at some pains to conceal his Nazi sympathies. Later I interviewed two captured Belgian pilots in Maputo. One of them had seen a wealthy-looking man with a limp and a silver-topped stick outside the Affretair office at Schiphol Airport, Amsterdam.'

'So what?' snapped Karl Petersen.

'Affretair is in reality a dummy company, a cover for Rhodesian Transport Services, which belongs to Coenraad Ventner – your father.

'Two weeks ago I was in Salisbury. I visited your father's house. Locked away in the wardrobe of the guest bedroom were three pairs of shoes with platform soles on the left heel, a silver-tipped walking stick and the Berlin photograph – carrying the bonus of a signature.'

'What – Krohl's?' exclaimed Rupin.

'No. Hitler's.'

'But why, why, why,' groaned Sol Enders, 'did Krohl issue a statement two weeks ago blaming the Americans for boycotting the Olympics? It doesn't make sense.'

'It makes perfect sense. Krohl wanted to stiffen the Russians' resolve, to reassure the Kremlin that the IOC won't withdraw recognition from the Games.'

'Because if the IOC did that, the Russians might capitulate and grant Tatiana a visa?'

'Exactly. Which would abort Operation Tatiana. You see,' Ellison went on, directing his remarks to the only woman in the room, 'you have believed all along that the people helping you wanted to see you win a gold medal for America in two weeks time. They wanted nothing of the kind. They wanted to destroy the Games.'

'And we will succeed!'

The voice was that of Karl Petersen.

July 5, 1980. California

Glassy-eyed, Lawson crawled across the floor to take the call. For the past three hours he and Ruth Leonhard had been stretched out on the carpet injecting one another with heroin and making love. Julie Beavan had averted her eyes from this degrading spectacle, but Magnus had watched every detail of it, fascinated. The appalling thing was he found Ruth Leonhard irresistibly attractive. Her moans and ecstatic convulsions during love-making brought Massey to a pitch of almost insane lust. He noticed that she was having the same effect on the three armed South Africans guarding the windows, Jacobsdal, Kruger and a type named Swanepoel.

Lawson, who insisted on cradling a gun and taking aim at Magnus whenever the journalist swam into his hazy line of vision, tried to talk to Stanley Lamont on the line, but the heroin had rendered him so incoherent that he could no longer make sense. Kruger seized the instrument.

'Have you conveyed our ultimatum to the *Sunday Monitor* and the *New York Times*?' Kruger demanded of Lamont.

'In whose name and on what authority is this ultimatum delivered?' Lamont asked. 'Pretoria insists that you are under instructions to release the two hostages.'

Kruger ignored this. The house's line to the outside world had been cut at the exchange: no doubt Lamont was bluffing. 'It's now 8:30 here,' Kruger warned. 'That means 16:30 in London. The first edition of the *Monitor* normally rolls at 17:15. Unless we receive independent confirmation by 18:00, London time, that the story has been killed, the hostages will be executed.'

'Now, Mr Kruger –'

'I am not arguing with you!'

In the corner of the living room the TV was permanently switched on, a perpetual murmur and flickering of light in the background of the drama. Now Kruger turned up the volume to catch a news bulletin reporting a successful Zanu guerrilla attack on the Salisbury, Rhodesia, home of Coenraad Ventner. Apparently Ventner had committed suicide when the guerrillas breached the electric fence and his white mercenaries began to surrender.

'I bet he killed his black Labrador, Polly, first,' Magnus said to Kruger. 'It would be a sporting gesture.'

The three South Africans glowered at him with venomous hatred.

Julie Beavan began to tremble.

July 5, 1980. London

The eight formes, iron chases filled with lead type and picture plates, moved from the composing room to the moulds. From the moulds the emergent flongs were transported to the foundry and inserted in the casters. From the casters emerged large, semi-cylindrical metal stereo-plates. These in turn were locked into the twelve giant Nohab-Ampress machines.

Stan Gilbert, the printer, phoned up to Ramsay Jordan's office. 'Ready to run,' he said.

'Thanks, Stan.'

It was 16:45 on his watch. By 17:00 at the latest he would have to make the decision – whether to run or whether to pull 'Operation Tatiana' out of the paper.

At 16:50 another call came through from Stanley Lamont in California. 'Just hold your decision thirty minutes, Mr Jordan, please.'

'But thirty minutes is too long! We have to catch the trains out of King's Cross and Euston to the far North. We run on an absolute schedule.'

'How long can you give me, sir?'

'Ten minutes.'

'Jesus Christ!'

July 5, 1980. New York

'And my husband,' Tatiana Larin-Petersen said bitterly, 'my handsome, honest, adored Karl – how did you get the measure of him? I'me sure it's all in your article but I'm not in the mood for reading right now.'

'We were first alerted to his racism by Barbara Floris.'

'She's just a cheap slut, a whore!' Petersen snarled.

'And Petersen's ancestry?' Rupin asked.

'Holzheimer discovered from Dorothy McGuire that Karl's father was not an American, that his name was Conrad (a very possible Anglicized mis-spelling of Coenraad), and that his accent wasn't like that of British film actors. The ruthless extermination of the McGuire women convinced me that someone was determined to prevent the penetration of Karl Petersen's actual ancestry. Then we had from Barbara Floris certain letters and photographs.'

'The goddamn bitch!' Petersen screamed. He wheeled round on Enders. 'You were instructed by Krohl to buy those back from her, you double-crossing yid kike!'

'I did, I did, Karl, I swear to you. . . .' Enders pleaded, mopping sweat from his chin.

Holzheimer leaned forward at this juncture towards Tatiana. He wanted to ask her: 'Tell me: how is it possible to love a man like your husband?'

'The photographs,' Ellison went on, 'tied Petersen to Rhodesia via the Selous Scouts and two young men who turned out to be Ventner's legitimate sons – not to mention a black Labrador. As for the letters he had sent to Floris, in not one instance did the date on the London postmark match the date on the letter. Why? Because the letters were really posted from Rhodesia to London, where the inner envelope was extracted and re-posted to Floris.'

'This man is real smart,' Petersen said. 'Someone should put him in a circus.'

Tatiana was now examining, fascinated and horrified, the pile of photographs which would be displayed in a few hours' time in the two famous newspapers:

—young Krohl saluting Hitler, Berlin 1936;

—Pieter Jacobsdal advancing on Massey with a drawn Webley, Hillingdon playing field, June 7, 1979;

—a female shop assistant planting two dresses in a carrier bag belonging to the Soviet athlete Bulganova; Bulganova's subsequent arrest by the store detective; Larin and Kitson leaving the shop accompanied by Jacobsdal and another agent;

—Karl Petersen arriving at Kitson's house in Ockenden Road with Ruth Leonhard; a chauffeur carrying a silver-tipped stick to the hidden occupant of a large American car; Larin, Kitson, Petersen and Leonhard, shadowed by Jacobsdal and another BOSS agent, emerging from the house and entering the big car;

—Joe O'Neill hospitalized; Magnus Massey hospitalized;

—Paul Shrivers murdered, his body booby-trapped;

—the machine-gunned ground-floor windows of Ellison's house in Chester Place; the warning note: 'DROP IT';

—Rhodesian Railway trucks at Lourenço Marques and at the Transport Services tank farm Bulawayo; Ventner fishing with Corbishley and his black Labrador;

—Karl Petersen wearing the Selous Scouts' emblem on his bush hat, in the company of Ventner's legitimate sons, plus black Labrador;

—BOSS and CIA agents snatching Tatiana from the Glenmore track area, May 1980; Jacobsdal at the same event; the angry faces of Lawson, Hans Kruger and Ruth Leonhard inside the Lincoln Continental;

—a *New York Times* telefoto lens shot of Massey being 'arrested' by Lawson, Kruger and Jacobsdal outside the UPI office, Oceanville, California;

—the note from Sol Enders delivered by an AAU official to Barbara Floris before the final 800 metre race at the Olympic Try-outs: 'Throw this race, Barbara, $10,000, Sol.'

'What is this?' exclaimed Tatiana Larin-Petersen.

'It was how Mr Enders bribed your rival, Barbara Floris,

to throw the race and allow you to qualify for the Olympics.'

'It cannot be true!' She confronted the impresario. 'You would not stoop so low!'

'He was under orders,' Ellison said. 'If Floris had finished within six metres of you in that race, the whole of Operation Tatiana would have aborted.'

Sol Enders began to sob. 'Mr Ellison, that one little message to Barbara, it's the end of Sol Enders . . . I mean, why don't you put a gun to my head and pull the trigger?'

'So you admit you tried to bribe her to throw the race!' cried Tatiana, who had been listening to the exchange with mounting anger. 'Karl, did you know about this?'

'Aw, come on.'

'Come on, nothing!' she yelled. 'You had those three McGuire women murdered in cold blood!'

'I never heard you turn down that Porsche or all those fine clothes, huh? Hell, it was out of my hands. Do you imagine that Krohl or Kruger or Lawson consult me? I'm just the stooge.' He turned to Ellison. 'You've got to believe that, sir.' The arrogance had evaporated now, Petersen had begun to whine. 'I never wanted any part of this business. . . .'

'Or of me!' cried Tatiana, eyes blazing. 'You never loved me at all! It was all a put-on!' She turned to Ellison. 'When I arrived in London with the Soviet team for the Crystal Palace match, I had no idea any of this was going to happen. Karl and I were semi-engaged, but it had been agreed that I would live in the Soviet Union until after the Olympics. I was happy with that. Then this woman, Ruth Leonhard, came to see me in my hotel. She handed me a letter from Karl, begging me to be his wife and swearing he couldn't live without me. It made me cry to read his letter. Ruth Leonhard told me that my one and only chance of marrying Karl was to make a dash for freedom immediately. Once they had me home in the Soviet Union, she said, I wouldn't be allowed to communicate with Karl in any way. Ruth Leonhard told me precisely how I must escape. I lay awake all night, undecided. Then, on the Saturday, I spent the morning watching Karl competing in the decathlon. I knew then that I couldn't live without him.

'As soon as we were on the American plane flying from Brize Norton to Maine, Lawson showed me the article, "Goodbye, Russia" and told me I had written it. I read it in amazement. Lawson and Karl both told me not to be naïve. Lawson said to me: "Listen, baby, you're not eloping with your gallant swain, you're defecting to the free, Christian West."

'Once I had burnt my boats with the Russians I became a stateless person, ineligible to compete in the Olympic Games. To qualify, I had to be naturalized, and fast, which meant making a big political issue of my case, to rouse people's emotions. I found myself trapped.'

'In the logic of Armand Krohl's operation,' Ellison commented.

'So you now tell me. And then I began to change inwardly. Once I had heard myself speaking the Cold War language at a press conference I began to relish the part, I began to believe in myself as a political refugee; I enjoyed the limelight, the fame.'

'And you like nice things, Tatiana,' Enders said mournfully. 'At heart you're a materialist. You like the American way of life.'

'Do you have anything else to say?' Ellison asked her.

She stared at him in amazement: only slowly did her gaze come to rest on the tape-recorder which had been turning quietly on his lap. Then her eyes filled with tears. 'I was very young. It wasn't my fault. Everyone was so kind to me, I loved Karl. . . .'

As she reached for a handkerchief in her purse, Ellison left the office to telex her statement to Ramsay Jordan. It would make the later editions of the *Monitor*.

July 5, 1980. California

The first mortar bombs dropped on the south side of the house shortly before 9:00 Pacific time. The prevailing wind swiftly carried the tear gas into every room. Wearing helmets, bullet-proof vests and gas masks, the FBI closed in. Two shots rang out.

Coughing and choking, the three South Africans emerged with their hands above their heads, followed by Lawson's CIA colleague and the two British journalists. Friendly hands assisted Julie and Magnus into a waiting ambulance.

Within the house Ruth Leonhard lay half-naked, blood streaming from a fatal wound in her temple. Besides her sprawled her lover, her last lover, Ray Lawson, shot through the mouth. He had botched both jobs badly: both would take a few hours to die.

Inside the ambulance a thin, almost emaciated man wearing a colourless brown suit and a 1940's trilby hat, and carrying, despite the fine weather, a grey raincoat over his arm, was watching Magnus and Julie intently. The Welsh girl was sobbing quietly in Magnus's arms. Weeks of tension, of living under the eye of a maniac and in constant danger of death, were now taking their toll.

'You seem all right,' Jack Knight said at last. Solicitude tended to turn to dust on his tongue. 'Nerves,' he added, indicating Julie.

'Could be that, yes.'

'You never discovered, I suppose, how Ruth Leonhard was recruited by the KGB?'

'She became very talkative, particularly towards the end when the game clearly was up.'

Jack Knight waited patiently, but Magnus only smiled at him like a cat.

July 5, 1980. London

At 17:05, London time, Ramsay Jordan flicked a switch on his intercom and instructed Stan Gilbert to pull 'Operation Tatiana' right out of the first edition. 'Kill it, Stan.'

'That's hard for you, Ramsay,' Gilbert said sympathetically.

'Shove in the eight-page supplement on investment opportunities in Saudi Arabia,' Jordan added bitterly.

At that moment the red light glowed on his outside line.

'We have your reporters alive and well, sir,' he heard Stanley Lamont say, six thousand miles away. 'You can run your big story. Good luck.'

Jordan flicked his intercom. 'Stan? Where is he? Get to him and tell him to keep the stereo-plates in position. I'm running "Operation Tatiana" after all.'

Fifteen minutes later his outside line glowed again. It was Massey.

'Just thought you might like this for your later editions. The history of Ruth Leonhard is the history of her lovers. She has always lived with and through men. When she was a student at the Hebrew University in Jerusalem, where Chaim Leonhard sent her to study philosophy, she fell in love with an Arab member of the Israeli Communist Party, the son of a Knesset Deputy representing Nazareth. Her lover took her up to Galilee and then across the Jordan River at night into Syria. In Damascus she talked about her father's work to the Security Service of the Ba'ath Party and was recruited by the KGB.'

'When did she first meet Lawson?'

'During the Montreal Olympics, soon after the MPLA released him in Angola.'

'So when she hooked Bill in Vienna, it was on behalf of the KGB; when she took him up to Quebec in '76, it was for the CIA?'

'Maybe. But it was always for Ruth Leonhard, too.'

The *Sunday Monitor* was roaring off the machines now at the rate of 150,000 copies an hour. Yellow vans were rushing the bundles to the overnight trains servicing the far North. The London offices of the major international news agencies were frantically digesting the 40,000 words of 'Operation Tatiana' and relaying the first reports of it to client newspapers and government offices round the world. In Moscow the lights would burn in the Foreign Ministry throughout the night. Alerted, the President of the United States had returned to Washington from Camp David.

Morale was not notably high that night in the offices of the *Sunday Dispatch*, particularly after Joe O'Neill phoned Tim Powerstock and offered him a job at the *Monitor* making the tea. Shortly afterwards Powerstock was summoned by his chairman, Lord Jacobs. After Powerstock had slunk away, Jacobs pencilled into his diary three possible dates for dinner at the Connaught. Then he called his chief accountant.

'How much can I offer Ellison this time?'

'On tonight's showing, the sky's the limit. The *Monitor*'s deal with Orbit Books is reported to be $1 million.'

At 22:30 GMT, a Soviet military vehicle drew up on the Eastern side of Checkpoint Charlie. After a brief conversation between officials from either side of the border, a small, bent man clutching a battered cardboard suitcase walked unsteadily into West Berlin. Alone. His name was Chaim Leonhard.

His daughter died two minutes later in a San Francisco military hospital.

CHAPTER 21

July 5, 1980. New York

She left the building alone, haggard and distraught. Karl Petersen followed her on to the sidewalk, attempting to calm her, to tame her fury, but she shook him off with a snarl. 'You bastard,' she hissed. 'You bastard!' She turned and ran down Park Avenue.

Petersen took a few steps in pursuit, then shrugged and hailed a cab.

Ellison walked twenty paces behind her, carrying only a Nikon camera. Everything else he had left behind in Holzheimer's care.

It was a hot day but Tatiana maintained an athlete's pace, a world champion's pace, looking neither to right nor to left, oblivious of her surroundings, the crowd, the traffic, the superb glass buildings towering above her. Her eyes were shielded by dark lenses and her hair was tied in a scarf: thus one of America's most widely exposed faces passed through the dense Saturday crowds unrecognized.

At Union Square she seemed to hesitate, then descended quickly into the subway, bought a token and passed through the turnstile onto the platform. Ellison took up position only a few paces behind her but Tatiana remained oblivious to her surroundings, locked into her own inner torment. Bleakly, fixedly, she gazed at the dark tunnel from which the downtown Local would emerge.

Unobtrusively he primed and focussed his camera. That he had a right to behave in this way he didn't doubt; besides, his professional pride had been badly wounded by his year-long failure to solve Operation Tatiana.

He could hear the train approaching now, rumbling in the tunnel. Tatiana moved her purse from her left hand to her right, then back again. The lights of the train appeared. Ellison raised his camera and focussed it on the edge of the platform, facing the oncoming train.

The train was beginning to slow down.

Someone shouted, someone laughed. A group of black teenagers were vaulting over the turnstile while the clerk yelled at them angrily. For a fraction of a second Ellison was distracted.

Tatiana made her dash. At that moment a force he could neither anticipate nor identify took possession of him: he dropped his camera and hurled himself desperately forward, clutching at her left arm. He was too late: the train, with a lazy, magisterial power, caught her shoulder and swept her from his grasp.

There was a single, horrifying scream.

It was night when the South African Airways Boeing 747 touched down at Jan Smuts Airport. In a screened-off, private enclosure at the back, closely guarded by agents of the Department of Internal Security, successor to BOSS, fourteen members of the Executive Council of the Broederbond gathered, grim-faced, to greet the fifteenth.

He who, alone among them, had lived abroad for thirty-five years.